Date with Mystery

Julia Chapman is the pseudonym of Julia Stagg, who has had five novels, the Fogas Chronicles set in the French Pyrenees, published by Hodder. *Date with Mystery* is the third in the Dales Detective series, followed by *Date with Poison.*

Julia Chapman

DATE WITH MYSTERY

PAN BOOKS

First published 2018 by Pan Books

This edition first published 2022 by Pan Books
an imprint of Pan Macmillan
The Smithson, 6 Briset Street, London EC1M 5NR
EU representative: Macmillan Publishers Ireland Ltd, 1st Floor,
The Liffey Trust Centre, 117–126 Sheriff Street Upper,
Dublin 1, D01 YC43
Associated companies throughout the world
www.panmacmillan.com

ISBN 978-1-0350-0240-5

3 5 7 9 8 6 4

A CIP catalogue record for this book is available from the British Library.

Map artwork by Hemesh Alles

Printed and bound by CPI Group (UK) Ltd, Croydon, CR0 4YY

For Brenda

One of Yorkshire's finest

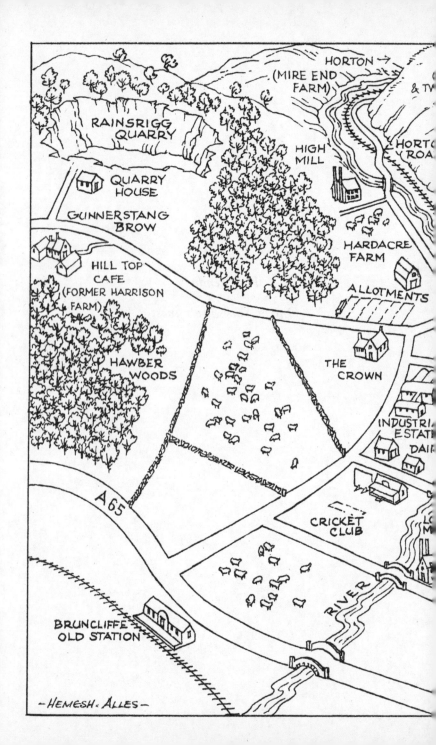

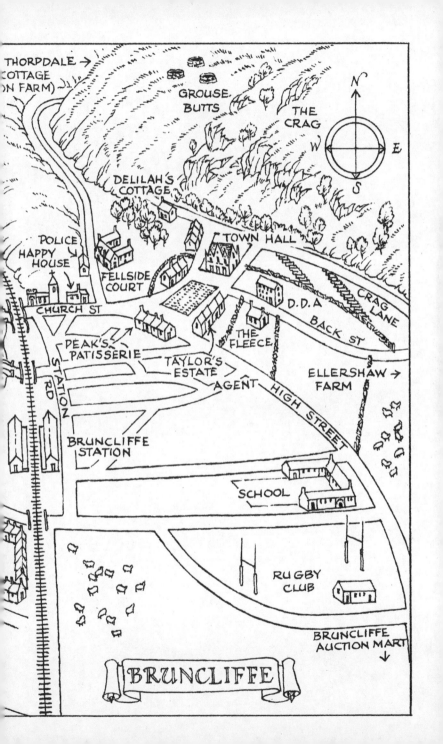

Prologue

Winter had a firm hold on the Yorkshire Dales. Bare trees scratched at the sky, the morning's frost still coating the land. Beyond the window the vegetable garden lay dormant, soil hard under the white layer, a few scraggly heads of cabbage left. February was proving to be a bitter month.

He hoped they were checking on the sheep. With lambing imminent, a few more nights like the last couple and there'd be trouble. Surely someone would have the sense to hop up and see they were right? Maybe not. He'd text them. When he got back to civilisation and could get a decent signal.

Whenever that would be.

Fighting a familiar feeling of confinement, Jimmy Thornton lifted his gaze to the scar that cut across the hillside behind the house. The quarry. Abandoned these many years, it remained a stark imposition, a coarse break in the fellside where the machinery had scythed through the rock. Funnily enough, it didn't look so bad in winter, the exposed limestone more fitting in this harsh season than when contrasted against the summer's green.

Even so, it felt like a cage around him. A violent interruption in the landscape he loved. It had ever been thus. Him here in the house, wishing he was elsewhere, hating the restrictions that chained him to the place. Hating the memories. Of this room in particular.

She should have left here, he thought. Long ago, when it all ended.

A sigh came from the darkened room behind him. His name, a mere susurration of air with very little sound.

'I'm here, Mother.' He crossed the threadbare carpet to the bed, her presence in it no more than a slight comma in the bedcovers, and gently took her hand. He felt the bones under his calluses. She was as fragile as a newborn chick. 'You're not missing much out there,' he said, voice hearty in the hope it would revive her, that his rude health would infect her and overcome the disease. 'Been a right old frost. Proper white and all.'

She sighed again, a longer one this time, her fingers twitching under his.

'What did you say? Ears aren't working right good this morning.' He leaned closer, aware of his bulk looming over her, cutting out the sunlight.

'*Sorry . . .*' She was looking at him, eyes clouded with pain, but she was seeing him. Struggling to make herself heard. '*So sorry . . .*'

'You've nowt to be sorry for, Mother.' He patted her hand, his fingers clumsy. Throat thickening. 'You hear me?'

He felt the slightest of pressure returning his touch. Then her gaze slid towards the photograph on the bedside table and he knew he was losing her.

'Come on, lass,' he muttered, the way he would to an ailing beast. 'Come on. Don't leave me.'

Downstairs he heard the click of the latch. The Macmillan nurse. Here too late. He'd been around death enough to know what it looked like. He heard the firm tread on the stairs, the footsteps on the landing.

By the time the nurse reached the bedroom door, Jimmy Thornton was all alone.

1

Delilah Metcalfe needed money. Lots of it. With everything that was coming round the corner, she was going to need substantially more income than she was used to making.

Taking the steps that led down to town from her cottage in energetic strides, she tried to convince herself that it would all be okay. Her bank manager, who also happened to be her uncle, wouldn't foreclose on the loans against her two businesses. Or the mortgage on her house. And her ex-husband would drop his demands for custody of their dog.

Up ahead, already turning at the bottom of the steps, Tolpuddle was eager to get to work. A grey shadow against the walls of the ginnel, he loped along and then stopped to wait outside the third gateway on the right, looking back at her with a distinct air of impatience.

The best thing to come out of Delilah's short-lived marriage – a Weimaraner with anxiety issues. She couldn't imagine life without him. But if Neil Taylor got his way, Tolpuddle would be heading south to live in London with Neil and his new girlfriend.

No more coming to work with her. No more running on the fells. No more chasing rabbits – a talent the dog was surprisingly lacking, choosing merely to hold point, indicating the direction of any bunnies he stumbled across rather than running them down. The experts would say this was typical Weimaraner behaviour; Delilah preferred to think Tolpuddle had a soft heart.

If she was going to keep that soft heart up here in Bruncliffe, she was going to have to find money.

It was the first working day of a brand-new week, she told herself as she opened the gate and entered the back yard of the office building. Surely that would bring customers to her door? People seeking her IT skills, looking for a website designer. Or even better, seeing as it was Valentine's Day, people looking for love. As the owner of the town's only dating agency, she ought to have the market sewn up. But in the lead-up to Christmas, that aspect of her business had taken a downturn, clients declining to renew subscriptions to the Dales Dating Agency and no new customers signing on. The weeks following the New Year had been just as fallow, Cupid's arrows falling short for the whole of January. And while the agency's speed-dating event to celebrate the patron saint of love the Friday before had been a success, it hadn't produced the surge of singles she'd been banking on.

All she could hope was that it was a winter blip. For her sake, and for Tolpuddle's. Because if she was going to fund a court case to fight for custody of her dog, she would need a lot more lovelorn souls turning up to seek her help.

Delilah followed the Weimaraner down the path towards the back door of the old three-storey house that was now her office, noting the absence of the scarlet-and-chrome Royal Enfield on the concrete inside the gate. Samson wasn't back yet, then.

She stifled the feeling of disappointment that had soured

her days since his abrupt departure. Bruncliffe had felt a duller place without him. Not just for her. Tolpuddle had been crestfallen all day Friday with no one to make a fuss of him. And she'd be lying if she said it hadn't crossed her mind that her troublesome tenant wouldn't come back at all. The way he'd shot off like that – if she hadn't bumped into him on Thursday night, she wouldn't have known where he'd gone. Calling in to pick up some paperwork she'd left on her desk, she'd met Samson coming out of the back door, a rucksack in his hand, startled to see her. When she'd asked where he was off to so late, he'd mumbled something about a long weekend in York with a friend. About needing a break.

'He's a free agent,' she muttered as she opened the door and entered the porch, Tolpuddle pushing past her in his haste to get to the downstairs office.

But Delilah Metcalfe couldn't help feeling hurt. After all they'd been through since October – Samson's unwelcome return to Bruncliffe; the way they'd been thrown together by the events that had shaken the town; and the fact that they'd celebrated Christmas in the heart of her family at Ellershaw Farm – after all that, to arrive at the office and catch Samson mid-flight had been like a punch to the stomach. She'd thought the last four months had brought them closer, repaired the fractures in their relationship caused by events fourteen years ago. Yet there he was, fleeing once more.

It was his background, she told herself. All those years undercover with the police down in London. It was second nature for him to dissemble. To be secretive. Why was she so upset?

Julia Chapman

Because she suspected she knew what was behind his sudden visit to York. What else merited a midnight flit in February?

It had to be the sophisticated woman whose call Delilah had intercepted on Samson's mobile before Christmas. One word from her and he'd gone scurrying over there. To spend Valentine's Day with her.

With her mood less optimistic about the future than it had been, Delilah walked through the small kitchen and into the hall. As expected, the door to the right of the hall-way was open, revealing Tolpuddle sitting in the middle of Samson's empty office, a forlorn expression on his face.

'He's not here, boy.' She crossed the tattered lino and rubbed the dog's head, a small whine answering her affection.

Tolpuddle and Samson O'Brien. Between the pair of them, very little else had occupied Delilah's mind since Christmas. Now she had a feeling she would lose them both before the year was out. One to her ex-husband. And the other to the mystery woman with a voice like velvet, who was no doubt in some luxurious hotel bedroom in York at this very minute, whispering sweet nothings into Samson's ears.

'Bloody Valentine's Day!' cursed Delilah, heading for the stairs in a foul mood.

'Did you miss me?'

Samson O'Brien tore his gaze away from the grey stretch of sea beyond the rain-smeared window of the caravan and glanced across the Formica table that separated him from his guest.

'More than I thought possible,' he laughed.

The bald head opposite dipped in acknowledgement, a grin forming on the weathered face. 'Thought as much.'

DI Dave Warren – more commonly known as Boss by those under his command – let the grin linger for a few moments, before turning serious. 'You weren't followed?'

Samson lifted an eyebrow in surprise. 'You think that's possible? Even up here?'

'With what's going on, anything is possible. You're up against ruthless people, son. Don't forget that.'

Turning back to the bleak seascape of Saltwick Bay, Samson didn't see how he could forget it. His entire life had been turned upside down because of events down in London. Events he didn't really understand.

'How's life in the sticks?' His boss was casting a disparaging eye at the interior of the caravan, which had seen better days. 'The locals treating you well?'

Samson gave a dry laugh. 'That's one way of putting it. Not everyone has welcomed me with open arms.'

'But you're okay? You know . . . up here?' A stout finger tapped a wrinkled forehead. 'Not planning on doing anything stupid?'

Suicide. Common amongst police officers cast out into the cold. It wasn't something that had crossed Samson's mind. Not even at the beginning when it was all so confusing; when he was being told to flee the city by his boss. And being encouraged to do so quickly by three men in balaclavas who'd used him for kicking practice.

And now? He thought of Bruncliffe and felt a sudden pang for the fells and the dales. For his office in the building on Back Street. And for the company of Delilah Metcalfe and her dog, Tolpuddle.

He wasn't planning on dying any time soon.

'You'll be the first to know,' he replied.

'Good . . . good.' DI Warren fidgeted on the bench seat, as uncomfortable being at rest as Samson was. 'And you're keeping your head down? Staying out of trouble?'

The image of a burning caravan played across Samson's mind. Closely followed by a delightful vision of Delilah in pyjamas as she accompanied him on a stake-out.

'Yes,' he lied. The drama that had arisen as a result of his newly formed Dales Detective Agency was better left untold. For a start, he wasn't sure how the higher powers in the police would take his new enterprise.

'Make sure it stays that way. You don't want to attract attention.'

A silence settled between the two men, awkward with the anticipation of bad news. Samson didn't believe that his boss had set up this meeting, stressing the need for secrecy, simply to enquire after his well-being. He decided to bite the bullet.

'Have they made any progress? With the investigation?'

DI Warren tapped his fingers on the table, the cigarettes that used to occupy his restless digits missing in the wake of his decision to quit smoking several years ago; his habit of playing with the packet was proving harder to shake. 'That's why I'm here,' he said. 'Thought you'd want to know in person.' His hands went still and he fixed Samson with the grey stare that had been one of the only constants through the six turbulent years Samson had spent under-cover. 'They're going to suspend you. Formally.'

Date with Mystery

Samson leaned back against the wall of the caravan. Finally. It was happening. For the past four months he'd hoped his boss was being paranoid. That the threat of an investigation was nothing but rumour in a profession that thrived on whispers and speculation.

But here it was. His career was about to be stripped from him. Because no matter how innocent, no one came out of the other side of a suspension without stigma.

'When?' he asked.

'Soon. A week. Maybe four weeks. But sooner rather than later. And you need to know,' his boss added with a grimace, 'they're talking about a prison sentence.'

Samson O'Brien stared back out to sea and wondered if it was too late to change his mind about dying.

Jimmy Thornton had lost his entire family. In the space of two and a bit decades he was the sole surviving Thornton.

He shuffled his feet on the plush carpet of the solicitor's office, glad he'd changed his boots before coming. Although why it couldn't wait, he didn't know. Mother was dead only a couple of days, the funeral not for another couple more. But Matty Thistlethwaite had been insistent and had asked him to drop in when he was next in town.

So here he was, feeling out of place amongst the glass table and the ash shelving. It felt more like a trendy cafe than a place of law. Old Mr Turpin, whose name still adorned the practice, had inhabited a much more traditional office with lots of oak and heavy furnishings, old books on the dark shelves. It had been a proper lawyer's den.

'Jimmy, thanks for stopping by.' Matty was at the door,

extending his hand. 'I'm so sorry for your loss. Your mother was a good woman.'

'Aye,' said Jimmy, shaking hands and resuming his seat. 'She was that. Too good for what she had to endure.'

The solicitor nodded, sitting down across the desk. 'Actually, that's the reason I asked you to call in.'

Jimmy fixed him with the unwavering stare of the outdoor man. And waited, in no hurry to pad life with words when others needed to be talking.

'It's about your mother. Was she in sound mind of late?'

'Not the last day or so, not with the morphine. But before that, aye. She was sharp as a tack.' He gave a dry laugh. 'Sharp enough to remind me more than once to look after the garden. Why?'

Matty arched his fingers in a steeple and looked down at the desk. Then he looked up at Jimmy. 'The thing is . . . it's her will.'

'Mother's will?'

The solicitor nodded again. 'There's a bit of a problem. Your mother has left half of her estate to you.'

'Half?' Jimmy scratched his head, wondering where this bizarre conversation would take him. 'Who got the other half? The Church?'

'No, not the Church. Your sister.'

'Livvy?' The shock propelled the big man to his feet. 'Our Livvy? You're joking, right?'

'It's not a joke. In a will deposited with us last month, your mother, Mrs Marian Thornton, left half of her estate to Miss Olivia Thornton.'

'But . . . but . . .' Jimmy turned towards the window, perplexed. 'But our Livvy . . .'

And he gestured towards the grey bell tower of St Oswald's that could be seen across the marketplace, the church where his sister's brief life had been commemorated a full twenty-four years before.

'Sorry to have been the bearer of such news,' said DI Warren, standing by the caravan door and preparing to leave. 'But it's best that you're forewarned.'

Samson nodded, still trying to take in the magnitude of what a formal suspension meant.

'And don't go thinking this means the people behind all this will back off. I'd be even more on my guard now, if I was you.'

'You think they'll still come after me? Even now that I'm in the frame?'

The older policeman frowned, fixing Samson with the stare he saved for stupid questions. 'Are you innocent?'

'Of course I am!'

'So there's your answer. They'll be doing everything in their power to make sure you don't look it. So watch your back. And trust no one.'

'Just like old times,' Samson muttered, trust not being something he'd granted to many of his acquaintances when he was living in London and working undercover.

His boss turned the door handle and then paused, twisting back to look at Samson.

'This is serious, son. Really serious. Don't underestimate the mess you're in.'

Being accused of corruption. Theft. Of running a racket that involved stealing drugs from evidence and selling them on the open market. Samson knew very well just what a predicament he was in.

'Believe me, I've no intention of taking it anything but seriously.'

A firm slap landed on Samson's back. 'I'll be doing everything I can to help. I'll have my ear to the ground and if anything comes up from the investigation, I'll let you know. Until then, just keep your head down and go along with the formalities. As for this conversation . . .'

'It never happened.'

DI Warren nodded. 'Best keep it under the radar.' He opened the caravan door and then turned to hand the plastic bag he'd been carrying to Samson. 'Here. Almost forgot. They're for you.'

Samson opened the bag and pulled out a box of expensive chocolates.

'Valentine's Day,' said his boss with a laugh. 'Walked into the office with them under my arm and now the lads all think I'm off seeing the mistress.'

'Glad you didn't choose lacy underwear instead,' said Samson with a wry smile as they shook hands.

'Look after yourself, son.' With one last nod, DI Warren walked down the steps and away from the caravan.

Standing in the doorway, Samson watched the only person on the planet who truly knew him recede into the distance. He had a disturbing sense that his chances of surviving the impending trouble were receding just as quickly.

Jimmy Thornton was staring at the document on the glass table in front of him. 'There must be some mistake,' he said. 'This must be one she made years back, before Livvy . . .'

Matty Thistlethwaite shook his head, leaning across to point at the date. 'It was drawn up over a year ago, Jimmy,' he said softy. 'Your mother knew what she was doing.'

A year ago. Jimmy didn't need to count back the months. He was a farmer, he marked time in seasons and the cycle of life, and he knew for certain that the day he found out his mother had terminal cancer had been in the middle of the tupping season. After a day on the hills checking the sheep – happy to see the coloured rumps that told him his rams were working hard – he'd called in at the house in the shadow of the quarry. Expecting her to be busy cooking or gardening as usual, he'd been surprised to find his mother sitting at the kitchen table, the stove unlit, the house cold.

She'd got the diagnosis that morning. Hadn't said a word about the tests until she had conclusive news. No point in worrying him – that had been her excuse for not telling him earlier. Now that there was no avoiding it, she'd told him bluntly. With no drama.

She hadn't told him about this, though.

'I don't understand,' he said, tapping the will with a broad finger. 'Why would she do this?'

The mixture of puzzlement and hurt in his client's voice moved Matty Thistlethwaite. Bruncliffe born and bred, he knew all about the Thornton family and the tragedies that had beset it, Jimmy having been in the year above him at school. The last remaining Thornton didn't need more trauma to add to the total he'd suffered already.

'I can't answer that,' said the solicitor. 'And I'm so sorry to be putting this before you so soon after your bereavement. But I didn't want to keep you in the dark.'

'Aye, I appreciate all that.' Jimmy lifted his troubled gaze to the solicitor. 'But what does this mean?'

'A bit more paperwork, unfortunately,' said Matty. 'We'll need to get a copy of Livvy's death certificate before we can proceed and settle the estate.'

Jimmy nodded absent-mindedly. 'Right, right,' he said. 'I'll leave it with you.' He stood, itching to be outside on the fells where he could think about this strange turn of events in comfort.

'I'll keep you posted,' said Matty, coming round the desk, hand outstretched. 'But it's just a formality. We'll have it sorted in no time.'

2

'How was York?'

Samson looked up from petting Tolpuddle to see Delilah standing in the doorway, hand on her hip. He'd left the coast early that morning, deciding to make the most of the caravan for one more night after his meeting with the boss. Riding along quiet roads in the dark, his Royal Enfield ate up the miles and he arrived at the office just after eight-thirty. Too late for his usual morning cuppa with the cleaner, Ida Capstick, but crucially Samson had been early enough to get his rucksack up to the second floor before Delilah arrived for the day.

Delilah, who had no idea that, thanks to a cashflow problem, he was not only renting the office space on the ground floor, but was also surreptitiously spending his nights in the spare room at the top of the house amidst her stored furniture. Sleeping in her old bed. It was a situation that required a lot of stealth and deception, so it had been a luxury to sleep without guilt in Whitby. And without the threat of being discovered.

But it was better to be back in Bruncliffe. Walking into his office with its peeling lino, old filing cabinet and red-flocked wallpaper, a slice of weak sunlight filtering through the window and highlighting the gold letters D D A that spanned the glass, it had felt like home. He'd let out a loud laugh at the irony of it. Being anxious to be back in Bruncliffe, a town he couldn't wait to leave when he was younger. He'd never have thought he could miss the place so badly when he was only away for four days. He was getting as bad as the locals. Next thing he'd be talking about visiting Skipton – thirty minutes down the road – as if it was a big deal. But he'd found himself pining for the fells and the dales. For the sheep dotted across the hills. And the stone walls that marched up and down the landscape. He'd even missed the unpredictable weather.

More than anything, Samson had missed the woman standing in front of him. Delilah Metcalfe, younger sister of his best friend. And her hound, who'd come crashing into his office with unfettered delight to welcome him home.

'York was lovely,' he said, rubbing Tolpuddle's stomach, the Weimaraner writhing on the lino in ecstasy. 'It was nice to get away.'

'And your friend?

He smothered a grin, knowing Delilah was ablaze with curiosity. 'Great. It was like old times.'

'When did you last see her?'

He noticed with interest the casual assumption as to the nature of his brief holiday. When Delilah had surprised him on Thursday evening as he was leaving, he'd given her the first destination that popped into his head. York. Although, to be truthful, he hadn't had many details to give. The call had been succinct, his boss merely telling him to set up a safe location for a meet sometime over the next four days. Samson had chosen Whitby. Far enough from Bruncliffe to avoid the chance of bumping into someone who knew him.

And not close enough to London to feel the repercussions of the trouble that was stirring.

Yet despite the lack of information, Delilah had turned his impromptu long weekend into a romantic tryst. Enjoying her unfounded suspicions, Samson didn't feel the need to set her right. It only helped maintain his cover. But he didn't lie either. 'Not since I came home.'

Delilah gave a slight tip of her head, her pursed lips the only indication that his truncated answers were as frustrating as they were intended to be. 'Are we going to get to meet her?'

'Maybe,' he shrugged. 'How about you? How was your Valentine's event?'

She pushed her hair back behind her ears, a bright smile lighting up her face. 'Very successful. A full house and lots of happy customers. And then Rick had a party Saturday night at his restaurant in Low Mill. It was brilliant.'

Just like that, Samson's mood soured.

Rick Procter. Bruncliffe's successful property developer. A man revered by many in the town for his work ethic, his philanthropy, even his classic good looks.

Samson hated him.

He couldn't help it. Rick had been a bully at school, and nothing Samson had witnessed since returning to town had led him to revise that opinion. The fact that his own father had been swindled out of the family farm by Procter Properties during Samson's absence didn't help, even if an addiction to alcohol on Joseph O'Brien's part had aided that particular deal.

And it was a hatred that was mutual.

Rick Procter had made his feelings clear several times in

the four months Samson had been back. Samson was to leave town. Quickly. And Delilah Metcalfe was off-limits.

Watching the woman in question, Samson wondered how she'd react if she knew that Bruncliffe's property magnate was so high-handed in relation to her; that Rick Procter considered her his. Samson suspected that famous temper would fly, and possibly a fist too – something he himself had experienced on his first day home. Delilah Metcalfe had a right hook to be feared.

But Samson wasn't about to enlighten her as to how the property developer viewed her. Not yet. He had a score to settle with Rick Procter, so he was biding his time. Plus, the little he'd witnessed of the man in the last few months had been enough to trigger his suspicions. Having spent fourteen years in the police force and six of those years working as an undercover operative, Samson's instinct for wrongdoing was finely tuned. That pile of cash he'd seen Rick with at Fellside Court, the retirement complex Procter Properties owned, had set it twitching. What had that been about? There was something shady about the property developer. Something Samson would enjoy investigating further, especially if it gave him the means by which to bring about Rick's downfall. And *then* he would tell Delilah.

Spirits rallying at the thought of Miss Metcalfe taking a swing at Rick Procter, Samson listened to the end of her tale about the Valentine's celebrations.

'Anyway,' she was concluding, 'you missed a really good night.'

'Sounds like it,' he lied, noting the forced cheer, the over-sunny smile. Delilah would be rubbish undercover.

Her Valentine's weekend had been every bit as miserable as his. 'Here,' he said, reaching into his desk and taking out a plastic bag. 'I brought you back a souvenir.'

'From York?' she said with a smile, already pulling out the box inside. A flutter of white paper drifted to the floor.

The receipt. Samson could have kicked himself. A slip-up of the biggest order. He hadn't checked the bag the boss had given him. Bending down, he casually picked up the piece of paper that was enough to expose his deceit, a Covent Garden address emblazoned across the top. He crumpled it in his fist and slid it into his pocket, Delilah too caught up in the pleasure of her unexpected gift to notice.

'Wow – Hotel Chocolat!' She laughed as she took in the elaborate box. 'Business must be going well.'

Samson shrugged nonchalantly, thrown by how lax he'd become. Four months in the Yorkshire Dales and he'd lost his touch, making the kind of errors that would get him killed undercover. Delilah Metcalfe had that effect on him.

'Business is great,' he said.

It was yet another lie. When he'd arrived back in Bruncliffe in October, he'd set up the town's only detective agency as a means to keep himself occupied while he served his time in exile from London. He'd also hoped it would be a much-needed source of funds. With a court case in the future a distinct prospect, Samson was reluctant to touch the money he was still being paid by the Metropolitan Police Service. In the coming months he might need every penny to pay for lawyers. So right now, with his bank balance depleted thanks to his unexpected trip to the coast, he needed a case. Something that would actually pay.

Unfortunately the good folk of Bruncliffe weren't exactly beating a path to his door. 'You?' he asked.

'Inundated.' Her eyes flickered down to the dog. 'Run off my feet, actually.'

'Good.'

'Well, I'd best get to work. Thanks for these.' She tapped the chocolate box and stood there for a pause, then turned to go. And at that moment the doorbell went.

'I'll get it,' she said eagerly.

'No need. It'll be for me,' he said, rising from his chair hopefully.

But she was already in the hall, opening the front door. 'Matty!' he heard her exclaim. 'Good morning. I don't suppose you're here looking for love?'

Matty Thistlethwaite laughed. 'No. Not today.'

'Well, come in anyway.'

Samson saw the disappointment on Delilah's face as she turned to close the door. She was as desperate for business as he was.

'Hi, Samson,' Matty was holding out a hand. 'How was York?'

After the anonymity of London, which had only been enhanced by his clandestine life, Samson still found himself caught off guard by the efficiency of Bruncliffe's grapevine and the fact that people knew all about his movements.

'Great,' he said. 'How are things with you? Busy?'

'Too busy! Christmas seems an age away already,' laughed the solicitor.

'Anything interesting?'

'That's why I'm here. I've come for help.'

'My help, I presume?' asked Samson, getting a glare from Delilah in return.

Matty nodded, oblivious to the office politics playing out behind his back. 'Yes. Have you got time to discuss it now?'

'Of course.' Samson gestured towards his office, but not before Delilah could interrupt.

'A cup of tea, Matty?' she asked with a sweet smile. 'I was just about to make one for Samson.'

Matty's eyebrows, thick and plentiful as befitted a Thistlethwaite, rose dramatically. 'Why, yes. Thanks. That would be great.'

He watched Delilah walk up the stairs to the kitchen on the first floor and then turned to Samson as they entered the office. 'You've got Delilah Metcalfe making your tea?' he asked, incredulous.

Samson forced a smile. 'She makes a wonderful secretary,' he said, in a tone calculated to be heard in the kitchen upstairs, where he knew Delilah was at that moment making tea strong enough to fell an elephant. He also knew she would arrive back downstairs with three drinks and her notebook, fully intending to sit in on the meeting with the solicitor. And there wouldn't be a thing Samson could do about it.

'Let me get this right,' said Samson as the three of them sat around his desk fifteen minutes later, mugs of tea to hand, Tolpuddle dozing in his bed in the corner. 'Mrs Thornton made a will leaving half her estate to Livvy, knowing that her daughter died years ago?'

Matty nodded. 'That's it in a nutshell.'

'So why do you need help?' asked Delilah. 'Surely it's an open-and-shut case?'

'It should be,' agreed the solicitor. 'Usually in a situation where there are only two beneficiaries, both issue of the testator, if one has predeceased the testator without issue themselves and there are no substitution clauses in the will, all assets pass to the remaining named beneficiary. Which, without the legalese, means that with Livvy having died without leaving any surviving children, all of Mrs Thornton's possessions should simply transfer to Jimmy.'

'But it's not that straightforward?' queried Samson.

'I wish it were.' Matty grimaced. 'As the executor of the will, I have to follow due process and establish proof of death for any beneficiaries before I can proceed.'

'Well, that's not going to be hard,' said Delilah. 'All of us can remember Livvy dying.'

Samson nodded, the incident shocking enough to have penetrated his own fog of grief all those years ago. 'Difficult to forget. She was such a gorgeous girl.'

For a second he saw her again. Auburn hair, a dazzling smile, against the backdrop of the scarred limestone behind her house – it had always seemed odd to him as a child that someone so vivacious could live up in the desolation of the quarry. He'd been eleven when she died. Caught up in the struggle to keep Twistleton Farm afloat and his father sober, he'd become a less frequent attendee at school, so he didn't hear the news straight away. It was his neighbour, Ida Capstick, who'd told him.

'That Thornton lass has died,' she'd said in her typically blunt manner, shaking her head and tutting at the loss. 'Another one gone who was too good for this place.'

She'd looked pointedly at Samson, letting him know that his mother wasn't forgotten. Even if his father was doing his best to drink away every memory he had.

Samson had made a rare appearance at school the next day. And the next. And every day after that, until young Jimmy Thornton came back to class. At the first break Samson had gone up to him, recognising the hunched shoulders, the defiant glare of a lad trying to hide his sorrow. He also recognised the absence around the boy, his friends unable to handle the magnitude of loss.

'You okay?' he'd asked.

Eight-year-old Jimmy had nodded, bottom lip trapped between his teeth.

'Let's play football then,' said Samson, leading the way across the playground to a group of lads his age who were kicking a ball around, a couple of the Metcalfe lads amongst them.

Jimmy had followed, mesmerised. He was being invited to play with the big boys.

For the next month Samson had attended school every day, and Jimmy Thornton had been a part of every playground activity. He still wasn't laughing much. And the aura of sadness never left him. But at least he wasn't on his own.

By the following September, Samson had moved up to the big school, where his attendance was to become even more sporadic. So he didn't really know much about Jimmy beyond that brief period after Livvy's death. But he knew the lad's pain.

And he knew the lad's sister had been a special person. For on Samson's own return to school after the death of his mother when he was eight, it had been Livvy Thornton who'd had the courage to cross that invisible line of grief. Just turned fifteen and already carrying the features that would make her beautiful, she'd walked up to him at the school gate and thrown her arms around him. He'd been entranced. By her vibrant hair. By her softness. By her smile. She'd kissed him on the forehead, told him how wonderful his mother was and, in doing so, added the young O'Brien to a list of boys in Bruncliffe who worshipped the ground Livvy Thornton walked on.

'What a woman she would have been,' Samson murmured, his sense of loss acute despite the intervening years.

'I can just about remember her,' said Delilah, casting a cheeky grin at the other two, 'not being as old as you. But I remember Will being devastated when he came home from school that day.'

'Him and most of Bruncliffe,' said Matty. 'There was something exceptional about Livvy. She was one of those people you just knew was going to go on and do something amazing. And instead of that, she's killed in a traffic accident. It's like all of us were robbed of something when she died.'

'How old was she?' asked Delilah.

'Seventeen.'

'Poor Jimmy. Imagine losing your sister like that.'

'And then his father not long after,' added Matty. 'Life can be cruel.'

'Not sure his father would have been as widely mourned,' said Samson.

'You knew Carl Thornton?'

'Not through choice. When I'd be trying to drag Dad

out of the Fleece, Thornton would be in there, getting drunk and shedding tears over his precious Livvy. Until someone knocked his arm and spilled his drink, and then he'd explode in violence.'

'He certainly took a violent way to go,' said Delilah, shuddering. 'Turning a shotgun on yourself is not the easiest option for leaving this world.'

'Grief tears people up in different ways,' said Samson, thinking about his mother's death and his father's decision to drink himself numb in the wake of it. 'Which makes me wonder if that's what this situation is. A manifestation of Mrs Thornton's grief.'

'You mean she added Livvy's name to the will deliberately, as a kind of tribute?' asked Matty.

'Yes. A final acknowledgement of her daughter from a woman who knew she was dying.'

'That makes sense. And in truth, that gesture in itself shouldn't complicate things unduly when it comes to executing the will. However, what does complicate things,' said Matty, a frown returning to his forehead, 'is not being able to prove Livvy is dead.'

'What?' Delilah was staring at the solicitor. 'How do you mean you can't prove it?'

'I can't find a death certificate. And I've looked everywhere. I've accessed the national database. I've tried the local register office. There is no paperwork to attest to her death.' Matty shrugged. 'As far as the state is concerned, Olivia Thornton is not deceased.'

'Which is why you need help,' said Samson.

'Precisely. I need someone to do a bit of legwork for me. Although,' added the solicitor, turning to Delilah, 'the more I think about it, this one might require some local knowledge, too. You know Jimmy Thornton quite well?'

'Well enough,' she said. 'He was good friends with my brother Chris when he was younger. They were in the same year at school, and Jimmy was up at the farm a fair bit. He was also a client of the dating agency.'

'Was?'

She grinned. 'Yes. Unfortunately, when I'm successful I lose my clients. He's engaged to a young woman he met through my website.'

Matty nodded. 'In that case,' he said, looking from Delilah to Samson and back again, 'I'd like to hire you both.'

Delilah's delight was clear to see, while Samson stifled a groan. He wasn't sure he could survive working with Delilah Metcalfe again.

Thorough in the way you'd expect of a conscientious solicitor, it took Matty a full fifteen minutes to satisfy himself that his hired help understood their remit: Samson and Delilah were tasked with finding the necessary paperwork that would testify to Olivia Thornton's death. Or, if that proved impossible, discovering why there was no official verification.

'Excellent,' said Matty, getting to his feet. 'How soon can you get onto this?'

Samson made a show of consulting his laptop while Delilah tapped her smartwatch and scrolled through her diary.

'If I move a few appointments, I can start tomorrow,' said Delilah. 'Would that suit you, Samson?'

'Yes. I can juggle things around to make that work,' he said, looking at a blank screen.

'I really appreciate it,' said Matty, bending down to fondle Tolpuddle's ears, the dog stretching in his bed. 'It's great to know you're both so busy, though. Helps keep this guy in dog biscuits.'

Tolpuddle closed his eyes, head flopping back onto his paws, and Matty laughed. Then he glanced at Delilah. The shake of her head was so slight, Samson almost missed it. But it was impossible not to notice the intensity with which she was regarding the solicitor.

'I'll walk you out, Matty,' she said, ushering him out of the room and closing the door behind them.

The second they left his office, Samson moved across to the door. And put his ear to it.

'Sorry,' he heard Delilah murmur. 'I didn't mean to be rude.'

'You still haven't told him, have you?' Matty asked.

'No. And I don't intend to.'

'You're making a mistake. The law can't help you with this. But Samson might be able to.'

'I don't see how.'

A pause. And then the sound of the front door opening, the voices harder to hear now.

Samson hurried back to the desk, gathered up the mugs onto the tray and, with a perfect excuse, headed out into the hall. He was in time to see Delilah closing the front door and turning round, a hand to her mouth, her face twisted in worry.

'Everything okay?' he asked.

She glanced up, a bright smile chasing away the frown.

'Yes. Fine. Just thinking about how much I'm going to have to rejig my schedule.'

She breezed past him and into the office, where he heard her making a fuss of Tolpuddle.

Rejig her schedule, indeed, thought Samson, not fooled for a moment by her lies as he made his way up to the kitchen with the tray. He'd bet everything he had – which wasn't much – on her calendar being as blank as his own. So what was bothering Miss Metcalfe? And how come Matty Thistlethwaite knew all about it and he didn't?

More importantly, if it was something Matty believed Samson could sort, how come she hadn't asked for help?

'What do you think, boy? Should I ask him?'

Tolpuddle regarded Delilah with his head tilted, one ear slightly cocked, delighting in the fuss she was making of him. It wasn't exactly an answer.

Trouble was, Delilah already knew the answer. Matty was right. She'd been to see him before Christmas to explain the situation, and Matty had been clear – the law wasn't going to be able to help her keep her dog. The paperwork from the Kennel Club was in her ex-husband's name, so she was fooling herself if she thought she could win a court case. Neil would be awarded custody the minute those documents were produced. Even though everyone in Bruncliffe knew Tolpuddle was her dog, bought by Neil in a rare thoughtful act to ease her heart-break after the loss of her brother, Ryan.

So, other than running away with Tolpuddle, Samson was Delilah's only remaining option.

But asking him for help would mean telling him she'd

been married. And divorced. Something she was certain he wasn't aware of, having been away from Bruncliffe in the years she lived to regret her reckless decision to wed Neil Taylor, son of the town's most successful estate agent and the current mayor. She was afraid Samson would think badly of her. Give her lectures on the perils of youthful romance just as Will, her oldest brother, insisted on doing every time her failed marriage was brought up.

Besides, she decided as she heard footsteps coming back down the stairs, what on earth could Samson do anyway? There was absolutely no point in telling him.

Slapping a smile on her face, she moved towards the door, Tolpuddle in tow. A run on the fells. That would help clear her head. After all, nearly two months had passed since Neil had contacted her to say he would be coming to Bruncliffe to take what he considered to be his dog. There hadn't been a word from him since. Given his fickle nature, there was every chance he'd had second thoughts and decided he didn't want Tolpuddle back in his life.

With her head firmly buried in the sand, Delilah headed upstairs to change.

3

Wednesday morning dawned bright and clear, a crisp sky above the Dales and a sharp wind blowing from the east. But inside the Dales Detective Agency, dark clouds were brewing.

'I said no. You're not coming.'

Delilah scowled, her right foot very close to being stomped on the tattered lino of Samson's office floor. 'I am coming. Matty hired both of us, or have you forgotten that already?'

Samson scowled back at her. 'How could I forget it when it's all you've talked about since yesterday morning? But that doesn't change anything. I work better alone.'

'Huh! Not much evidence of that lately. Who had to run across the fells chasing a killer?'

'Only because I was injured in a fight with said killer. And besides, the victims were all your clients, so in actual fact *I* was helping *you*.'

'What about at Fellside Court?' Delilah continued, referring to events just before Christmas. 'You couldn't have sorted that without my input. You haven't got a clue about surveillance cameras and spy software.'

'Gadgets which only work if someone doesn't tip a cup of tea all over them,' he replied pointedly.

'That's not fair! It was Tolpuddle's fault.'

'That's right. Blame the dog when he's not here to defend himself. Where is the hound, by the way?'

'Clarissa Ralph is looking after him,' said Delilah with a twinge of guilt. Normally Tolpuddle never left her side, his anxiety in the wake of her divorce such that he didn't cope well with being separated from her. Or rather, things around him didn't cope well. Shoes, trainers, cushions – when Tolpuddle got stressed, they took the brunt of his worries. All accompanied by a loud wail that could be mistaken for an air-raid siren.

Since Samson's arrival, however, the dog had been a lot calmer, happy to spend time alone with the returned detective to the extent that he now had a bed in both offices, and passed his days wandering between the two of them. He'd also taken a shine to Clarissa Ralph, one of the residents of Fellside Court, the retirement complex where Samson's father lived. And the place that had been the setting for the awful events that had come to light before Christmas.

Still coming to terms with the tragedy that had visited their peaceful world, Clarissa and her sister, Edith Hird, had leapt at the chance to look after Tolpuddle. But that didn't stop Delilah feeling guilty. Abandoning him for half a day when she had no idea how many more days she'd have with him.

'Maybe you're right,' she said to Samson, her enthusiasm for detective work fading. 'I'll stay here. With Tolpuddle.'

Samson stared at her, waiting for the laughter. But none came. Delilah Metcalfe had just backed down. In all the years he'd known her, he could never remember her capitulating in an argument quite so easily.

'Are you okay?' he asked.

'Yes. Why?' she snapped.

'It's just not like you to give in so soon. I was expecting this to carry on all the way up to Rainsrigg.'

She shrugged, already heading for the stairs and her office on the first floor. 'I've got better things to be doing than arguing with you.'

'But it's a lovely morning,' he urged. 'Come on. It'll do you good to get out.'

She paused on the first step, clearly wavering.

'We can take the bike. Come back the scenic route.' He was holding out the spare helmet, knowing how strong the pull of the Royal Enfield was.

'I suppose it wouldn't hurt,' she said, stepping back down into the hall.

Ten minutes later, not sure how he'd gone from refusing her company to begging her to go with him, Samson O'Brien was pulling out of the ginnel at the back of the office building, a pillion passenger up behind him. As they rode round the marketplace and down Church Street, passing under the high arches of the viaduct towards Gunnerstang Brow, he decided that working with Delilah Metcalfe would never be straightforward.

'How can anyone live here?' asked Delilah. Helmet in hand, she was staring at the road ahead and the brutal landscape it led to.

They'd turned off the main road just before they got to the top of Gunnerstang Brow to the west of town and Samson had pulled over, the motorbike idling beneath them. Like her, he'd removed his helmet, the wind whipping at his shoulder-length hair.

'I suppose some people don't have a choice,' he suggested, feeling anew the amazement that this place had produced someone as vivid as Livvy Thornton.

It was stark. A narrow road winding away into a ravaged hillside, bare rock cut into tiers, rusting machinery left abandoned. White. Grey. Black. Not a hint of green. It was as unlike the Dales around it as you could get.

Rainsrigg Quarry. Once a thriving industry providing work for many in Bruncliffe, now it was simply an empty pocket gouged out of the landscape. And just in front of it, like a defiant watchman guarding a burnt-out warehouse, was a cottage. The Thornton home. Although, with Mrs Thornton now deceased, it would probably be changing hands before long.

'When did the quarry close?' asked Samson, taken aback at the desolation ahead of him. When he'd left town it had been going strong, employing quite a few of his friends from school.

'Must be ten years ago. Maybe more. Now it's just a perfect setting for grief,' muttered Delilah, putting her helmet back on. 'It gives me the creeps.'

Samson pulled his own helmet on and they made their way down the road to the house, coming to a stop beside the Land Rover parked out front where the large figure of Jimmy Thornton was already waiting for them.

'I saw you coming,' Jimmy said, nodding back in the direction of the main road. 'Bit difficult to sneak up on anyone here.' He held out a large hand. 'Good to have you home, Samson.'

Unused to being welcomed so warmly in Bruncliffe, Samson felt his hand engulfed in the man's huge grip. 'Sorry we're meeting under these circumstances,' he said. 'I presume Matty Thistlethwaite filled you in on why we're here.'

Jimmy tilted his head to one side. 'Aye. Something about Livvy's death certificate being missing. Not as I see how I can help, but come on in. We'll have more comfort if we talk inside.'

He led them through the front garden, Delilah noting the small but immaculate lawn, the tidy borders dotted with snowdrops and the green tips of daffodils bright against the winter soil. Inside was just as well kept. A narrow hallway took them past the front room and into a kitchen at the back, which spanned the full width of the house. Wooden units ran along the walls, a range took up one side and a table nestled in the far corner against the window. The room looked out across a back garden with a sizeable vegetable patch and an old barn. And onto the quarry, the vista a complete contrast to the farmland that had formed the backdrop to Metcalfe family meals.

'What an unusual view,' Delilah said.

'That's one way of putting it,' said Jimmy, gesturing for them to sit in while he poured tea.

'Do you get used to it?'

'I didn't. Hated it when I was a nipper. Hate it now.' He shook his head in disgust at the bare rock cutting into the fellside. 'Mother liked it, though. Said it takes all sorts to make Nature.'

The wind gusted outside, swirling up an eddy of white dust which spattered against the glass.

'Spent her whole life trying to keep that damn dirt out,' muttered Jimmy.

'You weren't tempted to move after your father died?'

'I was.' He placed three mugs on the table. Delilah, noting the strength of the brew and the excess of milk, didn't dare look at Samson, whose southern tastebuds hadn't yet reacclimatised to Dales-style tea.

'Your mother wouldn't move?' Samson asked, not reaching for a mug.

'Wouldn't hear of it. When I left home I still couldn't get her to budge. And it wasn't for want of trying. I tried to persuade her to take one of those flats Rick Procter built in the old mill, but she always said she'd miss her vegetable patch. And her precious rhubarb. Even on her deathbed she was telling me to look after it.' Jimmy shrugged. 'Truth is, she associated the house with Livvy. Despite the fact that Livvy wasn't living here any longer when she died.'

'She was in Leeds, wasn't she?' asked Samson. It was a question he already knew the answer to. Because when he'd fled Bruncliffe that night fourteen years ago, he'd headed for Leeds himself. Partly because of Livvy Thornton. She'd been dead a while then, but even so, he'd liked the connection. Although she hadn't stolen her father's Royal Enfield to make the journey.

'Yes. I was only eight when she moved out so I can't remember exact dates,' said Jimmy. 'But she must have been there a few months before the accident, because I know she wasn't here when the curlews came back that year. We used to compete to see who could hear the first one of the season. I remember running home to tell her there was one above Hardacre's farm, forgetting that she wasn't there to tell.'

'So she left home in early spring?'

'Must have been. She never did hear that curlew.' He gave an apologetic shrug.

'We've got the date of the accident as May the twenty-ninth. Is that right?' asked Delilah.

Jimmy nodded. 'You think that might be causing the problem with the paperwork? A mistake with the date?'

'It could be that simple,' said Samson. 'But at this stage we're just making sure we've got all the facts. Like where Livvy was living in Leeds. Do you happen to know?'

'No. I never got to visit her.'

'Do you have any letters from her? Anything with an address on?'

A shadow crossed the big man's face. 'Nothing. All I know is that she worked at a hairdresser's called Snips. I remember thinking that was funny as a kid.'

'Your mother never talked about where Livvy was?' asked Delilah.

'No.' The answer was concise and clipped, as if Jimmy's lips had closed before other words could tumble out.

'So did she come home much in that time?'

'Not once.' Jimmy stared at the table.

'And you didn't go to Leeds, which means the last time you saw her . . .' Delilah paused, upset to think about the eight-year-old boy and all he'd lost.

'I last saw Livvy here,' said Jimmy with a long sigh.

'You poor thing.' Delilah reached out a hand to the farmer's arm.

'What about the accident?' Samson asked. 'What do you remember about it?'

'Not a lot. Mother didn't talk about it. And Father . . .' His gaze shifted to the old barn in the yard. 'I didn't get much chance to talk to Father about it.' He stared back down at the table, large hands toying with his mug. 'But the basics are that Livvy was run over crossing the road. They never caught the driver.'

'It was a hit-and-run?' asked Delilah.

'Yeah. Coward! Ruined our lives without so much as a glance back.' He looked at Delilah. 'Guess you were too young to remember any of this. But your brother was good to me. Ryan,' he added, realising that in a family with five sons, distinction was needed.

It was Delilah's turn to focus on her mug. Ryan. Middle son of five. Delilah's adored older brother and Samson's best friend. Killed in Afghanistan two years ago. She still hadn't got used to the loss.

'You too,' continued Jimmy, turning to Samson. 'You got me through the worst of it.' He gave a dry laugh. 'I reckon we've got a fair bit of experience of grief around this table. We should set up a counselling service or something.'

Samson laughed. 'Bruncliffe Bereavement Bureau?'

'That'd do the trick.' Jimmy smiled. Then he noticed the mug of tea untouched on the table. 'Here,' he said passing it to Samson. 'Don't forget your tea.'

'Thanks,' murmured the detective without conviction. He took a sip and placed the mug promptly back down. 'I don't suppose you have a photograph of Livvy to hand?'

Jimmy reached over to the dresser and pulled open a

drawer. 'Matty said you'd want something like that,' he said, taking out a framed photo and handing it to Delilah. 'This was on Mother's bedside table ever since the day Livvy left home. It's the most up-to-date one we have, taken just after her seventeenth birthday.'

Delilah took the frame, looking at the girl encased in it. Long hair in soft waves around her face, a bright smile on her lips, she was sitting on the grass looking up at the camera, both of her arms wrapped around a handsome border collie, the dog's distinctive colouring as auburn as her hair.

'They're beautiful,' she said.

Jimmy nodded. 'And inseparable. Livvy and Red went everywhere together. He wouldn't leave her side. Bit like you and that grey hound of yours,' he added.

'Unusual colouring for a collie,' said Samson.

'That's how Livvy ended up with him. Red was the runt of a litter and not the healthiest pup. And on top of that, his colouring wasn't what was in fashion. Livvy pestered the breeder until he caved and let her have the pup for almost nothing.' He smiled. 'She could be very persuasive.'

'Can we take a copy of this?' asked Delilah, getting her phone out of her pocket.

'Sure. If you think it will help.'

'Did Red go with Livvy to Leeds?' Samson was looking at the photo now.

'Of course. Like I said, they couldn't bear to be apart. I often wonder where he ended up.'

'What do you mean?'

'He disappeared. After the accident. Mother always reckoned he probably chased the car and then got lost.'

'Oh! How sad!' Delilah said, her hand going to her mouth. 'You never found him?'

'No. I even persuaded Mother to take me over there so I could put posters up. I must have covered every lamp post in the vicinity. But we never heard anything.' His face twisted in irony. 'Then Father went and killed himself, and Red faded into the past.' A heavy silence fell across the table before Jimmy Thornton got to his feet, large hands hanging by his side. 'I can't tell you any more than that. But I'm sure you'll find the paperwork you need. This is nowt but a hitch in the system.'

'You're probably right,' said Samson, standing too. 'Just one last question. Your mother didn't give you any indication as to why she left Livvy in the will?'

'I didn't know she had, until Matty called me in.' Jimmy scratched his head. 'Can't think what possessed her.'

'Could it have been for sentimental reasons?'

'Not Mother. She was tough. Had to be, with what life threw at her. She'd be right vexed if she knew what a fuss she'd created. Always hated a fuss, did Mother.'

'We'll get to the bottom of it,' said Samson, shaking hands with the younger man. 'Thanks for your time. Matty will let you know how we get on.'

'Aye. No doubt he will. He's thorough, I'll give him that.' He smiled, turning to Delilah. 'And remember me to Chris if you're over in Leeds. Tell him to give me a call next time he's home. Reckon we're owed a catch-up in the Fleece.'

'I will do,' said Delilah, knowing her brother would be pleased to hear from his old school friend. She followed the two men back out into the front garden, struck again by how odd the house was, sitting there on the edge of the quarry.

'It must have been noisy living here when this place was open,' she said as they reached the motorbike.

'I wasn't around much. I was at school during the day, and in the holidays I was off on the fells. Or working down at Tom Hardacre's.'

'Over on the Horton Road?' asked Samson, thinking of the farm which was situated on the way out of Bruncliffe to the north-west. 'Quite a trek from here.'

Jimmy tipped his head towards the copse to the right of the quarry. 'There's a path through there that leads straight down to it. Ten-minute walk.'

'Do you still work there?' asked Samson.

'No. I stayed on for a couple of years after I left school, but when his lad Oscar took over, I quit. Tom helped me get a tenancy on a place up near Bowland Knotts. Been there ten years.'

'That must be a change,' Samson laughed, remembering the wildness of the land to the west of Bruncliffe, where grouse, lapwings and curlews were a common sight. It was a far cry from the bleak panorama of Rainsrigg Quarry.

'Tell me about it. I hate coming back here. If it hadn't been for Mother . . .' Jimmy paused, then gave a bitter smile. 'Guess I won't need to come over much more. Once I've cleared out the house, I'll be done with it.'

'Will you sell it?' Delilah asked.

'Not mine to sell,' said Jimmy. 'It's rented. It came with Father's job as foreman at the quarry. When he died, the quarry owners agreed to let us stay on. I think they saw the writing on the wall and knew the site would be closing.' He looked at the squat cottage with unexpected sadness. 'Not sure they'll find anyone to take it on now Mother's gone. It'll probably go the same way as the rest of this place.'

Delilah squeezed his arm. 'It was good to see you, Jimmy. Despite the circumstances. And tell Gemma I said hello.'

The clouds that had swept across the farmer's face cleared at the mention of the woman's name. 'I'll be sure to,' he said. 'Best thing I ever did, calling in to your dating agency that day.'

'Make sure you tell all your single friends that,' said Delilah with a laugh. 'And when you two finally get married, I want an invitation.'

Jimmy blushed, foot swiping at the dust on the ground. 'Funny you should say that . . .'

'You've set a date?'

He grinned. 'Not exactly. What with Mother being sick and all, we haven't had time.' He paused, then spoke in an excited rush. 'Gemma is pregnant.'

'Oh, wow!' Delilah's face split into a smile. 'That's fantastic news. When is the baby due?'

'Not for a while. We only found out a couple of weeks ago so we're not telling folk just yet. But I thought you had a right to know. Seeing as you brought us together, like.'

'Did your mother know?'

'We came straight here from the doctor's. Just as well as she was gone not long after.' He gave a rueful smile. 'I promised her we'd call the baby Olivia, if it's a girl. Seems only fitting.'

'It's a lovely idea,' said Delilah, putting on her helmet. 'Take good care of Gemma.'

Jimmy laughed. 'Aye. And you take care riding round on that thing.' He gave the Royal Enfield an envious glance as Samson started the bike, the throb of the engine echoing around the walls of the quarry. Then he turned and went back inside the cottage.

Samson sat there for a moment or two, the motorbike rumbling beneath him, a feeling of disquiet settling on his shoulders. There was something about the place. An eeriness that had his heightened senses twitching. He stared at the blank face of the house for a moment and then let his gaze pass beyond it to the cluster of trees to the side of the quarry.

He could swear someone was watching them.

'Are we going to sit here all day?' Delilah shouted over the noise of the bike. 'It's just I've got a dog waiting back in town . . .'

Samson flicked his visor down, revved the engine and pulled away, glad to put distance between them and Rains-rigg.

They were gone. The vibrant bike disappearing up the track in a cloud of dust, the sound of the engine lingering in the echoes off the rocks. They'd disturbed the place. Uprooted it from its habitual quiet.

They'd begun to uproot the past, too. And that couldn't be allowed.

The gun was lowered, the barrel dropping below shoulder height. It had been trained on the man. O'Brien. If he kept digging, it would be used on him, too.

For the past needed to be protected. In whatever way necessary.

44

4

The ride back into Bruncliffe was cathartic. Instead of turning left out of the quarry road and heading straight into town, Samson turned right, taking them up over Gunnerstang Brow, past the cafe owned by Titch Harrison, a *For Sale* sign outside it. Once on the top, the views opened up before them, out across the edge of the Dales, the Lakeland Fells marking the horizon in the distance. They were so clear, their serrated outlines sharp against the blue sky.

Not feeling like he'd shaken all of the dust from Rainsrigg off him, Samson pushed on, down the hill to the main road. Turning left towards Skipton, he opened up the throttle and the Enfield sped away, cutting around the edge of Bruncliffe, the town a huddle of slate roofs topped by the dramatic rise of the limestone crag at the back.

Whenever he saw his birthplace of late, he marvelled at how impressive it was. And wondered at how he'd never appreciated that until he'd returned. This morning, with the sun shining down on it, the tall chimneys of the disused mills marking either end, it was a burst of colour, welcome relief after the reduced palette of Rainsrigg Quarry.

Soon they had passed Bruncliffe Old Station and Samson was turning left onto High Street, easing the bike back to a more moderate pace as they rode past fields towards town. The rugby ground appeared on their left, cement mixers and builders' vans parked up along the road. Three months after the clubhouse had been burned to the ground, work was under way to replace it, the heavy-set figure of the club secretary, Harry Furness, amongst the builders. Spotting the vintage motorbike, Harry waved, causing the man next to him to likewise turn his attention to the Royal Enfield. The blond head of Rick Procter was unmistakable.

Samson grinned behind his visor. Knowing his pillion passenger was instantly recognisable, the decision to ride the long way home suddenly felt more than justified. By the time they pulled up outside the front of the office building, he was in a good mood. A tap on his back from Delilah soon changed things.

'You've got a customer,' she said, helmet already in her hand as she got off the bike.

He looked towards the large window with the initials D D A stencilled across it. A man was standing in front of the glass, staring at the letters and tipping his head back to compare them with the window above on the first floor. Another window where D D A spanned the glass.

Dales Detective Agency on the ground floor; Dales Dating Agency on the first floor. It was something Delilah hadn't been happy about when Samson took on the tenancy, this ridiculous duplicating of letters, but in actual fact it hadn't proved a problem. Apart from the odd person getting the offices the wrong way round, which soon became apparent.

'Do you know you two have got the same initials?' the man asked, pointing out the obvious as he turned round. 'Bit daft is that.'

Date with Mystery

Samson stifled a groan and reluctantly pulled off his helmet. Clive Knowles. The farmer from Mire End who had occupied so much of his time before Christmas on a hunt for a missing ram.

'I can smell him from here,' murmured Delilah with a delighted grin. 'You might want to open the office window.'

'Morning, Clive,' said Samson, crossing over to the man, a stale smell of manure oozing from the farmer's stained clothes. 'How can I help you?'

'What makes you think it's your help I need?' he demanded gruffly, before turning to Delilah. 'Come on, lass. Get the office open and a brew on. Haven't got all day for chit-chat.'

Samson looked at Delilah with a wide smile. 'Yes, lass. Make me one while you're at it.'

He was wise enough to stand well back as he said it.

'What took you so long?' Ensconced in a chair in front of the desk, Clive Knowles reached forward to take a mug of tea off the tray Delilah was holding. 'No biscuits?'

'No, sorry. I can offer you a Dog-gestive, if you'd like?' Delilah said through gritted teeth, not convinced the farmer would refuse one of Tolpuddle's treats.

He waved her suggestion away, releasing yet more odour into the room. The man had only been in her office a mere five minutes and already there was a farmyard fug clouding the air. She walked around the desk and pointedly opened the window. In the yard below, Samson, having parked the Royal Enfield on the concrete, was heading out of the gate on his way to Fellside Court. When Delilah had asked him to collect Tolpuddle for her, he'd agreed with alacrity, happy to be out of an environment that included Clive Knowles. At the sound of the window opening, he looked up and grinned, pegging his nose at the same time.

She glowered at him, before turning back to her client. Because that's how she had to view the man sitting across the desk from her, no matter how odoriferous he was. And if she was going to raise enough money for a court case to secure custody of Tolpuddle, she needed every client she could get. Even the smelly ones.

'So, Mr Knowles,' she said, sitting a bit further away from her desk than usual as she pulled up his account on the computer screen, the farmer having been a member of the Dales Dating Agency for a while. Without any success. 'You're fully paid up for the next three months. And I see you've already signed up for the next speed-dating event.' Delilah looked up from the screen. 'So how can I help you?'

The farmer leaned in across the desk, white stubble bristling along his jaw, his breath reeking. 'I need a wife,' he stated.

'I know. You keep telling me.'

'I've been on over ten dates with this agency and three of those Speedy Date nights, and what have I got to show for it? Nothing!'

Delilah bit her tongue. Hard.

'Well the waiting is over, missy. I need a wife.' He pointed a dirt-creased finger in her direction. 'And *you* are going to find me one.'

'Mr Knowles,' Delilah began, finding a patience she didn't know she possessed. 'I've done all I can—'

'I'm willing to pay.' The farmer slapped an envelope on the desk, ten-pound notes stacked thickly inside it.

Delilah faltered, the refusal she had been forming dying on her lips. She stared at the money, then lifted her gaze to the man opposite.

Could she do it? Find a wife for a man who paid scant attention to personal hygiene and whose attitude to women languished in the nineteenth century? Was it possible that there was someone out there who would want to marry such a person?

She put a hand on the envelope and reluctantly pushed it back towards the farmer. 'I'm sorry. I don't think I can help.'

He blinked. His mouth opened but it took a beat before anything emerged. 'Are you saying it's not possible?' he finally asked, all of the bluster knocked out of him. 'That I'm unmarriageable?'

'No . . . yes . . . I mean, it's not that simple,' Delilah stuttered, taken aback by Clive Knowles' obvious upset.

'So you'll do it then?' he said, pushing the envelope back across the desk. 'Please?'

Tolpuddle was basking in the attention. Two elderly ladies were making a fuss of him and he was loving every minute of it.

'He's been such a good boy,' cooed Clarissa Ralph, tickling the dog behind his ears. 'Not a peep out of him all morning.'

'He can be good when he wants to be,' said Samson.

'Can't we all.' Edith Hird, Clarissa's sister, was patting

the dog with affection. She cast a wry glance at the two other men standing with them. 'Well, most of us.'

'It just takes some of us more of an effort,' said Arty Robinson with a laugh that came from the depths of his ample belly. 'Doesn't it, Joseph?'

Joseph O'Brien nodded, a ghost of a smile flitting across his worn features.

They were standing in the courtyard at the back of Fell-side Court, the wall of glass that linked the two wings of the building towering over them. Samson had arrived to pick up the dog from the two sisters some time ago, but had been pressured into staying for a cup of tea and a slice of cake. And of course they'd insisted his father joined them. And Arty Robinson, the former bookmaker in good humour on this clear day.

It seemed a lifetime removed from the dark weeks that had beleaguered the retirement complex in the run-up to Christmas. Samson observed the four friends and marvelled at their resilience. They'd been put through a lot and yet here they were, laughing and joking and enjoying the pleasures life sent. Or rather, three of them were. His father seemed preoccupied. Wary. As though his son's visit was a strain.

Given the history they shared, it was understandable. They'd never win any awards for familial affection. A childhood dominated by a father's alcohol abuse, followed by fourteen years without any communication – four months was hardly enough to overcome the shadows of the past.

'Eric's moving back in today,' Edith was saying. 'You'll have to come round and have a drink with us one evening. Delilah too.'

'And Tolpuddle,' interjected Clarissa.

'That goes without saying,' her sister said, giving the dog another pat. 'Delilah and Tolpuddle are a pair.'

'How is Eric?' asked Samson, the frail elderly gentleman having been hospitalised in December following a fall in his apartment. A fall that had been part of an attempt on his life.

'Better. Although I would imagine he's apprehensive about being back living on his own.' Edith's lips pressed together. 'Who wouldn't be, after what he went through?'

'He's lucky to be still with us,' murmured Clarissa.

'Give him a week back here and he might be arguing that fact,' quipped Arty.

Samson grinned, catching his father's eye. Joseph looked away.

'It'll be lovely to have him home,' Edith continued. 'And Rita.'

Rita Wilson. Yet another resident at the complex who'd fallen foul of the spate of malice that had visited the place.

'Any word on Rita?' Samson asked.

Clarissa nodded. 'I had a call from her a couple of days ago. She's on the mend. It'll be a month or so before she comes back, but she can't wait.'

'And how about the new manager?' Samson looked towards the office in the foyer behind them. 'How are you getting on with her?'

'Fine. We're showing her the ropes,' said Arty with a grin. 'We've almost got her trained.'

'Talking of trained . . .' Samson looked down at Tolpuddle. 'It's time we got back to the office. Give my regards to Eric.'

'We will. And don't be a stranger,' said Edith as Samson clipped a lead onto the Weimaraner's collar. 'You know where we are.'

His father just smiled vaguely, his gaze shifting when Samson looked at him.

'Yes, if you need any assistants for your detective work, don't hesitate to ask,' added Arty.

'Oh!' said Clarissa as Samson turned to go. 'I forgot to ask. How was York?'

'It was great, thanks,' said Samson, already walking off before he could be grilled, an art which the good folk of Bruncliffe excelled at. 'And thanks again for looking after Tolpuddle,' he called back over his shoulder.

Dog at his heels, he walked around the side of the building and down Fell Lane towards town, pondering on his father's behaviour. It had been several weeks since Samson had made the time to call in at Fellside Court, and even then, it had been a brief visit. In fact, now he thought of it, he'd hardly seen his father since Christmas. Not properly. So it was hard to know if this was a new development. But either way, Joseph O'Brien didn't seem himself. Or at least, not the man Samson had begun to know since returning in October – a very different person from the one he remembered staggering out to meet him with a shotgun on his last night at Twistleton Farm all those years ago.

Perhaps the events over Christmas had taken their toll? Or maybe he wasn't well?

Or perhaps . . .

Samson hated himself for it. Instantly suspecting the worst. Anticipating failure. But as the child of an alcoholic, he was conditioned to expect his father to fall back into drinking.

'Give him a break,' he muttered.

Approaching the end of the road, his head rooted in the unwelcome past, he was glad to see a familiar figure coming towards him.

'Morning, Samson.' The passing months had seen no change in Constable Danny Bradley's physique, his uniform still hanging off his thin shoulders. They were shoulders that had borne a lot recently, as tragedy hit Bruncliffe in quick succession and the small rural police force found themselves dealing with murder. But the young policeman had proven himself to be more than capable. More capable, despite his inexperience, than many of those he worked with.

'Hi, Danny. How are things?'

'Great. All quiet on the crime front, for once.' The constable looked up from patting Tolpuddle. 'How was York?'

Samson shook his head. 'Is there anyone in this town who doesn't know I went to York?'

'I doubt it,' Danny said with a grin. 'Mrs Pettiford from the bank knows, so that just about covers things.'

'What I can't understand is why anyone is interested in what I get up to,' said Samson with genuine puzzlement.

'Of course they're interested. You're exotic! It's not every day we get a returned Met detective living amongst us.' The young man's face became serious. 'You must be itching to get back to it. I know I would be. I'd give my right arm to have a chance like that. So exciting.'

'It's not exactly been quiet around here of late,' said Samson, aware the lad had him on a pedestal. Aware that, before long, the pedestal would be smashed. He was also aware that all of Bruncliffe, including his own father, were under the impression that Samson had served his time with the Metropolitan Police. It was a fact he hadn't rushed to dissuade them of. Partially true, he'd actually only been in the Met for six years before being seconded to work undercover with Britain's top crime-fighting agency.

Which was where the trouble had started.

'It's not the same,' Danny murmured. 'London must be a world away from this. No one down there would know you've been to York.'

Samson laughed. 'True. I lived in a flat for years and never even saw my neighbours.'

'Like I said,' moaned Danny. 'A world away from Bruncliffe, where people know everything about you before you even know it yourself.'

'Talking of which,' Samson said, 'it's good to hear Eric's moving back in at Fellside Court.'

Danny nodded. Grandson to Eric Bradley, he'd seen evil come perilously close to his own family in the events before Christmas. 'That's where I'm heading. I want to make sure the apartment's all ready before he gets there.'

'I hope he's up to a welcoming committee. They're excited about having him home.'

The policeman smiled. 'I suppose that's where Bruncliffe beats London.'

As they went their separate ways, Samson couldn't help thinking that it wasn't the only thing his home town had over the capital. There would be a lot of things he'd miss once his suspension was lifted and he resumed his undercover work. *If* his suspension was lifted . . .

A soft tug on the lead brought his attention back to Tolpuddle, who had crossed the marketplace and was trying to pull Samson towards the butcher's. Inside the shop window, with her apron stretched across her generous frame, Mrs Hargreaves was waving at them.

'Fancy a pie, eh, Tolpuddle?' Samson asked.

The dog pulled even harder in response.

She'd said yes. Half an hour later, as she saw Clive Knowles off the premises, Delilah was wondering what had possessed her.

The man was impossible. His dating profile was a catastrophe. And yet she had agreed to find him a wife.

In two months.

The farmer had dropped that bombshell once she'd submitted to his demands, swayed by the man's misery at being considered an impossible case. He was only giving her two months to find him a bride. If she succeeded, he would pay her a handsome bonus.

It was a very big 'if'.

They'd spent some time going over his profile, Delilah trying to point out the areas where he could improve his answers. Clive Knowles had rebutted every one.

'I don't see why I need to change it,' he'd argued, leaning in over the desk to underline his point, his finger leaving a trail of greasy smears across the screen. 'It gives all the necessary information.'

Delilah sighed. 'Mr Knowles, a dating profile is like a shop window. It's supposed to tempt people inside to see what's on offer.' She'd gestured at the monitor. 'Let's just say yours isn't exactly John Lewis.'

He'd grunted. 'What's up with it then?'

'The photograph, for a start. When was it taken?'

'A bit back.'

'How far back?'

'Couple of years, maybe.'

'Couple of decades more like!' She'd pointed at the image of a young Clive Knowles, hair swept back off his forehead, a dashing air about him as he smiled for the camera. The reality sitting across from her was starkly different. Bald head under a tatty cap, eyebrows meeting in a perpetual frown and many years' worth of lines tracking across his weathered face, the farmer could easily be mistaken for the grandfather of the man in the picture.

'So we update the photo. Will that be enough?'

'I think it might take a bit more than that,' Delilah had said. She'd cast her eyes over the text that formed the heart of the profile. 'I mean, *Farmers Weekly* doesn't really count as your favourite book.'

'But I don't read much else. *Craven Herald* and the *Weekly*. That covers all I need to know,' he'd protested.

'There's plenty of people would agree with you. So just ignore the questions that don't apply. Like naming Bruncliffe brass band as your favourite group – it limits you to rather a niche market.'

'There's not much'll beat a good brass band,' grumbled the farmer. 'They fair entranced folk at Malham Show last year. Besides, any woman will have to take me as I am, and be glad about it.'

When she'd tried to diplomatically suggest that this attitude was the problem, Clive Knowles had slapped his hands flat on her desk, sending a warm waft of farm odour her way.

'I'm a man of property,' he'd declared. 'There's many would be happy to have me.'

Delilah had bitten her tongue. Again. For Mire End Farm, with its dilapidated barns, neglected farmhouse and weed-infested fields, was hardly the Promised Land. If anything, it reduced the man's worth on the marriage market. And that took some doing.

They'd finally come to a compromise. Delilah would take a week to work on the profile and would then call over to Mire End with the result. She'd bring her camera, too.

Kicking herself for being too soft and taking on the job in the first place, she climbed back up the stairs and washed her hands in the kitchen – a wise precaution after dealing with Clive Knowles – before heading into her office. She sat down at the computer and stared again at the self-portrait the farmer had compiled for himself.

A strangled laugh escaped her throat. How on earth was she going to make him sound appealing? And if she was successful in tempting someone to meet him, surely the reality of the man would be enough to send any sane woman running for the fells?

She let her eyes drift to the envelope of cash still sitting on the desk. It was a lot of money, which she badly needed. So if she was going to accept it, then it was only fair that she did her best by the lonely farmer. And pray for a miracle at the same time.

The ping of an incoming email sounded on her mobile. Still thinking about the mammoth task ahead of her, she glanced at the screen, saw the sender and froze.

The email was from Neil. It could only be about one thing.

She tapped it open.

In typical Bruncliffe fashion, it had taken a full ten minutes for Samson to emerge from the butcher's, three pies in a bag in his hand and an impatient dog waiting for him. There'd been a couple of other customers ahead of him, all chatting to Mr and Mrs Hargreaves, who were working hard behind the counter. But when Samson entered, the focus had turned on him and he'd had to answer a barrage of questions about his recent sojourn in York. And about his father and the residents of Fellside Court.

'Let's get out of here while we still can, Tolpuddle,' he muttered as he untied the dog's lead and set off across the marketplace for Back Street, Tolpuddle loping along beside him.

Insatiable curiosity backed up by a directness unique to the Dales – Bruncliffe thrived on it. It was the kind of community that would have made his life undercover almost impossible. It made his current life, with its half-truths and deceits, uncomfortable.

Samson found himself unaccountably saddened by that fact.

'I'll miss the place,' he murmured. 'You too, boy.' He reached down to pat the dog, who used the movement as an excuse to nose the bag in Samson's other hand. 'Even if you're only with me for my pies.'

Another couple of months. If he was lucky, he'd have another couple of months here. But even that hung in the balance. After the meeting with his boss, his life in the Dales seemed more precarious than ever.

Everything seemed more precarious.

It wasn't simply that he was going to have to fight to prove his innocence, which was going to be hard enough. It was the trouble that was coming with it.

For he'd been warned. Not just by his boss, but also by the mystery woman who seemed to know all about him. She'd called out of the blue in December, alerting him in her sultry tones that his past was catching up with him. He hadn't recognised her voice. Couldn't think of any woman who would fit her profile. Or one who would be willing to help him. Then on Christmas Day she'd called again. This time she'd told him they were going to make him take the fall. Whoever 'they' were. She'd told him to run.

Could he trust her? Should he take her advice? But where would he go? Besides, he hated the thought of turning tail yet again. It had been bad enough the first time, fleeing London when things went sour and his boss advised him to leave town. With the bruises from the balaclava-clad men fresh on his face, he'd come home. The only place he could think of. Hoping to have time to lick his wounds and work out what the hell was going on. And at least be amongst people he knew, even if they weren't all happy to see him back. He'd felt safer here. There was little chance of strangers arriving in Bruncliffe without him knowing.

But now he was suspended from the police force. Formally. Pending investigation into drugs offences.

That's what was hanging over him and he was stuck up here kicking his heels, waiting for goodness knows what to arrive.

His grip tightened on the lead, Tolpuddle shifting in closer to him as though sensing his unease.

'Make the most of it,' he told himself as he walked across the cobbled square in the sunshine, taking in the busy shops, the sense of security that came from being in a community like Bruncliffe. All too soon, he would have to leave. Because even if the trouble that had been threatened never materialised, when news about the investigation broke, he would be hounded out of town anyway.

It was a despondent Detective Constable Samson O'Brien who entered the ginnel that ran parallel to Back Street and let himself into the back yard of the office building. He glanced up at Delilah's window as he walked up the path, continuing to the porch when there was no sign of her.

Yet another reason not to cut and run. Delilah Metcalfe. He smiled, knowing what she'd have to say on the subject. She wasn't the sort of woman to turn her back on trouble. And she'd come to be a big part of his life.

He wondered if she knew how lucky she was being a part of this world. Not having to fear what was coming round the corner.

He turned the key in the door, let the dog off the lead and made his way to the hall, Tolpuddle already trotting towards the stairs.

But the Weimaraner didn't make it that far. Delilah Metcalfe came running down to meet them, tears on her cheeks as she flung herself at Tolpuddle, wrapping her arms around his grey body.

Both dog and man reacted, Samson dropping the pies,

the dog setting up a loud wail of distress as Delilah sobbed into his neck.

'He's coming,' she cried, lifting her face to Samson. 'He's coming. And you have to stop him.'

5

'My ex-husband is trying to get custody of Tolpuddle.'

Delilah kept her gaze fixed on the hallway tiles, not wanting to see the reaction her statement had triggered. It had taken a while for Samson to prise her from Tolpuddle, and a further couple of minutes for her to calm down sufficiently to explain her behaviour. Now she was mortified at having lost control. And at having to divulge her past in order to get help. But the email from Neil had pushed her over the edge.

'You were married.' It was more of a statement than a question, devoid of any nuance. Samson was sitting next to her on the second-from-bottom stair, while the object of her despair was lying in the hall, staring longingly at the plastic bag Samson had dropped on the floor when he'd been confronted by the sobbing Delilah.

'Yes,' she conceded miserably. 'To Neil Taylor.'

She risked a glance at the man next to her. If he shared her brother Will's contempt for the son of local dignitary Bernard Taylor, it didn't show. But then Samson was a master of dissemblance.

'How long for?'

'Long enough. Three years.'

'When did you get divorced?'

'We spilt up two years ago. Shortly after Ryan was

killed. It wasn't a great year,' she said with deliberate understatement. It had been a brutal time for her. Losing her brother. Finding out Neil had had another affair. Struggling to keep their joint web-design business alive and kick-start the Dales Dating Agency. The only highlight amongst all the turmoil had been the arrival of Tolpuddle. 'Neil moved down to London with his new girlfriend and the decree absolute came through almost a year later, on my twenty-eighth birthday.'

'That's well over a year ago.'

She nodded.

'And yet Neil's only asking for custody now?' Samson raised an eyebrow. 'Why the sudden change of heart?'

'God knows,' muttered Delilah. 'He contacted me out of the blue in mid-December. I thought it was about his belongings. I have them stored up on the top floor.' Heat rose up her cheeks, turning them crimson. 'Daft, I know, but I couldn't bear the thought of using anything of his afterwards. Especially not the bed.'

'But it wasn't about that?'

'No. He said he wanted custody of Tolpuddle.' Her voice caught on the name and she fought another swell of tears. 'I was trying to convince myself it wouldn't come to anything. That it was just another of Neil's whims. He can be like that – blowing hot and cold over things.' She gave a dry laugh. 'Me included. So when I didn't hear anything more, I told myself there was nothing to worry about. But then I got an email just now . . .' She faltered, her hand going to her mouth.

'He's coming up?'

'Sunday afternoon. He's bringing his girlfriend, Abbie.' She pulled a face. 'Reading between the lines, I get the feeling she's the driving force behind this.'

'And they're planning on taking Tolpuddle back to London with them? Without a fight?'

Delilah's shoulders slumped. 'What fight can there be? I've been telling myself I'd go to court, but Matty's been really clear. Thanks to the paperwork being in Neil's name, I don't have a leg to stand on.' She pressed the tissue she was holding to her lips, her eyes welling up once more. 'There's nothing I can do.'

'Rubbish!' Samson stood. 'There's always something that can be done. We just need to think this through.'

Tolpuddle rose too and crossed the hall to nose the discarded bag, before looking at Samson wistfully.

'But first things first,' said Samson. 'As Tolpuddle is trying to tell you, we've got some of Mrs Hargreaves' pies, so let's eat before the hound loses patience and starts without us.' He held out his hand and pulled Delilah to her feet. 'And then we'll sort it.'

Mrs Hargreaves' steak-and-ale pie did the trick. Sitting across from Samson at the table in the first-floor kitchen, Delilah placed her cutlery down on her empty plate and smiled.

'Thanks,' she said.

He smiled back at her, relieved to see her spirits lifting. It had been painful witnessing her distress, knowing that she wasn't the type to fall apart easily. It had been equally painful listening to her telling him things she would clearly have rather kept to herself. Especially when he already knew most of it.

Thanks to Bruncliffe's grapevine, he'd heard about Delilah's adulterous husband. And about her divorce. He also knew that he spent each night in the marital bed she couldn't bear to keep.

But as she'd blurted out the whole sorry tale, things had begun to make sense. The whispered conversation with Matty Thistlethwaite; Delilah's sudden reluctance to leave Tolpuddle with Clarissa that morning. Since mid-December she'd been worried sick because her ex-husband was claiming custody of her dog.

Yet it wasn't until Neil Taylor emailed her to say he was coming to town to make real on his threat that she'd seen fit to confide in Samson. It was a fact that hurt the detective irrationally.

'Everything feels better after a pie. Doesn't it, Tolpuddle?' he said.

The dog glanced up from his bowl, a distinct look of satisfaction on his face and a trail of gravy on his chin. Delilah laughed.

'I hope for our sakes that wasn't steak-and-ale he had,' she said. 'You know what he's like after beer.'

Samson grinned, having already witnessed Tolpuddle's adverse reaction to bitter a couple of times since making the dog's acquaintance. Neither had been a sweet-smelling experience. 'Don't worry. He's not going to be toxic. Well, no more than normal.'

As quickly as Delilah's spirits had risen, they plummeted back to the depths of depression. 'I can't bear the thought of life without him,' she whispered.

'You won't have to,' said Samson, feigning a confidence he didn't feel.

'How can you be so sure? Even Matty doesn't think I have a chance.'

'Matty has to operate within the law. We're going to operate outside it.'

'You've got a plan?'

'No. Not yet. But I'm working on it. Tell me more about this girlfriend.'

'I only met her the once.' Delilah's lip curled in disdain. 'She's pretty, if you like waif-thin types. Other than that, I can't really remember her.'

'She didn't make much of an impression?'

'It wasn't that. More that I was concentrating so hard on not thumping Neil, I didn't really take her in. But she seemed high-maintenance. Not the sort to be at home on a farm, you know?'

Samson laughed, knowing that the Metcalfes judged most people by the farmyard barometer. 'Not the sort to go tearing across the fells, either, I suppose.'

'No.' Delilah sounded miserable. 'I doubt Tolpuddle will get much running down there.'

'Tolpuddle isn't going anywhere,' said Samson, rising to his feet and clearing the plates. 'Leave it with me. In the meantime, we need to decide what our next step in the Livvy Thornton case is.'

The reaction was immediate, as he'd known it would be.

'I've been thinking about that,' she said, already tapping at her mobile, distracted by the prospect of being part of the investigation. Samson hid a smile as he placed the dishes in the sink.

'We should go to Leeds,' she was saying. 'See if we can find the hairdresser's Jimmy mentioned. There might be someone there who remembers Livvy.'

'If it still exists. We're better off calling in at the register office. They should have the original paperwork.'

'And *then* we'll go to the hairdresser's,' said Delilah, brandishing her mobile in triumph, a website for Snips Hair Salon showing on the screen.

Samson laughed. 'There won't be any need. I keep telling you this will be straightforward. A simple oversight in the records department. We'll be done in no time.'

'When do you want to go?'

Samson made a pretence of consulting his mobile. 'I'm free tomorrow,' he said. 'How about then?'

'Suits me. I'll call Chris and see if he can get the day off. We can take the train over and then he can chauffeur us around, seeing as he knows the city.'

'Is he averse to O'Briens, too?' asked Samson, trying to remember this Metcalfe brother who'd made the rare decision to move away. Trained as a doctor and working in Leeds, Chris had been at Ellershaw Farm on Christmas Day when Samson, his father and Arty Robinson had joined the Metcalfes for dinner. But the day had been a bit of a blur and Samson hadn't spent any time with him. All he could hope was that as another of the clan with the fair hair, height and slender frame that was typical of the family, Chris – lacking the darker, shorter features shared by Delilah and Will – would lack their temper, too.

Delilah laughed. 'Not that I know of. He's been gone from Bruncliffe a long time. I doubt he'll hold any grudges. But I can't promise anything. Anyway,' she added, holding her mobile to her ear, 'I don't think Chris is allowed to cause injury, as a doctor.'

'Great,' muttered Samson, beginning to wash up the plates as Delilah started talking to her brother. 'I'm relying on the Hippocratic Oath to protect me from the Metcalfe wrath.'

He felt a nudge against his thigh. Tolpuddle, leaning into him, whether in gratitude for the pie or in the hope of more, it was hard to tell. Samson scratched the grey head, filled with sadness at the thought of the dog no longer being part of his life. Or Delilah's. Because despite the assurances he'd given, he didn't see how Tolpuddle could be kept in Bruncliffe. Apart from hiding him. Or faking his death . . .

'Sorted,' Delilah announced, putting her phone away. 'Chris is off duty tomorrow, so we can go over.'

'He's fine with me coming too?'

Delilah grinned sheepishly. 'I didn't tell him. Thought it was best to let him find out in person. Just in case.'

Samson sighed. It was bad enough having to work with one Metcalfe. Having to spend the day with two of them would be hell.

'Right,' said Delilah, getting up from the table. 'I've got to go over to the bank. And then I'm going to run off that pie. What do you reckon, Tolpuddle? Does a blast up on the fells sound good to you?'

The dog barked and began heading for the stairs. Delilah followed him and then paused in the doorway, turning back to Samson.

'Fancy joining us?' she asked.

She made it sound casual, when Samson knew it was

anything but. Delilah Metcalfe, former champion fell-runner who had shunned the sport for so many years, was inviting him to run with her. Like they used to when they were younger.

'I'd love to,' said Samson.

'Excellent. How long do you need to nip home and change?'

He thought of his fictional flat in the village of Helli-field five miles down the road, and then of the reality – the rucksack containing all his belongings up on the second floor. 'I've got my kit with me,' he said, offering the bare truth, knowing from experience that people seldom ques-tioned it.

'In that case, I'll see you at the gate in half an hour. Feel free to change in the bathroom upstairs,' she added gener-ously as she walked off.

Samson finished the washing up, vowing to himself that he would find accommodation soon. Even for a seasoned liar like himself, the deception was getting hard to maintain.

They ran up Crag Lane, concentrating on the changing terrain, the increasing steepness as they approached the looming shape of the crag that rose up at the back of town. Three figures: one small, compact, pacing easily as she ran smoothly upwards; the second one tall, powerful, breath-ing heavily, his dark hair flicking his shoulders; and the third, a grey shadow of muscle, outstripping the others as he bounded gracefully towards the fells.

They were unaware of the binoculars trained on them. The man assessing them, watching her movement in par-ticular – the former champion. And her running companion, returning to the hills after a hiatus of fourteen years. The condition wasn't there yet. But the instinctive style was.

He tracked them up the path that snaked around the outcrop of limestone that towered over Bruncliffe. They were heading for the tops, where the bright skies above would be tempered by the raw east wind. That'd test them.

And when they came back down, he'd be waiting for them with a far-from-welcome surprise.

'Christ, I'm out of condition!' An hour later and Samson was still panting, despite the last half of the run having been downhill. Trying to keep up with Delilah and Tolpuddle as they flew down the fellside was almost as hard as tracking them up it.

Almost.

'A few more runs and you'll get there,' said Delilah with a grin as she jumped down onto Crag Lane, Tolpuddle already waiting for them. 'Of course, it'll take a bit more than that to keep up with me.'

'I'm not sure I'll ever get to that level again,' muttered Samson, joining her on the tarmac.

It had been like old times, out on the hills on a Thursday evening with the Bruncliffe Harriers, the two of them so much better than the rest. Especially Delilah. She was born to run the fells. National junior champion, she'd been heading for the same at senior level when Samson left town. He still didn't understand why she'd walked away from what could have been a bright future. Although her revelations about her youthful marriage went some way towards explaining it.

But she was back running now and the potential was still there. All she needed was a push.

Legs screaming at him, Samson began running down the lane, Delilah and Tolpuddle either side of him. They were almost at the steps that led down to the town when a door was flung open in one of the small cottages that faced the Crag.

'Hold up, you two!'

They both jumped, startled. Seth Thistlethwaite, retired geography teacher, former athletics coach and uncle to Matty, was standing in the doorway, a pair of binoculars around his neck.

'Been spying on folk, Seth?' asked Delilah with a grin as they walked over to him.

Then she spotted the red folder in his hand.

'Is that . . .' she murmured.

'Oh God,' groaned Samson, realising what she'd spotted in Seth's grasp. 'No, please no.'

'Don't start moaning,' barked Seth, tapping the folder. 'If you're going to start running, you might as well do it properly. With a plan.'

The dreaded training plans. Seth had been infamous for them. Gruelling sessions designed to make better runners out of all of them. Although Samson had sometimes suspected they were actually designed to kill. There'd been many an evening when he'd crawled upstairs to bed at the farm, legs buckling under him from the interval training and hill repetitions that Seth had subjected them to. At the time, dealing with his father's drinking and trying to run the farm, Samson had relished the pain, a release from his everyday life. Now, he wasn't so sure he would.

'Give it a try,' muttered Seth, slapping the file into Delilah's hand. 'And re-join the Harriers, the pair of you. It's time you gave a bit back.'

He turned, cutting off any argument with the slam of his front door, leaving Delilah and Samson feeling like the kids they'd been when he first started training them.

From Seth Thistlethwaite's house, tucked in under the Crag at the back of Bruncliffe, there was a direct line of sight across the roofs of the town below and up towards Gunnerstang Brow. A copse of trees shielded the top of the fell, hiding from view the quarry that lay behind them. For Jimmy Thornton, sitting at his mother's kitchen table, there was no hiding from it. Outside the window the exposed stone glared white in the sunlight, the wind kicking up eddies of dust across the deserted space.

But for once, Jimmy didn't notice. After his visitors had left that morning he'd sat alone in the empty kitchen, remembering the violence, hearing the ghostly echo of tears as the past crowded in on him in a room that never felt warm, no matter how much he stoked up the range. Secrets he'd kept buried since childhood, and of which he was now the sole custodian, had been stirred up by Samson and Delilah's questions, threatening to overwhelm him. In an effort to escape the memories, he'd decided to make a start on the task of clearing out the house.

He'd begun in his mother's bedroom, emptying the wardrobe item by item – sorting out the clothes, folding up the good ones and putting them into bin bags to be taken to the Age Concern shop once the will was settled. There hadn't been a lot to pack, his mother having been a frugal woman and not one for hoarding or sentimentality. Which is why he'd been surprised when he'd found the shoebox at the bottom of the cupboard.

Beige in colour, it had a swirl of script across the lid: *Beryl's Shoes.*

Lifting it onto the bed, he'd known from the weight that it contained more than just shoes. He'd taken off the lid, stared at the contents for a moment, and decided this was a job to be done over a cup of tea. More than an hour later he was still sitting at the kitchen table, a mug to one side, the tea untouched and long cold.

First he'd come to postcards from his sister's penfriend in Melbourne, a thin strata across the top of the box. He'd gathered them up and put them aside, revealing the treasures underneath. A bundle of photos of Livvy, auburn hair vivid in the summer sun or tucked up in winter hats; Livvy with her little brother; Livvy at school. He flicked through the thick pile and then placed them beside the postcards.

Next he pulled out a tiny shoe, the buckle shiny, the sole barely worn. Underneath that, a Mother's Day card, home-made egg-box daffodil protruding from the background and daubed in yellow. Inside, Livvy's unsteady hand had signed her name in bold crayon, kisses covering the bottom half of the page. A swimming certificate. A rag doll with a fabric eye peeling, red hair straggly with age.

Only two items were left. A small jeweller's box. And a Yorkshire Tea caddy.

He pulled out the jeweller's box, the burgundy leather scuffed at the edges. He recognised it straight away, even though he hadn't seen it in years. His mother's engagement ring had always nestled inside, the single diamond an object of fascination for him as a child, something so precious that it was never worn apart from on Sundays when Mother went to church.

He flipped open the lid. The box was empty. He stared at the deep fold in the white interior where the ring was supposed to reside, puzzled. Had she lost it and never said? Or perhaps sold it, given the way Father had been. But why keep the empty box?

He laid it on the table along with the rest of the contents and turned to the tea caddy, the last thing in the shoebox. It was heavy. Inside, a stack of letters, tied together with a red ribbon. The first thing he noticed was the Leeds postmark and the unusual address. The second thing he noticed was the handwriting.

Jimmy Thornton felt the past collide with the present and the letters fell to the table, spilling out of their ribboned constraints. He waited a couple of heartbeats before picking up the top envelope, pulling out the letter and beginning to read. Then he reached for the phone.

6

'Livvy was writing to her mother in secret?' Delilah looked up from the image of a letter on Samson's phone, the question asked in a lowered voice, respecting the fact that the train they were travelling on was filled with folk from Bruncliffe.

Samson nodded. 'Jimmy called me when we got back from the run yesterday, just after you'd gone home. He was on his way into town so he dropped by to show me what he'd found.'

'How many letters were there?'

'Twelve. Almost one a week for the time Livvy was in Leeds. The last one was two weeks before her death.'

'And Jimmy didn't know about them before now?'

'He says not.'

'How odd.' Delilah stared at the sloping handwriting and felt a pang of sadness for the girl. 'She couldn't even write to her mother openly.'

'It appears that way. And look who was the intermediary.' Samson flicked to a photograph of an envelope on his mobile.

Born and bred in Bruncliffe, Delilah didn't need telling. The envelope was addressed not to Mrs Thornton at Quarry House, but to Croft Cottage in Thorpdale, a small house that sat at the start of the remote dale to the north of town.

'Ida Capstick,' she muttered, thinking about the straight-talking cleaner who lived in the immaculate cottage with her brother, George. She was responsible for keeping Delilah's office building – and its occupants – in order. 'It's not like Ida to get involved in another family's business.'

'Not at all. Which makes me think there must have been more to Livvy's departure from town than we know.'

'Like what?' asked Delilah.

Samson shrugged. 'Family stuff,' he said, knowing from experience how complicated that could get. Knowing also that outsiders rarely had a true understanding of what happened within families. His own was a prime example. One fight at a christening and he had been cast as the black sheep by Bruncliffe, just because the fight happened to be with his father. The christening was that of his best friend's son – Ryan Metcalfe's lad, Nathan, who was now a strapping fourteen-year-old. The fact that Samson had been godfather to the infant had cast further condemnation on his behaviour. That he'd fled the town that night on his father's motorbike had sealed his reputation. Yet not one person had ever asked him what had been the catalyst for the argument which had ended in violence. Or knew about the shotgun he'd had pointed at him when he'd returned to the farm after the fight.

If there was anything Samson had learned in his thirty-four years on the planet, it was that families were a law unto themselves. One best not interfered with.

'Well, if Livvy did fall out with someone, it must have

been her father,' said Delilah, pointing to the photo on Samson's phone. 'Which would explain why she was writing to her mother on the quiet. It would also explain why her parents never talked about her.'

'Don't forget we only have Jimmy's word that they never spoke about her,' cautioned Samson.

'What are you suggesting?'

He shrugged. 'I got the sense young Jimmy was holding back when we were up there yesterday. I think he knows more than he's letting on.'

Delilah laughed. 'You've been away too long! While folk around here are happy to spread gossip about neighbours and friends, no one in Bruncliffe airs their own laundry willingly. Least of all farmers. Jimmy was behaving the same way anyone would if someone was prying into their affairs.'

'Especially if that someone's an offcumden?' asked Samson with a wry smile, knowing that the local term for outsider would always be applied to him by his fellow townsfolk.

'Which is exactly why Matty asked me to be on the case,' said Delilah with a triumphant grin. 'So,' she continued, 'we think Livvy's move to Leeds might have been more than just a change of scenery. I wonder what it was that drove her away?'

'Luckily we're not tasked with investigating the Thorntons,' Samson said, noticing the gleam of speculation in his partner's eyes. 'We simply have to get a copy of Livvy's death certificate.'

'And this?' Delilah indicated the photo of the envelope. 'If we don't have any success at the register office, it might come in handy. Livvy was helpful enough to write her own address at the top of her letters. It'll be a good starting point, if we need it.'

Delilah handed him back his mobile and turned to stare out of the window. It had been an early start, standing on a cold Bruncliffe platform by seven-fifteen to catch the first train. Huddled inside her thick winter coat, hands thrust deep in her pockets, she'd pitied the commuters around her who had to make this journey every morning. She'd been amongst their number herself after she left school, taking the train to Skipton each day for six years, working her way up in a newly established tech company and studying at college in the evening.

She didn't miss it. The freezing wait in winter. The unbearable waste of precious hours on the train in the summer when she could have been out running. She'd been more than happy to give it up when she'd set up her web-design business with her then-husband, basing themselves in Bruncliffe, where her commute became a walk down the hill into town.

But Delilah had to admit – if she had to commute, it would be difficult to beat this journey. Pulling out of Bruncliffe, the train was almost immediately in the open countryside, gliding down the dale, the fells rising up around it. In the half-light of a winter's morning, the stone walls that cut across the fields were black grid-lines corralling the white smudges of sheep like a giant game of noughts and crosses. It was hard for Delilah Metcalfe, Bruncliffe to her bones, to imagine living anywhere else. To imagine wanting to live anywhere else.

Yet Livvy Thornton had been eager to leave all of this.

To escape to the vibrancy and bustle of Leeds, for whatever reason. But within a few months of leaving, she was dead, her life cut short by a reckless driver.

It put things into perspective. Delilah's troubles – the debt, the struggling businesses, the failed marriage – amounted to nothing in light of the price Livvy had paid for trying to change her destiny. As for Tolpuddle . . . She glanced down at the grey shape curled up on the floor between the seats, the dog having managed to place a part of his body on both Samson's and Delilah's feet, binding them all together even in his sleep.

'We'll sort it,' Samson said softly, guessing the direction of her thoughts.

Delilah forced a smile. Because while Matty had been right about telling Samson, the weight of this problem made lighter by having shared it, she didn't for a moment believe that there was anything Samson O'Brien could do to prevent Tolpuddle leaving their lives. She was resigned to making the most of the next four days. She would deal with the aftermath when it came.

'You haven't told me yet what Clive Knowles wanted yesterday,' continued Samson.

Delilah's gaze lifted from the dog and she grimaced. 'A wife.'

Samson let out a loud laugh of surprise, startling some of the commuters from their half-slumber. 'You're joking?'

'I wish I was. He's given me a two-month deadline.'

'No pressure, then!' Samson was grinning now. 'Where are you going to start? With giving him a bath?'

She smiled in response. 'Wouldn't be a bad idea. Then

I'm going to work on his profile. See if I can't tweak it a bit and invite some suitable replies.'

'*Tweak* it? It'll take more than that. The man's a Neanderthal. No sane woman would touch him.'

'You don't need to remind me,' Delilah groaned. 'But I have to try, no matter how impossible it seems.'

She didn't mention that her motivation was more than simply job satisfaction. The handsome bonus that the farmer had promised would coincide with the end of the six months' grace period granted to her by the bank on her loans; those extra funds in her account would mean the difference between solvency and ruin. The very success of her businesses rested on her finding a wife for Clive Knowles. She would give it everything she had.

'Somewhere out there someone is waiting for him,' she murmured, trying to convince herself. 'I just have to find them.'

'Good luck with that. But if you want my advice, stick Ralph up as the profile photo,' quipped Samson, referring to Clive Knowles' prize-winning Swaledale tup. 'That lad has no problem attracting the lasses!'

Delilah gave a hiccup of a laugh. 'Why didn't I think of that?' Then she sighed and pulled her laptop out of her rucksack. 'I suppose I'd better do a bit of work. A woman willing to marry that man is going to take some finding.'

Samson watched, amused, as her fingers flicked across the keyboard, her attention totally on her hopeless assignment. He looked down at the snoozing dog, pleased to have diverted Delilah's attention from that particular problem, if only for a while.

As to how he would manage to keep Tolpuddle in

Bruncliffe, he still didn't have a clue. The woman sitting opposite wasn't the only one facing mission impossible.

'Delilah didn't mention you were coming.'

The tall figure of Chris Metcalfe hailed them at the entrance to Leeds station, fair hair falling carelessly across his forehead in a way that made him look too young to be a doctor. Fourth son of the Metcalfes, he was three years older than Delilah, the same age as Jimmy Thornton. But whereas the farmer from Bruncliffe carried an aura of maturity about him that was common to most folk who worked the land, Chris still had the youthful air of a student. Although, from the bulk of muscle straining against his down jacket, there was nothing immature about his physique. It was with some relief that Samson noticed the hand being held out towards him wasn't clenched.

'Good to see you again,' continued the doctor.

'Likewise,' said Samson.

'So, where first?' Chris looked from Samson to Delilah and back again. 'My car is at your command.'

'The register office—'

'Snips Hair Salon—'

The two voices cancelled each other out, making Chris laugh.

'We're here to find a copy of the death certificate,' Samson stated. 'So it makes sense to start at the register office.'

'But if they had a copy, it would have been online and Matty would have found it,' replied Delilah, hand on hip and jaw thrust forward in a way her brother recognised. It didn't bode well for the day ahead. 'So we're better off going to Livvy's place of work and doing some proper investigating.'

'I keep telling you, there's nothing to investigate. This is simply a matter of a computer error. You, of all people, should appreciate that.'

'Computers don't make errors,' snapped Delilah, 'humans do.'

'How about,' interjected Chris, 'we start at the place closest to us?' He gestured to the town centre behind him. 'The register office is only a short walk away and will be open in fifteen minutes. So,' he added, sweetening Delilah's defeat, 'we can get a coffee on the way. I know a place that does an excellent bacon butty.'

Tolpuddle let out a bark at the mention of bacon, settling the argument, and Chris led the way into town, a town that Samson was already struggling to recognise from his time as a trainee policeman. Following the Metcalfes through the swarm of morning commuters, he bizarrely found himself already pining for the open spaces of Bruncliffe.

An hour and a half later, Samson and Delilah were exiting the register office on Great George Street.

'Don't say it!' Samson warned.

Delilah grinned, a finger on her lips as they crossed to the low wall where Chris was waiting with Tolpuddle. 'I didn't say a word.'

'Any luck?' asked Chris.

Samson shook his head. 'Not a trace. No Olivia Thornton on any registration covering the period she was here.'

'So it wasn't a simple mistake with the date. Or a computer error,' added Delilah with a smug smile.

'Where next, then?' Chris asked.

'Snips Hair—'

'The library,' said Samson, overriding Delilah. 'We need to check the archives for the day of Livvy's death. A fatal accident would have been headline news in the local press, and it might give us a pointer as to why her death doesn't seem to have been recorded.'

Chris nodded. 'That makes sense, and the library is just around the corner.'

'*Then* we're going to Snips,' muttered Delilah as she tagged along behind the two men and Tolpuddle, feeling exactly as she had all those years ago when Samson and Ryan had endured her presence.

'Nothing.' On the second floor of the library in a room dedicated to local history, Samson scrolled through the newspaper archives once more, shaking his head. 'No mention of an accident, fatal or otherwise. And no mention of Olivia Thornton at all.'

'Do you think it just got overlooked?' Delilah was sitting beside him, peering at the screen. For the past hour they had diligently trawled through old editions of *The Yorkshire Post*, the *Yorkshire Evening Post*, the *Wetherby News* and the *Craven Herald* from the year Livvy died, looking not just at May the twenty-ninth, but at the days and weeks around it. They hadn't found a thing.

'If it was a mere accident, maybe. But not a fatality. Local papers thrive on news like that.' Samson sat back in his chair, staring at the headlines from more than twenty years ago. 'I don't get it,' he muttered. 'No official record of her death. And now no account of it in the press, either. Something isn't right.'

'Maybe we're looking in the wrong place,' said Delilah.

'What do you mean?'

'Leeds. Maybe she wasn't here.'

'You mean she lied about where she was living?'

Delilah nodded. 'Her family had no contact with her during those few months, apart from the handful of letters she sent home. It would have been easy for her to tell her mother she was in one place, while living in a completely different part of the country. Who would know?'

Thinking of his own situation and the double life he was leading in terms of accommodation, Samson knew she had a valid point. Who would know? Except . . .

'What about this?' He took out his mobile and pulled up a photo of one of Livvy's letters. 'Why would she bother putting an address at the top of the page unless she was getting replies?'

'Perhaps Livvy had her own Ida Capstick.'

'Another intermediary?' Samson considered the idea. 'Perhaps. Either way, there's nothing more we can do here.' He pushed his chair away from the desk and stood to go.

'So, next stop Snips,' said Delilah, following him.

Samson was already shaking his head as he started down the library's ornate staircase. 'Not yet. I want to check out the house on North Park Avenue, the address on Livvy's letter.'

'But that could be miles away,' protested Delilah. 'And what can you possibly learn from it anyhow? It's over twenty years since she lived there. *If* she lived there.'

'Right now it's the only firm connection we have to her, so that's where we're going. Besides, it's nearer than the hairdresser's.'

'You're just saying that,' Delilah argued, picking up her pace in order to keep up with his longer stride as they headed down the final flight of stairs.

'Fine,' said Samson. 'How about we let Chris decide, seeing as he's the local?'

'Let's do that,' Delilah said, marching through the door he was holding open and down the steps onto the pavement.

They crossed the road and headed into the pub on the corner where Chris and Tolpuddle were sitting by a window, Chris reading a paper and drinking a coffee, Tolpuddle stretching next to him as he spotted their approach.

'Did you find anything?' Chris asked.

Samson leaned down to scratch behind Tolpuddle's ears. 'No. Not a thing.'

'So what now?'

'Whichever is nearest – Snips Hair Salon on Street Lane or North Park Avenue.' Samson smiled at Delilah.

'They're both in Roundhay,' said Chris, folding his paper and getting to his feet. 'But North Park Avenue is definitely closer.'

Samson grinned, taking a step back as Delilah turned on him.

'How the hell did you know that?' she muttered.

'You forget,' he said, ushering her ahead of him as they all trooped out of the pub. 'I used to live here. Roundhay was on my beat.'

Delilah cursed under her breath. How could she have forgotten the years Samson had spent in the city? Whenever she thought of his life away from Bruncliffe, she associated him with London. Yet Leeds had been the first place he'd lived when he left home, where he'd trained as a policeman.

'Fine,' she said, with a bright smile. 'Your choice of destination, so my choice of seat in the car. And I'm taking the front one.'

When they arrived at the car park five minutes later, it was easy to see Delilah had insider knowledge.

'It might be a bit of a squeeze,' Chris was saying as he unlocked the midnight-blue Mini Cooper convertible. 'But we're not going that far.'

'Be my guest,' said Delilah with a grin, opening the passenger door and folding forward the front seat. Tolpuddle was fastest off the mark, hopping in and sprawling out in the back.

'I thought you Metcalfes liked cars that can carry sheep,' muttered Samson as he squeezed in next to the dog, getting a lick on his cheek from his travelling companion.

Chris laughed. 'You're thinking of the farming Metcalfes. The urban variety prefers a bit of style.'

With dog breath on his neck and a heavy paw on his lap, as they headed out into the suburbs Samson couldn't help thinking that style was vastly overrated.

North Park Avenue wasn't what Delilah had expected. When she'd envisioned young Livvy Thornton making her life away from home, she'd pictured a bedsit above a takeaway or a shared house in a down-at-heel area. A tree-lined avenue with large houses set back behind high hedges didn't really fit with that image.

'Wow!' she said, stepping out of the car, Samson and Tolpuddle spilling out onto the pavement behind her. 'Are you sure you've got the right road?' She turned back the way they'd come, the tennis courts of Roundhay Park visible on the other side of the T-junction just yards away, the park stretching out beyond them. Its expanse of green was another thing Delilah hadn't anticipated in the heart of the city. She wondered if its proximity had made leaving the Dales easier for Livvy.

'Certain,' said Samson. He pointed away from the tennis courts. 'It should be this way.'

They set off along the pavement, Tolpuddle tugging at his lead as he took in all the new scents, Chris and Delilah craning their necks trying to see some of the residences hidden down driveways.

'Here,' said Samson, coming to a halt at a property bordered by overgrown hedges, a solid fence towering up behind them. 'This is it.'

'Bugger!' Delilah stared at the fence. It was impossible to see anything through it. Or over it.

'It's being developed,' said Chris, pointing at the wrought-iron gates which had been similarly barricaded. Fixed to the metal railings was a sign:

Danger. Construction Site. Keep Out.

'I guess we're not going to learn much here, then,' said Delilah, turning to Samson with the beginnings of a smug smile.

'I don't know about that,' he muttered. He'd moved

over to the gate and was looking at the sign. 'Guess who the developer is.'

Delilah shrugged. 'Does it matter?'

He stepped aside, letting her get close enough to read the small writing at the bottom of the sign.

'Procter Properties?' she exclaimed, turning to Chris. 'Rick Procter has development projects over here?'

Chris nodded. 'I've seen a few of his placards on buildings that are being renovated. He buys big houses like these and converts them into flats. There's good money in it.'

'Crikey.' Delilah stared at the sign and then at the fence, disconcerted to find a slice of Bruncliffe in the middle of this city. 'What a coincidence. He's developing the house that Livvy Thornton lived in.'

Samson grunted. 'Coincidence indeed.' He stepped back, assessing the line of fence, trees and bushes growing on the other side of it. 'Reckon I might take a look.'

He grabbed hold of the stone gatepost, put a foot on a bar in the gate and hauled himself up onto its top railing, a hand on the fence keeping him balanced.

'What are you doing?' hissed Delilah, whipping round to check the empty street. 'That's trespassing.'

Samson grinned down at her and held out a hand. 'Coming with me?'

Tolpuddle's lead was thrust at Chris and Delilah was scrambling up onto the gate in seconds.

'Delilah!' protested Chris, doing his best to be the older brother. 'Come back down. You'll get hurt. Or arrested. Or both!'

Her grin mirrored Samson's. 'We won't be long. If you see anyone coming, whistle.'

And with that, she pulled herself over the top of the fence after Samson and disappeared.

'It's massive!' Delilah whispered, head tipped back to take in the house.

Sitting at the top of a winding drive that kept it hidden from the road, the property was built from stone. A lot of stone. It was bordered on each end with wide double-bow windows topped by gables, the arched windows in the gable peaks indicating a third storey. In between these magnificent bookends, a set of generous double doors sat above curved steps, a mullioned window above them. With a rack of chimneys on both ends, the house was magnificent. If slightly eerie.

It was the stone. Dark, almost black in places, it gave the building a sombre air. It wasn't a place Delilah would want to spend a night alone in.

'Have you noticed the windows?' murmured Samson. 'Boarded up from the inside, every one of them.'

'It's a development project. Surely that's normal?'

'Maybe. But I don't see much evidence of any developing going on.'

It was true. The building seemed untouched. Merely closed up and closed off from the road beyond. There were no builders' tools outside, no cement mixer and definitely no white van.

'Come on,' said Samson, heading towards it. 'Let's have a look around the back.'

They walked round the house and got their first glimpse of the overgrown rear garden. With mature trees ringing the boundary and bushes growing up between them, it was completely private, even in the depths of winter with the branches bare of foliage.

'It's not quite what I imagined when I thought of Livvy's accommodation,' Delilah admitted.

Samson gave a low laugh. 'No, it's not what you'd expect a student hairdresser to be living in.'

'So do you think I might be right? That Livvy used this purely as a delivery address?'

'Possibly. But that still means she knew whoever lived here so there has to be some connection. It's just discovering what it is.'

They turned to take in the back of the house. Less ornate than the front, it faced blankly onto the untended lawn, each window shuttered with plywood. Apart from one on the top floor. As Samson was looking up at it, he saw a shift in the light behind the unblinkered glass, the outline of a figure pulling back out of sight.

'We might have company,' he murmured, taking Delilah's arm and beginning to retrace their steps around the house. 'Let's get out of here.'

They were past the front edge of the house and hurrying down the drive when they heard the door open. Prepared to try and charm his way out of the situation, Samson turned towards the sound. But no one appeared on the steps, the yawning door revealing nothing but a dark interior.

'Should we go and apologise?' asked Delilah, a guilty look on her face.

Before Samson could reply, a shrill whistle cut the air. Not from beyond the fence where Chris Metcalfe was waiting. But from within the house. It precipitated the scrabble of paws on tiles.

Date with Mystery

'Run!' shouted Samson, as a bundle of black bristle and muscle came tearing out of the open door.

A Rottweiler. Looking far from friendly.

7

There was no leash on the dog. It was running free. And after them.

Following Delilah's fleeing figure, Samson raced for the fence. The fence that was on their side of the gate with no handy foothold to help them get over it. Without the benefit of that leg-up, it would be impossible to scale.

'The trees, Delilah,' he yelled. 'Head for the trees.'

He saw her veer to the left, making for a broad oak, its branches low to the ground. Behind him he could hear the fast approach of the dog. He risked a glance over his shoulder and wished he hadn't. The Rottweiler was closing rapidly. There was no way to reach the trees before it would be upon him.

Faster – run faster. Legs pounding across the gravel, lungs bursting, he raced for the oak, where Delilah was already swinging herself up onto a bough.

'Come on,' she screamed back at him, her hand held out as though to pull him on. 'Samson! Run faster!'

He was running as fast as he could. But he could hear the approach of the dog, paws scattering gravel, the heavy pant of pursuit. It was impossible. He was never going to outrun it.

Making a snap decision, he yanked down the zip of his jacket, managing to shrug it off one arm as he ran. Then he wheeled around, with the jacket bundled over his other arm, and faced the dog.

Teeth bared, it was already bunching, ready to jump. As it sprang towards him, a ferocious barking set up from the other side of the fence. Tolpuddle. Deep, anxious barks. Paws slamming on the fence, rattling the boards.

It was enough to distract the Rottweiler, its leap losing momentum as its attention was pulled towards this newer, louder threat. Making the most of the distraction, Samson swung his jacket towards the beast, loose sleeve trailing, and with a flash of sharp teeth, the Rottweiler bit into the flapping fabric. Teeth tearing at the cloth, the dog landed back on the gravel, Samson throwing the rest of the jacket over it before turning on his heel and running for his life towards Delilah's outstretched hand.

It gained him a couple of seconds. No more. But it was enough.

Reaching the tree, he grabbed hold of the bough and Delilah's hand and hauled himself up beside her, the Rottweiler already stretched up along the trunk, snapping at his heels as he pulled his legs up behind him.

'You took your bloody time,' she muttered, staring down at the snarling canine prowling beneath the tree.

Samson didn't reply, his lungs sucking deep breaths of air into his body.

'You're going to need to go shopping,' she added. She nodded towards the drive, where the Rottweiler had returned to the discarded jacket and was savaging the material in a frenzy of teeth and paws.

A second whistle split the air, sharp, high. The dog froze. Looked back over its shoulder. Then bounded back up the drive towards the house. From the safety of the tree, they watched it disappear inside the building, the door slamming shut behind it.

'Next time you suggest we go trespassing,' murmured Delilah, cheeks flushed, eyes wide, 'remind me to pass.'

Samson grinned. 'Next time I suggest we go trespassing, remind me not to give you a head start.'

'Head start?' she exclaimed. 'I was simply faster than you and you know it.'

'Have you two finished arguing over there?' Chris Metcalfe's voice carried to them from the other side of the fence. 'Because if you have, I've got a dog here that's frantic to see you.'

A whine from Tolpuddle underlined Chris's words and with one last mournful look at the black strips of lacerated fabric on the drive, Samson followed Delilah up the tree and out over the fence. It was the second jacket he'd lost in his time as a private detective, the first having been burned to a cinder in a fire. At this rate, he was going to have to start putting them on expenses.

'You could have been killed!' Chris muttered, spearing a chip with his fork and glaring at Delilah.

They were sitting in a pub on the edge of Roundhay Park, the three of them having decided that food was needed after a close brush with the sharp side of a Rottweiler. With a fire blazing in the grate nearby, now that drinks and plates were in front of them and Tolpuddle was lying under the table munching contentedly on some dog treats, shock was setting in.

'How were we to know there'd be a massive hound the

other side of that fence?' demanded Delilah, taking attack as her form of defence. 'There was no sign on the gate.'

'That's precisely my point. You had no idea what you were getting into, yet you still went over there. Imagine if something had happened. How the hell would I have explained that to the rest of the family?'

Delilah rolled her eyes. 'You're as bad as Will. One day you're all going to have to accept that I'm no longer the little sister tagging along.'

'When you stop being so reckless, perhaps we'll take note,' said Chris.

'Great burger,' interjected Samson brightly, holding up his eight-ounce Chef's Special in the hope of breaking up the familial tension. In return he got two hard stares from the Metcalfe siblings, as ferocious as that of the snarling Rottweiler.

He sighed, putting the burger reluctantly back on his plate. Reluctantly because it really was good. Although after being chased by a savage dog, anything would taste good. 'It wasn't Delilah's fault, Chris,' he said. 'I talked her into going in there. So if there's any blame to be had, it rests with me.'

'Rubbish!' snapped Delilah. 'I'm old enough to make my own decisions. And it's time my overprotective brothers realised that. They've always tried to wrap me in cotton wool but since Ryan got killed, it's been worse. It drives me mad.'

Whether it was the mention of his deceased brother or an attempt – as the older sibling – to bring an end to the argument, Chris didn't respond, focusing instead on his meal, his jaw clenched as he cut into his Yorkshire ham and eggs. Apart from the crackling of the fire, the clink of cutlery and the occasional contended sigh from under the table, a strained silence settled on the group. Samson was wishing he could join Tolpuddle out of range of the Metcalfe ire when Delilah, unable to bear the awkward atmosphere or hold a grudge, finally spoke up.

'Besides,' she muttered, 'you're missing the point. Instead of berating me for going over the fence, you should be asking what on earth a guard dog was doing there.'

'Guarding the place?' replied Chris wryly.

'What, though? There was nothing in there.'

Samson looked up from his plate. 'Good point,' he murmured, wondering why he hadn't thought of that. 'No tools. No sign of development. No workers. Yet there's a guard dog.'

'And at least one person on site. That door didn't open on its own.'

'Did you see anyone?' asked Chris, Delilah's curiosity becoming contagious.

'The windows were all boarded up. But Samson thought he saw someone on the top floor.'

'It was the only unshuttered window,' Samson explained. 'I saw a shift in the light, as though someone had moved behind the glass. But it could have been nothing.'

'It saved us,' said Delilah. 'Gave us the head start we needed.'

Samson laughed. 'So you admit it, you did have an advantage.'

He was relieved to see a grin appear in response. 'I'm admitting nothing of the sort.'

'Are you going to report it?' asked Chris.

'What?' Samson turned to him. 'That we were attacked by a guard dog while trespassing? I don't think the police will see our side of it.'

'Even if the dog was deliberately set on you without any warning?'

'It'd be our word against the testimony of whoever is guarding that place.' He shook his head. 'There's no point.'

'You could sue them for a new jacket,' Delilah said, still grinning.

'I'm thinking of putting it on expenses. Let Matty pay.'

'Knowing Matty Thistlethwaite,' said Chris, smiling too now, 'I think he'd find a way to wriggle out of that. After all, you didn't discover anything pertinent to your case by going in there.'

'Chris is right,' agreed Delilah, the dispute of moments before forgotten as the Metcalfes united against Samson. 'That house didn't lead us any further on in the investigation. I told you it would be a waste of time.'

Samson laid down his knife and fork and pushed his empty plate away. 'Maybe,' he conceded, unwilling to reveal that, for him, the house had been yet one more piece in the puzzle that was Rick Procter. Some day all of those pieces would be linked together and Samson would be able to show Bruncliffe the true nature of its golden boy. For now, he was content to have brother and sister gang up on him if it brought about peace. 'Perhaps you were right too, Delilah, when you suggested Livvy never lived in Leeds.'

'You think that's a possibility?' asked Chris.

'It's looking more and more likely. It would explain why there's no record of her death here, either in official documents or in the press.'

'So she was using the house in North Park Avenue as a drop box?'

'Yes. Which means we need to get a look at the deeds and trace ownership back to the time Livvy was supposed to be in the city. There must be a connection there worth following up.'

'And in the meantime?'

'Police records,' said Delilah, looking at Samson. 'A fatal accident would have to have been investigated. Surely you've got some contacts on the force from your time here that we could ask to check for us?'

Samson gave a non-committal shrug, ruing Delilah's shrewdness. He knew the accident would be on record. But, to his frustration, he no longer had access to the police database and wasn't in any position to go calling in favours. Least of all in Leeds, where his career had started and his current status would cause the most disappointment.

'I lost touch with everyone,' he lied. 'Being undercover doesn't exactly lend itself to sustaining friendships.'

'Well in that case,' said Delilah, accepting his reply without question, 'next up is Snips. Finally.'

'And then back into town to get me a jacket,' added Samson. It was only mid-February and he knew, from bitter experience, that winter in North Yorkshire lasted well into what should be spring. He wouldn't get through it without a substantial outer layer.

'What about Tolpuddle?' queried Chris.

'What about him?' asked Delilah.

Her brother nodded towards the bar with a grin. 'Is he coming with us or staying with his new friends?'

Samson and Delilah turned to see what had captured

Chris's attention: Tolpuddle, sitting between the bar stools of two old men, soaking up their attention.

'Good boy,' one of the men was saying, patting the grey head. Tolpuddle pushed into the offered hand and then nosed towards the almost-empty pint glass the other man was holding.

'Here, be my guest,' the second man laughed, extending the glass towards the eager dog, who began lapping at the dark-brown beer.

Samson was the first to react. 'Bagsy front seat!'

'That's not fair,' Delilah groaned, while Chris looked nonplussed.

'What's the problem?' he asked as Delilah left the table to retrieve her dog from his admirers, a trace of froth on the Weimaraner's muzzle.

'You'll see,' said Samson. He stood up and followed Chris in the wake of Delilah and Tolpuddle out of the pub. 'How far away is the hairdresser's?'

'A couple of minutes. We could walk it in ten.'

'Oh no,' said Samson with a sly grin as they stepped out onto the pavement, Delilah already heading for the car. 'Let's drive. And take the scenic route.'

Chris shrugged. 'If you're sure.'

A minute later they were pulling away from the kerb, Samson and Chris up front, Delilah squashed in the back with a sleepy Weimaraner. By the time they drove past the boarded-up property on North Park Avenue, the Mini's windows were all open and Chris was contemplating putting the top down, while focusing on the quickest route possible to their destination.

*

The sound of the Mini driving past didn't disturb the man standing on the drive of the large stone property on North Park Avenue. Concealed behind the solid fence, he wasn't worried about being seen. Nor was he worried about the aggressive dog that had roamed the garden just hours before.

What he was worried about was the person on the other end of the phone.

'I don't know who they were,' the man stuttered into his mobile, looking at the remnants of a black jacket in his hand. 'It was a man and a woman.'

'How the hell did they get in?'

'Over the fence.'

'And the dog? Did you let it loose?'

'Yes. As soon as we noticed the intruders.'

'But it didn't catch them?'

'Not quite. The guy threw his jacket at it.'

A scornful bark of derision came down the phone. 'Some guard dog. I should have it shot. And you with it.'

The man on the drive paled, sensing it wasn't an idle threat.

'What about the jacket? Anything in it?'

'That's why I was calling,' said the man, feeling more confident. 'There was something in the pocket.'

'What?'

'A business card. For a detective agency.'

The silence on the line turned ominous.

'There's a name on it,' the man continued, his burgeoning confidence quashed beneath the lack of response. 'It says "Samson O'Brien".'

A hiss of released breath and then a chilling question. 'Were you seen?'

'No. I don't think so . . . No. Definitely not.' The man stumbled over the words, desperate to reassure.

'You don't seem certain.'

The man gulped. 'I'm certain, Mr Procter. Very certain. They didn't see me.'

The click told him he was talking to thin air. Jacket trailing in his hand, he walked back towards the house, a sheen of sweat on his top lip and the chill of fear in his stomach.

'Bloody hell!' Chris was standing by the open door of the car, face aghast as Samson and Delilah scrambled out after him, Delilah looking green. 'What was that?'

'Beer,' muttered Delilah as her dog roused himself and sauntered out onto the pavement to regard them all with a bemused expression, ears half-cocked, head to one side. 'Tolpuddle's allergic to beer.'

'I think you mean we're all allergic to Tolpuddle once he's had a beer,' countered Chris, hand over his mouth as he closed the car door. 'In all my years in the hospital I've never smelled anything so bad.'

Samson grinned. 'He's our own chemical weapon.' He ruffled the dog's ears with affection.

'Well he can wait outside while you two go and do your investigating,' said Chris. 'He's not getting back in my car until he's been fully disarmed.'

'Come on,' said Samson, clipping on Tolpuddle's lead. 'A bit of exercise might do you good.'

With Delilah next to him, he led the dog along Street

Lane, the wind cutting through his jumper in the absence of his jacket as he took in the changes since he'd patrolled the area in his newly acquired police uniform.

It was a part of Leeds that had always had a suburban chic, but whereas that chic had veered towards shabby in Samson's time, now it was the trendy bustling heart of Roundhay. Delicatessens, wine bars, restaurants, a couple of independent boutiques, a bakery and the usual smattering of charity shops, all being frequented by an astounding number of people for a weekday afternoon. It spoke of an affluence that Samson didn't remember. But then he hadn't been on the beat long here before he was transferred to the more troublesome Harehills to the south. That had been an altogether different experience.

'There it is.' Delilah broke into his reminiscences, pointing towards a hairdresser's sandwiched between an estate agent's and a tanning parlour.

SNIPS Hair Salon.

Silver writing on a black background, a pair of scissors cutting through a lock of hair cleverly forming the 'N' in the name, it looked sophisticated. Not the sort of place Samson would brave when it came to getting his hair trimmed.

'I'm guessing this isn't somewhere you frequented,' said Delilah, reading his thoughts with a grin.

He laughed, running a hand over his mane. 'No. I had a crew cut back then. I used to keep it in check myself with a pair of clippers.'

Delilah smiled, remembering the cropped hair of the young man who'd fled Bruncliffe. 'I'm happy to do the talking,' she said as they approached the smoked-glass frontage of the salon.

'Be my guest,' Samson replied, silently relieved. Hairdressers were on a par with lingerie boutiques in terms of places that made him break out in a cold sweat. 'Although I still think it's a long shot. The place has probably changed hands several times in the last two decades.'

'Not according to Companies House.' Delilah gave him a smug look. 'I checked and it's still registered to the same owner as back in Livvy's day – a Mrs Paula Atkins. Let's hope this isn't her day off.'

She opened the door, releasing a blast of feminine scents – shampoo, hairspray, perm lotion – all carried on the noise of hairdryers and female chatter. Already unnerved, Samson edged behind Delilah, Tolpuddle tucking in next to him as though he too felt out of place in this woman's world.

'Here for a cut, love?' called out a large woman wielding a pair of scissors.

'No, actually—'

The lady laughed, cutting Delilah off. 'Not you. Him.' She tipped her head towards the awkward figure of Samson. 'Wouldn't mind getting my hands on those locks.'

Samson blushed while the women in the salon burst into laughter, made more vociferous when they noticed the crimson creeping up his cheeks.

'He's shy,' Delilah said with a grin. 'Be gentle with him, ladies.'

'So how can we help?' continued the first lady, coming over to them.

'We'd like to speak to Mrs Atkins, if possible. Is she here?'

'That's me. What's it about?'

'It's about someone who might have worked here twenty-four years ago.'

Mrs Atkins gave a wry smile. 'You'll be lucky. I can barely remember last week, let alone that far back. Have you got a name?'

'Livvy Thornton,' said Delilah, pulling up the photo on her phone and showing it to the lady.

Mrs Atkins took the mobile and ran a finger over the girl's face. 'Livvy,' she murmured softly. 'Aye, she was a bonny lass. Quick learner, too.'

'She worked here?' Samson stepped forward, wariness forgotten.

'Not for long. Couple of months or more.'

'But you remember her?'

'Hard to forget, that one. She had a quality about her, you know? Like she would go on to be something extraordinary. Gorgeous hair, too.' Mrs Atkins passed the phone back to Delilah. 'Why are you asking about Livvy after all these years?'

'We're trying to track down her death certificate—'

'She's dead?' The salon owner's hand went to her mouth. 'What a shame. She can't have been that old. When did she die?'

Samson glanced at Delilah, who was frowning. 'You didn't know?' she asked.

'How could I? We didn't keep in touch when she left. I wasn't right pleased with her, disappearing the way she did.'

'So you're saying you don't know anything about her accident?'

'What accident?'

'Livvy Thornton was killed in a hit-and-run two decades ago,' explained Samson. 'While she would have been working here.'

Mrs Atkins was shaking her head. 'No, no, that can't be true. We'd have known. Seen it on the news or something.'

'What's he saying?' A younger woman had joined them. Judging by the similar facial features, Samson was guessing it was the salon owner's daughter.

'Livvy Thornton,' said Mrs Atkins. 'They reckon she died in a hit-and-run back when she was training here.'

'No way,' said the younger woman, shocked. 'We'd have heard.'

'But she did work here? That's definite?' Samson asked.

Both women nodded.

'I don't suppose you happen to remember where she lived?'

'Not a matter of remembering,' Mrs Atkins replied with a frown. 'We never knew. Livvy gave us an address and phone number which turned out to be false. When she didn't turn up for work we tried calling, but the old lady there said she'd never heard of her. It was all a bit of a mystery.'

'What about that address?' asked Delilah. 'Can you recall where it was?'

'North Park Avenue, down by Roundhay Park. I only remember because I thought it was a bit swanky for a trainee hairdresser. Bit above the salary I was paying.' She glanced at the clock on the wall and towards the client who was waiting for her. 'If that's all . . .' she said apologetically.

'Thanks,' said Delilah. 'You've been a great help.'

'Just one last thing,' Samson interrupted. 'When Livvy went missing, did you contact anyone in authority? The police, maybe?'

'No . . .' The salon owner had a look of contrition. 'In retrospect, I suppose I should have. But I just presumed . . . I thought she'd moved on.'

'I understand. Thank you for your time. And if you think of anything else, don't hesitate to call.' Samson passed her his business card. She looked at the name and burst into laughter yet again.

'Samson? Really?' she asked. She wielded the scissors, snipping at the air. 'Are you sure you don't want me to cut your hair?'

He grinned sheepishly, the same heat as earlier creeping up his cheeks. 'Maybe another time,' he said, backing towards the exit, Tolpuddle with him, the pair of them grateful to get out of the fug of hair products and into the cold of the winter afternoon.

When Delilah joined them on the pavement, Samson was deep in thought.

'So Livvy must have lived in Leeds,' he muttered. 'Given that she worked here.'

'Seems like it,' Delilah agreed. 'And there was a connection to that house. Whether she stayed there or it was a drop box, who knows?'

'None of this makes sense.'

'No. It doesn't. Those women remember Livvy working here, but not dying here. How can that be possible?'

Date with Mystery

A blast of hairdryers made them turn to see the salon door reopening and the younger of the two women hurrying out after them, a couple of business cards in her hand.

'Here,' she said, passing one each to Samson and Delilah. 'Mother thinks I'm touting for business, but I couldn't say back there – Livvy had another name.'

'Like a middle name?' asked Samson.

The woman shook her head. 'No. A stage name. She sang down at the Fforde Grene pub. I used to sneak in to listen, as I was only sixteen. Mother didn't know about it. Still doesn't.'

Samson wasn't surprised. He remembered the pub from his days in the town. Situated at the southern end of Roundhay where Harehills began, it hadn't been the kind of place a parent would want a young daughter going to.

'What was her name?' he asked.

'Olivia Nightingale.' The woman gave a fond smile. 'She was good. Bloody good. I was always telling her she should give up hairdressing and take up singing professionally. When she disappeared, I thought that was what she'd done.' She shrugged, pulled her cardigan tight across her chest against the chill wind and hurried back into the salon, where her mother was still watching them.

'Olivia Nightingale,' murmured Delilah. 'I reckon that pub might be worth a visit. What did she say it was called?'

'The Fforde Grene,' said Samson.

'Do you know it?'

'Unfortunately, yes. I was in on a couple of drugs raids there. Not a pleasant place. Or at least it wasn't in my time. It might have changed in twelve years.'

'So we head there then? See if anyone has anything else to add to this mystery about Livvy Thornton?'

Samson nodded, already turning back towards Chris and the warmth of the car and wondering why this investigation, which should have been so straightforward, was proving to be so complex.

8

'Not much of a pub.'

Delilah sounded less than impressed. A short drive back through Roundhay Park and down the Roundhay Road had brought them to the edge of Harehills. The change couldn't have been more dramatic. From the tree-lined streets of the northern suburb and the green expanse of open parkland, they had driven into a more urban area, delicatessens being replaced with loan shops and cash converters, a busy road wrapped around the lot, its traffic incessant.

'It must have been closed down,' said Samson. 'No surprise, given its past.'

They were standing in a car park looking at a large redbrick building rising up three storeys, marble surrounding what had once been the grand entranceway of the Fforde Grene pub. Now the double doors looked permanently closed, a large sign across the front declaring the premises to be a continental supermarket, its entrance on the side.

'So another dead end.' Delilah sighed. 'We're not having much luck.'

'No. But at least we know more than we did this morning.'

'I reckon I might know someone who could help us find out a bit more,' said Chris, Samson noting with amusement the use of 'us', in a manner typical of the Metcalfes. 'Are you in a hurry to get back to Bruncliffe?'

'Not particularly,' said Delilah. 'As long as we catch the last train.'

'Same here,' added Samson. 'We'll take any help you can give.'

'It'll probably involve going to a pub,' said Chris, taking out his mobile and turning away.

Delilah and Samson both looked down at Tolpuddle.

'No beer allowed,' Delilah warned the dog. 'Or we'll get chucked off the train home.'

Tolpuddle lifted an eyebrow, his martyred expression revealing the aptness of his name.

A couple of hours and a new jacket later, Samson was following Delilah and Chris along Briggate in the heart of the town, Tolpuddle trotting next to them. The pedestrianised area was busy with office workers and shoppers heading home under street lights, the sun having already set in its customary winter habit. With the air turning colder, Samson was glad to be able to pull his collar up to his chin, feeling snug after an afternoon of shivering.

'It looks good on you,' said Delilah, giving him an approving glance.

She'd taken pity on him when they'd arrived in the city centre amongst a labyrinth of shops, his horror at the task facing him painfully clear. Lodging her brother and Tolpuddle in a coffee shop, much to their relief, Delilah had slipped an arm through Samson's and marched him into an outdoor clothing store. Forty minutes later he walked out in the warmest jacket he'd ever owned. Having rejected the temptation of the exorbitantly expensive down jackets, given the rigours of his job and the fate that had befallen his last two, he'd opted for a hard-wearing, waxed parka. Black – despite Delilah's attempts to get him into something more vibrant – and lined in fleece, it was worth the cost, Samson decided as he walked along the precinct. It was a jacket that would withstand the worst of a Bruncliffe winter. As long as he didn't lose it to fire or a rabid dog.

'This way,' said Chris, veering down a narrow alleyway between two shops and into the dark beyond.

'We're meeting your friend down here?' queried Delilah as the high walls of the buildings closed around them, cutting off the glow of the street lamps. She glanced back at Samson and he shrugged.

Despite having lived in Leeds for two years, this wasn't a place he knew. He'd spent most of his time in the city on the edge of Harehills, finding a cheap room in a house share with a couple of student nurses when he'd arrived. Working in a pub at first, he had little money or inclination for visiting other drinking establishments, especially when he didn't touch alcohol himself. When he'd started his training with the police he'd been travelling to Wakefield every day and coming home late, no time for socialising. And once he'd begun his probation, up in Roundhay and later on in his own patch of Harehills, he'd been even busier. Even though he'd been earning enough by then to move to a better part of the city, he'd grown attached to Harehills, in spite of its social problems. Or maybe because of them. Whatever it was, he'd always felt more at home in the terraced streets with their subcultures and diverse ethnic mix than he had in the leafy avenues of Chapel Allerton or the student-magnet of Hyde Park. It was an experience that would set him up perfectly for a life undercover.

Which explained why, as Chris led the way further into the alley, Samson didn't have a clue where they were going.

'Here we are!' said Chris, throwing out an arm as they rounded a corner to welcoming lights and a whitewashed facade, bright against the walls around it.

The Angel. A small pub hidden away between two major shopping thoroughfares.

Chris opened the door, a couple of rooms branching off either side of a small entranceway and narrow stairs twisting out of sight ahead. He turned right into a compact bar, a low buzz of conversation coming to a halt as they trooped inside.

'It's just like the Fleece,' murmured Samson with a grin, recognising the guarded looks of the regulars at this intrusion by strangers.

Delilah laughed. 'Only we're the outsiders for once.'

'Speak for yourself,' said Chris. 'This is my local. And the landlord isn't as moody as Troy Murgatroyd.'

'That's not saying much,' quipped Samson.

Acknowledging the truth of the statement with a wry smile – the owner of Bruncliffe's oldest tavern being renowned for his sullen nature – Chris took their orders and made his way to the bar, leaving Tolpuddle to pull Delilah towards the roaring fire. Samson, meanwhile, was taking in the pub. It was a drinker's haunt. Cosy. Uncomplicated. Good beer on the taps. No frills. It was the kind of place his father would have loved in his drinking days. The days when he was still discerning, before the desire for alcohol removed any refinement from his choice of establishment.

'O'Brien!' An authoritative voice hailed Samson from the larger room across the hall. He looked over and instantly felt the years peel away.

A set of bushy eyebrows beneath a bald head marked the man out as a Thistlethwaite. His accent marked him out as a native of Bruncliffe. Gabriel Thistlethwaite, brother of Seth, uncle of Matty and the person who had persuaded Samson O'Brien to join the police. Samson hadn't seen him in twelve years.

'Sir!' Samson was already crossing towards him. 'Chris didn't mention it was you we were meeting.'

'It's not,' said Gabriel, shaking hands with a firm grasp. 'My days of policing are over. This is who you're here to see.'

He moved to one side and, at a corner table next to another blazing fire, Samson saw a man of about his own age, possibly a bit older, with the same distinctive eyebrows but this time underneath a thick thatch of brown hair. The man stood, his hand extended in welcome, a wariness in his dark gaze.

'I heard the prodigal son had returned,' he said. 'Dad's itching to hear all about it.'

Frank Thistlethwaite. He'd been in the intake the year before Samson, following his father into the police but opting to do his probation in Bradford, away from the long shadow of Chief Superintendent Gabriel Thistlethwaite. Samson had seen very little of him during his time in Leeds.

'Not much to tell,' lied Samson. 'How about you? Still over in Bradford?'

Frank shook his head. 'Back here now. Have been for some time.'

'He's a DCI,' said Gabriel, proudly.

Detective Chief Inspector. Samson was impressed. Frank was climbing the ranks at a tremendous rate.

'Not as exciting as undercover, I'm sure,' said Frank with a self-effacing smile.

'Don't believe everything you hear,' said Samson as Chris arrived with a tray of drinks, Delilah and Tolpuddle with him.

'Delilah Metcalfe!' announced Gabriel, pulling her into a bear hug. 'You're all grown-up. I remember you as a tiny thing, running after those five brothers of yours and getting into more trouble than all of them put together.'

'Nothing much changed there then,' muttered Chris with a meaningful stare at his sister.

She ignored him, holding out her hand towards Gabriel's son instead. 'I don't think we've met,' she said.

Frank grinned, eyes twinkling as he took her hand. 'We have. When you were a nipper with a hell of a temper. Shame you don't remember, because I'd prefer the welcome you gave Dad. I'm guessing you save that for old friends?'

Delilah blushed, fussing with Tolpuddle's lead while Frank pulled a chair out for her.

Gallantry. Samson had always felt it was overrated. He took a seat next to his former boss.

'So what's brought you home, lad?' asked Gabriel with a directness that was as hereditary in the Thistlethwaite line as unruly eyebrows.

'Time for a change.' Samson held the older man's gaze, knowing he wasn't easy to fool.

'And the force?'

Acutely aware of everyone listening, Samson kept it casual. 'I've taken a sabbatical.'

Gabriel gave a slow nod. 'Understandable, with the kind of work you were doing. But don't leave it too long, son. It's hard to go back to undercover. The nerves go.'

'That's presuming they'll have him back,' said Frank with a light laugh.

'One of the best coppers ever to come out of this district. Of course they'll have him back,' barked Gabriel. 'Not many get called up to the Met and then go on to be seconded to SOCA.'

'SOCA?' asked Chris.

'Serious Organised Crime Agency. Been rebranded since as the National Crime Agency, but it does the same job. Top-notch crime-fighting unit.'

'I thought you were just in the Met?' asked Delilah, looking at Samson with open admiration.

'It's no big deal,' he muttered. The attention and the subject matter were both making him uncomfortable. But his old chief superintendent wasn't about to let it drop.

'Don't go hiding your lights under a bushel!' boomed Gabriel, slapping his protégé on the back with a hefty clout that almost shook the drink from Samson's grasp. 'You were hand-picked, and I have it on good authority that you excelled.'

Frank dipped his focus to his pint. When he looked back up, there was a hardness to his gaze, enough to make Samson paranoid that the younger Thistlethwaite knew what was coming down the line. And that it would tarnish Samson's stellar reputation forever.

'How's retirement?' Samson asked, steering the conversation onto safer grounds.

'Endless golf. Long walks with the dog. Three holidays a year.' Gabriel picked up his pint, took a drink and grimaced. 'I bloody hate it,' he cursed.

Delilah laughed. 'You sound like my father. He gave up farming, supposedly, but we can't keep him out of the fields. Drives Will mad.'

'They're intense professions,' said Gabriel. 'A way of life more than a job. And Samson here has tasted both.'

Tasted both and lost both, thought Samson, picturing the abandoned farmhouse in Thorpdale that now belonged to Procter Properties. In a few weeks' time he could be walking away from his police career, too.

'So what brings you to Leeds?' asked Frank, with a hint of impatience. 'Chris mentioned an investigation.'

'We're working for Matty,' said Samson. 'He's trying to locate a death certificate for a local girl who died twenty-four years ago.'

'What's the connection to here?'

'She was working in Roundhay when she was killed in a hit-and-run. But there's no record of her death at the register office, or in the local papers for the time—'

'Samson's too polite to ask,' chipped in Delilah with a smile aimed at Frank, 'but it would help if we knew whether there was a police file on the accident.'

The frown that had marred the policeman's forehead during his exchange with Samson disappeared as he turned his attention to Delilah. 'I'd love to be able to help,' said

116

Frank, with a warmth that had been missing in his earlier conversation, 'but if you haven't had any success with the register office or the newspapers, I wouldn't rate your chances of finding anything in our files. It sounds like the whole thing is a wild goose chase. What was her name?'

'Olivia Thornton. She went by the name of Livvy. Does the name mean anything to you?'

'I'm afraid not. She was here way before my time in the force.' He looked at his father but the older Thistlethwaite was shaking his head.

'Doesn't ring a bell with me, either,' said Gabriel. 'Was she one of the quarry Thorntons?'

'Yes,' said Delilah. 'They're not Bruncliffe, are they?'

Samson noted the phrasing of the question, so typical of people who could trace their ancestry back multiple generations, all within a five-mile radius.

'No,' concurred Gabriel. 'The mother was from down south somewhere. And the father was from Bradford.'

His son glanced at him. 'Not one of the notorious Thorntons?'

'A branch of them. He didn't have a criminal record, but I seem to remember he had a reputation for being quick with his fists. What was his name . . . ?'

'Carl. And I can vouch for that reputation,' said Samson, thinking of the times he'd seen the man throwing his weight around the Fleece.

'So it's his daughter you're investigating?' continued Gabriel. 'I don't remember her coming over here. Normally I've got my ear to the ground whenever folk come from home, but she must have slipped the net. Unless . . . when did you say she was here?'

'Twenty-four years ago,' said Delilah.

Gabriel nodded. 'I was on secondment over in Bradford. Otherwise I'd have kept an eye out for her. Poor lass. She can't have been that old.'

'She was only seventeen when she died.'

The retired policeman sighed. 'Youngsters running away from home. They always think the city will offer up something more dramatic than the fells and dales of Bruncliffe. Trouble is, they're not always equipped to handle it.' He glanced at Samson. 'Not sure how you'd have turned out if I hadn't found you in that dive of a pub you were working in.'

Samson grinned, thinking back to the day when big Gabriel Thistlethwaite had walked into the Anvil, the regulars almost choking on their pints at the sight of a high-ranking policeman in full uniform striding up to the bar. It had been deliberate, the uniform. He'd greeted Samson like a long-lost son and marked him out as connected to the police. Tainting him in the eyes of the suspicious locals who didn't take kindly to law enforcement. Or to the bar staff having affiliations to it.

Then he'd told Samson to join the force. That if he didn't have an application in within the week, he would be visited every day by a constable in uniform, until his job became untenable. Looking over Gabriel's shoulder at the angry stares of the old timers, Samson knew his time at the Anvil was already up. He'd gone home that night and applied to the police.

'I'd probably be living off illicit earnings and a lot happier,' laughed Samson.

Gabriel laughed with him, but Frank merely raised an eyebrow and picked up his pint.

'So you don't remember Livvy, then? Either of you?' continued Delilah.

'Sorry, no,' said Frank.

'What about Olivia Nightingale? Apparently Livvy used to sing at the Fforde Grene under that name.'

Gabriel was already shaking his head. But Livvy's stage persona had caught Frank's attention.

'Olivia Nightingale?' he said with pleasant surprise. '*Her* I remember. I used to sneak into the Ffordy with a couple of mates and while I've happily forgotten most of the bands we saw, she was special. She had a voice like an angel. Stunner, too.'

'Do you have any idea when that was?' asked Samson.

'Sure. The spring I turned sixteen. I can remember hearing her for the first time. I didn't touch my pint for the entire session.'

'Your *pint*?' queried Gabriel. 'You were underage. How the hell did you get served?'

Frank shot a grin at his father. 'Fake ID.'

Gabriel grunted and clipped his son around the ear. 'Better late than never,' he muttered, shaking his head at this revelation.

'So you actually heard her perform?' asked Delilah, as Frank rubbed his ear, still grinning.

'Many times. She wasn't around for long, though, a couple of months or so. When she stopped appearing, we were all heartbroken.'

'And you never knew why she just disappeared?'

Frank shook his head. 'We just presumed she'd gone on

to better things than the Ffordy on a weeknight. She had the talent for it.'

'So Livvy Thornton was definitely here,' murmured Samson. 'Working in the hairdresser's and performing at night.'

'Trouble is,' said Delilah, 'people remember her being alive. But no one remembers her death. Maybe we're looking at this the wrong way round?'

'In what sense?'

She shrugged. 'Perhaps there was no accident.'

'You're not suggesting she's alive?' asked Chris.

'Yes . . . no . . . I mean, I don't see how that can be. But logically, if there's no evidence of the incident, wouldn't that suggest there's some hope?'

The look Gabriel gave Delilah was world-weary. 'I love your optimism, young lady. But when you've been in the police as long as I have, you soon realise that hope is best reserved for lottery tickets. I'm afraid not having a paperwork trail doesn't preclude someone from having met a sad fate.'

'He's right, Delilah,' said Samson.

'Besides,' added Chris, 'there *are* people who remember Livvy's death. The whole of Bruncliffe, for a start. It's simply that there's no record of it in Leeds.'

The three policemen turned in unison to the doctor, his words striking a chord of suspicion in all of them.

'He's got a point,' said Gabriel, frowning. 'Perhaps it's not the death you need to be questioning, but the location of it. And the person who told you about it.'

'You mean . . . ?' Delilah looked around the table, perturbed by the grim expressions displayed there.

'He means,' said Samson, darkly, 'there's probably more to this than meets the eye. And the answer may well lie closer to home.'

Darkness pushing against the carriage windows, the Bruncliffe-bound train rattled along the tracks towards home. Relieved to be out of the city, Samson stared into the night, occasional lights from isolated farmhouses pin-pricking the distance. Even though he couldn't see the fells, he could feel them, a sense of openness and expanse that was lacking amongst the high-rises and terraced streets of Leeds. It was as though he could breathe more easily, feel lighter.

He smiled ironically at his own reflection in the glass. He was turning into a country bumpkin. God knows how he was going to be able to go back to London when the time came.

Sidestepping the thought, he let his gaze shift, the mirror-like window allowing him to covertly study the woman in the seat opposite: Delilah curled up asleep, shoes off, head resting on her bunched-up coat. Below her, Tolpuddle lay sprawled along the floor, the heater blasting out over him, soft doggie snores just about audible. At least he was only snoring. They'd been vigilant in the pub, making sure no one fed the hound beer while they fussed over him.

It had been a strange encounter. Catching up with his old boss after all these years had been a treat for Samson. Meeting his boss's son again, less so. There was something about the way Frank Thistlethwaite had regarded him that made Samson suspect the worse. Already at the rank of detective chief inspector and only a few years older than Samson, the younger Thistlethwaite was tracking his father's footsteps and heading for heights that Samson would never attain. Even without the threat of dismissal and possibly prison hanging over him. So it was entirely feasible that Frank, with a network of contacts in the force, knew all about Samson's impending problems. And being a Thistlethwaite, he would hardly approve.

But at least he hadn't mentioned his suspicions to his father. If Gabriel had had an inkling of what was going on, he'd have tackled Samson about it, regardless of the setting or who was present. It wasn't in his nature to tippy-toe around a subject. Especially not one as toxic as a suspension, pending investigation. The thought of his old boss's inevitable disappointment when the news did finally break made Samson sick to the stomach. Yet another person he'd have let down.

He turned from the window, not caring for the image it was throwing back at him. At least meeting the Thistlethwaites had given them a bit more insight into Livvy Thornton's life before she was killed. And with Frank promising Delilah – pointedly, Delilah and not Samson – that he'd run a check through the police files for the accident, one more avenue of enquiry had been duly investigated. That his offer of assistance had given DCI Thistlethwaite the perfect excuse to elicit Delilah's phone number hadn't escaped Samson's notice. Nor had he missed the warmth with which Frank had bid Delilah goodnight. A warmth which had been reciprocated.

Overcome with a disgruntlement he wasn't in the mood to analyse, Samson forced his attention back to the case. It was getting more complicated by the hour. And the fact that the evening had brought into question where – and possibly how – Livvy had been killed was something Samson would have to broach with Matty. The solicitor had approached the Dales Detective Agency over the simple matter of finding a death certificate. Samson wasn't sure how keen he would be to extend that into solving what was turning out to be a mystery. One that might involve something darker than a missing piece of paper.

First thing in the morning, Samson decided, he'd speak to Ida Capstick when she came in to clean the office. Over their regular cup of tea, it would be interesting to hear how she'd come by her role of intermediary, and how exactly letters had been passed between Livvy and her mother. Then he'd call over to the solicitor's and report back on the day in Leeds. Although, given that the Bruncliffe grapevine tended to include members of families who'd long left the town, there was every chance Matty was getting an update from his uncle or even his cousin right now. Perhaps an update that covered more than the investigation Samson was working on, if Frank was the one doing the calling.

It wouldn't be long before all of Bruncliffe knew.

Impatient at the way his thoughts kept turning, Samson pulled up the collar on his new jacket and shuffled down in his seat, closing his eyes in an effort to shut out the trouble. And instantly he saw the sharp teeth and strong jaw of the Rottweiler lunging for him. With a jerk he snapped back upright.

Procter Properties. What on earth were they doing with a dog like that roaming their premises? Yet another puzzle he needed to work on. With a sigh he closed his eyes again and was asleep before anything else could disturb him.

Bruncliffe was winter-dark, thick cloud cover having blocked out the moon and stars, leaving the street lights to do battle with the night alone. In the marketplace they held their own, the cobbles glinting underneath their soft glow. But away from the shop fronts and the majestic facade of the town hall, down the narrow streets and ginnels that radiated out from the square, it was a different story.

Bereft of all but two lamp posts and with only the furthest of those in working order, Back Street was pooled in darkness. Plastic Fantastic was shuttered. Shear Good Looks likewise. The unlit windows of the Dales Detective Agency and its partner dating agency stared out on the empty street. Only the Fleece provided any illumination, a muted yellow spilling from behind the glass. It wasn't enough to dispel the pockets of shadow that stretched along the road. It wasn't enough to highlight the hunched figure that slipped out of the ginnel beyond the hairdresser's to make its way along the pavement opposite the pub.

To the casual observer, it was just an evening walk in the cold. Black winter coat. Collar pulled up. Hat pulled low. A scarf wrapped around the lower half of the face. There was nothing to remark about any of it. Even the pause outside the door opposite the Fleece. Just a brief rest during a bit of exercise.

In the gloom that pervaded, it would have taken sharp eyes to see what happened next. The gloved hand moving swiftly, pushing something through the letter box with haste. But careful enough to ease the flap closed quietly after it. Then a swift turn and the figure was walking away from the gold lettering on the darkened window and the closed office building, melting back into the night.

He was asleep at last. As the train pulled out of Gargrave station, Delilah peeked across at her dozing tenant, his sleep-softened features making him look vulnerable.

She'd been feigning slumber herself since they boarded the train in Leeds, uncomfortable at the thought of having to talk to him in the intimate setting of the sparsely populated train carriage as it trundled through the dark, given what she'd been told.

Was it true? Was he trouble?

Through the fabric of her coat, she could feel the hard edges of the business card Frank Thistlethwaite had given her when she was leaving. While Samson had been saying goodbye to her brother and Gabriel Thistlethwaite, Frank had leaned in to kiss her, pressing the card into her hand. And as his lips had brushed her cheek, he'd whispered a warning.

'O'Brien is bad news. Keep your distance.'

Frank Thistlethwaite. She knew of him, even if she didn't remember him from her childhood. He seemed as solid as his father. As his uncle Seth. And his cousin Matty. All men she would trust. Yet Frank was telling her to steer clear of Samson O'Brien. Why would he say that if he didn't mean it?

Added to her brother Will's misgivings about the returned black sheep, and Rick Procter's clear mistrust of the man, Frank's words had worried her. Were they right?

Could they all see something behind the charming smile and the good humour that she couldn't?

Samson had his secrets, of course. That woman with the voice like honey who'd called him before Christmas. The same woman he'd been to see in York. There'd been other instances since his arrival back in Bruncliffe, too, when Delilah had witnessed first hand the ease with which he lied. Covering for her nephew Nathan after the disaster up at High Laithe in November was just one of them.

Lying was a part of his job. It had been something he'd excelled at, all those years down south. Good enough a dissembler that he'd been chosen to join some crack law-enforcement group – what had Gabriel called it? The National Crime Agency? Four months home and even with all they'd been through in that short time, Samson hadn't uttered a word about it. Or corrected anyone when they mentioned he worked with the Metropolitan Police.

She stared at the sleeping figure, the mass of dark hair tumbling over his jacket collar, long legs stretched out between the seats.

Just how well did she know Samson O'Brien?

A grey head lifted up from the floor, amber eyes regarding her intently. She put a hand out and stroked Tolpuddle, feeling the pressure under her touch as he pushed back into the embrace.

'You think he's all right, don't you, boy?' she whispered, scratching behind his ears.

Tolpuddle gave a sigh, his head falling back onto his paws and, before long, he'd returned to his dreams, legs twitching, tail giving an occasional thump. Delilah was left

alone with her worries, wondering if she could base her
trust on the opinion of a dog.

The cold walk back from the station was enough to rouse
Samson from his train-induced drowsiness. He'd accompanied Delilah and Tolpuddle as far as the marketplace,
bid them goodnight, and then turned back towards the
ginnel that led to the office. Ostensibly to collect his motorbike and ride back to his non-existent flat in Hellifield.

He would tell her, he promised himself as he opened the
gate, a few spots of rain starting to fall. Come clean and admit
to abusing his tenancy agreement. When he got paid for the
Thornton case and he had a bit more money in his pocket
and could honestly claim to be looking for somewhere.

Walking past the Royal Enfield, Samson let himself into
the building, keeping the lights off as always. No need to
alert the neighbours to his unauthorised presence. He made
his way through the small kitchen and into the hallway,
the passage darker than usual, the council still not having
fixed the street light that normally provided illumination
through the fanlight above the front door. Which is why he
didn't see it. But as he turned to go up the stairs, his right
foot caught the edge of it. Enough to make it crackle.

Samson froze at the noise. Lifted his foot. Then
crouched down to the floor, took his mobile out of his
pocket and turned on the torch. In the harsh light that
splashed across the tiles he saw a rectangle of white. An
envelope. Face-down.

Laughing at his thumping heart, he picked it up, expecting a flyer. Or perhaps a payment for either himself or
Delilah. Maybe someone wanting to hire them.

But it was none of those. Samson could tell without even opening it. For splayed across the front of the envelope was a selection of letters of varying fonts, roughly cut and pasted into place to spell out a single word:

O'Brien.

Somehow Samson didn't think it would contain a request for his services. He slid his finger under the seal and opened it.

9

Rain. Falling from the leaden sky onto the fells. Trickling over the limestone and down the hills, flooding the fields and spilling out onto the lanes, leaving deep puddles and blocking roads. Streaming down pavements and pooling in the potholes in the ginnels. Seeping under cottage doors and saturating gardens. The Dales winter had turned decidedly soggy.

Samson stood staring through the window of Turpin's solicitors at the marketplace below. It was deserted, the cobbles slick with water, shop windows misted up. Having started the night before as Samson and Delilah arrived back from Leeds, at nine-thirty the following morning there was no sign of the rain easing. Friday was in danger of being a washout – both in terms of weather and business.

First, Ida Capstick hadn't turned up to clean at the office, so Samson had been unable to find out more about her role in the exchange of letters between Livvy and her mother. Then Delilah had arrived to inform him rather brusquely that Frank Thistlethwaite had called her that morning. The policeman had found no records of a fatal accident involving Livvy. If the conversation between Delilah and Frank had strayed onto more personal matters, she didn't say. And given the sour mood she was in, Samson hadn't lingered to ask.

With the day already shaping up to be a dud, Samson had left for Turpin's solicitors to give a report on the case – alone, thanks to Delilah spurning his invitation to join him. He'd laid the bare facts out before Matty who, as Samson had anticipated, didn't relish how tangled the situation had become – a dead girl everyone remembered alive, but whom no one could recall dying. The solicitor had digested the news sitting back in his armchair, deep in thought, leaving Samson to appreciate the exceptionally good coffee that clients could bank on at the law firm. And to prowl across the office to the window. The investigation into Livvy Thornton was troubling them both.

With his mood as heavy as the clouds stretching across the town, Samson turned back to Matty.

'I don't get it,' the solicitor said. 'How can there be no record of her death, official or otherwise?'

'It's an odd one all right.' Samson resumed his seat and placed his empty cup on the coffee table between them, wondering if it would be impolite to ask for another, while, fingers steepled under his chin, thick eyebrows drawn together in a frown of concentration, his friend tried to process everything he'd been told.

'The women at the hairdresser's knew Livvy,' Matty murmured, 'cousin Frank can even remember her singing at a gig, and the address on the letters Jimmy found correlates with what Livvy told the hairdresser. But we have nothing. No paperwork. No newspaper clippings. No police report. Nothing to prove she is dead. How can that be possible?' He sat forward, noticed Samson's empty cup and reached for the cafetière. 'More?'

'Please.' Samson tried not to look too keen.

'Any idea where we go from here?' asked Matty, topping up his own cup, too.

'We don't have a lot of options. From what we've uncovered, we have to accept that it's highly unlikely Livvy Thornton died in Leeds. So we need to start looking elsewhere.'

'Where?'

'Up at Rainsrigg.'

Matty looked shocked. 'You think there's something more sinister going on here?'

Samson reached into his pocket and placed a ziplock plastic bag on the table. Inside was a single sheet of A4 paper and an envelope.

'What's this?' Matty pulled the bag towards him and peered at the contents. Then he stared across at Samson. 'Where did you get it?'

'It was waiting for me at the office last night. I called in to get my motorbike and it was by the front door.'

'You think it relates to the Thornton case?'

Samson shrugged, rereading the odd assortment of black and yellow letters that had been pasted across the page to form two sentences:

StoP digging into the Past.

You won't Like THE ConseQuEnces.

'I can't think of any other case it could be referring to,' he said, not wanting to acknowledge that the only investigation he had on was the one Matty had given him. When he'd read the note the night before, for a brief moment Samson had wondered if it could be part of the corruption that had wormed its way into his life. But somehow he didn't think the men he'd encountered in London, with their heavy boots and powerful fists, were the type to cut out letters and paste them on paper in order to get a message across. Their threats tended to be more physical. And delivered in person.

'Do you think it's serious?' asked Matty.

'Someone took the time to produce this,' said Samson. 'I'd say they were serious enough.'

'Enough to involve the police?'

Samson had been expecting this question from the cautious solicitor. 'Not yet. It's a lead of sorts and we're precious short of those, so I'd prefer to keep this between us for now.'

'Fine. But if it escalates into anything else . . .' Matty was looking at Samson, both of them aware of the recent Dales Detective Agency cases that had turned dangerous.

'You'll be the first to know.'

Satisfied, the solicitor placed the letter back on the coffee table. 'So,' he said, 'enlighten me. How is this connected to the search for Livvy's death certificate?'

It was something Samson had been giving a lot of thought. He took another sip of the delicious coffee as he tried to form the words needed to articulate the kernel of suspicion Chris Metcalfe had triggered in the Angel pub the night before; a suspicion which had fermented into a tangible sense of deceit pervading everything about the case, only strengthened by the anonymous warning letter and the news from Frank Thistlethwaite that morning.

'Let me put it this way,' he began. 'In all your years of

settling wills, have you ever come across an unrecorded death?'

'Never. The odd complication, but usually it's down to a computer error.'

Samson smiled, thinking of Delilah's protestations about computers and errors. 'But never a situation like this.'

'No.'

'Exactly. Yet we're trying to make Livvy's death fit in with the scenario of a hit-and-run in Leeds because that's what we've been told, despite the fact that all the evidence is telling us that Leeds is not where she died.'

'But what you're saying . . .'

'I'm saying that someone has been lying. Possibly more than one person. And this,' he gestured at the letter, 'just reinforces that belief. If Livvy's death was straightforward, why would someone be trying to dissuade me from looking into it?'

Matty tapped the arm of his chair as he contemplated this unexpected turn in what he'd thought was a simple case. 'It's plausible,' he muttered. 'All we know about Livvy's death has come second-hand.'

'And from the Thornton family,' added Samson, pointedly.

Matty's fingers stopped their staccato beat and he stared at Samson. 'You're right. We – the town, everyone – that's how we heard back then that Livvy had died. Carl Thornton told us. But why would the Thorntons lie about it? And how could they get away with it?'

'Your Uncle Gabriel gave me the answer to that. He said Marian Thornton came from down south somewhere and

Carl was from Bradford. They had no immediate family in Bruncliffe. No one to dispute whatever they wanted to say.'

Matty slumped in his armchair. 'Christ! You realise what you're suggesting?'

Samson nodded. While he wished he could share Delilah's optimism, years of experience led him to agree with his former boss, Gabriel, that in the face of what they knew, there was little to be hopeful about when it came to the fate of Livvy Thornton.

'Thing is,' he said, 'it's not just me suggesting it. Both Gabriel and Frank came to the same conclusion last night.'

At the mention of his relatives, Matty gave a small smile. 'I'm happy to proceed on your analysis alone, as you know. But I have to admit I'll feel happier going forward with this – given how distasteful it will be – knowing those two agreed with you.'

'So you want me to take this further?' asked Samson.

'What choice do I have? The will can't be settled without that piece of paper, wherever we get it from.'

'We could be about to unearth a lot of misery. And anger, if this warning is anything to go by.'

Matty grimaced. 'I'm aware of that. But it's unavoidable.' He glanced out of the window. 'Poor Jimmy,' he muttered. 'He's been through so much.'

Samson knew that Jimmy Thornton was about to go through a hell of a lot more. Because the questions Samson was going to have to ask him would throw suspicion on the people he had cared about most – his family. And possibly even himself.

'I'm presuming that's where you'll begin this new line of enquiry?' Matty asked. 'With Jimmy?'

'At first. But there's a couple of other things I want to have a look at. It will involve expenses.'

'Such as?'

'The deeds for the house in North Park Avenue, for a start,' said Samson. He'd elected not to include his trespass onto the property, or the ensuing race with the Rottweiler, in his report to the staid solicitor. Nor had he mentioned anything about Rick Procter's interests in the house, never one for playing his cards anywhere but close to his chest. 'Livvy Thornton was using the address to collect her post, so she must have had some form of contact with the owner, even if she wasn't living there. It would help us to know who that person was.'

'I thought you said Livvy's old boss at the hairdresser's tried that address and had no luck? Isn't it going to be a dead end?'

'Mrs Atkins didn't remember the house number. Just that it was on North Park Avenue. It's possible she tried the wrong place.'

'Possible, but unlikely. You're right, though. It won't hurt to check out who the owner was back then. We might hit lucky for once in this case. Anything else?'

'Burial records,' said Samson. 'I'm presuming we know where Livvy was buried – or Jimmy does? We should at least be able to get proof of her internment, and that should lead us closer to getting the essential proof of death.'

Matty slapped his forehead and smiled. 'Excellent idea. I don't know why I didn't think of that already.'

'That's what you're paying me for,' replied Samson with

a grin. He stood up and put his jacket on, preparing to take his leave.

'I'm clearly paying you far too much,' joked the solicitor, giving Samson's black parka an approving nod. 'New jacket, I see. Wasn't your last one up to our Bruncliffe winters?'

'Something like that,' murmured Samson. He had an unwelcome flashback of snarling teeth and shredded fabric.

'So how soon do you think you might have something for me?' Matty asked as he held open the office door.

'As soon as I can. I've cleared my schedule and I'm giving this my full attention. And as for our mystery letter writer,' said Samson, tucking the ziplock bag back in his pocket, 'I'd rather you didn't mention it to anyone for now. Especially not Delilah.'

'You haven't told her?'

'Not yet. I don't want her worrying about it. She's got enough on her plate with the threat of losing Tolpuddle.'

'Ah!' Matty looked relieved. 'I'm glad to hear she's told you about that. Are you going to be able to help her?'

Samson grimaced. 'I wouldn't bank on it. I've had no bright ideas so far and time's running out. Neil Taylor is coming up on Sunday to make good on his threat.'

'Damn!' the solicitor cursed softly.

'Precisely,' muttered Samson, hating the thought of letting Delilah down. And Tolpuddle, too.

'Well, if anyone is capable of taking the wind out of Neil's sails, it's you,' said Matty, patting Samson's back with a confidence the detective didn't share. 'I'm sure you'll think of something.'

They shook hands and Samson made his way through

the outer office and down the stairs to the marketplace, where the rain was bouncing off the cobbles. Pulling up the lined hood of his parka, he stepped out into the damp winter morning, marvelling at the wonder of his new jacket. It wasn't long before that wonder had been replaced by thoughts of Livvy Thornton and the mystery surrounding her death.

Approaching Jimmy Thornton seemed the most logical way to commence this second round of digging into the past. But as Samson walked down Back Street, passing Plastic Fantastic on the corner, its piles of gaudily coloured plastic items slick in the rain, his attention was drawn to the shop on the far side of the Dales Detective Agency.

Of course! A grin split his face. It was the perfect place to start.

Ten o'clock and already Delilah was in despair.

Throwing her pen onto the desk, she pushed back her chair and crossed to the window. Through the rain-streaked glass she could see the motorbike in the back yard, its chrome marred with water, the scarlet struggling to shine in the gloom.

What awful weather. It was worse than a full-on storm, this constant drip-drip-drip from the sagging skies.

With a sigh of impatience she turned her back on it, leaving the office and heading for the kitchen. A cup of tea. That would take her mind off her impossible task for a while. Filling the kettle occupied her for a couple of seconds, but as soon as she switched it on, her thoughts returned to Clive Knowles.

A wife. For a man unfit to be in polite company. How

on earth was she ever going to do it? It was little wonder she wasn't getting anywhere.

Although, if she was honest with herself, her lack of progress was more to do with a lack of concentration.

Bloody Frank Thistlethwaite. The words he'd whispered in her ear the day before had wormed their way into her heart and she'd spent the night tossing and turning under her duvet, wondering what she should do. Then he'd called first thing, just as she'd been persuading herself that he was being over-dramatic. He'd told her about his lack of success in finding anything relating to Livvy Thornton's accident and then asked her out. Just like that.

After a night of no sleep, Delilah had been caught off-guard. She'd mumbled something about being busy, promised she'd be in touch next time she was in Leeds to visit Chris, and hung up quickly, as flustered as a fourteen-year-old schoolgirl. But not before Frank had reiterated his exhortation about her tenant.

O'Brien is bad news. Keep your distance.

While Delilah could ignore her older brother's advice in the way siblings tended to, and Rick Procter's protestations about the calibre of the returned black sheep could be put down to a mutual dislike between the two men, Frank's repeated words of caution had struck a chord. He had no axe to grind when it came to Samson O'Brien. If anything, given his father's clear respect for the man and their shared background in the police force, Frank should surely be inclined to give Samson the benefit of the doubt when it came to character assessment.

Painfully aware of what happened the last time she failed to heed advice when it came to men – the fallout from her disastrous marriage having repercussions even now, threatening to take Tolpuddle from her – Delilah had resolved to take a step back and give herself a chance to make an objective assessment of the man sharing her office space. And a lot of her life. Since his arrival in October they'd been thrown together, first in the spate of murders that had targeted her dating agency and then in the horrible events up at Fellside Court. It was time to take a breather and let her head be the judge of Samson O'Brien, rather than her way-more-impulsive heart.

She'd taken the first steps by turning down Samson's invitation to accompany him to Turpin's for his meeting with Matty, figuring that quelling her burning curiosity when it came to the Livvy Thornton case was a small price to pay. If Samson had been surprised by her refusal, he hadn't said. And so now Delilah was trying to make the most of the empty premises by getting down to some work that would cover the bills. She was finding it impossible, however, to remain focused on finding a bride for Clive Knowles.

Hearing familiar voices in the street outside, she glanced out of the kitchen window. Talk of the devil. Samson was speaking to Seth Thistlethwaite in the doorway of the Fleece.

Damn! He was back already. She was preparing to flee, tea untouched, when he looked up and saw her there, throwing up an arm in greeting, a smile accompanying it. She waved back instinctively. Then he turned and walked away, and Delilah cursed herself for the sense of disappointment that welled up when she realised he wasn't coming into the office.

Taking her tea with her, she went back to her desk and resumed her work. She would find the farmer a wife. Even if it bloody killed her. Because she needed something to take her mind off the conundrum that was Samson O'Brien.

A small whimper from the curled-up shadow in the dog bed across the room reminded her that she wasn't the only one obsessed with the returned detective. Tolpuddle had barely seen Samson today and he wasn't appreciating the change in habit. He'd spent the majority of the morning lying down in the doorway of Samson's office, giving her reproving glances whenever she tried to tempt him upstairs to his bed.

'It's for our own good, Tolpuddle,' Delilah muttered as she forced herself to focus on her computer screen. She wasn't sure the dog believed that, any more than she did herself.

Shear Good Looks. The sign, decorated with a sheep and a pair of clippers, hung on the front of the premises next to the Dales Detective Agency. Through the misted window, Samson could see it was busy. Of course it was. The hair salon served as a news service, attracting people who wanted to catch up on local events as much as get themselves a new haircut. With trepidation, he pushed open the door and entered.

Three chairs facing mirrors along the left, all full, with hairdressers working over clients at various stages of being coiffured. Two sinks on the back wall, a young girl bent over an elderly lady as she washed her hair, chatting away. And on the right two chairs, both occupied by waiting customers, and two more chairs under dryer hoods, both empty.

'Finally!' exclaimed Jo Whitfield, looking up from the curlers she was applying to a grey head of hair. The same age as Samson, the intervening years since they'd both left school had seen Jo rise from a trainee to owner of the salon. They'd also seen her figure soften, the whip-thin, self-confident teenager who'd intimidated the boys now a plumper, more approachable woman. The cheeky smile aimed in Samson's direction, however, was exactly the same. 'Are you going to let me loose on those locks?'

Samson laughed. 'Not yet.'

'Thought it was too good to be true. You're here about Livvy Thornton, I'm guessing.'

The comment caused Samson to pause, shocked yet again by the speed with which news travelled around the town. 'How—?'

'How did I know?' Jo grinned. 'You're not the only one capable of making deductions around here, Sherlock. Everyone's talking about Mrs Thornton's will and the fact you're chasing down a death certificate.' She shrugged. 'Livvy trained here for a while, so I presumed you'd call in at some point. Grab a seat and I'll be with you in a bit.' She nodded towards the bank of dryers.

Samson had no choice but to duck under one of the dryer hoods and sit down. It was only then that he noticed the person sitting next to him. Mrs Pettiford from the bank – Bruncliffe's equivalent of a tabloid newspaper.

'How was York?' she asked, a glint in her eye.

In the mirror across the room, Samson saw Jo Whitfield grinning back at him. It was going to be a long wait.

'Sorry to keep you waiting.'

Half an hour later, having withstood a barrage of questions from Mrs Pettiford about his detective agency, his private life and his father, Samson was relieved when Jo Whitfield beckoned him towards a door at the back of the salon.

'It's not normally this manic in February,' she explained as she led the way into a small staffroom. 'But I can't complain. How was your chat with Mrs Pettiford? Did she get anything out of you?'

Samson gave her a wry look. 'That woman has the tenacity of a terrier. The merest scent of a story and she starts digging.'

'Careful! That's my mother-in-law you're talking about,' said Jo, before bursting into laughter at Samson's stricken expression.

'Really? I had no idea,' he said. 'Sorry.'

She waved away his apology. 'Ex-mother-in-law, in truth. The marriage lasted ten years, but she thinks that gives her the right to a family discount on haircuts for life. Still, it means there's not much goes on in town I don't know about.'

Marvelling yet again at the network of relationships that ran through Bruncliffe, a myriad of interconnections that he, as a relative outsider, would never fully uncover, Samson took a seat at the small table in the corner while Jo filled two mugs from a coffee machine on the counter.

'You've done well for yourself,' he said. 'Running your own business. Employing staff.'

Jo laughed. 'It's a long way from being told off for talking in class. God, I look back at my teenage self and I feel sorry for the teachers.'

'And the boys,' said Samson. 'We were all terrified of you. You seemed so much older than us. Wiser, too.'

'I don't know about that. I'm in my mid-thirties, with a failed marriage and two kids. I don't feel very wise.' She passed him a mug and took a seat opposite him. 'And you never struck me as being afraid of anything. Or anyone. You always had an aura of independence about you.'

He smiled. 'I just hid it better than the other lads. Believe me, you girls with your short skirts and make-up were more terrifying than much of what I've faced since.'

She smiled back at him. 'Those were the days. Talking of which – Livvy Thornton.'

'You knew her well?'

'Quite well. Mum worked here part-time back when Mrs Walker ran the place, so I used to hang out in the salon on Saturday mornings. I remember Livvy starting her training.' Jo laughed softly. 'She turned up with her dog, Red. A beautiful collie. Well, Mrs Walker went apoplectic, telling Livvy she couldn't have a dog in the salon, that it was unhygienic and all that. By the end of the day, Red was curled up by the hairdryers and Mrs Walker was worshipping the ground Livvy walked on. As were the rest of us.'

'Sounds like she was quite a character.'

'She was amazing. She'd walk in the place and it was like someone had turned the Christmas lights on. So vibrant. And so patient with me. I was only ten, but I was given full responsibility for Red every Saturday, walking him, feeding him. God, I loved that dog. I don't know which I was more upset about when Livvy went to Leeds – losing her or losing him. And then for that accident to happen . . . What a waste!' She sighed, then a slow smile crossed her face. 'Livvy even allowed me to cut her hair once. It was only a couple of snips off the end, but even so, I felt like a proper hairdresser. I reckon that's how come I ended up becoming one.'

'How long did she work here before she left for Leeds?'

'I couldn't tell you exactly, but it can't have been that long because I was eleven when she died. So just under a year, maybe.'

'Do you know why she left?'

'I always presumed it was to complete her training somewhere a bit more exotic than here.' She shrugged. 'It's not exactly demanding, working in a small town like this. Perms. Colours. The odd wedding. If you want to be more creative, you need to go somewhere like Leeds.'

'Do you still think that's the reason Livvy moved away?'

'I don't know. I thought about her a lot as I was training. Still do. There was something about her.'

'Charisma?' suggested Samson.

'Certainly that, but also . . . a sadness.' Jo took a sip of her coffee, Samson allowing her the space to continue her thoughts. 'Despite the confidence and the bright persona, I always thought she seemed a bit sad.'

'Any ideas why?'

'Not then. Now?' She shrugged again. 'Perhaps her home life. I don't think it was that great.'

'In what way?'

Jo shook her head. 'Listen, I'm not the one you should be asking all this. I was only a kid. Go and talk to Mrs

Walker. She trained Livvy. She'd know more about her than I do.'

'Mrs Walker's still around?' asked Samson, recalling the sharp-faced older woman who'd run the salon before he left town.

The hairdresser burst out laughing. 'Yes, she's still around, as you put it. And living in the same place as your father.'

'She's in Fellside Court?'

Jo nodded. 'She moved in a year ago when her house got too much for her. Reckons it was the best decision she ever made – even after all that nastiness before Christmas.' The hairdresser shot Samson a look of admiration. 'You're making friends fast in town, you know. What with all these villains you keep catching.'

He grimaced. 'Not fast enough. There's still folk that would prefer me to leave.'

A manicured hand flicked the air in dismissal. 'A minority. One that's best off ignored. You keep this up and you'll be running for the town council next, mark my words!' She glanced at her watch and rose from her chair. 'Sorry. Got to get back to work. Good luck with the investigation. And if I can be of any more help, let me know.'

'Thanks for your time,' said Samson, walking with her to the door. 'Oh, one more thing. Were you aware that Livvy was a singer?'

'In the church choir? Yes. She had a beautiful voice. Sometimes she'd sing when she worked, without even knowing she was doing it. At first Mrs Walker used to get cross, muttering about disturbing the clients. But then, as with everything connected to Livvy, it just became normal, having "Amazing Grace" floating out over the noise of the hairdryers. It was lovely. We all missed it when she went.'

Thinking it doubtful that 'Amazing Grace' would have been in the repertoire of Olivia Nightingale at the Fforde Grene pub, Samson left the busy salon, wondering what had torn Livvy Thornton from her life in Bruncliffe. And what had happened to her afterwards.

A quick check of his mobile showed no emails requiring immediate attention, so deciding to strike while the iron was hot, he walked past the Dales Detective Agency and up Back Street to the marketplace. If he picked up the pace, he could reach Fellside Court just as the pensioners were having their coffee and cake.

Grinning at himself for knowing the timetable of the local retirement complex, he pulled up his hood and walked through the rain towards the far side of town.

10

Samson timed it perfectly. As he stood in the foyer of Fell-side Court, shaking the worst of the wet off his parka, the residents were beginning to file out of the lounge, heading for the cafe that was in the front corner of the building.

'Why, if it isn't young Samson!' exclaimed a loud voice, Arty Robinson standing at the end of the corridor, arms open wide in welcome. 'Come and join us for a brew and a bite, lad.'

Samson didn't wait for a second offer. With his break-fast several hours past, he was more than ready for some sustenance. Falling into step with the former bookmaker, he entered the cafe, Arty steering him towards a table by the windows that already had several people grouped around it, Edith Hird, her sister Clarissa and Joseph O'Brien amongst them. Samson noticed the guarded look on his father's face as he approached.

'You take a seat and I'll get your tea,' said Arty.

'Coffee,' said Samson hastily, not trusting the tea in Bruncliffe to be drinkable unless he made it himself. 'And a cake,' he added, reaching for his wallet.

Arty's hand on his arm forestalled him. 'My treat, lad.' Samson began to protest, but the bookmaker overrode him. 'I insist. We're still in your debt in here. Let me at least buy you a coffee by way of thanks.'

'Don't argue, Samson,' said Edith Hird, a smile on her face. 'It's not often Arty gets his wallet out.'

'There'll be moth-collectors in here in a minute,' muttered an elderly man next to her, an oxygen cylinder by his side and a grin on his face.

'Good to see you back, Eric,' said Samson, accepting defeat and taking a seat at the table. He shook hands with the old man, grandfather of the young constable, Danny Bradley. After the events that had seen Eric have to leave Fellside Court, Samson was genuinely happy to see him home and amongst friends. 'Are you settling in okay?'

'As good as can be expected with this lot,' wheezed Eric Bradley, a chuckle concluding in a coughing fit.

'We're looking after him,' said Clarissa. 'Or at least we're trying to. Keeping him out of mischief is a full-time job.'

'Talking of mischief,' said Edith, the former headmistress regarding Samson with her head tipped to one side, in a way he remembered from primary school. It had never boded well. 'What's this I hear about you trying to find a copy of the death certificate for poor old Livvy Thornton?'

'You heard correctly. In fact, that's partly why I'm here.'

'Oh, good!' Clarissa Ralph clapped her hands in delight. 'Are we going to do another stake-out?' she asked, referring back to the events before Christmas when Samson had had to rely on the residents of Fellside Court to help him stop the terrible chain of events besetting the place.

'Can't believe I missed that,' moaned Eric, as Joseph put his mug down with a clatter.

'Sorry,' Joseph muttered. He dropped his hands into his

lap, but not before Samson saw the tremors. They were worse than normal. A sign of stress. Or a relapse?

'Did I hear someone say stake-out?' Arty had returned, carrying a tray laden with mugs of coffee and a couple of slices of Yorkshire tea loaf. 'When do we start?'

'Stop!' Samson held up his hand to quash the growing excitement. 'There's not going to be a stake-out. Never again, if I can help it.'

'Not even a bit of one?' asked Arty.

'Seeing as the last one nearly ended in tragedy, no.' Samson sighed, knowing how the pensioners valued the excitement his work brought into their lives. 'But I do need your help.'

'In what way?' asked Edith, as practical as ever.

'I'd like to know more about Livvy Thornton. Jo, from the hairdresser's, suggested I speak to Mrs Walker.'

Edith was nodding. 'Jo gave you good advice. Phyllis Walker took that girl under her wing. She's the perfect place to start. But why are you asking about Livvy? I thought you were just trying to sort out a paperwork error?'

Not for the first time, Samson was impressed by the perspicacity of the headmistress, her faculties as sharp as ever.

'Just tying up a few loose ends,' he said. 'Trying to get a better picture of Livvy's background, which might help us sort out this mess.'

Edith stared at him, lips pursed, and then tipped her head towards the door. 'Phyllis doesn't leave her apartment much these days. She has difficulty getting around. If you want to see her, I'll take you.'

'I'll come, too,' said Clarissa.

'We might as well all go, eh, Eric and Joseph?' said Arty, finishing off his drink and cleaning the last crumb of cake from his plate. 'It'll do Phyllis good to have visitors. And a couple of men amongst them, too,' he added with a wink.

Knowing there was little point in arguing, Samson ate his tea loaf and gulped down his coffee. When he looked up, the pensioners were already standing, waiting eagerly for him. Apart from his father.

'You not coming, Dad?' he asked as he got to his feet.

Joseph shook his head. 'I'll leave you to it. Got a few things to sort out. Make sure you keep that lot in line.' He gave a small smile.

'I can't promise anything,' said Samson, returning the smile and taking the chance to have a good look at his father. Searching for the telltale signs . . . 'Is everything all right?'

'I'm fine,' Joseph said brusquely, turning away from his son's scrutiny. 'Don't keep them waiting.'

'Right. I'll catch you around.'

Samson crossed the cafe in the wake of the amateur sleuths, persuading himself he was wrong. They'd have noticed, this band of pensioners who looked out for each other. They'd spotted something was amiss when evil visited their retirement home. They'd have noticed if Joseph O'Brien was drinking again.

He watched them leave, pushing the remnants of a scone to one side of his plate, his appetite gone.

Or not gone. That was the problem.

Joseph O'Brien, recovering alcoholic, rose reluctantly, knowing where he was going. Knowing what was waiting for him there. He had a horrible feeling his son knew too.

While Joseph had been able to conceal it from his friends, when those piercing blue eyes turned on him – *her* eyes – there was nowhere to hide.

Leaving the cafe, he entered the stairwell in the corner and slowly climbed the stairs, like a prisoner heading for execution. Reaching the first floor, he walked along the corridor towards his flat, not bothering to glance out of the wall of glass which was streaming with rain.

Key in the door. Latch clicking shut. He was alone. Alone with his nemesis.

Taking a chair from the small dining table in the open-plan living space, he moved into the kitchen area, placed the chair by the sink and stood up on it. Stretching up high above the wall unit, he felt the familiar shape, the cold welcome of an old friend hiding on top of the cupboard.

Grabbing hold of it, he stepped back onto the floor and returned to the lounge, where he placed the bottle on the coffee table.

Demons. Caught inside the glass. Swirling around in the amber liquid. All he had to do was unscrew the top and he could release them, like his body was crying out for him to do.

He sat in his armchair and stared at his potential downfall. One taste of it before Christmas. One swig, which had been forced upon him in circumstances beyond his control. And now this. The craving was back as strong as ever.

He gripped the chair, fighting the urge to drink. Willing himself to conquer this affliction which he had beaten into submission once before. It was his own version of Russian roulette. He'd been playing since the end of December and, so far, he'd won every round.

He didn't think he could win many more.

'Livvy Thornton? Why, that's a name from the past.'

Phyllis Walker peered at Samson from over her glasses, not flustered in the least at having a group of people descend on her. She'd graciously invited them all in, observed Bruncliffe customs by offering tea – which was universally declined, to Samson's relief – and had retained an air of elegant refinement as she'd gestured towards the seating area in her lounge. All while shuffling across the apartment with the aid of sticks, clearly in pain.

'He's on a case,' said Clarissa, sitting on the couch next to her sister. Eric was in an armchair opposite Phyllis, while Arty and Samson were sitting on dining-room chairs by the balcony doors. 'And we're helping him.'

'A case? About Livvy? But she's been dead a long while.'

'I'm trying to locate a copy of her death certificate,' explained Samson, the elderly lady turning her attention back to him, her eyes watering, hands gnarled and knotted in her lap.

'Rheumatoid arthritis,' she said in explanation, noting Samson's glance. 'I was diagnosed in my late fifties. Not the best thing for a hairdresser to get,' she added with a dry laugh. 'It makes holding a pair of scissors rather difficult. I managed to keep going well into my sixties, but then it all got too much.'

'Is that when Jo took over?'

Phyllis nodded. 'I thought at one stage it would be Livvy who would take it on. But that wasn't to be. Poor girl.'

'Do you remember her well?'

'Very well. She was like a kaleidoscope of colour dropped into my life. No day working with Livvy was like the last, but all were vivid. I was sad to see her leave, and distraught to hear she'd died.'

'Did you go to the funeral?'

'There was no funeral.'

Surprised, Samson looked at Edith Hird, who was nodding in corroboration.

'Phyllis is right,' she said. 'There was a church service here in Bruncliffe, but no funeral. Livvy had already been cremated.'

'Where was she cremated?'

Edith shrugged. 'Leeds, I presume. The story from the family was that they wanted a private ceremony. But it was a bit odd.'

'So she's not buried here?' Samson tipped his head in the direction of St Oswald's on Church Street, just along from the police station.

'No. I don't know what they did with her ashes. Marian Thornton wasn't the most outgoing of people and she never really spoke about what had happened. As for Carl . . .'

Phyllis Walker let out a snort of contempt, completely in contrast to her genteel demeanour. 'Carl Thornton was a waste of space. He didn't deserve a daughter like Livvy.'

'What makes you say that?' asked Samson.

The former salon owner drew her shoulders back, sitting more upright, a prim expression on her face as if realising she had transgressed her self-set boundaries of propriety. 'I'm not partial to tittle-tattle,' she said. 'Either dispensing it or collecting it.'

'This is different, Phyllis.' Edith Hird leaned forward and placed a hand on the other woman's arm. 'Samson isn't after gossip. He's trying to help young Jimmy by sorting out the bureaucratic mess Marian left behind. If you know anything, you can tell him in confidence. And if it makes any difference, I share your opinion of Carl Thornton.'

Phyllis Walker gave a brief nod of her head and turned back to Samson. 'The man was a bully.'

'In what way? Did he physically abuse his family?'

'I can't vouch for that. Livvy never bore any visible bruises. But she came to work quite upset several times, and it took a lot to upset that girl.'

'Did she confide in you at all?'

'Not specifically. She was very defensive of her family. Especially her mother. But reading between the lines, I'd say things weren't great at home. And the father was the cause.'

'You don't think it was typical teenage angst? A daughter rebelling against her parents?'

'No.' The response from Phyllis Walker was adamant. 'Livvy wasn't that type. This was something more . . . more adult. As though she was the responsible one in the family. For example, she was always talking about going to work on cruise ships when she finished her training. But when I suggested she start applying, she clammed up. Said she couldn't. Not yet.' The old woman let out a long sigh. 'Turns out she never got the chance.'

'Did you notice this too, when Livvy was at school?' Samson asked Edith.

'A bit. Obviously she was only a nipper when she was in my charge, but she was always precocious. In a good way.

Date with Mystery

I didn't have that much to do with her parents – a couple of parents' evenings, that was about it. But I'd agree with Phyllis. There was something cowed about Marian Thornton when her husband was alive. Even more so in the weeks between Livvy's death and Carl's suicide. Whether he was abusive or not, I couldn't say. But it wasn't healthy.'

'I can vouch he had a temper,' Eric Bradley added. 'I used to drink in the Fleece and Carl Thornton was a man you'd walk round carefully. Any excuse and he'd fly off the handle.'

'I remember,' muttered Samson. 'Was he ever arrested?'

'Never got that far, from what I saw. He'd flare up, throw a few wild punches and old man Murgatroyd would have him by the ear and hauled out of there quick-smart.'

Old man Murgatroyd, father of the current landlord and, likewise, an ex-rugby player, broad of shoulders and hard of fists. Samson remembered him as a man that no one messed with. He'd have been more than a match for a bully like Carl Thornton.

Could the same have been said for Livvy? Samson wondered what kind of relationship the young woman who'd been brimming with character could have had with such an aggressive father – a man who would have been top of Samson's list for penning the threatening letter that had arrived at the Dales Detective Agency. But for the fact that Carl Thornton was dead.

As it was, Samson didn't have any idea as to the identity of the anonymous author. With both Livvy and her mother also deceased, there was only Jimmy left who was directly affected by the investigation. And while Samson didn't think being a grieving son precluded the farmer from being a suspect, he decided to make the most of the repository of Bruncliffe history represented by the pensioners around him and do some discreet digging.

'Sounds like Mr Thornton wouldn't have appreciated me raking over the past,' said Samson with a smile. 'Are there any other toes I need to be wary of treading on in this case?'

'Huh!' retorted Edith Hird, arms folding across her chest, her piercing stare fixed on her former pupil. 'Not like you to start worrying about offending folk.'

Samson grinned. 'Forewarned is forearmed,' he quipped.

She stared a moment more, scrutinising Samson in a way that some of the toughest gangsters he'd dealt with would have been proud of. Then she spoke. 'Most round here are quick to take offence, whether they have a right to or not. But apart from young Jimmy, I can't imagine any would have a legitimate cause to be upset about you asking questions.'

'That's good to know.'

'Although I'd tread carefully with Oscar Hardacre,' added Phyllis.

'Oscar?' asked Samson, thinking of the farm on the Horton Road. And the path that linked it to Rainsrigg Quarry. 'Tom's son?'

'The very same. He had a thing for Livvy. Always hanging around the salon on a Saturday waiting for her to finish, come rain or shine.'

'Was he her boyfriend?'

Phyllis laughed softly. 'He'd like to have been. But she was out of his league.'

'Did she lead him on?' asked Samson, thinking of the

unwitting cruelty of teenage girls when vulnerable hearts were strewn before them.

'Not Livvy. She wasn't like that. She was always friendly with him, letting him walk her home. Perhaps, though,' mused Phyllis, 'that was worse. Giving the lad hope, even though she didn't mean to.'

'How did Oscar react when she left?'

'Ah! That was awful. The poor soul was waiting for her outside the following Saturday, as usual. It was pouring down, so I went out to him in the end. To tell him she'd gone.' Phyllis shook her head at the memory. 'He was soaked through. But when I told him, he just stayed there, staring at the salon as though Livvy would appear at the door, despite what I'd said. I left him to it. At some point in the afternoon he disappeared.' She shrugged. 'I can't imagine he'll relish being cross-examined about his first love after all these years.'

'Thanks for the advice,' said Samson. 'And for giving me some context to the case.'

'I'm glad to have been of assistance,' she smiled. 'Although I don't see how any of this can help get you the paperwork you need. But it's been lovely to have the chance to talk about Livvy. She and that gorgeous dog of hers brightened up my life, even if it was only for a year. I just wish I'd had more notice that she was leaving. Perhaps I could have persuaded her to stay and then she never would have been killed.'

'You didn't know she was going?' asked Samson.

'Not a clue. I got a phone call from her mother on the Monday morning to say Livvy was gone. And then a letter from Livvy herself, full of apology. I never saw her again.

'Do you still have that letter?'

In reply, Phyllis Walker struggled to her feet and limped across to the writing bureau in the corner of the room. She opened the sloping hatch and took an envelope from one of the shelves within.

'Here,' she said, handing it to Samson.

He checked the date and the postmark. Early March the year Livvy left Bruncliffe and a Leeds stamp, like the letters to her mother. But when he pulled out the familiar writing paper, there was no return address on the top. Livvy hadn't given Phyllis Walker – or anyone else – the chance to get in touch with her.

'May I?' he asked, gesturing at the letter.

'Of course. Although I don't think it will reveal much.'

It didn't take long to read. Two paragraphs telling Mrs Walker how grateful she, Livvy, was at having had the chance to train under her. And how sorry she was to be moving on so suddenly and without notice. According to Livvy, an opportunity had arisen that was too good to turn down. She hoped Mrs Walker would forgive her.

The letter concluded with a flourish of a signature and two kisses.

Samson folded the paper and slid it into the envelope before standing and putting it back in the bureau.

'Thank you for saving my legs,' said Mrs Walker with a smile. 'But like I said, it doesn't tell you anything new. Not even a mention of Red, either. I always wondered what happened to that poor dog.'

'You know he disappeared after the accident?'

Phyllis Walker nodded. 'After I heard the news about Livvy, I went to see Mrs Thornton to offer my condolences and to ask her what was going to happen to Red.' She gave a small smile. 'I was going to offer to take him in. Me, someone who had no time for dogs, before Livvy and Red came into my life. But Mrs Thornton told me about him running away. So sad. To think of him roaming the streets of Leeds looking for Livvy. It breaks my heart. The two of them were inseparable.'

Standing over by the writing bureau, Samson froze. What was it? Something in what Mrs Walker had just said.

He closed his eyes, tried to concentrate, but whatever it was, it was disappearing, slithering away from his consciousness.

'Sorry,' he muttered, reaching for his coat and slipping it on, already heading for the door. 'I've got to go. Thanks, everyone.'

The door closed behind him, the remaining people in the room sharing a surprised look at the sudden departure, before Arty Robinson burst out laughing.

'Like a hound on the scent, that boy!' he said, shaking his head. 'God help the person at the other end of it.'

11

The office building had echoed to his call when Samson returned from Fellside Court. No Delilah. No Tolpuddle. He'd gone up to the first floor to double-check she wasn't simply in a meeting but he'd been met by a locked door, her office closed up. In the kitchen along the corridor, a hand on the cold kettle told him she'd been gone a while.

Feeling strangely put out by her absence, he'd returned downstairs. So much for an assistant on the Livvy Thornton case. He'd barely seen Delilah today and now that he needed someone to bounce ideas off, she wasn't around. The elusive thought triggered by Mrs Walker's words had remained beyond his reach and he'd been hoping that talking to Delilah might bring it out into the open. He also needed to find out where Ida Capstick had got to, the cleaner normally a regular presence in the office buildings every morning. He was pretty sure Delilah would know where she was, but having been blindsided by the mention of Frank Thistlethwaite this morning, it had slipped his mind to ask her.

Resigned to working in isolation, he'd put the bag of sandwiches he'd bought at Peaks Patisserie – enough for him, Delilah and Tolpuddle – on his desk and pulled out his laptop. Maybe going through his case notes again would yield whatever it was that was niggling at him. Several hours later, with the rain now falling under illuminated street lights and half of the sandwiches eaten, Samson rose from his desk and stretched his aching back.

In all his years undercover he'd never felt as stiff after a day's work as he did sitting in front of a computer.

Spotting his running kit spilling out of a plastic bag under his desk, he glanced out of the window. The rain had eased, becoming more of a mist than a serious downpour. It wouldn't hurt to go for a run. It would help him sort out everything he'd processed during the day. Maybe even unblock his thoughts. He could have a go at some of Seth's training plan, too.

Changing quickly in the cloakroom next door, Samson was letting himself out of the back porch within minutes. Through the yard and a gentle jog down the ginnel to the steps that led up to the Crag. Up the steps and then across Crag Lane to begin the gruelling climb up to the tops.

It was only when he had crested the steep slope, the land levelling out above the town and the twilight giving him enough light to see the path, that Samson found his mind settling, the facts of the day slotting into place.

His work on the internet had yielded some success. After a bit of searching, he'd discovered that a Mrs Larcombe had been the owner of the big house on North Park Avenue during Livvy's time in Leeds. Cross-referencing the name, he'd also ascertained that a Mrs Jean Larcombe had died three years ago. The house had subsequently been bought by a Mr Phillip Kingston.

So Rick Procter, Bruncliffe's property developer, was renovating the place on behalf of someone. Someone who felt the need to keep a Rottweiler.

Filing that thought for another day, Samson had returned to his computer search: the cremation certificate for Livvy Thornton. Thanks to Phyllis Walker, he now knew that Livvy hadn't been buried. But crematoria kept records, too.

An hour later and he'd had no luck. None of the facilities in Leeds or Bradford held a file on Olivia Thornton. So where had she been cremated?

Feeling the hillside kick up once more, Samson concentrated on his running, one foot in front of the other as he pushed himself, the rain blowing softly on his face. He was soaked. But he didn't care. The exercise felt good after a day being cooped up inside. He simply wasn't used to long hours indoors.

With a final effort, he reached the top of the fell, pausing to catch the breath rasping in his chest. Hands on his thighs, bent double, Samson wondered if he'd get back the ability to run these hills with ease. Or perhaps he was kidding himself. Maybe they had been just as difficult to conquer when he was younger, but he'd simply forgotten the pain.

Either way, it was going to take more than Seth Thistlethwaite's training plan to get him into shape. A miracle would be more like it.

Hoping the rhythm of the running would eventually free his thoughts like it had done so many times before, he started the descent, his mind emptying as his feet followed the route home. He was halfway down when he found himself thinking about the visit to Leeds with Delilah and Tolpuddle; about Chris standing by the car on Street Lane, an appalled look on his face. He laughed out loud.

Tolpuddle. What a star that dog was! Delilah would be distraught if Samson failed to come up with a way to keep him in Bruncliffe. But it was becoming a distinct possibility. The days were passing and inspiration had yet to strike when it came to rescuing the hound.

Tormented by the prospect of dashing Delilah's hopes, by the time Samson bounded out onto the tarmac of Crag Lane he was more agitated than when he'd set out. The impasse with regards to the Thornton case hadn't lifted, nor had he found a way to deal with Tolpuddle's looming fate. Frustrated, he turned left, the lights of town spread out below him, and began running down the steps that led to the ginnel at the rear of the office building. He was at the bottom when he stopped short.

An idea. A brilliant one.

He wheeled round and raced back up the stairs.

The smallest cottage on Crag Lane was ablaze with light, a beacon against the darkening night beyond it. Not wanting to be in the office when Samson came back, Delilah had returned home early. She'd also wanted to make the most of her precious last few days with Tolpuddle. It was Friday evening. Neil would be arriving on Sunday and then she would be living life without a dog. Without *this* dog.

She put an arm around the grey shape taking up a large slice of the couch next to her and heard a sigh of contentment. Tolpuddle thought it was Christmas all over again. She'd cooked him some chicken for tea. He'd followed that with some dog biscuits. And now he was lying crashed out on the sofa with his head on her lap and the wood-burner going full blast. He was in doggy heaven. The only thing that could make it more perfect . . .

Bloody Samson. Despite his blissful state, Tolpuddle jumped at every sound, a log falling on the fire, the wind rattling at the back door. He was on tenterhooks, hoping that Samson would appear after the best part of a day without seeing him. The dog was pining for the black sheep of Bruncliffe.

Delilah fondled the dog's ears, wondering if she was being over-dramatic. Frank Thistlethwaite hadn't offered any evidence; just a whispered condemnation of a man everyone was quick to denounce, thanks to his past. Herself included. She'd been amongst the not-so-welcoming party that had met Samson on his arrival back in Bruncliffe, seething about his casual disregard for her brother, Ryan, his supposed best friend. Samson's unexplained absence from Ryan's funeral two years ago had been compounded by compete neglect of his godson, Nathan, as the lad tried to come to terms with the loss of his father. Combined with his outrageous behaviour prior to his departure from town fourteen years before, it had been enough to condemn Samson in the eyes of the Metcalfe family. And most of Bruncliffe.

But from what Delilah had seen of him over the last four months, the present-day Samson O'Brien didn't deserve such vilification. He'd saved her business from certain ruin, stopped the malicious incidents at Fellside Court and offered to help her thwart Neil's ambition to take Tolpuddle. He'd also developed a good relationship with Nathan, the teenager always keen to spend time with his godfather. What's more, Bruncliffe's returned reprobate was a model tenant.

Surely present conduct was far more important than previous transgressions when passing judgement on someone?

Easing the dog's head off her legs, Delilah stood up slowly, not wanting to disturb him. When she was satisfied he was still asleep, she crossed to the kitchen and opened the fridge. There wasn't much she missed from her years living with Neil, but the evenings when they'd cooked together was one of them. Making lasagne seemed pointless when she was the only one eating it. Yet in a moment of exasperation at her single life, she'd bought the ingredients that morning on her way home and there they were, sitting on a shelf in the fridge staring back at her. Beside them, a ready-made cottage pie.

She reached for the pie, resigned to having another meal for one, when out of the corner of her eye she saw Tolpuddle jerk upright, head twisted towards the small back yard that wrapped around the cottage.

He barked. Sharply. A warning. Then he leapt off the sofa and raced towards the back door. He was there before the knocking began.

'It's okay, boy,' she said in an attempt to soothe the dog, his loud woofs echoing off the walls. 'Just someone at the door.'

On a Friday evening. She rarely had callers. Never of an evening. With a hand on Tolpuddle's collar, Delilah stepped into the porch and saw a bedraggled figure in running shorts and a T-shirt standing out in the yard, the rain streaming off him.

'Samson,' she exclaimed as she opened the back door, beckoning him in. 'What on earth . . . ?'

'I've got it!' he said, a grin on his face, arms spread wide. 'I've got a way to save Tolpuddle.'

She didn't hesitate. She threw her arms around him and hugged him.

She started making the lasagne while Samson was in the shower. It had been an automatic response to the excitement his words had triggered: the soothing routine of putting ingredients together while her brain whirled in anticipation.

Delilah hadn't given him a chance to explain. Having extricated herself from his damp embrace, embarrassed at how she'd reacted, and with Tolpuddle jumping up at him in a frenzy of happiness, she'd decided it was best to impose a bit of calm before Samson revealed his plan. So she'd sent him upstairs with a towel, told him where to find a box of Neil's clothing – a box that still hadn't found its way to the charity shop in town – and had set about making something to eat. She was stirring the ragu as he came down the stairs. Wearing a pair of Neil's joggers and an old hoodie and with his wet hair curling on his shoulders, Samson looked disconcertingly different. And younger.

'That smells amazing.' He sniffed appreciatively while putting a hand down to the shadow that had appeared at his side. 'Doesn't it, Tolpuddle?'

The dog followed him into the compact kitchen, lying on the floor at his feet as Samson took a chair at the small table against the back wall. Delilah placed a cup of tea in front of him, lighter than her usual brew in rare deference to his taste, and set out cutlery. For two.

Samson looked at the table and up at her. 'I'm staying for tea?'

'Have you got somewhere better to be?' she asked, the words coming out more brittle than she'd intended.

'No,' he said quickly. 'Nowhere other than home to a meal for one.'

'Well then. You might as well stay and we can discuss this scheme of yours.'

She put the ragu in the oven, took her tea over to the table and sat down opposite him. She was trying hard to act naturally at having this man sitting in her kitchen but her hands weren't getting the message, beset with tremors. She clasped them around her mug before he noticed.

'Fire away,' she said. 'But bear in mind that I'm not an accomplished liar. So if you need me to play a part in this plot, it's probably better if you don't give me all the details. Neil knows me too well and he'll spot it a mile off if I'm bluffing.'

Samson grinned and leaned forward, elbows on the table. 'Don't worry,' he said. 'You don't have to do anything. Leave it to me and Tolpuddle.'

'Sunday morning at the office, then,' said Delilah, standing in the porch in bare feet as she saw him out, Tolpuddle leaning against her leg.

'Be there by eleven,' said Samson. 'Both of you. That should be plenty of time.'

'And that's all I need to do?'

He grinned, sensing her desire to know the details.

Recognising the truth of what she'd said – Delilah Metcalfe being as easy to read as the first signs of spring in the Dales. Samson hadn't told her anything about his plan to scupper her ex-husband's custody attempt, apart from asking her to bring Tolpuddle to the office on Sunday morning. Being kept in the dark was killing her.

'Just bring Tolpuddle to me. That's all you have to do.'

She glanced down at the dog and then back up, biting her lip. 'You're not going to do anything illegal? Anything that would get you into trouble?'

'Me?' he asked with the innocence of a choir boy. 'Would I?'

She laughed softly, a flutter of sound in the quiet of the night. It was gone midnight, the evening having passed in a comfortable blur of good food and easy conversation. They'd discussed the Thornton case, Delilah insisting that Samson bring her up to date. So he'd told her about his visit to Matty – omitting all mention of the warning letter – and had relayed his conversation with Mrs Walker, including her memories of lovesick Oscar Hardacre, which Delilah had found heartbreaking. Then they'd talked about what the next step should be. And while Delilah hadn't been able to help Samson pinpoint whatever it was that had been nagging at him since his visit to Fellside Court, she had been able to tell him the whereabouts of the elusive Ida Capstick. The cleaner was over in Bridlington on the east coast, her cousin having been recently bereaved. Ida had gone to offer support. And no doubt clean the woman's house from top to bottom.

From the topic of work, they'd moved on to the past, their childhood and their memories of her brother Ryan, the best friend Samson had ever had. They'd also talked about Delilah's failed marriage, Delilah opening up in a way that surprised Samson, as though being in the security of her own home had lowered her natural guard.

Her story hadn't flattered Neil Taylor. The man had taken Delilah's heart and stomped on it from a height. Two affairs that she knew about, the last with a student from Leeds. And then walking out and leaving her burdened with two business loans and a mortgage on the cottage. To compound it all, out of the blue he was demanding Tolpuddle back. It wasn't going to happen if Samson could help it. And he was pretty sure he could.

'Thanks for a lovely evening,' he said, meaning every word. When he'd noticed how late it was he'd had to tear himself away, reluctant to leave the cosy cottage, the sofa where he'd been sitting with Delilah, Tolpuddle splayed out between them, the wood-burner ticking over and the lights of Bruncliffe sprinkled across the darkness beyond the window. 'And thanks for the clothes. I'll get them washed and back to you.'

She waved a hand, dismissing his thanks. 'No hurry. They're destined for the charity shop anyway.' Then she leaned forward and kissed his cheek. 'That's for Tolpuddle,' she said, a smile creasing her cheeks.

'Right.' He coughed. Looked over the low wall at the town splayed out beneath him. Turned back to Delilah and knew that if he stayed a moment longer, he would do something they would both regret. 'See you Sunday.'

He turned from the porch and the dog and the young woman, and headed into the night. Towards a sleeping bag on a borrowed bed in an empty building, telling himself the whole walk back that, with his past about to catch up with him, it was better this way. Less complicated. For him and for her.

Delilah Metcalfe had had enough failure in her life. She didn't need another man letting her down.

'*Bad news* indeed,' she muttered, closing the door to the porch and leaning back against it.

But not in the way Frank Thistlethwaite had meant. Samson O'Brien was bad news for her sanity. And for her heart. She'd had to fight every instinct not to grab hold of him and pull him back inside the house as he stood there saying goodbye.

So much for taking a step back after Frank's warning.

'And so much for having a guard dog,' she murmured, her gaze falling on the shape of Tolpuddle in his basket by the fire, head on paws, eyes already closing.

He'd had the best evening of all.

Hoping that Samson could ensure there would be many more of them, Delilah started up the stairs to bed. Even though she knew she wouldn't sleep a wink.

12

'You ready?'

Delilah nodded and passed Tolpuddle's lead to Samson. Sunday morning, eleven o'clock on the dot, the scarlet-and-chrome motorbike had already been parked in the back yard of the office building when she'd come through the gate with the dog. With the rain having finally stopped, a fragile blue sky was peeking through the white puffs of cloud above, a bitter wind blowing from the east, reminding the people of Bruncliffe that winter hadn't finished with them yet.

Inside the office of the Dales Detective Agency, the cold that Delilah was feeling came more from fear than from the temperature outside. She leaned against Samson's desk, her fingers drumming nervously on its surface.

'Promise me you're not going to do anything stupid?' she asked, her imagination having provided numerous scenarios in the intervening hours since Samson's visit to her cottage.

'Don't worry,' he said with a wicked smile. 'I'm not planning on getting any of us arrested. Text me when they get here.'

She nodded. Then she knelt down and wrapped her arms around Tolpuddle, lying her head against his. 'Just in case . . .' she murmured. Feeling tears forming, she stood, wiped the back of her hand across her eyes and forced a smile, the dog's amber gaze regarding her solemnly.

'Be good,' she said to him. 'You, too,' she added in Samson's direction.

'We'll try.'

Samson led the Weimaraner to the front door and Delilah had a moment's panic, worried that she was sacrificing her final hours with Tolpuddle for the sake of some foolhardy attempt to save him that would end in failure. It was only her grip on the desk that stopped her from flinging herself at him.

'It'll all work out,' said Samson. No trace of a smile. Totally understanding the torment she was going through. 'Trust me.'

She stared at him and then at the dog. 'Go, quickly,' she muttered. 'Before I change my mind.'

The front door opened and closed and she heard a muffled bark from the other side. It was enough to start her crying.

Two hours. More than enough time for Samson to activate his plan. With a glance over his shoulder at the windows spanning the front of the office building to make sure Delilah wasn't watching, he hurried across the road, Tolpuddle beside him.

'Let's see how this goes down,' he muttered, pulling open the door of the Fleece and slipping inside.

It was like stepping back in time to the pubs of his youth. Dark floral carpet, brass hangings on the walls, low beams and a fire burning in the grate. Not a twee reproduction of the past, but simply the result of a tight-fisted

owner who refused to waste money on upgrading the decor. And who wasn't bothered about attracting a more refined clientele. The regulars of the Fleece kept coming back because they knew the pub had the best beer in town.

Glad to be out of the biting wind, Samson paused in the doorway, his eyes adjusting to the gloom of the interior. Despite the relatively early hour, a handful of other people were also taking shelter from the wintry conditions outside. Three hikers were sitting in the corner, maps spread out on the table. Tucked in by the fire were some farmers Samson recognised. And at the bar, Seth Thistlethwaite was talking to Will Metcalfe.

Samson felt his courage fail. This wasn't an environment he felt comfortable in, the scene of so many of his father's alcoholic collapses. As a child and teenager he'd only frequented the place in order to drag his father home, and since returning to Bruncliffe in October, he hadn't entered the pub apart from with Delilah. Standing here on his own, as a non-drinker and someone Bruncliffe hadn't accepted to its bosom, he was feeling very exposed. Having Will Metcalfe – the oldest of the siblings and one still wary of the returned detective – in the vicinity wasn't going to help any.

'Bloody hell!' Troy Murgatroyd, landlord of the Fleece, was behind the counter drying glasses, a surly expression on his wide face. He'd spotted Samson in the doorway. 'To what do we owe this honour?'

The greeting was loud enough to override the muted conversations; to make everyone look up at Samson and Tolpuddle.

'Morning, all.' Samson crossed to the bar. 'A coffee and a full English, please, Troy.'

Troy threw the tea towel over his shoulder, glared at Samson and strode off towards the kitchen, forgoing his usual lecture on the hateful habits of people who came in a pub and ordered anything but beer.

'Reckon he's missed you,' quipped Seth, shaking hands with Samson and then leaning down to pet the dog.

'Morning.' Will Metcalfe nodded in Samson's direction and then looked at Tolpuddle, jaw clenching. 'How come he's with you?'

Seth, too, was regarding Samson with a raised eyebrow and a definite twinkle in his eye, making the detective realise how it must seem – him walking into the bar at this hour on a Sunday morning with Delilah's dog.

'It's not what you think,' he stammered, Will still holding him fixed in his fierce gaze. 'Honestly.'

Seth Thistlethwaite was grinning now, delighting in watching Samson squirm.

'Why don't you tell me how it is, then?' growled Will, a strong hand grasping his pint. Trained as a boxer in his youth, Delilah's oldest brother was reputed to have a lethal right hook. It was a claim Samson didn't want to put to the test.

But at the same time, he didn't think the truth was something Delilah would want him sharing with her over-protective brother.

'I'm just looking after him,' he said lamely.

Will stood up, placed his pint back on the counter. 'I'm warning you, O'Brien. I don't mess around where my sister is concerned.'

Date with Mystery

Samson glanced at the dog, who was sniffing the carpet, unperturbed, and then over at the office building across the road. Tolpuddle wouldn't spill the beans, and Seth was the epitome of discretion. So as long as Will could be persuaded to stay quiet, Delilah need never know. But that was the problem. Will was an unknown quantity when it came to protecting his sister. When he heard why Neil Taylor was in town, could the oldest Metcalfe sibling be trusted not to go over and throttle the man?

It briefly crossed Samson's mind that this would be a more certain solution to the custody problem than the one he was about to attempt.

'Okay,' he conceded, taking the risky decision to move closer to the brooding figure, but keeping Seth between them. 'I'll tell you why we're here, but you both have to promise not to let on to Delilah that I told you.'

Puzzlement replacing belligerence, Will nodded, while Seth Thistlethwaite put a finger to his lips. Samson leaned in towards them.

Delilah was pacing the floor. Having confined herself to her office, hoping to use work as a distraction from what the day would bring, she was walking back and forth between the window and the open door, a worried frown on her forehead.

Neil Taylor would be arriving in an hour and a half. Her ex-husband. She hadn't seen him properly – apart from fleeting glimpses around town on the odd occasion when he was back visiting family – since he'd fled two years ago, worried about the legendary wrath of Will Metcalfe. He'd been right, too. Will had been livid when he'd found out about Neil's infidelity. From all accounts, her over-protective brother had been in the Fleece when Rick Procter had told him. How the hell Rick had found out, Delilah didn't know. But perhaps it was just as well it had been Rick who was the messenger, as anyone else would have struggled to hold Will back as he went charging for the door, intent on finding Neil. As it was, Rick had needed the assistance of Harry Furness, the livestock auctioneer, to restrain her brother and talk some sense into him.

That Will had been the one to break the news to Delilah had only added to her mortification at having been duped a second time by her cheating husband. Wisely, with two enraged Metcalfes on the warpath, Neil had left for London with Abbie, his new woman. Girl. Not woman. The slip of a thing had barely been out of her teens.

And very shortly the pair of them would be waltzing in here and demanding Tolpuddle.

Delilah's throat constricted at the thought. She wasn't ready to face them. She certainly wasn't ready to lose Tolpuddle.

A quick check of her watch told her she still had an hour and a quarter left to wait. That was a lot of time to fill with pacing.

She forced herself to sit at her desk. Clive Knowles. If finding him a wife couldn't distract her, nothing would. Clicking open the profile for the lonely farmer that she'd begun compiling, she skimmed through the text, making a few changes. Nothing significant. Nothing that would yield success.

Five minutes later she was back on her feet, wearing a track across the floor. There was nothing that could take

her mind off the magnitude of what lay ahead. Nothing that could reassure her that Samson's plan – whatever it was – would work.

'Will it work?' asked Seth, casting a sceptical glance at Tolpuddle after hearing the detective outline his idea to keep the dog in Bruncliffe.

'It's all I've got,' said Samson. He shrugged. 'It's not like we have a lot of options open to us.'

'We could kill that peacock Taylor,' muttered Will, a murderous look in his eyes.

Samson didn't dare ask if the suggestion was a serious one. 'Legal options,' he added for clarification.

Will grunted and took a swig of his beer, leaving Samson to eat some of his breakfast, which had arrived and which Tolpuddle was watching avidly with a keen expression of hope, tracking every movement of Samson's knife and fork as sausage, bacon and egg passed from plate to mouth.

'But will it work?' demanded Seth a second time. He'd been as shocked as Will to hear that Tolpuddle's life in Bruncliffe was under threat and astounded to learn that Neil Taylor was the cause of it.

'We'll know in an hour or so.'

'Is that when the Taylor runt is arriving?' asked Will, shaking his head. 'His father should be ashamed of him.'

Seth snorted at the mention of Bruncliffe's mayor. 'I doubt our esteemed leader would care one way or another. That man is only bothered about lining his own pockets. It's no wonder his son is a waste of space. Poor old Delilah getting mixed up with that one.' He shook his head in dismay. 'I tried to tell her, but she wouldn't listen.'

'That's Delilah,' said Will with exasperation. 'Stubborn as hell. The more she was warned about that bloody idiot, the more she mooned over him. She won't take telling.'

Samson felt a sudden sympathy for the youngest of the Metcalfe brood. It was bad enough growing up in Bruncliffe, where everyone considered themselves your extended family, without having five older brothers watching your every move as well. There was something to be said for being an only child, after all.

'Anyway,' said Will, finishing off his pint and signalling Troy Murgatroyd to fetch him another, 'I'll be in here for a while yet, waiting for the kids to finish at football practice. So if your plan doesn't work out, give me a shout and I'll come over and make Neil Taylor change his mind.'

'I'm sure it won't come to that,' said Samson, relieved for once not to be the one in Will Metcalfe's crosshairs. 'But thanks.'

Will grunted, the closest he had come to approval of the black sheep of Bruncliffe. 'Thanks are due to you, I reckon.'

'Seems like a lot of Bruncliffe have been thanking you lately, young man,' said Seth with fatherly pride. 'Heard you're working to help Jimmy Thornton out of a spot of bother.'

'I wouldn't go that far,' protested Samson.

'Is it true then? Mrs Thornton listed Livvy as an heir?' asked Will.

Samson nodded, knowing he was giving nothing away that wasn't already common knowledge.

'Why on earth would she do that?'

'Search me. Perhaps she wanted to acknowledge her

daughter. But to be honest, that's not what I'm focusing on,' said Samson, deliberately neglecting to mention that Delilah was on the case with him. He didn't need to give Will a fresh reason to get het up – and considering the way the last two cases Delilah had been involved in had ended, her brother had ample reason to be worried. Even more so if he got wind of the threatening letter that had landed at the Dales Detective Agency. 'I'm only bothered about finding a death certificate for Livvy,' he said.

Both men stared at him.

'There's no death certificate?' Seth asked.

'None that's surfaced so far.'

'Bizarre,' muttered Will. 'Perhaps it's just lost after all this time?'

'It's not that simple.' The detective finished his breakfast, offered a grateful Tolpuddle the last piece of sausage and pushed the plate aside. 'Did you know Livvy well at school?'

'Not as well as I'd have liked,' admitted Will with a sad smile. 'She was something special, was Livvy.'

'I hear Oscar Hardacre had a soft spot for her.'

Will laughed. 'Him and every other lad in town. We were all besotted with her. Even though we knew we didn't stand a chance.'

'So Oscar never went out with her?'

'No way.'

'Do you have much to do with him nowadays?' asked Samson, knowing how tightly knit the farming community was.

'A bit. We catch up at auctions and the like. Why? What's Oscar got to do with any of this?'

Samson shrugged. 'I just wondered if he talked about her at all.'

Will shook his head. 'I've never heard him mention Livvy Thornton. Not since she left town. But then I haven't heard anyone talk about her in years. Not until you started going around asking questions.'

'Not even Jimmy? He doesn't speak of her?'

'Not to my knowledge. Although I've always wondered if that's why he left his job at the Hardacre place so suddenly.'

Samson kept his sudden interest hidden behind a casual lift of an eyebrow. 'What do you mean?'

'There was bad blood between him and Oscar. Ever since Jimmy was young. Oscar used to tease him. Pick on him, you know? So when Tom began handing over the reins of the farm to Oscar, Jimmy quit.' Will took a sip of his pint before continuing. 'I don't know the cause, but I've always thought it was connected to Livvy somehow.'

'What about Livvy's home life?' asked Samson, making the most of this outburst of conversation from the normally taciturn Will Metcalfe. 'Did you know anything about that?'

'Nothing more than the usual. I knew her parents to see around town, but they didn't mix too much. They were offcumden,' Will added, using the term as a statement of fact rather than an insult. Although Samson suspected the insult was intrinsic whenever the expression was applied. 'Mrs Thornton seemed nice enough. I hear he had a bit of a temper, though.'

Seth was nodding. 'You heard right. Carl Thornton was a mean-spirited bugger. Wasn't he, Troy?'

180

The landlord looked over from the far end of the bar. 'Wasn't who what?'

'Carl Thornton. What do you remember of him?'

Troy Murgatroyd's face darkened as he walked towards them. 'Bad lot, that one,' he muttered. 'I wouldn't wish anyone dead, but there was no sadness in here the night he passed.'

'Was he a troublesome customer?' asked Samson.

'Aye, and some. Couldn't set foot in the place but he had to try and start a fight. Many's the time I watched Father chuck him out. And there weren't many folk Father would turn away if it meant making a bob or two.'

'Was Carl Thornton violent at home, too?'

'I never heard directly. But after all my years working behind this bar, I've yet to meet a man who doesn't show his true nature after a sup or two. And Carl Thornton's nature wasn't a pretty one.'

'True enough,' vouched Seth. 'There was never anything said in the open about what went on up at that quarry cottage, but given how the man behaved down here . . .' He shrugged. 'Draw your own conclusions.'

'You think this has something to do with your case?' asked Will, his steady gaze on Samson.

'Not necessarily. Just trying to see the whole picture. The more I know, the easier it'll be to solve this mystery.'

'Huh!' grouched Troy, staring pointedly at the empty plate and the empty cup in front of the detective. 'I'd like to solve the mystery of how people expect this place to stay open when they sit over a bloody coffee for an hour or more.'

Samson laughed, glanced at the clock behind the bar and

nodded towards the beer taps in front of the landlord. 'Another coffee, in that case, Troy. And a half of Black Sheep while you're at it.'

Troy's eyebrows shot up into his hairline. Samson had never ordered an alcoholic beverage in the pub. Never been known to drink anything stronger than tea and coffee in fact. 'Black Sheep?' he questioned.

Samson nodded while Seth and Will grinned.

'You sure? Won't go to your head, you being teetotal and all that?'

'Just pour the man a drink,' said Will, 'before he changes his mind. He's in need of a bit of Dutch courage.'

With great ceremony, Troy placed the glass of amber liquid in front of Samson and held out a meaty hand.

'No discount for first-timers?' asked Samson with a smile as the landlord's fingers curled over the money. Troy glared at him and strode off to get the coffee.

'Is it time, then?' asked Will.

Samson nodded. Time to put Operation Save Tolpuddle into action.

'Let's hope it works,' murmured Seth.

Samson silently echoed his entreaty. The next couple of hours would decide the fate of the grey shadow lying on the floor at his feet. If it went wrong, would Delilah ever forgive him?

Delilah heard the car pull up outside. From the kitchen window she saw a silver BMW convertible parking at the kerb. Typical. Neil still as flash as ever, but with more money now. His father's money, no doubt.

Running her hand over her hair, she fought the urge to

nip upstairs to the bathroom to check how she looked. Despising herself for it, she'd changed out of her usual attire of jeans and a jumper and instead was wearing a russet woollen dress with black boots. She was fully aware that she was using the form-clinging outfit as a substitute for armour. With an impatient toss of her head, she pulled her shoulders back and headed down to the hallway, where the doorbell was already pealing.

She was ready for them. She only hoped Samson and Tolpuddle were, too.

Through the pub window the occupants of the Fleece watched Neil Taylor get out of the car.

'Bloody hell,' muttered Samson, taking in the razor-sharp cheekbones, the mop of tawny hair flopping across the forehead and the effortless grace of the man he'd last seen as a scrawny youth. 'When did young Taylor turn into a Greek god?'

'Good looks are skin-deep,' growled Will, fists clenched on his lap.

'And easily achieved on his father's money,' added Seth.

Neil had crossed to the pavement and was now holding open the passenger door, proffering a hand to his companion.

'A real gent,' snarled Will as a pale arm emerged from inside the BMW, delicate fingers latching onto Neil's hand.

She rose silkily from the car, a vision in a bright-red knee-length coat, the hood pulled up around a beautiful face framed with jet-black hair. Red Riding Hood in downtown Bruncliffe. In a pair of boots that even had Seth shuffling closer to the window for a better view.

'Wow!' murmured Samson.

'Indeed,' said Will. 'Still, she wouldn't last a second in the ring with Delilah. Jaw like glass, that one.'

Samson laughed, slapping Will on the back at his brotherly pride. 'Right, Tolpuddle,' he said, the dog stirring himself at the rattle of his lead. 'Showtime.'

Tolpuddle stretched, yawned, gave a last sniff of the carpet and looked up at Samson.

'Good luck,' said Will, reaching down to pat the dog. 'Make sure you keep him with us. He's bloody useless as a farm dog but our Delilah would be lost without him.'

With a stirring of nerves, Samson followed the nonchalant dog out of the pub and across the road.

13

She'd done exactly as Samson had requested. With the thermostat set high all morning, Samson's office was uncomfortably warm as Delilah led Neil and Abbie across the hall and into the room, gesturing for them to take a seat and closing the door behind her.

'I like what you've done with the place,' said Neil with a wide smile, ignoring the invitation to sit as he strode across to the window, hands in his pockets. He was taking in the red-flocked wallpaper, the same old coffee-stained desk, the lino peeling up in the corners and the battered metal chairs that had been there when they bought the building together. 'Still not had the decorators in?'

Delilah forced a smile. Having graduated in graphic design, Neil had always been concerned with appearances. When they'd set up the website company, he'd insisted that the more pragmatic aspects of running the business be left to her, as though it was beneath him to concentrate on something so prosaic. And they'd had many an argument over his desire to spend money they couldn't afford on refurbishing the offices.

Memories crowding her, Delilah bit back a retort. Don't antagonise them. That's what Samson had told her before he left. On no account make them annoyed.

Easier said than done when Abbie, also a designer, was

sitting on the very edge of a chair, as though the seat itself might be infectious, wide eyes scanning the room. If the office was scruffy and unkempt, the same couldn't be said of her. With her hood pushed back, her ebony hair was splayed out over the red of her coat, making a dramatic contrast with her ivory skin and giving her an ethereal beauty. And below the hem of the coat a pair of killer boots extended, ending in sharp heels. She looked immaculate, everything about her was stylish, making Delilah feel decidedly second-rate in her russet dress.

'How are things?' Neil was asking.

Delilah shifted her gaze, letting herself really look at him for the first time. He'd put on a bit of weight. But those cheekbones remained magnificent, giving him Holly-wood features, his hair slightly longer on top than when they'd been together. He still had the charm too, the way he was regarding her now, brown eyes focused on her as though she was the only person in the room.

'Things are fine,' muttered Delilah, a prickle of per-spiration forming at the back of her neck. Bloody stupid woollen dress and the heating cranked up high. 'You?'

'Great. I'm working for a dynamic company that's really going places, and Abbie has almost completed her Masters.' Abbie smiled sweetly up at him, hands folded neatly in her lap. The perfect girlfriend. 'We're planning on setting up our own design business when she's finished.'

Combined with the heat and her nerves, it was enough to untether Delilah's self-control.

'Let's hope you don't run out on this one,' she snapped.

Neil laughed. 'Still as feisty as ever, eh, Dee?'

'Delilah,' she said pointedly, hating the sound of the

nickname Ryan had bestowed on her in childhood coming from her ex-husband's mouth. Only family – and Samson – got to call her Dee.

Smile undimmed, Neil dipped his head in acknowledgement. 'Fair enough. How are the businesses doing?'

'Great. Going from strength to strength.'

'I hear you have a new tenant.' A cocked eyebrow accompanied the comment. Clearly moving away from his home town hadn't softened Neil's judgement of Bruncliffe's black sheep. 'I'm surprised you took O'Brien in. After everything.'

'Everyone deserves a second chance,' Delilah retorted, chin tilting in defiance. 'God knows, I gave you enough of them.'

There was a beat of silence, during which Delilah caught herself wishing Samson would walk in the door and save the situation she seemed so intent on spoiling. But then Neil raised his hands in surrender, a grin on his handsome face.

'Touché,' he said. 'I'd forgotten how much fun it was to spar with you.'

A delicate cough from Abbie and a glitter of blue eyes as she looked from Neil to her watch, a perfectly varnished nail tapping it gently.

'Yes, time is pushing on,' said Neil. 'We don't want to put you out any longer. If Tolpuddle's here . . . ? Abbie can't wait to meet him.'

'It's so true,' said Abbie with a smile, her gaze turning coy. 'I've been pestering Neil for a pooch for ages, and when he told me about Tolpuddle – he just sounds perfect.'

Perfect. Delilah thought of all the other adjectives she'd

use to describe the Weimaraner and a hard lump formed in her throat. Her desire to have Samson there was replaced with a fierce hope that he'd absconded with her dog in tow. 'Erm . . . he's—'

'Afternoon, all!' The office door opened and in walked her tenant, dark hair curling on his broad shoulders, his new jacket giving him a roguish air, and a sleepy-looking Tolpuddle by his side.

'Oh, he's adorable!' Abbie cooed, getting to her feet. 'Such a lovely boy.'

'He has his moments, don't you, Samson?' said Delilah, sparking a grin from the man in the doorway while Abbie blushed furiously.

'I didn't mean . . . I was talking about . . .' she stammered.

'Nice to meet you,' Samson said, stepping forward and extending his hand, smoothing over her awkwardness with a charm matching that of Neil Taylor. A charm that had Abbie fluttering her eyelashes at him.

Bloody hell! Delilah didn't know whether to laugh or launch herself at the woman and make her just a little bit less perfect. The only consolation in the ridiculous charade was Neil's deep frown.

'Tolpuddle,' Samson was saying, 'this is Abbie.'

The dog looked up at Abbie's proffered hand, sniffed it and then allowed it to pat his head. Within a minute he was lying on the lino having his stomach rubbed.

'What a gorgeous dog,' Abbie gushed, crouched down next to him. 'A real beauty. Aren't you, my darling? A real beauty.'

Neil Taylor crossed the room, nodded a curt greeting at

Samson and bent to pat Tolpuddle, genuinely delighted at seeing the Weimaraner again, even if the delayed custody bid had been provoked by a desire to pander to his girlfriend.

'He looks great, Delilah,' he said. 'You've been looking after him well.'

'Someone had to,' she retorted, the situation becoming unbearable. The heat. The scratchy wool of her dress. The facade she was having to maintain. She was stretched to snapping point, being asked to just stand and smile while they took her dog.

'He's going to be so at home in our flat,' continued Abbie, rubbing the dog's head now, his legs sprawled out across the floor.

Their *flat*? Delilah whipped round to stare at Samson, willing him to do something. Say something. There was no way Tolpuddle could live in a flat.

But Samson just gave a shake of his head, making her want to throttle him as well as the two visitors.

'And we've got lots of toys, so you won't be lonely during the day while we're at work.' Abbie glanced up at Samson. 'I've been reading that it's important to keep them active. It stops them getting anxious when we're out of the house.'

A surge of anger crashed over Delilah. Sod Samson's non-existent plan. Neil and Abbie didn't deserve Tolpuddle and she wasn't going to let them have him. She wasn't about to condemn him to a life locked up inside a bloody flat!

She took a step forward, intending to put an end to this farce, but firm fingers encircled her wrist. Samson, standing next to her. There was another subtle shake of the head, a brief wink. He wanted her to think he had it under control. But from Delilah's perspective, Neil and Abbie were about to walk away with Tolpuddle. The same Tolpuddle who had rescued Delilah from the depths of despair after the death of her brother; the dog that had given her life purpose when her husband walked out and everything she'd believed in had come crashing down around her ears.

The dog she couldn't live without.

'Trust me,' Samson whispered, his hand moving to the small of her back. 'Please.'

She stared at him, his blue gaze holding hers, then she closed her eyes to hold back the tears, and placed her faith in him.

Ringing. The sound of a mobile being ignored sounded in his ear.

She was probably out on the fells making the most of her Sunday. A day of rest. But not for the wicked. Or alcoholics.

Joseph O'Brien feared he was both. Sitting in his armchair, a cold sweat on his forehead, he shoved his phone back in his pocket. There'd be no help from that quarter. And he couldn't face calling Samson. Exposing this weakness to a son with whom he was still trying to piece together the fragments of a relationship. It would kill any chance of them reconciling properly stone dead, because Samson wouldn't understand this. Not after everything Joseph had put him through as a child.

Gaze never leaving the bottle on the coffee table, he swallowed, the taste of whisky raw in his throat. Imagined.

But all the stronger for that. The smoky flavour, the soft warmth . . .

He reached out. His fingers splayed around the curve of glass separating him from his addiction, daring himself. One small shot. It wouldn't hurt. And no one could blame him. It hadn't been his fault. He hadn't fallen off the waggon so much as been pushed by a deranged woman determined to kill him.

He wished she'd succeeded. The agony he was going through, trying to live each day as though nothing was wrong. As though he was still sober, when all the time he was obsessed with drink.

His hand worked up the bottle, all the way to the screw top. A quick twist and it would be off. He tightened his grip, the top beginning to rotate under the pressure. He heard it click. Open.

'Joseph?' A hammering at his door and a loud voice shouting. 'You in there?'

In one swift movement, the top was screwed back on and the bottle stowed down the back of his armchair. Habits learned long ago. The furtiveness of the compulsive drinker.

When Joseph O'Brien opened the door, slightly flushed, Arty Robinson had no idea how close his friend had been to giving in.

'Right. I think we're all sorted.' Neil Taylor was straightening up, clipping a lead onto Tolpuddle's collar.

'I can't believe he's ours,' cooed Abbie, still patting the Weimaraner. 'He's so beautiful.'

Samson felt Delilah stir next to him and knew he didn't

have much longer before she snapped, his plea for her trust having gained him only a modicum of time.

Tolpuddle, for his part, was getting to his feet, giving himself a shake. Still looking happy with all the attention. Still looking his normal self.

Which wasn't what was supposed to be happening.

'Come on, boy,' Samson muttered under his breath. Willing his plan to kick into action.

'Thanks for being so understanding, Delilah,' said Neil, heading for the door, the dog at his heels.

'Yes, thank you so much.' Abbie was giving Delilah a simpering smile. 'I know it must be hard for you to part with him. But he'll be happy with us.'

A strangled sound from Delilah, part cough, part sob. She stared at the dog as he followed Neil out into the hallway, Abbie on their heels. The front door was opening . . .

Still nothing happening.

Fingers dug into his arm. Delilah. Next to him. Hissing in his ear. 'Whatever your plan is, now would be a good time for it to start working!'

The click of a car unlocking. Samson hurried over to the front door, still convinced there was time.

'It'll work,' he muttered. It had to.

But he could see Neil encouraging Tolpuddle into the rear of the BMW. Could see Abbie getting gracefully into the passenger's side. Then Neil was glancing over, raising a hand in farewell.

Delilah had moved alongside Samson. Grey-faced. 'They're leaving,' she said, turning to him, tears in her eyes. The simplicity of her words more wounding than any screams. 'I thought you were going to do something?'

Date with Mystery

A wrench of anxiety tore at Samson's guts. He'd been so confident. He'd asked Delilah to trust him. Could he have got it all wrong?

The car door closed. The engine started. And a low murmur of pain issued from the woman standing next to him.

Delilah wasn't aware of anything. Not the whimper coming from her own throat. Not the cold air against her flushed cheeks. Not even the small crowd that had gathered on the pavement outside the pub.

All she saw was the smudge of grey in the small rear window of the silver car. The car that was pulling away from the kerb.

Tolpuddle. She could see him looking back. He'd be confused. Upset. Then she realised. She hadn't even got to say goodbye.

'What the hell . . . ?' An angry voice. Her brother, Will, storming across from the pub. 'I thought you had this sorted, O'Brien!'

Samson next to her, face twisted in contrition. 'I'm so sorry,' he was saying. 'I'm so very sorry.'

Then Will was upon them, advancing on Samson, fists curled in rage. 'You let that scumbag take her dog!' he was shouting. 'You didn't even try to stop him.'

Samson was taking a step back and Seth Thistlethwaite was there, trying to calm the two men. And all the while Delilah was watching the car heading down the road; the flash of the indicator as it began turning right. Then it was gone. Out of sight.

'No.' She felt her knees tremble. 'No . . . no . . . no!'

A strong arm caught her elbow, helping her stay upright.

'We'll get him back, Delilah,' Samson was saying. His eyes bright with distress. 'No matter what it takes. I promise.'

She turned her head slowly, the world still not in focus. Then she stared at him and felt the flood of anger and grief overwhelm her. Ripping her arm from his grip, she pushed both hands against Samson's chest, sending him staggering backwards.

'I trusted you!' she spat. 'I should have known better.'

Turning on her heel, she entered the office building and slammed the front door behind her. Only when it was closed and the eyes of Bruncliffe could no longer see her did she let the tears fall. She collapsed onto the stairs, her head in her hands, sobs convulsing her body.

Tolpuddle. She'd lost him. For good.

'Leave her alone,' Will Metcalfe growled as Samson approached the door that had slammed in his face only moments before. 'Take my word for it, she's best left alone. Unless you want a black eye.'

'Not particularly,' muttered Samson, his hand still raised, key grasped within it.

'He's right, lad.' Seth Thistlethwaite stepped forward, putting himself between Samson and the lock. 'Leave her be. She's not one for wanting folk seeing her when she's upset.'

And she was upset. For Samson could hear faint sobbing coming from within the office building, each hiccup of sound tearing at him, making him feel distressed and angry and concerned all at the same time. He'd let her down. Badly. All because he'd had the arrogance to think he could solve the situation with Tolpuddle.

Instead, he'd allowed Neil Taylor to drive off with the dog without the least bit of a challenge. He hated himself. Enough that he would happily allow Delilah free range with her fury, letting her do her worst with those fists of hers. He'd welcome the pain. Deserved it, in fact.

'Come on.' Seth was leading him away, steering him towards the pub and out of earshot of the small crowd of spectators which had gathered in the street. 'Let's get inside and talk this over.'

'What's there to talk about?' snapped Samson. 'I've messed up. This is all my fault.'

'You won't find me disagreeing,' muttered Will as he made a path through the onlookers and entered the Fleece. Troy Murgatroyd looked up from behind the bar.

'Thought you were going saving that dog, O'Brien,' said the landlord as the three men filed in. 'Didn't look like whatever you had planned worked out too good.'

'Bloody understatement of the year,' growled Will, slumping onto a bar stool and pulling the remains of his pint towards him.

'Easy Will,' said Seth as Samson collapsed on a stool, head in hands. 'Getting angry isn't going to help anyone.'

'Might have bloody helped if I'd decked that peacock, Taylor. At least we'd have had the satisfaction of seeing him suffer.'

'And the satisfaction of being in the holding cell at the police station before the day was through,' retorted Seth. 'Old man Taylor would have you locked up in seconds if you so much as touch his lad. So ease up on the testosterone and give Samson a break. He was trying to help.'

Will glowered at Seth and finished off his pint.

'What went wrong?' Troy asked.

Samson's shoulders slumped. 'I don't know. It's always worked before.'

'What has?'

'Beer,' said Samson, glancing up at the landlord. 'It has an unwelcome effect on Tolpuddle.'

Troy stared at him. 'That was your master plan? To make the dog fart?'

Samson nodded miserably. 'To make him undesirable. But it didn't work. Tolpuddle wasn't bothered by it.'

'Bloody hell. I've heard some things in my day, but that . . .' Troy was shaking his head in disbelief.

'It must have been the beer,' said Seth.

'Now hang on a minute!' Troy straightened up, chest puffing out in indignation. 'Don't go blaming my merchandise. There's nowt wrong with any of the ale on tap in here.'

'I'm not saying there is,' said Seth, hands up to soothe the irate landlord. 'Just that it didn't have the same effect on the dog as usual.'

'No matter what it was,' muttered Will darkly. 'End result is the same. That blasted Taylor whelp has got Tolpuddle, and our Delilah is across the road crying her eyes out. So what I want to know, O'Brien, is what are you going to do about it?'

Samson stared at the floral carpet swirling across the floor and wished he could start the day all over again.

*

He was in a car. He'd been in cars countless times. But never without her.

Anxiety rising, Tolpuddle twisted round on the cramped rear seat, his tail brushing across the passenger seat as he did so.

'Oh!' An exclamation from the front. 'He just swiped me with his tail! Sit down, Puddle-kins, there's a good boy.'

'Puddle-kins?' A laugh from the man. 'I'm not sure Tolpuddle will respond to that.'

'Perhaps he'll respond to this.' A sharp slap on his flank. Then a raised voice. 'Sit down!'

Startled, Tolpuddle fell back against the seat, flopping onto it. He felt the panic building. A burbling in his stomach, too.

'See. He knows who's boss.'

The man was looking in the mirror. He caught Tolpuddle's eye. A wink. 'Not too far to your new home.'

Tolpuddle shifted on the uncomfortable leather, the smell unfamiliar. A strong floral scent wafting back from the front. Overpowering. He sneezed loudly. Shook his head.

'Oh God. He just sneezed. All down the back of my seat. Didn't Delilah train him at all?'

Delilah. Tolpuddle's ears picked up at the word. He knew what it meant. He barked. A sharp ricochet of sound in the confines of the car.

'Tolpuddle! Be quiet!' She was turning back to stare at him. Angry.

The bubble of disquiet grew, engulfing him. Making him whine. Making his stomach flip. And gurgle.

'What's that noise?'

'It's the dog. I think you've upset him.'

Tolpuddle put his head on his paws, eyes watching mournfully as the trees and the fells flashed by. The whine grew louder.

'You have to make him stop it.' She had her hands over her ears. 'We can't go the whole way back like this.'

'You wound him up. You stop it.'

He could keep it up for hours. A wail of despair. Of grief. Of distress. But on its own, it might not have been enough to save him. When his stomach churned again with a gaseous burble, that was what changed things.

'Oh, Jesus! What the hell is that?' A face peering back at him, hand clamped across the nose.

Tolpuddle simply whined all the more.

14

She'd put the kettle on without even realising it. The motion of filling it and placing it down to boil a routine reaction in times of stress. And this was a stressful time.

Leaning her forehead against the kitchen window, Delilah stared down at the road below. Numb. A deep pit of anguish in her gut.

What was she going to do? Because she couldn't leave things as they were. She couldn't allow Tolpuddle to fester in a cramped flat down in London, spending long days on his own. It wasn't fair.

The kettle clicked off but she made no move to cross to the worktop and make tea.

Across the road she could see the shadows of people inside the pub. Samson and Will had gone in there. With Seth to keep them apart.

She felt a pang of sympathy for Samson. For whatever his plan had been that had failed so spectacularly. He'd be gutted. Distraught at losing Tolpuddle, too. The sympathy was tinged with contrition for the way she'd reacted, lashing out at him like that. But she couldn't help it. He'd promised her he'd save her dog. He'd even stopped her when she'd been going to step in and put a halt to Neil's casual assumption that Tolpuddle was his for the taking.

Samson O'Brien was going to have to shoulder the blame for this one.

And he was going to have to come up with a way to get her dog back. Because his life wouldn't be worth living if he didn't.

She turned from the window and opened the cupboard above the kettle, reaching for the teabags and seeing instead the packet of Dog-gestives. Tears streamed down her face once more.

'You promised her,' Will was saying, his temper still simmering. 'You said you'd get him back. So you'd best get thinking, O'Brien.'

'I know, I know,' muttered Samson, staring at the floor and hoping for inspiration.

'Haven't you got contacts who could help out? Someone down in London handy with their fist, who might persuade that runt to give up the dog?'

Samson could think of plenty of people he'd come across while undercover who would frighten the life out of Neil Taylor. Perhaps that was an option?

'Is that your answer to everything, Will? Resort to violence?' Seth Thistlethwaite asked. 'I think this will take a bit more finesse.'

'Like trying to get a dog to fart?' scoffed Will. 'Not much finesse there. No success, either.'

'For what it's worth,' said Troy from behind the bar where he was wiping glasses, 'Seth's right. You can't beat a Taylor with brawn. They're too powerful. If you want to get that dog back, you're going to have to come up with something clever. Something that would hit them where it hurts.'

'Like what?' asked Samson, lifting his head to look at the landlord.

Troy leaned across to the three of them, voice lowered. 'Kidnap.'

'What?'

'You heard,' he said, straightening up. 'There's no way they'd pay a ransom. Tighter than a duck's you-know-what, the lot of them.'

Seth was already shaking his head. 'You're suggesting Samson goes down to London and kidnaps the dog?'

Troy stared back at him. 'I'm suggesting no such thing. That would make me an accessory.'

But Will was already standing up, ready to act. 'It could work,' he muttered. 'Grab Tolpuddle from a busy street. Send a ransom note.'

'And then what?' asked Seth with a sigh. 'Bring the dog back up here, where Neil's entire family lives, and hope no one notices a Weimaraner is back in town? I can just see that working out.'

Will thumped a large fist down on the bar. 'Well, what then?' he shouted. 'We've got to do something.'

'Oh, I don't know about that . . .' Samson was standing too, crossing to the window where he'd just seen a flash of silver go past. A BMW. 'I think,' he said, with a grin beginning to form, 'we've already done all we need to.'

Seth and Will hurried over to his side and then they were opening the door, heading out into the street where the sound of an air-raid siren was issuing from the car parked outside Samson's office.

'Jesus!' said Will, as the car doors shot open and two people spilled onto the pavement, gagging. 'What the hell . . . ?' He stuttered to a stop as the faint odour of rotten hops wafted across the road. 'I'll be damned.' He turned to say something to Samson, but the detective was already running towards the office.

Mug in hand, she was leaning against the worktop when she heard the car. She didn't think anything of it. But then she heard that unmistakable whine. A high-pitched keening that she knew from experience could last for hours. She was crossing towards the window when footsteps pounded up the stairs.

'Delilah! Delilah!' Samson's head appeared above the bannisters, a wide grin on his face. 'Come quickly!'

Heart thudding, she thrust the mug on the table and hurried across the landing, following him down the stairs two at a time. Out onto the doorstep and there was the BMW, doors wide open, a dreadful wail coming from within and Neil and Abbie standing some distance away, Abbie's ivory skin a shade of green. She was holding a lace handkerchief to her nose while Neil was staring at the vehicle with a mixture of disgust and respect.

Then Tolpuddle emerged from inside the car. He saw Delilah and Samson, his ears picked up and the whining cut out mid-yowl, to be replaced with enthusiastic barking. The dog had gone from depressed to elated in a matter of seconds, bounding over to leap up at the pair of them.

'Down, Tolpuddle,' Delilah said half-heartedly as she wrapped her arms around him. She glanced across at her ex-husband with raised eyebrows. 'Whatever's the matter?' she asked. 'Did you forget something?'

Neil shuffled closer, taking a circuitous route around the car. 'We've changed our minds,' he murmured.

There was a snort of smothered laughter from the vicinity of the pub doorway where, yet again, a small cluster of people had gathered.

Delilah glanced from Neil to Abbie and then at Samson, an unconcerned look on the detective's face. And then it reached her. A fetid smell oozing from the interior of the BMW, an invisible mushroom-cloud of stink.

'Oh, really?' Delilah fought back a coughing fit, blinking to stop her eyes streaming. 'How come?'

'Erm . . . Abbie's not sure about taking Tolpuddle.' Neil shrugged, apologetic. 'She thinks it'd be a problem. His size in our flat.' He stared at the pavement, cheeks reddening at the lie.

Struggling to keep a straight face, Delilah nodded. 'I understand.'

'She's not a country girl, like you,' he continued. 'She's not used to animals.'

Delilah stifled a laugh.

'That said,' Neil added, looking down at the dog, 'I don't remember Tolpuddle being . . . well – so . . .'

'Smelly?' Delilah gave him a sympathetic look. 'It's age. No doubt it'll come to all of us.'

Looking slightly appalled at the thought, Neil nodded. He made to go and then turned back. 'Thanks, Dee. For being so understanding about everything.' He leaned in and kissed her on the cheek, the citrus tang of his aftershave a memory of happier times. And a welcome respite from the foul odour still emanating from the car. 'You might as well take this,' he said, thrusting an envelope in her hands. 'Bye.'

He walked towards the BMW, Abbie reluctantly coming over to join him, her lips in a tight line. With a swirl of red coat she got in the car and slammed the door, head leaning towards the open window, handkerchief pressed to her face. Neil got in beside her and the BMW pulled away.

Watching them leave, Delilah felt a nudge on her hip. Tolpuddle, leaning against her, surveying the world, and next to him, Samson, waving at the departing car.

She waited until the vehicle disappeared around the corner, then she sank to her knees, arms thrown around Tolpuddle, hugging him to her in a mixture of laughter and tears of relief.

'Thank you,' she said, looking up at Samson. 'I don't know what you did, but thank you.'

'It worked then?' Seth Thistlethwaite was crossing the road towards them, Delilah's brother, Will, next to him, the pair of them grinning.

'Finally!' said Samson.

'They couldn't get out of that car quick enough,' laughed Will, slapping Samson on the back. 'I owe you an apology, O'Brien.'

Still kneeling next to Tolpuddle, Delilah looked from her brother to Samson and then to the pub, Troy Murgatroyd standing in the doorway, a rare smile on his face.

'Beer!' she exclaimed, comprehension dawning. 'That was your master plan? You fed Tolpuddle *beer*?'

Samson grinned down at her. 'Just a couple of sips. It worked, didn't it?'

'Took a while, but aye, it worked a treat,' Will said, surprisingly in agreement with the black sheep of Bruncliffe.

'I thought she was going to be sick,' chuckled Seth.

Delilah shook her head in despair. 'You're all incorrigible.'

'No point fighting fair with the Taylors,' said Will. 'Gets you nowhere. And we don't even have the assurance that the runt won't try something like this again.'

'Oh, I don't know about that.' Delilah was holding out a set of papers.

'Are they from the Kennel Club?' asked Samson, taking the papers from her and unfolding them.

She nodded, a large grin on her face. 'Yes. Neil's given me Tolpuddle's official documents. I can get him registered in my name.' She started laughing, wrapping her arms back around her precious dog.

'Thanks,' Will murmured to Samson, tipping his head in Delilah's direction. 'I think losing that dog would have killed her.'

'What did you say?' Samson had turned to Will Metcalfe and was staring at him intently.

'Thanks. I said thank you.'

Sensing a shift in atmosphere, Seth Thistlethwaite stepped forward, preparing to intervene between the two men again.

'No. The other bit.' From lounging in the doorway having a joke, Samson O'Brien was now standing bolt upright, his face fierce with concentration.

Will looked puzzled by the dramatic change in the

detective's demeanour. 'That losing the dog would have killed her,' he repeated.

Samson gripped his arm. 'My God. That's it. That's what's missing.' He wheeled round and headed into the office.

'What did you say to him?' demanded Delilah, aware of Samson's abrupt departure.

'Nothing,' protested Will. 'For once, I didn't say anything.'

Delilah stood up and walked across the hall to poke her head through the doorway of Samson's office.

'Everything all right?' she asked.

He glanced up from his laptop. 'Livvy Thornton,' he said. 'I think I know what we've been overlooking.'

'It's the dog.'

'Red? Livvy's collie?' asked Delilah, cutting into a Yorkshire pudding, thick gravy oozing from it. She'd persuaded Samson to accompany her across the road with Tolpuddle for a celebratory Sunday roast. With plates of Kay Murgatroyd's delicious beef in front of them, Samson was telling Delilah about his revelation.

'Something's been niggling me ever since I called in to see Mrs Walker at Fellside Court on Friday. I just couldn't put my finger on it. But then Will made a comment earlier about the impact losing Tolpuddle would have had on you.'

'Don't,' Delilah said, stricken with a mixture of relief and dread at what could have happened. She glanced down at the hound sitting by her feet, watching her patiently. 'I can't bear to think about it.'

'Precisely. Given what everyone has said about Livvy, I don't think she could have, either.'

'Which is why she took Red to Leeds.' Delilah was frowning, failing to see the breakthrough Samson was excited about.

'Exactly!' he said. 'So how come he's missing?'

'Because he ran after the car?'

'I don't mean in the past. I mean in the present.'

Samson saw her thinking it through, the fork placed back on the plate, the furrow on her brow as she contemplated his question. Then the dawning comprehension. She was sharp. He had to give her that.

'They didn't mention him,' she said, with growing excitement. 'At Snips. Neither Mrs Atkins nor her daughter mentioned that Livvy had a dog.'

Samson nodded. 'Exactly. Everyone in Bruncliffe we've spoken to has referred to Red – Jimmy, Jo Whitfield, even Mrs Walker. The common consensus is that Livvy and Red were inseparable. To the extent that she brought him to work with her on her first day.' He gestured towards the empty hairdresser's on the other side of Back Street.

'But if that were the case, how come she didn't do the same in Leeds?' Delilah had temporarily abandoned her meal, leaning eagerly across the table. 'We need to talk to the owners of the salon again. See if they remember Red.'

'I agree. Unfortunately it's Sunday, so I doubt they'll be there.'

Delilah groaned. 'Of course. How frustrating.'

'Welcome to the reality of being a detective. And talking of frustrating . . .' Samson was looking at Tolpuddle, who'd moved closed to Delilah, his head now resting on her lap, big eyes gazing up at her. 'I reckon he's earned a bit of beef.'

'He can have all the beef he wants,' said Delilah with a smile as she rubbed Tolpuddle's head and then gave him a morsel of meat. 'But beer . . . Never again!'

Sunday. A day the same as every other for farmers. But for Jimmy Thornton's mother, it had been a holy day. A day set aside for church.

Jimmy hadn't inherited his mother's faith. He'd stopped going to St Oswald's down in Bruncliffe once he started working at Tom Hardacre's farm. His mother had objected at first, but gradually he'd made her see that being out on the land was as good as religion for him. When up on the fells, he felt closer to anything resembling a god than he did cooped up inside the four cold walls of the church.

Today, he'd decided to honour his mother. Not through prayer but through tending her beloved rhubarb. Having spent the morning doing chores on his farm, he'd driven over to Quarry House after a superb roast – Gemma's Yorkshire puddings every bit as good as those his mother used to make – and had arrived at the cottage intending to sort through the kitchen. He'd set about his task diligently, packing up pots, pans and dishes. But with the will still unsettled and Matty having advised him not to be hasty in getting rid of things, given the legal uncertainty, he'd soon become frustrated by the increasing pile of boxes cluttering up the floor.

'Typically over-cautious solicitor,' muttered Jimmy, annoyed at the inability to tie the loose ends of his mother's passing. What the hell could be taking so long to sort out?

Date with Mystery

Leaning on the kitchen counter and watching the clouds moving fast over the top of the quarry, a delicate blue sky behind them, he'd decided some fresh air would ease his exasperation at the unexpected mess that had followed his mother's death. Abandoning the open cupboards and the contents of the kitchen strewn across the worktop, he headed outside.

Sort out her rhubarb. She'd been pressing him to look after it before she'd died and he still hadn't got round to it.

Which is how he found himself walking the length of the garden, mentally preparing to enter the outbuilding that marked the end of the property. With its stone walls and small windows, it resembled so many other barns that dotted the landscape of the Dales. As a farmer, Jimmy had been in his fair share of them. None of them made him feel the way this one did.

Taking a deep breath, he unlocked the door and entered. It was innocuous to the outsider. A workbench crossing the wall opposite the door, plastic shelving to the right groaning under the weight of half-filled cans of paint and rusting tools, a couple of old bikes hanging from the roof, one of them Livvy's, and another set of shelving to the left where the gardening equipment was kept. And in the middle of the floor, directly opposite where he was standing, a brown stain.

The place where his father had killed himself.

He crossed to the gardening tools stored in a rack he'd made for his mother in woodworking classes, the joinery rough, the design functional. She'd refused to allow him to buy her something better when he had the money – rakes, spades, hoes and forks all standing upright in his first and only attempt at carpentry. Feeling the familiar unease in the space, his eyes always drawn to that patch of concrete, he grabbed the spade and a bucket and got back out into the fresh air.

Split the crowns.

It would give him something to do. Even though no one would be living here. The garden that she'd tended so carefully would be left to go wild, abandoned like the quarry looming over it.

He approached the sad mass of dying leaves and stalks in the rhubarb patch, the plants not having been tended since his mother's illness really took hold in the late autumn, and his heart ached. Standing there in the shadow of the scarred cliff, everything bleak, it seemed to Jimmy Thornton that his life had been surrounded by death.

'Get a grip,' he muttered. Mother would have had no time for such maudlin nonsense.

He'd take a crown with him, he decided, trying to shake off his dark mood. A mere bit of rhubarb wouldn't be missed if ever he was called to account over his mother's will. He'd have a go at making rhubarb-and-ginger jam. The thought brought a smile to his face. Mother had made it ever year in the back end, stocking the pantry with jars of it. Chutney, too. And crumble every Sunday. She'd loved her rhubarb, loved the fact that her adopted county was famous for it.

He wielded the spade and shoved it hard into the soil around the first plant, his foot pushing it deeper. He was preparing to lever it when his mobile sounded. Gemma's ringtone.

With the panic of all fathers-to-be, he whipped the phone out of his pocket and answered.

'You okay?'

A burst of static was the reply. Bloody quarry and its dodgy reception. He moved across the garden to the barn and was rewarded with a fractured sentence from Gemma.

'. . . dog running amok . . . yows . . . bring the gun.'

It was enough to tell him what was happening. Pregnant ewes, being harried around a field by a strange dog. Lives could be lost.

'Bloody hell! I'll be right back,' he shouted into the phone. But the line was already lost.

Leaving the spade and bucket where they were, he hurried towards his Land Rover, cursing people who let their animals loose when out walking, always with the same claim that their dog wouldn't do anything to harm the sheep – until one day the dog does go after them and chases them. And kills them.

His shotgun. He'd pick that up from the farm in passing and then head for the field.

He got in the Land Rover and, in a cloud of quarry dust, raced off up the track and into the distance. The house and garden settled back into quietness, the empty windows looking out onto the sharp edges of the cliff, the ground dappled in light and shade as the clouds passed above. And the spade, upright, its blade buried in the soil. The soil that still held its secrets.

15

'No doubt tha's got washing for me?'

Monday morning, seven o'clock, and Ida Capstick was coming up the stairs to the first-floor kitchen, metal bucket of cleaning supplies in one hand, a big shopping bag in the other.

Samson started pouring the tea that was part of their daily ritual – a ritual that had begun the morning in November when the unsuspecting cleaner had walked in on him in his makeshift bedroom upstairs. Taking pity on her homeless former neighbour, Ida had agreed to keep his illicit use of Delilah's top floor a secret. The price? A cup of tea waiting for her every morning at seven, with a plate of biscuits next to it. 'Posh ones, mind,' she'd stipulated. 'None of that Rich Tea rubbish.'

As she muttered her way up the stairs, Samson realised how much he'd missed the ritual while Ida was away.

'How was Bridlington?' he asked.

'Too much sand for my liking. Blowing up all over the place.' She sat, pulled her mug towards her and reached for a biscuit. 'Even on a dry day it's difficult to get washing out.'

Samson grinned, picturing Ida ranting at the elements that were hindering her obsessive cleaning.

'Aye, tha can grin. Wasn't tha underwear that was collecting half a beach.' She glowered at him before handing him the shopping bag, which was filled with cleaned and ironed laundry.

Samson knew better than to protest. Part of the bargain that had secured Ida's silence had been her insistence on doing his washing in order to prevent him hanging it up to drip-dry in the bathroom on the top floor. All attempts to persuade her otherwise had failed, so instead Samson meekly handed her a bag loaded with dirty clothes in return.

'And your cousin? How is she?' he asked.

'Humph.' Ida raised the mug to her lips and took a drink before expanding on her disapproving opener. 'Not so bereaved as she can't be planning what's next. She was already packing boxes when I left.'

'She's moving?'

'Reckon so. Wouldn't be surprised if she didn't happen over this way.'

'She's coming to Bruncliffe?'

'Maybe.' Ida pursed her lips and Samson knew that was as much as he would get out of her. Ida Capstick had never had time for gossip. Which meant he had to tread carefully if he was to get anywhere with his next line of questioning.

'Have you heard about the case I'm on?' he asked, casually.

A shrewd look was his reply. 'Aye. And I know why tha's raised it. Spit it out, whatever it is tha wants to know.'

He grinned, hands raised in surrender. 'You're right. I need your help. It's about the letters Livvy was writing to her mother.'

Ida nodded. 'Thought as much.' She shook her head,

staring into her tea. 'What a mess that was. Poor Marian not able to write to her own daughter without him kicking off.'

'Carl Thornton?'

'Aye. A right devil of a man. He had that family living in fear.'

'Is that why Livvy left?'

'Marian never said, and I never asked. But I'd lay money on him being at the back of it.'

'So how did you get involved?'

'I knew Marian through church. Livvy, too. That lass could sing like an angel.' Ida smiled sadly.

'Mrs Thornton asked you to be an intermediary, then?'

'If that's the fancy word tha wants to put on it. She took me aside one morning after service and asked if I would hold letters for her. She didn't go into great detail, but it was clear her husband didn't want her in communication with Livvy. I didn't see the harm in helping her out. No more than I do in having George collect tha post from the farm.'

Her reply was accompanied by a defiant glare, making it clear that if there was any blame to be apportioned for her actions in the past, Samson was guilty of a similar sin, seeing as he had given his old home in Thorpdale as his address to contacts in London. Not wanting the trouble that was brewing in the capital to find him, or relishing a repeat performance of the beating he'd been given before he left there, he'd decided it was best to hide his exact whereabouts for now. As a result, Ida's brother, George, who had been appointed caretaker of Twistleton Farm by Rick Procter, was picking up Samson's mail.

'How often did Livvy write to her mother?' Samson asked, neatly sidestepping the issue.

'Once a week. Up until a couple of weeks before she was killed.'

'So Livvy stopped writing before she died?'

'Aye. A couple of weeks before.'

'What made her stop?'

Another purse of the lips. Prying secrets out of Ida Capstick wasn't easy. 'I'm not sure as it's my place to divulge confidences. Especially when all them that's involved are dead,' she said.

'It could help sort out the mess Jimmy's having to deal with.'

The cleaner's face softened. 'Poor lad. What a life he's had,' she murmured. She reached for another biscuit, ate it in silence, wiped the crumbs off the table into her tissue and then looked at Samson. 'Carl Thornton threatened to kill her.'

'He threatened to kill his wife?'

Ida shook her head. 'No. Livvy. His own daughter.'

Samson stared at the cleaner, shocked. 'Did Mrs Thornton tell you that?'

'Not in so many words. She came to see me in a complete state and said Livvy wouldn't be writing any more. It wasn't safe.' Ida's face screwed up in distaste. 'Combined with the bruises Marian had that day, I put two and two together. Carl Thornton must have found out what was going on and he put a stop to it. He was always handy with his fists.'

'But why would he threaten to kill Livvy?'

Ida lifted her chin, eyes sparking with anger. 'Because

threatening his wife would have made no difference. Marian Thornton would have died for her daughter. But she wouldn't allow her daughter to die for her.'

'Bloody hell!' Delilah sank onto the chair opposite Samson's desk, stunned. 'You're sure about that?'

Samson raised an eyebrow. 'Have you ever known Ida Capstick to exaggerate?'

Since his conversation with the cleaner two hours before, her words had been haunting him. What kind of father threatened to kill his own daughter? And what light did this shed on Livvy's death and her missing death certificate?

'Crikey. Do we need to tell the police?'

'What would we tell them? That a man, now dead, threatened to kill his daughter, who is also dead, and the only witness to it has passed away, too? I hardly think they'll break their necks to investigate it.'

'But it's . . .'

'Shocking. Yes. It still doesn't tell us anything more about the missing death certificate.'

'So what next, then?' asked Delilah. She'd arrived at the office at nine, a bit later than normal as she'd lingered over breakfast with Tolpuddle, still awash with relief at his unexpected reprieve. On entering the building, they'd found Samson sitting at his desk, staring into space. Not even a cup of tea in front of him. He'd quickly filled Delilah in on what Ida had revealed. 'Should we go and see Jimmy?' she suggested. 'Get his version of events?'

'It's worth a shot. We might be able to prise a bit more

out of him with everything we've learned over the last couple of days.'

'You still think he's holding back?'

'I'm sure of it,' said Samson.

'And the women at Snips? Have you contacted them?'

Samson laughed. 'Yes, boss. First thing this morning. I left a message—' The ringtone of his mobile interrupted him. 'Talk of the devil,' he said, recognising the number on the screen as he answered the call. 'Hello?'

'Mr O'Brien, it's Paula Atkins from Snips. How can I help?'

'Mrs Atkins, sorry to trouble you again. I just wanted to know if Livvy Thornton ever brought her dog to work?'

'A dog? Livvy didn't have a dog.'

'Are you sure? She didn't mention one at all?'

'Not to my knowledge. Just a moment.' Samson heard the click of the phone being laid down and the hum of a hairdryer in the background. Then muffled voices before a younger woman spoke.

'Hello? Mr O'Brien? It's Viv Atkins here. We spoke the other day when you called in. Mother said you were asking about a dog?'

'Yes. Did Livvy ever refer to one? Perhaps when you were out together?'

'Never. She talked about her brother. A bit about her mother. But she never talked about having a dog.'

'Thanks.'

'So did she have one?' Samson could hear the curiosity in the woman's voice, wanting to know more about the enigma that was Livvy Thornton.

'Yes. She was supposed to have brought it to Leeds. They were inseparable, apparently.'

'Oh.' There was a small silence. Then, 'Perhaps it died? Like her father?'

'Did she tell you her father was dead?'

'Not exactly. I just presumed that was the case because she never mentioned him. Maybe it was the same with her dog.'

'Perhaps,' said Samson. He thanked the woman for her time and hung up.

'Well?' Delilah was leaning across the desk, where she'd been straining to hear the other side of the phone conversation.

'Nothing.'

'How odd!'

Samson nodded. 'Very peculiar. According to Jimmy Thornton, his sister left for Leeds with Red. Yet neither Mrs Atkins at Snips nor her daughter knew anything about the dog's existence.'

Delilah shrugged. 'It could be that Livvy just didn't talk about him.'

'Maybe. Just like she didn't talk about her father.'

'Sorry?'

'Viv Atkins, the daughter at Snips. She thought Livvy's father was dead because Livvy never referred to him.'

'Hardly surprising, given what we've been learning about Carl Thornton,' said Delilah, getting to her feet. 'Besides, there's plenty of folk don't talk about their parents. You don't exactly mention yours much, and your father lives just down the road.'

The reprimand was typical of Bruncliffe and one that

had been levelled at Samson many a time. Even so, it brought colour to his face. And guilt hot on its heels. He hadn't had time to go back and check on his father since visiting Mrs Walker at Fellside Court. Or if he was honest, he hadn't wanted to. He wanted to take his father at his word. Everything was all right. Because Samson couldn't face it if it wasn't.

'Tea?' said Delilah brightly. 'I think better with a brew in front of me.'

She hurried out of the room, leaving Samson to brood. On families. On relationships that soured.

A snore from the corner took his attention. Tolpuddle. Fast asleep. Unaware of how close he'd come to being a London-based dog. Was it as difficult for a canine to adapt to such a change in surroundings, Samson wondered, thinking about the shock his system had taken when he'd moved to Leeds. The traffic. The noise. Not sheep noise. Or birds calling the dawn. But sirens and loud voices. Drunken laughter. It had taken him a while to adjust.

Had it been the same for Red?

Whichever way he looked at it, that dog seemed to be the key. Beautiful Red. The collie that wouldn't leave Livvy's side. The faithful hound which had chased the driver of the car that killed Livvy, according to Mrs Thornton.

How come no one in Leeds knew anything about him?

Still brooding, he heard Delilah coming down the stairs, humming, her mood like an early spring.

'Tea,' she announced, placing a mug in front of him. 'Solved it yet?'

'It's the dog,' Samson muttered in return. 'Red is the clue we need to crack.'

'I agree. I've been thinking about it. You know I suggested Livvy had never gone to Leeds—'

'I think, with the evidence of her working at the hairdresser's and singing at the Fforde Grene, we can dismiss that theory now. She was definitely living in the city. We just don't know for sure whereabouts.'

'That's what I was going to say. We have to accept that Livvy was in Leeds,' said Delilah. 'But what if Red wasn't?'

Samson froze, hand outstretched for his mug, his gaze fixed on Delilah. He stood, grabbed his jacket off the back of the chair and walked out of the door.

'Hey! Where are you going?' demanded Delilah, rushing after him.

'To see a man about a dog,' he called back over his shoulder. 'You coming?'

George Capstick was anxious. From the open door of the barn next to Croft Cottage, he'd watched the car go past. An outsider's car. Not one that would have any business in going past the cottage and into Thorpdale, an isolated valley that began at the Capstick home and ended at Twistleton Farm, formerly home to the O'Briens, now owned by Procter Properties. With nothing in between the two properties apart from fields and stone walls, there was no cause for anyone to venture up the rough track that ran beyond the Capstick gate.

No cause unless they were up to no good.

As official caretaker of Twistleton Farm, appointed by Rick Procter himself, George knew he had to go and investigate. Even though he didn't want to. He'd just started stripping down a David Brown 850 Implematic, tractor bits now strewn across the floor of the large barn. He stared into the distance at the outline of Twistleton farmhouse, his hands restless, twitching.

Ida wasn't there to ask. He'd have to decide for himself.

He paced back into the gloom of the barn, muttering. 'Eight-fifty two-point-five-litre four-cylinder diesel dry disc clutch . . .'

The unpunctuated recital of tractor statistics. It was George Capstick's equivalent of worry beads, calming his natural inclination to anxiety. Helping make sense of a world he didn't entirely understand. And one that certainly didn't understand him.

'. . . thirty-five-horsepower liquid-cooled I should go up there—' He scurried across the farmyard, scattering the hens, and entered the house, leaving his shoes by the back door. The gun cabinet was in the cupboard under the stairs.

A few minutes later, shotgun in hand, George Capstick started towards Twistleton Farm.

If it wasn't for the satnav, the woman would have thought there was a mistake.

A couple of outbuildings in various stages of disrepair leading to a farmhouse, empty and neglected, slates slipping on the roof, windows in need of painting.

Surely no one lived here.

She got out of the car, taking in the steep rise of the fells at the back of the house, the two streams running across the land. It was a dramatic setting. One that would take some beating. But she wasn't here to admire the scenery.

Crossing the broken concrete of the yard, she called out a greeting, expecting a dog to come hurtling out of the shadows. There was no response. Although she noted the shiny new padlock and huge doors on the largest of the barns. Someone had been here recently.

She walked round to the front of the house. Knocked on the door. Nothing. No curtains twitching. No sign of life. The windows cobwebbed and dirty.

Twistleton Farm was a dead end, in more senses than one.

She turned back towards the car and came face-to-face with a man wielding a shotgun. Disconcertingly, the man was twitching rather a lot.

With Tolpuddle precluding the use of the Royal Enfield, Samson and Delilah ended up taking Delilah's Nissan Micra. By the time they reached the edge of town, Samson – knees cramped against the dashboard and the dog breathing down his neck – was already regretting his generous invitation. If Delilah Metcalfe was going to continue to work with him, she was going to have to get a better car. One a bit less compact and that didn't groan every time it was faced with an incline, a serious shortfall in a place like Bruncliffe where the fells rose on all sides. It wouldn't hurt for her to go on a couple of anger-management courses, either. Not that it was anger that was causing her reckless driving right now. Excitement seemed to have the same detrimental effect on her motoring skills.

'Watch out!' Samson yelled as the Micra screeched round a corner on the narrow Horton Road and came face-to-face with a tractor barrelling along towards them.

A slam of brakes, Tolpuddle letting out a yelp of protest and Delilah cursing. 'Road hog,' she muttered, backing up into a passing place as the tractor pulled past, the farmer lifting a finger in recognition as he went.

'Tom Hardacre,' she continued, pulling back out onto the road as if nothing had happened. 'Why are we going to see him?'

'Because he knew Jimmy well back then. And the Hardacres are the closest thing to neighbours the Thorntons had. There's a chance they'll know what was going on in that house up at the quarry.'

Samson was surprised he hadn't thought of it before. The farm tucked under the fellside that led to Rainsrigg Quarry. The place where Oscar Hardacre had nursed his crush on Livvy. Where Jimmy had worked as a youth. It was a good starting point before speaking to Jimmy himself, a conversation Samson wasn't looking forward to having.

'Huh,' said Delilah as she turned into a farmyard and parked the car by a well-kept house. 'I wouldn't bank on the Hardacres knowing anything. Plenty of families keep secrets around here, despite all the gossip that abounds. Some walls don't leak,' she said, getting out of the car.

Samson didn't challenge her. He knew too well from his own experience that she was right. Twistleton Farm had kept its secrets from his time living there. He wondered if the four walls in the shadow of the quarry had done the same.

Tom Hardacre was a lot smaller than Samson remembered. As the Micra pulled up outside, a wiry old man had emerged from the back porch of the farmhouse, a thatch of white hair above a ruddy face, thick jumper on over a checked shirt, hands broad-backed where they rested on the doorframe. He was joined by a man from the barn on the right. Oscar Hardacre. A good few years older than Samson, he was a more youthful version of Tom. Broad-shouldered but short of stature, he stood next to his father, hands on hips, sleeves rolled up, the frantic bleating of newborn lambs resonating from the building behind him.

The two men watched Samson get out of the car, the same suspicion etched onto weathered features. It was a greeting Samson had been used to as an O'Brien in Bruncliffe. Seemed like nothing had changed in his fourteen-year absence.

'Mr Hardacre, Oscar,' he said, by way of greeting.

'O'Brien,' muttered the older Hardacre, with the merest inclination of his head. Oscar simply stared, brow knitted together in a deep frown.

'Morning, Tom, Oscar,' breezed Delilah, having finally extricated Tolpuddle from the back seat of the Micra, the hound not eager to exchange the warmth of the car for the cold of the farmyard.

At the sight of a Metcalfe – a species that inspired trust in farming folk, unlike those reprobate offcumdens, the O'Briens – the old man's face split into a smile.

'Delilah! Come on in, lass. The kettle's on.' Tom gestured towards the house, turning to his son as he did so. 'Will tha be joining us?'

Oscar shook his head, his stare never leaving Samson's face. 'Got two yows about to lamb.' But he made no move to go. Just stood there, watching, making Samson think of the heartsick teenager standing outside the hairdresser's in the pouring rain, waiting for Livvy Thornton. There was no trace of affection in Oscar's gaze right now.

With that brooding stare on his back, Samson followed Delilah into the cottage, aware that Matty Thistlethwaite's insistence on having her on the case was proving wise. Without the lovely Miss Metcalfe, Samson doubted he'd have been allowed across the Hardacre threshold. Perhaps not even out of the car. As if to underline his point, as they entered the kitchen a tall, angular woman turned from the stove.

'Delilah Metcalfe!' Mrs Hardacre exclaimed, setting down the teapot she'd been in the act of filling and pulling Delilah into an embrace. 'Been a while since we've seen you down here. How are things at Ellershaw? Lambing under way?'

While Delilah was welcomed into the Hardacre home joyfully, Samson stood to one side, taking in the room and overcome with nostalgia for Twistleton Farm. Farming calendars on the wall, copies of *Farmers Weekly* stacked on an armchair under a pile of magazines – most notably the *Dalesman* and *Yorkshire Life* – a sideboard groaning under sporting trophies and souvenirs from snatched holidays away, the smell of fresh baking coming from the stove and an overall air of homeliness. It was a room well lived in.

'Sit, if tha's staying.' Tom was pulling out a chair at the table, gruffly gesturing Samson towards it.

'Yes, do sit in, Samson,' Mrs Hardacre added with more warmth than her husband. 'You too, Delilah.'

They all settled around the pine table, Tolpuddle making himself at home on a rug in front of the fire, and

Samson waited patiently while the Hardacres caught up with the news from the farm up on the fells above Bruncliffe, where Delilah had been raised and Will now farmed. Cattle auctions. The price of sheep. The weather. The increase in rural crime. All this had to be discussed over a cup of tea and thick slices of fruitcake before the true purpose of their visit could be embarked upon. Samson knew there was no point in fretting about the passing time; it was how things were done in the Dales.

'So,' said Tom after a good twenty minutes of catch-up. 'Tha didn't come out here for farming chat.' He looked pointedly at Samson.

'No,' said Delilah. 'We're working on a case for Matty Thistlethwaite. We've got a few questions we'd like to ask you.'

'Matty? Is it about Marian's will?' Mrs Hardacre looked out of the window and up at the fellside at the back of the farmhouse, in the direction of the quarry. 'We heard there was a problem with Livvy's death certificate.'

'Aye, poor Jimmy was down here last week, fair unsettled by it all,' added Tom, a stern gaze in Samson's direction insinuating that he was the cause.

'I'm sure it's just a formality, Mr Hardacre,' said Samson. 'We're doing all we can to sort it.'

'So what does tha want to know?'

'We're trying to piece together a picture of Livvy's life here in Bruncliffe before she left—'

'What's that to do with a piece of paper?' the farmer demanded brusquely.

'Thing is, Tom,' Delilah intervened, 'we've hit a bit of a

dead end with the official route. You know how it is with these bureaucrats.'

'They'd drown a body in paperwork,' he grumbled in agreement. 'Nowt but making work for decent folk.'

'Exactly. So we thought we'd find out a bit more about Livvy, try and trace her movements and see if we can't sort all this out for Jimmy that way.'

'I still don't see how we can help,' said Mrs Hardacre.

Delilah turned to her. 'You were the Thornton's nearest neighbours. We were wondering if you could tell us anything about why Livvy left Bruncliffe in the first place.'

The glance between husband and wife was that of a couple who'd spent their married lives living and working alongside each other. There was no need for words for them to communicate.

'Not sure we can help,' Tom Hardacre said firmly. Lips closing shut once he'd said his piece. His wife was toying with the teaspoon on her saucer.

'We're not after gossip.' Samson looked at them both. 'What you tell us will go no further than this room. But it could help Jimmy move on. He can't even clear the house out until the will is settled. And it won't get settled if we can't find that paperwork.'

Another glance between man and wife.

'We don't know for sure why Livvy left,' said Mrs Hardacre.

'But if you had to guess?' asked Samson.

'Carl Thornton.'

'She didn't get on with her father?'

'Wasn't much of a father, by my reckoning,' grunted Tom.

'Tom!' his wife rebuked him gently, before expanding on her answer. 'Carl and Livvy clashed a lot. Over lots of things.'

'And the day she left? Do you know if they argued then?'

This time Tom Hardacre and his wife turned to each other and Samson sensed a hesitation. He'd seen it before. Usually in witnesses who were sure they'd seen something incriminating but were afraid to say it out loud in case they were mistaken; in case they wrongly accused someone.

'It's okay. Whatever you know, it won't get anyone into trouble,' promised Samson.

'Go on, Tom,' his wife urged softly. 'Tell them.'

Tom Hardacre gave a deep sigh. 'Lambing had started,' he said, staring at his hands as he recalled the past. 'A bit early that year as we normally hold back until March, but we had a few arrive in mid-February. A couple of them were needing care so we were busy, as tha'd expect, and glad to have young Jimmy helping us out, it being half-term.'

'He was always down here,' said Mrs Hardacre with a smile, gesturing towards the copse of trees beyond the yard. 'That track back there was well used. And he was already a hard worker, for such a nipper.'

'So at the end of this particular day,' continued Tom, 'I walked him home, up through the woods. It would have been about six, dark out, and I know I hadn't had my tea as my stomach was fair rumbling. Jimmy's, too. We were halfway up the fell when we heard a shotgun.'

'From the Thorntons' place?' asked Samson.

Tom shrugged. 'Hard to say at that point. Shotguns

aren't exactly uncommon in these parts. I didn't think much of it until we got to the house, as Jimmy was prattling on about Leeds United and some Frenchman they'd just signed.' He sighed again at the memory. 'Poor lad. He was high as a kite. Leeds were in with a chance of winning the league and for Jimmy, life was perfect. By the end of the season he'd have lost his sister and his father – and his interest in football.'

'So what happened when you got to the house?' prompted Delilah gently.

'It was odd, straight off. Lights on upstairs and down like it was Christmas. And when I knocked on the kitchen door it took an age before it was opened, and then only a crack, big enough to let Jimmy in.'

'Was it Carl at the door?'

'No. Marian. A red welt under one eye, though she was twisting her head so I couldn't see it properly. She didn't invite me in like she would do normally. Just pulled Jimmy inside, thanked me and shut the door.' Tom Hardacre was shaking his head, the memory upsetting him even now. 'I should have kicked the door down and gone and throttled him,' he growled.

'Tom, love,' his wife said, laying a hand on his arm. 'Don't get worked up. There was nothing you could have done.'

'Carl was beating her?' asked Delilah.

Mrs Hardacre nodded. 'We suspected it. But that was the first time there was any evidence.'

'You didn't see him at the house that night?' Samson asked.

'No sign of him,' muttered Tom. 'Apart from a strong smell of gunpowder.'

'In the house?'

'Definitely. When Marian opened the door, I caught it straight away. Like bad eggs.'

'So you're saying Carl Thornton fired the shotgun *in the house*?' Samson asked again in disbelief.

'Someone fired it. I've no knowledge as to who. Or why.'

16

In the wake of Tom Hardacre's story, silence fell across the table, finally broken by Mrs Hardacre rising to place the kettle back on the stove.

'Tea,' she said briskly. 'We need more tea.'

'And you're sure this happened around the time Livvy left for Leeds?' Delilah asked Tom as Mrs Hardacre bustled around the kitchen.

'Certain. It was the night before. I know, because the next day Jimmy came down in floods of tears. His mother had put him straight up to bed after I left, and in the morning when he got up, Livvy was gone.'

'She didn't even wait to say goodbye?'

'Nope. He never saw her again.'

'So whatever happened the night you walked Jimmy home, that was the catalyst for Livvy leaving,' Samson mused.

'It seems that way.'

'And it involved a shotgun,' added Delilah.

'Did you ever ask Mrs Thornton about it?' asked Samson.

'I tried,' said Tom, wearily. 'She wouldn't have any of it. Walked away when I broached the subject of Carl hitting her. In hindsight, it probably would have been best to let

Annie talk to her.' He nodded towards his wife. 'Probably would have been better coming from a woman.'

'To be fair to Tom, he did his best,' Annie Hardacre said from over by the stove. 'But Marian wasn't the kind of woman you'd talk to about stuff like that. She wasn't one for opening up.'

'Aye. She could be a bit odd, could Marian,' agreed Tom.

'In what way?' Samson caught the look between husband and wife, and the slight nod Annie gave. But this time Tom stayed silent.

Annie sighed. 'I'll tell them, then.' She turned to Delilah and Samson. 'The following May, when Livvy had been in Leeds a good three months or so, Tom was up to the house. Jimmy had asked us to fetch him some chicks from the feather auction at Skipton, so Tom went up to the quarry to make sure Marian knew about it. We didn't want her landed with hens out of the blue. Anyroad, when he got to the door, he knocked and then just went in, like we do round here. Next thing there's a clattering on the stairs and down comes Marian, all flustered.' Annie looked at her husband fondly. 'Tom thought she was having an affair.'

'That's how it seemed,' Tom admitted, breaking his silence and running a hand over his thick brush of white hair. 'I asked about the chicks and Marian agreed, and then she near as much kicked me out. Couldn't get rid of me fast enough.'

'Was she? Having an affair?' asked Delilah, incredulous, having trouble picturing the demure Mrs Thornton in the throes of passion.

Tom shook his head. 'No lass. As I walked away, a bit

disgruntled like, I heard someone singing. Beautiful singing coming from the house.' He gave a sad smile. 'Turned my mood right round. I came home and said to Annie it was worth the trek up there just for that.'

'Livvy?' asked Samson.

'Aye. A week later, she was dead.' The farmer picked up his mug, clearly not planning on elaborating any further.

'But that wasn't all,' said Annie, taking up the tale. 'At the memorial service down at the church, Tom and I went up to talk to the Thorntons. Carl Thornton was all red-eyed and teary. Marian was like a piece of marble, white with shock. And Tom put his foot in it.'

'How was I to know?' retorted her husband.

'What did you do?' asked Delilah.

'I made the mistake of saying how fortunate it was that Livvy had come home the week before she died. How that must have been a consolation for them.' Tom looked at Samson, the puzzlement of two decades ago still on his face. 'Marian said she didn't know what I was talking about. Livvy hadn't been home since February.'

'And you're certain it was Livvy you heard?' Samson asked.

'I'd bet my bloody life on it.'

'So Marian lied,' mused Delilah. 'Why would she lie about her daughter being home?'

'To protect her,' said Samson, 'from her father.'

Tom Hardacre shifted uncomfortably on his chair. 'Time I was getting out and giving Oscar a hand.'

'We'll come with you,' said Delilah. 'We can ask Oscar about Livvy while we're out there.'

'Oh, I wouldn't do that!' said Annie Hardacre, getting to her feet. 'Oscar's not too keen on that topic.'

'Why not?' Delilah asked, the picture of innocence.

Annie shot a glance at Tom and then looked out towards the barn. 'She broke his heart,' she said softly.

Tom snorted. 'Perhaps he should have aimed a little lower,' he grunted.

'He couldn't help it,' said Annie, quick to defend her son. 'Livvy was like that, you know, she entranced every-one around here. Oscar just fell harder than most, that's all.'

'Were they seeing each other?' asked Delilah, keeping up the pretence of being in the dark when it came to Oscar and Livvy.

'No, nothing like that—'

'He mooned over her,' interrupted Tom. 'Made a fool of himself, traipsing up and down that wretched path to the quarry. Waiting for her outside the salon. Livvy was never anything but kind to him. But he took it to mean more.'

'He must have been distraught when she told him she was leaving,' said Delilah.

Annie Hardacre sighed. 'That was the problem. She didn't tell him. He found out from Mrs Walker that Livvy had gone to Leeds. He wasn't best pleased.'

'And we lost the best worker we had because of it,' muttered Tom, rising from his chair and heading for the porch.

'That's why Jimmy Thornton stopped working for you?' Samson asked.

'Aye, lad.' Tom was pulling on his coat. 'There was bad blood 'twixt the two of them ever since the day Livvy left.

And if I don't get out in that barn and give Oscar a hand with them two yows about to lamb, there'll be bad blood 'twixt father and son, too. Give my regards to tha folks, Delilah.'

The back door slammed, waking a snoozing Tolpuddle on the hearth, and Tom Hardacre could be seen walking across the yard towards the barn.

'Sorry,' said Annie. 'The past is a bit of a tender subject around here.'

Delilah reached out and laid a hand on the older woman's arm, a warm smile on her face. 'Thanks for your time,' she said. 'We appreciate your help. And I'm sure Jimmy will, too.'

'Speaking of help,' Annie began, twisting the edges of the apron she was wearing between nervous fingers and shooting an uncomfortable glance at Samson. 'I've been meaning to ask you something, Delilah.'

Sensing Mrs Hardacre didn't want him privy to whatever it was she was about to ask, Samson roused Tolpuddle from his cosy spot and led him to the door. 'We'll head outside,' he said.

Annie waited until the door closed before continuing. 'It's about that dating agency of yours,' she said, cheeks going pink.

'You're not thinking of leaving Tom?' asked Delilah with a laugh.

'Lord, no!' Annie laughed in return. 'No. It's not for me. It's for Oscar. He's forty in a couple of months and still single.' She shrugged. 'There's never really been anyone in his life. Not properly. And working on a farm isn't exactly going to help his chances of meeting the right woman. I just thought . . .'

'Do you want me to have a word with him? See if I can persuade him to join up?'

'Would you?' The words came out in a rush of relief. 'I think it would do him the world of good. But if I suggest it . . .'

'I understand. Men can be delicate about dating,' Delilah said with a grin. 'They like to think they have everything under control. That they don't need any help.'

Annie laughed. 'Exactly. And certainly not a mother's help. But if you could persuade him . . . It would be lovely to think he wouldn't have to go through the rest of his life alone.'

'I'll see what I can do,' said Delilah, looking out across the yard to see Samson approaching a sullen Oscar Hardacre. She wondered if she'd just accepted another mission that would prove to be impossible.

'I've nowt to say on the subject. Now bugger off! We've work for doing.'

A simple enquiry about Livvy Thornton had provoked the sharp response Oscar's mother had predicted, and Samson wasn't about to argue. Not with the solid block of muscle that was the younger Hardacre.

'Sorry to have bothered you,' he said, turning to lead a sleepy Tolpuddle across the farmyard where a bitter wind was blowing, the sky dark with the threat of snow. The plaintive bleating of tiny lambs echoed between the buildings.

'Can't say Annie didn't warn thee,' muttered Tom

Hardacre, accompanying them to the car under the baleful stare of his son standing in the doorway of the barn.

'It was worth a try,' said Samson.

It was always worth a try. Years of police work had taught him that. It had also taught him not to push too hard when faced with the brooding anger of a man like Oscar Hardacre.

'Hopefully us older folk were of some help at any rate?'

'Definitely,' said Samson, holding out a hand. 'Thanks for being so honest.'

The farmer shook the proffered hand, reassessing the detective. 'Aye. Maybe I was wrong about thee, O'Brien. Seems like tha's trying to do right by Jimmy, and that's right by me. Let me know if I can help with anything else.'

Samson nodded, feeling ridiculously touched by the farmer's change of heart.

'And take care of this one,' Tom added, gesturing towards Delilah as she joined them. 'She's a keeper.'

'Oh, we're not – I mean, she's not . . .' Samson stuttered while Delilah busied herself with getting Tolpuddle into the rear of the Micra, her cheeks pink.

Tom laughed. 'Aye, lad. Of course not.' He turned to go back into the barn, still chuckling.

'Oh, one more thing,' said Samson, the farmer pausing in the doorway next to his son. 'Red, Livvy's collie. I forgot to ask – do either of you remember what happened to him?'

Oscar Hardacre scowled and walked off out of sight, leaving Tom rubbing his head, hair sticking up like wayward thatch. 'Red?' the farmer muttered. 'Haven't thought of him in years. Gorgeous dog.'

'Do you know if he went to Leeds with Livvy?'

'Can't say I ever asked. But he must have.'

'What makes you say that?'

Tom grinned. 'Ask the postie. Red was a good dog but if anyone came to the door, he went berserk. Very protective of Livvy, he was. Once she left, there was never any barking at the Thorntons' place.'

'Thanks again,' said Samson.

Tom just nodded and continued on into the barn.

'Did you get anything out of Oscar?' asked Delilah as they got into the car.

'Nothing. Apart from a suggestion that we vacate the premises, expressed in Bruncliffe dialect.'

Delilah laughed. 'So where next? A talk with Jimmy Thornton?'

'Yes,' said Samson with a heavy heart. 'I'll give him a call and see if he can meet us at Rainsrigg. Are you free to come with me?'

Delilah glanced at him. 'Of course. I wouldn't let you do this on your own.'

As Samson made the call, she put the car in gear and turned out onto the road, heading back towards town and Gunnerstang Brow. And the small house tucked in against the white rock face. A house that was still keeping its secrets.

It took George Capstick a while to calm down. Never good at interacting with other humans, confrontation was something he avoided as best as he could. This morning he'd had no choice; the car going past had triggered his responsibilities.

Luckily she'd gone quietly. The woman with the big bag

over her shoulder, a blue file sticking out of it. He'd found her round by the front door of the farmhouse. Knocking on it like a real outsider. No one used the front door. Always the back.

'Private property,' was all he'd had to say. The shotgun said the rest.

She'd walked towards her car – not a make or model that interested George, although he'd memorised the number plate. Then she'd asked him the question.

'Does Samson O'Brien live here?'

'No,' George had replied.

'Do you know where he is?'

'No.' It wasn't a lie. George never lied. It was the simple truth.

When she'd driven off, he'd walked home, replaced the shotgun in the cabinet and then spent a long time pacing the barn. He should call Samson. But he didn't like using the phone. All those words travelling through the air without context.

It never crossed his mind that perhaps he also ought to call Rick Procter and explain about the trespasser, Mr Procter being very particular about the privacy of his property. But then George Capstick's mind wasn't wired like that of most folks.

When he did get round to calling Samson, it was a while later. Standing in the hallway of the cottage, receiver pressed hard to his ear as he listened to the ringing tone, he rehearsed the words in his head, mouth dry. As soon as he heard a voice start to speak he blurted out the message. Then he hung up.

'Unsynchronised gear liquid-cooled back to work,' he

muttered, crossing the yard towards the waiting David Brown tractor, eyes on the ground, the black clouds gathering on the horizon of no interest to him.

Jimmy Thornton arrived at the quarry fifteen minutes after Delilah had pulled up in front of the empty house.

'Sorry,' he said, ushering Samson and Delilah round to the back door and into the kitchen, Tolpuddle having been left asleep in the car. 'I had to drop Gemma home. We've been at the hospital. First scan.' His face split into a beaming smile, making Samson feel awful. They were about to take the shine off Jimmy Thornton's day.

'Everything go well?' asked Delilah, taking a seat at the table.

'Seemed to. Although it was strange seeing Gemma getting scanned instead of one of the yows,' he laughed. 'Tea?'

Delilah nodded.

'Coffee, if you have it,' said Samson, already awash with tea but wanting to delay the interview. He sat next to Delilah, taking in the open cupboards, the contents cluttering the surfaces, the pile of boxes in the corner. A life being dismantled, piece by piece. He thought of all Tom Hardacre had told them. The shotgun. The bruises. What else had this room witnessed? And would the secrets come spilling out as the house was emptied?

'So,' said Jimmy, sitting opposite Delilah and distributing mugs. 'Any sign of that blasted certificate?'

'Not yet,' began Samson. 'Our investigation has taken an unexpected turn. We've got some questions we need you to answer.'

'Hard questions, Jimmy,' said Delilah softly. 'But we need you to answer them honestly.'

The farmer looked from Delilah to Samson and then stared down at his tea. 'How will this help find the certificate?'

'We're not sure.'

He looked back up, wary. 'Okay.'

'First of all, the address on the top of Livvy's letters,' said Samson, consulting his notes. 'It's for a house that was owned by a Mrs Jean Larcombe at the time. Does that name ring any bells?'

'Mrs Larcombe? That's where Livvy stopped in Leeds?' Jimmy looked puzzled.

'We think so. You knew her?'

'Not as such. She was Mother's primary-school teacher down in Dorset. She moved up to Leeds when she retired.'

'Did your mother talk about her much?'

'A bit, when we were younger. She used to get Christmas cards from her and the odd present for us. That kind of thing. But not to the extent that Livvy would go and stay with her.' He shook his head in amazement. 'I can't believe Mother never mentioned it.'

Delilah shot Samson a look. There was a lot Marian Thornton had never told her son.

'On the subject of Leeds,' continued Samson, 'when we spoke last week, you said Red went with Livvy when she left. Are you certain of that?'

Jimmy frowned. 'Of course I'm sure. The dog wasn't here. Where else would he be?'

Sensing his irritation, Delilah intervened. 'We spoke to

some people who knew Livvy over there. None of them remember a dog, that's all.'

'Why would they? It's a long time ago. Look, I don't see how this is connected to the death certificate. Is there something you're not telling me?'

Samson ran a hand through his hair, hating what he was about to do. 'We think Livvy wasn't killed in Leeds,' he said.

'What? Whatever's made you think that?'

'There's no trace of her death over there. No certificate. No newspaper reports. Not even a cremation record.'

Jimmy blinked. Looked down at the table. And then back up at Samson. 'No cremation? You're sure?'

'Certain. I checked all the crematoria in Leeds and Bradford.'

'How can that be? She was cremated in Leeds. That's what Mother said.'

'You weren't there?'

'I wasn't allowed. Father didn't go, either.' A strained expression crossed the farmer's face. 'He said Livvy left the family the day she left here.'

'So your mother went on her own? To Leeds?'

'That's what I thought . . . but now?' Jimmy got to his feet, crossed to the window and leaned on the wall, looking out at the sharp edges of the quarry. 'None of this makes any bloody sense.'

Samson made to speak but Delilah put a hand on his arm, shaking her head.

'Perhaps it would help if you tell us everything you know, Jimmy,' she said gently.

The farmer turned back to them, looking weary. 'I'm not sure what I know any more.'

'So start with Livvy leaving. What do you remember about the night before?'

He slumped back onto his chair, scratching his head. 'Not much. I came back from a day down at Tom's, and Mother put me straight to bed.'

'That was it?' asked Samson. 'You didn't hear any argument?'

'No. Mother met us at the door. She said Livvy and Father were out. I went to bed and she brought me up a sandwich and a glass of milk.' He shrugged. 'When I got up the next day, Mother told me Livvy was gone.'

'You don't remember hearing a shotgun being fired?'

Jimmy shook his head.

'And your mother?' Delilah asked. 'Do you remember – was she . . . bruised?'

A dark stain crept up over Jimmy's cheeks. 'Who have you been talking to?' he asked, voice curt.

'Is it true?' Samson leaned forward. 'We wouldn't ask if we didn't think it was important.'

The farmer pulled his mug towards him and finished his tea, knuckles white around the handle. 'Aye, she was bruised,' he muttered. 'She was trying to hide it the next morning, but when I burst into tears at hearing Livvy was gone, she gave me a hug and I remember seeing this mark under her eye. She'd got make-up on it, but that close up . . . I burst into tears again.'

'Your father used to hit her?'

Jimmy nodded, miserable.

'Did he hit you, too? Or Livvy?'

'Never. He saved his temper for Mother.'

'What about threatening you?' asked Delilah.

The mug was placed back on the table, Jimmy staring into it, the past consuming him. 'Once,' he finally said. 'He threatened me once.'

'What was it over?'

'God knows. I was upstairs and I heard him shouting. It was after Livvy died. I came running down, trying to do what Livvy had always done. Trying to be the man I thought I was. At eight years old.'

'You tried to protect your mother?'

'Tried to. He'd backed her into that corner.' Jimmy glanced up at the range. 'His hand was raised as though he was about to hit her. I ran over and grabbed hold of his arm.'

'Did you stop him?'

A bitter smile twisted Jimmy's face. 'Kind of. He flung me across the room and said he'd deal with me next. Then Mother asked whether he meant the same way he'd dealt with Livvy. Father just deflated. Turned on his heel and walked out.'

'That was the only time he was violent towards you?'

'He didn't get another chance. He came home from the pub that night and shot himself in the old barn.' Jimmy ran a hand over his face. 'I've never talked about this before.'

Delilah reached across the table and took his other hand in hers. 'It's not easy, Jimmy. But it may well help us.'

He shook his head. 'I don't see how airing the Thornton dirty laundry will help you get a death certificate for Livvy.'

'With no record of her death or cremation in Leeds,'

said Samson, 'we need all the information we can get. In fact,' he continued, 'we have reason to believe Livvy came back here just before she died. Were you aware—'

'Whoever told you that is lying,' Jimmy said with vehemence, pulling away from Delilah's attempt to comfort him. Then his eyes narrowed. 'It's that bastard Oscar Hardacre, isn't it? Filling your head with his nonsense.'

'What makes you say that?'

Jimmy snorted. 'He was always spying on her. Watching the house with binoculars from the track. He was obsessed.'

'Is that why you fell out?'

'Kind of.' The farmer's shoulders slumped, his anger dissolving into weariness. 'Oscar hated Livvy in the end. When she left like that. Even after she died, he couldn't get over it. That she'd gone away without a word. So he took it out on me, always baiting and jibing, making snide comments about her. Until one day he went too far.'

'What did he do?' asked Delilah.

'Let's just say he called Livvy a name I couldn't tolerate,' said Jimmy with a wry look. 'So I went for him. I was in my twenties by then, taller than him, but he was stronger. We had a right do, until Tom arrived and pulled us apart. I knew I couldn't keep working down there after that. So Tom helped me get the tenancy and the rest is history.' He shrugged. 'Might have been for the best in the end.'

'You don't believe Livvy was home the week before she died, then?' asked Samson, choosing not to set Jimmy straight as to the source of the news.

'No.'

'You're certain? She couldn't have been here without you knowing? While you were at school, perhaps?'

'I'm more than certain.'

'How can you be so sure?' persisted Samson, earning a frown from Delilah.

'Because,' said Jimmy with a deceptive calm, studying his hands splayed on the table, 'Father said he'd kill her if she ever set foot over the threshold again. Livvy wouldn't have risked that. Mother wouldn't have let her.'

Delilah threw a shocked glance at Samson. But the detective didn't say anything. Just let the silence settle in the partially dismantled kitchen. Then he spoke.

'So what if Livvy did risk it? What if she did come home?'

Jimmy looked up at him. Frowning. Putting it all together, as Samson had known he would. Then he stood, a look of horror on his face. 'You think – Father? You think . . . ?' He shook his head violently, backing away from them. 'Livvy died in Leeds,' he said. 'A hit-and-run.'

'I'm sorry, Jimmy, but that's looking more and more unlikely.'

'Go!' The strangled command came from the distraught farmer as he held the back door open. 'Just go.'

Not even trying to argue, Samson and Delilah rose from the table and walked past Jimmy Thornton, who was barely holding back the tears. The door slammed behind them, cutting off the sound of a choked sob.

'Christ!' muttered Samson as they followed the path to the front of the house. 'I hate myself right now.'

'I don't know how you do this for a living,' Delilah

murmured, her face pale. 'We can't leave him like this. I'm going to call Gemma.'

'Have you got a signal?' Samson was holding out his mobile, the screen devoid of the bars that indicated reception.

Delilah checked her own phone and cursed. 'I'll try a text.'

Leaving her to compose the message, Samson stared at the bleak quarry that encircled them, and at the old barn with its horrible past. The gathering clouds closing in, sullen and brooding with the possibility of snow, only added to the malignancy of the setting. He shivered, the sensation of being watched as strong as the first time he'd visited.

What a place. What an awful place.

17

They waited in the warmth of the car until Gemma arrived some minutes later. Not feeling up to the task of explaining the situation to Jimmy's pregnant fiancée, Samson took the coward's way out and allowed Delilah to do all the talking. When Gemma entered the house and they got back in the Micra, he let out a sigh of relief.

'I don't ever want to have to do that again,' he said, as they drove away.

'I thought you'd be used to it. Being in the police.'

He shook his head. 'One of the upsides of being undercover, you don't get emotionally involved. Plus I was mostly mixing with people you wouldn't have a shred of sympathy for. Not decent folk like Jimmy and Gemma.'

'Was it worth it?' Delilah asked, glancing at Samson. 'Putting him through all that?'

'Depends how you measure it. We learned a lot.'

'We learned Carl Thornton was a bully,' muttered Delilah.

'That, too. But we also know that Mrs Larcombe was Marian Thornton's teacher. Which explains how Livvy could afford to live in the big house on North Park Avenue.'

'So she really was living there?'

'I'd say so. As for Red . . . We're no clearer on what happened to the dog.'

'Or to Livvy.' Delilah glanced at Samson again. He was staring out of the window, frowning. 'Do you really think Carl Thornton had something to do with her death?'

'Everything points that way, despite what Jimmy said about his mother being the only target of Carl's violence.'

'Except when Jimmy intervened.' Delilah shuddered.

'Or Livvy, too, maybe. Did you notice what Jimmy said?'

Delilah nodded. 'About doing what Livvy had always done, when he tried to stop the argument? Yeah, I noticed that. Do you think that's what happened?'

'That Livvy came home the week before she died and interrupted a domestic incident of some sort and something happened? Sadly, it's looking possible. But we need to prove it.'

'How awful,' murmured Delilah. 'I'm never going to complain about my family again after this.'

Samson smiled. 'I'll hold you to that,' he said, as they approached the end of the Rainsrigg track, his mobile pinging loudly as reception was finally restored. The detective reached into his jacket pocket while Delilah began turning onto the narrow road that led back down to town.

A Micra. Not the biggest of targets. But that was no problem. That's what the telescopic sight was for.

Hunkered down on the side of the fell overlooking the Bruncliffe back road, an outcrop of limestone providing cover, the shooter waited as the car turned off the Rainsrigg track. Rifle steady. Stock nestled in against shoulder and chin. No other traffic around, a clear line of sight down onto the exposed tarmac before the trees offered shelter further along. It was perfect.

A deep breath. Calming the nerves. Watching the car approach the zone. One squeeze of the trigger and it would be done. The past would be protected.

Unaware of the crosshairs trained on the car, Delilah was pulling onto the road and into danger.

A muffled curse came from next to her. Samson had fumbled his mobile and dropped it on the floor, the cramped conditions making it difficult for him to reach it. 'Damn it,' he muttered, head down, scrabbling for the phone, which was slipping beneath his seat.

'Do you want me to pull over?' Delilah asked, her eyes leaving the road for a split second as she glanced over at him.

Samson didn't get a chance to reply.

There was a deafening crack. And then the passenger window shattered, shards of glass showering over them, Tolpuddle startled into wild barking on the back seat.

Instinct made Delilah swerve away from the explosion, the car veering to the right across the white line, then she was correcting it, pulling it back to her side of the road, applying the brakes in a squeal of tyres.

But Samson was shouting, 'Drive! Drive!' his hand reaching for the steering wheel, leaning across from where the window had just exploded. 'Don't stop!'

Delilah floored the accelerator on a spike of adrenalin, the Micra picking up speed again, the bare fellside whipping past as they hurtled down the steep hill, unforgiving stone walls at the edge of the tarmac. Seventy miles an hour. On a road not made for more than fifty. And a car not made for much more. 'What's going on?' she shouted, pulse pounding. 'What's happening?'

'Just keep driving! Don't pull up!' He was scanning the rocks to the left as they raced downwards, Delilah praying there would be no traffic coming against them.

On the back seat Tolpuddle stopped barking, sitting upright, anxious. Then he began to wail.

'Is he cut?' Delilah asked, skidding the car around a bend, into the trees now, aware of the glass beneath her feet, the cold air rushing in through the empty space where the window had been. 'Are you?'

'I'm fine. Concentrate on the road.' Samson was twisting back to check on the dog. 'We're both fine.'

Another screech of tyres, the car juddering around a tight left-hander, the grey wall precariously close. Then the allotments, coming up ahead. The normality of green-houses and sheds, the Crown pub opposite. The safety of the outskirts of town.

'Ease up,' Samson was saying, a hand over hers on the wheel. 'You can ease up now.'

'What *was* that?' she asked, the panic still in her voice as she slowed to the speed limit. 'What the hell was that?'

'Pull over. In there.' He was gesturing towards the Crown and the car park down the side of it.

Delilah did as he said, turning off the road and into the empty yard, stopping the Micra straddled across the white lines of two spaces. She turned to face him and saw blood trickling down his left cheek.

'You're cut! Here.' She pulled a small packet of tissues

out of the glove box and handed him a couple. Then she turned to the back seat, held out a hand to Tolpuddle, the dog no longer wailing but still looking unsettled.

'You okay, boy?' she asked, patting his head, feeling him calm down. 'No wounds?'

Tolpuddle licked her hand, no evidence of harm.

'So,' Delilah said again, turning back to Samson, who was dabbing at his bloody cheek, 'what was that?'

'An air rifle.' He said it so nonchalantly. Like it was an everyday occurrence.

'Someone *shot* at us?'

He nodded, concentrating now on brushing the worst of the glass off himself and into the footwell. 'I'd say so.'

She stared at him until he looked over at her. 'You'd *say* so? Is that the extent of your reaction? Someone takes a potshot at us on the back road into town and you react like I've just asked you how the weather is.' She could hear the nerves rippling along her words and hated that Samson was so unfazed by it all. 'If you hadn't dropped your mobile . . .'

'It's probably just kids,' he said, voice calm. 'Trying out a new rifle. They probably weren't even meaning to hit us.'

Delilah's jaw dropped. 'You're joking. Kids round here don't try out air guns on moving cars. And either way, we need to tell the police.'

'There's no point. They won't be able to do anything. And besides, there's no harm done.'

'My bloody window's been smashed out,' snapped Delilah. 'And they frightened the life out of me. And Tolpuddle.'

Finally Samson reacted, a frown creasing his brow, his lips compressing into a thin line. He reached out a hand to her cheek but she pulled back, too angry to be mollified. 'Sorry,' he muttered. 'You're right. Let's get back to the office and I'll give Danny a call.'

Delilah shoved the car into gear and pulled onto the road, feeling her heartrate settling, her anger fading to be replaced with tiredness. She turned towards the market-place and the safety of town, trying not to notice that her hands were trembling on the steering wheel.

He'd lied to her. Again. As the Micra headed into town at a much more sedate pace than it had come down Gunner-stang Brow, Samson was pondering his instinct to keep the truth from the woman sitting next to him.

He'd told Delilah it was kids, when he knew the shoot-ing had been the work of someone with a much calmer head. Because while the glass from the car window had still been settling on the floor, Samson had been scanning the exposed fellside, looking for movement, a scampering of teenagers running from the crime.

There had been nothing. No flash of colour against the limestone. No rapid flight. Whoever it was had known to stay still. To remain hidden in the cover they'd fired from, until the car had gone out of sight. Which meant it had been deliberate. Planned. Not the rash action of lads with a new toy.

And given that it had happened on the way back from Rainsrigg, Samson was convinced the shooting was a mani-festation of the threats made in the letter he'd received four days ago. The one he still hadn't told Delilah about.

He'd had the ideal chance to be upfront with her just now in the car park of the Crown, yet he'd lied. As she sat there next to him, her hands shaking, eyes wide, he'd felt a strong desire to protect her from whatever was going on. A sentiment she wouldn't appreciate.

But his reluctance to be frank with Delilah wasn't simply about shielding her. Samson knew that once Miss Metcalfe had an inkling of what was really behind the incident that had destroyed her car window and shaken her so badly, she would insist on telling the police everything – about the shooting and the letter. Samson wasn't keen to have Bruncliffe's finest involved just yet. He had a feeling that, in this complex case where leads were scarce, unmasking the person trying to derail the investigation into Livvy Thornton's death certificate would lead them to the truth. Any chances of that happening would vanish like the mist over Pen-y-ghent on a summer's morning the minute the police were called in.

Was that reason enough to lie to Delilah?

Bizarrely, after a lifetime of falsehoods, Samson was having a crisis of conscience. Surely he owed Delilah Metcalfe the truth? She was working alongside him on this case. She had the right to know what she was getting into. Especially if it was going to involve people firing guns at them.

Besides, if he didn't come clean and tell her, when she found out – which she would do eventually, as this was Bruncliffe – she'd kill him.

Stifling a grin at the thought, he turned to Delilah as they drove past St Oswald's church and the marketplace came into sight. 'Drop me off at Peaks Patisserie and I'll pick up some sandwiches. We're owed a treat after that morning.'

She glared back at him. 'I think I'm owed more than just sandwiches,' she growled, pulling the car up on the cobbles. 'Some cake at the very least.'

'Don't push your luck,' he said with a laugh, spotting the hint of a smile on her lips.

He was out of the car and walking away when he heard her shout after him through the broken window.

'Make sure it's a big bit! And something for Tolpuddle, too.'

With a grin on his face, Samson entered the quiet Peaks Patisserie, a Monday in February not enticing the crowds out to eat. He was in and out in minutes, stopping only for a brief chat with the owner, Lucy Metcalfe, Delilah's sister-in-law, before grabbing the bag of sandwiches and cake and heading back to the car.

He'd tell Delilah everything over lunch, he decided as he approached the Micra with its missing window. It would be good to have her input as to the identity of their anonymous adversary, even though she would insist on involving the police. And he'd feel better about himself. It'd be one less thing he was lying to her about.

He opened the car door to see Delilah putting away her phone.

'Change of plan,' she said before he had a chance to get in. 'I've got to go somewhere. I'll drop you back if you like.'

Samson looked at the bag in his hand and then at the glass strewn all over the passenger side of the car, before looking at her. 'It can't wait?'

She shook her head. 'Sorry. No. Tolpuddle will help you out.'

A glance into the rear of the Micra revealed that the dog was watching the Peaks Patisserie bag with great interest.

'You're not taking him with you?' he asked.

'I was hoping you'd look after him for me,' she said, already starting the engine. 'He's had a stressful morning. He'd benefit from some quiet time at the office. Is that okay?'

'What about you?' he asked. 'Don't you need a bit of quiet time?'

She smiled, the brightness not making it all the way to her eyes. 'I'm fine. Like you said, it was probably just kids playing around. So if you could take Tolpuddle . . .'

Caught in the snare of his own lies, Samson had no option. 'Sure,' he muttered, putting two and two together.

Rick Procter. He couldn't stand Tolpuddle. Or rather, having exceptional taste, Tolpuddle couldn't stand him. So whenever Delilah met the property developer, she left her dog with Samson. Had Rick called her and invited her to lunch? A prospect more enticing than a couple of sandwiches over the office kitchen table with Samson? One she couldn't turn down, even after what she'd just been through?

'Hop in then and I'll drop you back,' she said.

He shook his head, feeling surly. 'Don't worry. We'll walk.' He pushed the front seat forward and beckoned Tolpuddle, who scrabbled out, easily tempted by the bag in Samson's hand.

'Sorry,' Delilah said again, her words cut off as he slammed the door.

Clipping on Tolpuddle's lead, he led the dog across the cobbles without a backward look, his mood dark.

*

Date with Mystery

From the marketplace to the office building was only a matter of minutes on foot. It was long enough for Samson to brood on Delilah's sudden desertion.

She'd stood him up for that idiot Procter. It shouldn't matter. But it did. It also hurt that she was so coy about it. Why not just say the man had called?

Aware of the hypocrisy in feeling piqued by Delilah's lack of candour, Samson turned down Back Street, berating himself for his adolescent behaviour. Instead of dwelling on Delilah's choice of lunch partner, he should be trying to identify the culprit from the morning's shooting. Someone willing enough to target a car. A good enough shot to hit it, too.

If it hadn't been for a dropped mobile, more than just the car might have been hit.

At the thought of his mobile, Samson pulled it out of his pocket. He still hadn't checked to see what the message was that had possibly saved him from getting badly hurt. Looking at the screen, he recognised the number straight away.

The Capsticks. With Ida at work, it must have been George. What would George be calling him about?

Trying to juggle the phone, the sandwiches and a Weimaraner thinking only of his stomach, Samson paused to trap the mobile between his shoulder and ear and lift the bag out of the dog's reach. He heard the voicemail click in and then a garbled message.

'George Capstick. Someone here. Samson.'

That was it. Brief. A note of panic in George's voice, which could have been caused by the stress of having to use the phone, an instrument he had no time for. But the fact

George had felt compelled to use the phone – that in itself told Samson something was up.

Or someone. Looking for him out in Thorpdale.

It could only mean one thing. Trouble. Today of all days, his past was catching up with him. What form would it take? More balaclavas? More boots?

Turning abruptly back towards the marketplace, Samson veered round the corner and into the ginnel at the rear of the office building. If there was a welcoming party waiting for him inside, he'd rather have the upper hand. And the single avenue of attack which entering through the rear porch afforded.

A low whimper by his side reminded him he wasn't alone. Tolpuddle. So much for giving the dog some quiet time. It had become a concept sorely lacking in Samson's life of late.

'Stay,' he whispered, putting a hand down to the Weimaraner and unclipping his lead.

Tolpuddle sat and Samson began creeping along the alley, tucked in against the high wall to the right, shielding his presence from the windows overlooking the back yards he was passing. At the third gate he stopped. The gate was ajar.

Inching forward, Samson put his eye to the gap. His motorbike stood on the concrete. And reaching out to touch the engine was a hand. A female hand.

Was it her? The woman who'd called him. Warned him about the trouble that was coming from London. Why was she here? And was she alone?

He shifted, trying to see, but it was impossible, the opening too small to afford a better view. Gently he pushed the gate, easing it open a fraction more, all the while assessing his options.

Date with Mystery

Go in through the gate fast and hard. Go up over the wall and get the element of surprise. Or walk away.

After several months out of action and a stressful morning, Samson was tempted by the third option. But he knew it would merely delay the inevitable confrontation. Better to get it over with now. Glancing up at the high wall, he knew option two wasn't going to happen. Which meant he was going in fast and hard.

Having already been shot at, this was the last thing he needed.

Stifling a sigh, he left the sandwiches on the ground, stuffed his mobile back in his pocket and zipped up his jacket, praying it wouldn't get damaged in what was about to follow.

'Ready,' he muttered to himself. He stepped back and kicked the gate open with force, throwing himself across the yard before anyone inside could react.

A squeal. A bark. The thud of his body hitting hard concrete. Then he was up on his feet and preparing to fight. Only there was no one to do battle with.

Both hands up in the air, a young woman was standing with her back against the wall looking terrified, long blonde hair tumbling out of its clasp, eyes wide, a blue file clutched to her chest.

'Samson O'Brien?' she squeaked, her glance darting from the figure in the garden to the large dog at the gate, which was nosing a bag on the floor.

'Depends who's asking.'

She carefully pulled a slim wallet out of her coat pocket and flipped it open. 'We need to talk,' she said.

18

'How did you find me?'

Samson was talking to the top of the woman's head as she bent over her large handbag, scrabbling round inside it for goodness knows what.

DC Jess Green. She'd flashed her credentials at him in the yard, but had offered nothing more. It had to be something to do with the case. And if she had his official address at the farm, albeit one he wasn't using, then she had to be in touch with his boss. Which meant she was a friendly. Possibly. So he'd invited her into his office, simply to get her out of sight of any prying neighbours, and they'd sat at his desk, Tolpuddle happily eating one of the sandwiches that had been meant for Delilah. Samson had also taken the precaution of closing the office door, not wanting his landlady walking back in on this unscheduled interview.

'Sorry?' DC Green said, looking up, a biro clutched in her hand, hair falling over her face.

'How did you find me?'

'Oh,' she blinked. 'Easy. I bought some motorbike magazines.'

Samson blinked back at her. 'What?'

She shrugged, a shy grin forming below freckled cheeks. 'I come from a small village. I know how people are about outsiders. So I figured there was no point in asking for you outright when you weren't at the address I'd been given.

Especially when I was met with a shotgun at the farm . . .' She looked at Samson, an eyebrow raised. 'Your neighbour is protective of your property.'

'It's not my property any longer,' said Samson. 'And George means no harm.'

'I'm presuming his shotgun licence is in order?'

'Knowing George, yes. He's not one for breaking the law. You were saying about the magazines . . .'

'Ah yes, so I came back into town and decided to start with your Royal Enfield Bullet 500. A distinctive bike.'

'You asked where you could find one?'

She shook her head, smiling. 'No. That would have been too obvious. You'd have had a phone call before I could even get here. I went into Whitaker's newsagents in the marketplace and spent a few minutes obviously browsing the motorbike magazines. Then I went to the counter with three of them and struck up a conversation, in the process of which I might have confessed to being a fan of British bikes . . .'

'And Mike Whitaker told you there was an Enfield in town. Even told you where to find it.' Samson was impressed. She was smart. The scatterbrained appearance deceptive. Whereas Bruncliffe folk would be slow to point out the whereabouts of another inhabitant to an outsider they knew nothing about, they were happy to boast about the town's attributes, even to the extent of a vintage motorbike. Civic pride had been Samson's downfall. 'So what now?'

'Now we talk about what's going on with you.' DC Green opened the blue file, uncapped her biro and wrote the date at the top of the page.

'Before we start talking about me, why don't you tell me why you're here,' said Samson.

'Oh! Sorry! I forgot.' A flutter of papers as she rifled through the file, some of the pages falling to the floor, her fingers clumsy. 'Here it is.'

Samson leaned across the desk to read the document being presented to him. Then he looked at the woman.

'I'm your SSO,' she said almost apologetically. 'Your Suspension Support Officer. I'm here to support you through what's coming.'

'Sorry. I just didn't know what to do.'

In an apartment on the first floor of Fellside Court looking out over a Bruncliffe that was growing darker by the minute, Delilah took Joseph O'Brien's hand in hers. 'You did the right thing.'

He'd phoned her while she was waiting outside Peaks Patisserie. Having missed a call from him the day before with all the excitement surrounding Tolpuddle's last-minute reprieve, this time Delilah had answered, even though she wasn't exactly feeling sociable after being shot at. She was glad she had. Something about Joseph's simple request that she come round to see him as soon as possible had alerted her. Perhaps the plea that she keep it a secret from his own son.

She hadn't liked deceiving Samson, but now she was here she realised how serious the situation was. For sitting on the coffee table between Joseph and the balcony doors was a bottle of whisky. The cap had been taken off. But the liquid itself remained untouched. For now.

'Do you want to tell me about it?' she asked.

Joseph hung his head, tears forming in his eyes. 'It was when I was attacked. I can't remember a thing about it apart from the blasted taste of whisky.'

The shadow of Christmas Day morning fell across the room, Delilah remembering the mayhem, the fight. The syringe that hadn't reached its target. The Rohypnol that had been used to drug Joseph O'Brien. And the bottle of whisky they'd found under his chair.

'You never said about the whisky. We presumed it hadn't been used.'

'Oh, it was used all right,' said Joseph morosely. 'Enough to give me a hankering for it like I haven't had in a long time. Two years sober and I'm thrown off the wagon by this. I'm nothing but a useless drunk.'

'But it's not your fault,' protested Delilah. 'If anything, we're to blame for not asking about it. For not making sure you were okay. You need to tell Samson. Get his help with this.'

'No!' Joseph looked at her, eyes wild. 'Don't tell him. He'll be so disappointed in me. You have to promise you won't say a word.'

Against her better judgement, Delilah acquiesced. 'Okay. But you have to do something. Don't you have an AA sponsor?'

'Not any more. He moved away to be nearer his family and I don't have the energy to go through the whole process again. I think it would kill me.'

'Well, you can't be left on your own to deal with this.' She pulled out her phone, Joseph watching warily as her fingers flicked over the screen.

'Are you googling "hopeless cases"?' he asked with a dry laugh.

She grinned at him and slipped her mobile back in her pocket. 'Something like that. How about we begin right here?' She pointed at the whisky on the table.

Joseph reached out, picked up the cap in shaking hands and slowly screwed it back on. 'Take it,' he said, gruffly, thrusting the bottle at her. 'And get rid of it.'

A knock at the door made him start in his chair.

'No visitors,' he said, panicked, but Delilah was already crossing to the hallway, opening the front door. She returned with two people behind her.

'Meet your new sponsors, Joseph O'Brien.' She stepped aside to reveal Arty Robinson and Edith Hird, both looking concerned.

'We came as soon as Delilah texted,' said Edith, taking a seat opposite Joseph.

'Why the hell didn't you tell us sooner, you daft bugger?' Arty had moved to the other side of the coffee table, staring at the bottle of whisky in Delilah's grasp.

'We don't have any training,' said Delilah. She raised a hand as Joseph began to protest. 'But we care about you. A lot. So I reckon with the three of us by your side, you'll be back on track in no time.'

Arty was nodding. 'Whatever you need to beat this, Joseph. We'll be there for you.'

Joseph O'Brien rubbed the back of his hand across his eyes to wipe away tears. Not for the first time, he thought Fellside Court and its residents had been the saving of him.

*

A rookie. They'd sent a bloody rookie to check up on him. To make sure he wasn't about to throw himself off the Crag in despair. Samson didn't know what to make of it. According to DC Green, she'd been hand-picked for the job by Samson's boss.

A detective straight out of uniform.

For the past thirty minutes she'd been asking anodyne questions about his mental health, about the support network he had around him. She hadn't once touched on the topic of his suspension. Or the seriousness of the imminent investigation.

'Just one last thing,' she was saying as Samson got to his feet, ready to show her to the door. 'DI Warren doesn't have your current address listed in the file.'

His boss. DI Warren. The man who'd saved his life by telling him to get out of London when things became toxic. When men in balaclavas started calling by and leaving boot prints on Samson's body as calling cards.

'If you could fill me in on your correct place of residence, I'll make a note of it,' she concluded.

He paused, hand on the door, formulating a lie.

'And I will check it out,' she said quietly, pre-empting his instinct to deceive.

'Is it entirely necessary?' he asked.

'It's procedure. You have to reside at the address on file during suspension. Technically you're breaking those terms right now.' She glanced around the room, so clearly an office, the golden letters arching over the window. 'I'm already pretending this isn't your place of work, because moonlighting during suspension would be another infraction. So lying about where you're living is a whole load

265

more trouble you don't want to bring down on yourself. Not with the mess you're in already.'

It was her first mention of the extent of his problem.

'And if I told you I would be endangering myself by committing my address to record?'

She studied him from under the mass of blonde hair that was now free of the clasp which had so ineffectually tried to hold it back. 'You have proof of that?'

He laughed. 'Four months ago, yes. But the bruises have healed. You'll just have to take my word for it.'

Her pen hovered over the file and he could see her thinking it through. His undercover work. The connection to drugs. The seriousness of the allegations laid against him. The kind of people who would be involved.

She tapped the end of the biro against her mouth, not realising she'd got the pen the wrong way round and was leaving a trace of ink on her lips. 'You think your life is in danger?'

'Yes.'

DC Green glanced at the paperwork in her hands. Then she closed the file and slipped it into her bag along with her biro. 'Here's the deal,' she said. 'I'll arrange a meeting with you in person once a month. As long as you turn up, we'll leave your address as it is. If you fail to attend, then I will inform the authorities that you have broken the conditions of your suspension. Agreed?'

Samson sighed. 'I don't need babysitting—'

'Agreed?' She had her arms folded, a steeliness to her tone. There would be no dissuading her. He either complied with her demands or had his whereabouts put on file.

Date with Mystery

A file that could easily be seen by people who wanted him out of the way.

'Okay. But don't just turn up unannounced. This isn't something I want everyone round here knowing about.'

Her face softened – was it sympathy, pity? An awareness of the nature of small-town gossip, given her own upbringing? 'Agreed.'

'Until next time, then.' Samson opened the office door.

Delilah Metcalfe was standing in the corridor.

She'd caught the end of it. Arriving back from Fellside Court, stressed from the morning's incident and the worry of seeing Joseph O'Brien so close to giving up his battle with alcohol, Delilah hadn't been in the best of moods. Weighed down by the secret she'd been asked to keep from him, she'd headed straight for Samson's office, intending to pressure him to contact the police over the air-rifle incident. She dreaded the thought that someone more vulnerable might be the next target of the irresponsible idiots behind it. When she'd seen his door closed, she'd been surprised. In the few months he'd been her tenant, she'd rarely known him to hold a meeting with it shut. He said it went against his nature to be cooped up with people he didn't know – a remnant, no doubt, of his years undercover.

So when she'd spotted the anomaly, she'd walked up to the door. She'd heard the voices, one of them a woman. And curiosity had overcome her. She'd pressed her ear against the wood. Pressed so close that she'd had seconds to step away before the door swung open and Samson was standing there, a blonde-haired woman behind him.

'Delilah?' Samson was frowning.

'Hi,' she said, trying to control the heat that was coursing up her face. 'I was about to ask if you wanted a coffee. I didn't realise you had visitors.'

'No, no need for coffee.' He turned to the woman, ushering her out of the office and towards the back door.

No introductions. The woman giving the smallest of smiles as she walked past.

Delilah kept an eye on them as they walked into the yard, Samson saying something, the woman nodding. Then he was opening the gate and she was gone.

Who was that woman? And the bit Delilah had overheard – Samson declaring he didn't need babysitting – what the hell was that all about? And what was it that Samson didn't want the people of Bruncliffe to know?

The back door slammed and Samson was coming towards her, a smile on his face.

'Didn't take you for someone to listen at doors, Delilah.'

She blushed. 'And I didn't take you for someone so secretive.'

'Can't a man even have a private life around here?' he asked, grinning. 'Or do I have to go to York to get away from prying eyes?'

It threw her. The mention of York. Was that the woman he'd spent Valentine's Day with? The one with the sultry voice? She'd been expecting someone more . . . sophisticated. Not a child with ink smeared on her lips and her hair all over the place.

Thoughts churning, she turned towards the stairs, only for Samson to call after her.

'I've changed my mind about that coffee. Drop one down when you've made yours. Cheers.'

Delilah Metcalfe swore she could hear him chuckling as she marched off to make a drink she didn't even want. But she didn't get far. The white envelope on the tiles inside the front door pulled her up short. She picked it up and stared at the odd lettering across the front.

O'Brien.

Normally she wouldn't open Samson's mail. But there was something sinister about the cut-and-pasted letters. She pulled out the single sheet of paper, unfolded it and gasped.

Next Time I won't Miss. Leave the Past alone.

Above her, through the fanlight over the door, the first flakes of snow were visible, beginning to fall.

'What do you mean this isn't the first one?'

Anger mounting, Delilah was standing in front of Samson's desk, the opened envelope lying on the surface and next to it, the threatening message it had contained.

'I was going to tell you—'

'Of course you were.' A roll of her eyes accompanied Delilah's retort. She pointed a finger at the sheet of paper with the hotchpotch of yellow and black lettering staggered across it. 'You had the audacity to lie to me. Telling me it was just kids shooting at us up there, when you knew differently all the time.'

'I'm sorry. Really, I am. I should have told you sooner.'

'Too bloody right!' She turned away, feeling her anger mixing with the stress of the day and threatening tears. She was damned if she'd cry in front of him.

'If it's any consolation,' Samson was saying, 'I don't think you're in any danger.'

She whirled back to face him. 'Oh, really? So it wasn't my Micra someone was firing at? With myself and Tolpuddle both in it?' She had the satisfaction of seeing him flinch.

'Yes, fair point,' he muttered. 'But it was me they were targeting.' He tapped the envelope. 'Both letters were addressed to me.'

If he was trying to reassure her, he failed miserably. A shaft of concern shot through her fury, making her even more annoyed at his cavalier attitude. And his exclusion of her. She thought of the ease with which he told lies. The way he kept things secret. The mystery woman with the blonde hair . . .

Frank Thistlethwaite's warning was beginning to make sense.

'And that makes it all okay?' she snapped. 'You knew someone was threatening you, but you saw no need to tell me. Or to go to the police. Honestly, Samson, when are you going to realise that real life isn't lived undercover?' Calling Tolpuddle from his bed, she clipped on his lead and strode out of the office, holding her head high and willing the tears to stay back. At least until she was out of the building.

The back door slammed, rattling the windows and making the ensuing silence even more pronounced.

Date with Mystery

Damn it! Samson O'Brien let his head fall into his hands and roundly cursed his inability to maintain a working relationship with Delilah Metcalfe. Or any kind of relationship. Every time he thought he'd made progress, he messed up and put them right back to that day in October when she'd greeted his homecoming with a punch.

He should have told her. He should have at least explained to her why he didn't want the police involved. The letters were their only lead in a case that was going nowhere. If he handed them over to Sergeant Clayton, Bruncliffe's plodding policeman, word would get round and the perpetrator would go to ground, eliminating whatever slim chance Samson had of finding them and getting closer to the mystery behind Livvy's death.

It was too late to tell Delilah that now. He stared at the sheet of paper that had caused the trouble.

He hadn't even had the chance to get the benefit of her insight into the source of the letters. Delilah would have been able to tell him who had air rifles in the area. Who was a good enough marksman to hit a moving car – presuming that was what had been intended. She'd have been able to corroborate the suspicion forming in his mind. Two names. Both involved with the Thornton case.

Oscar Hardacre. A man who didn't want to talk about the past. Whose love for Livvy had turned bitter. Did he know the truth behind what had happened? Had he been involved somehow? The shooting trophies Samson had seen in the Hardacres' kitchen suggested Oscar was a feasible candidate for the role of sniper.

And Jimmy Thornton himself. Samson sensed the farmer still wasn't telling them everything. If he knew what fate had really befallen his sister – possibly at the hands of his own father – would he try to keep it quiet?

Both could have a motive for trying to silence Samson. Both had had the opportunity to fire on the Micra that morning. Although Jimmy would have had to move fast to get from the house to the fellside before they drove past.

Other than that, Samson didn't have a clue who would want Livvy Thornton to stay well and truly buried. Wherever that was.

Faced with a mystery in the town he was born in, Samson had never felt more like an outsider.

He glanced up from his desk and saw thick snow falling beyond the window, isolating the office from the world beyond. As metaphors went, it was fairly apt.

At Rainsrigg the snow was already settling. Soft white flakes fluttering out of the sky and lying gently upon the exposed stone like a gauze dressing. The sound of a door closing echoed in the silence and two figures emerged from the house which stood sentry over the disused quarry. Arms around each other, they hurried towards their cars, the track leading out to the world beyond patched in white.

A burst of engine noise and the vehicles set off in convoy, leaving the quarry to settle back into a winter's hush. Leaving the snow to fall on the vegetable patch, covering the bare soil, the last of the cabbages. To coat the roof of the old barn and blur the edges between path and garden. To lie across the handle of the spade, its blade still buried deep in the earth, and to smother the rhubarb, hiding it from sight.

19

The winter that had abated somewhat since mid-February came back with a vengeance in the days following Samson and Delilah's visit to Rainsrigg Quarry. Snow fell across the Dales, blanketing the fields in white and masking the contours of the fellsides. Sheep huddled up against walls, farmers tracked to and fro with feed, worried by the drifts that were forming, drifts capable of killing their pregnant stock and the newborn lambs that were beginning to dot the hills. Down in the town, roads were mired in grit and slush, pavements covered in a treacherous mixture of compacted snow and ice. Those who ventured out on foot wore sturdy boots. And walked carefully.

Those who ventured out by car put a snow shovel in the boot. And a flask. And a blanket.

Delilah had all three stowed in the Micra – and a Weimaraner on the back seat – as she turned off the main road in Horton, a village to the north of Bruncliffe, and onto the small lane that led to Mire End Farm. Even so, she didn't feel overly confident. It was foolhardy. Making a trip out in this weather. In a Nissan Micra. Will would have a fit if he knew. But she'd had no choice. Plus, if she'd stayed indoors another moment, she would have gone mad.

A week. An entire week of nothing much happening. No one had taken a shot at her from the fells. And to her knowledge, there'd been no more threatening letters delivered to the Dales Detective Agency. Not that she could vouch for that as she hadn't spent much time in town, apart from leaving her car at the garage to get the window fixed. She'd told them it was a casualty of debris on the road. If they were puzzled as to how the passenger window and not the windscreen had come to be shattered by a flying piece of rock, they didn't say.

So seven days of humdrum mediocrity had passed. Other than watching the snow falling and stopping and falling and stopping, Delilah had spent them working from home on a new website for Taylor's Estate Agents. The commission had come out of the blue, her former father-in-law calling her into his office for a meeting six days ago and asking her to redesign the site she'd created several years before – the website that had brought Neil Taylor into her life. If Delilah's surprise at being asked to take on the role had shown on her face, Bernard Taylor hadn't commented. He'd just outlined the brief and told her to get on with it. And mentioned, as she left, that Neil would want some input on the final product.

Of course he would. Her ex-husband wouldn't allow her to have free rein on a project that had once been his baby. It wasn't a condition that alarmed her. She was confident that she could work with him without killing him. Especially now the whole farce over Tolpuddle was sorted, the dog's registration papers having been reissued under her name.

No, what alarmed Delilah about Mr Taylor's insistence on his son's collaboration was the danger of her family finding out. Or more specifically, Will. So she hadn't mentioned the commission at all. Not even to Samson – which, as she'd barely seen him since she stormed out of his office the day of the shooting, was hardly surprising. Her silence wasn't due solely to a lack of opportunity. For some reason, she was just as averse to her tenant knowing that she would be working alongside Neil as she was to her brother discovering the fact. Unfortunately, however, the Taylor contract wasn't one she could afford to turn down.

Even with spring just around the corner, a time for new life and new love, the Dales Dating Agency was still struggling for new customers. Admittedly some regulars had renewed their subscriptions, but a handful of repeat payments didn't represent a business model that would lead to success. Or even survival. To keep the company afloat she needed fresh blood. She'd placed adverts in the local press, hit the internet with targeted marketing – as much as she could afford – and crossed her fingers. Sometimes it felt like the latter had more chance of succeeding than anything else.

Her hard work had yet to yield much – a couple of enquiries. Nothing definite. So when Bernard Taylor had summoned her to his office and told her what he wanted, she hadn't been in a position to refuse. By the end of April she had to have sufficient income to prove to the bank that she could maintain the loans on her businesses. And her house. Two months. It was a challenge that woke her up at night, gripped in panic.

If the price of alleviating that stress was working with Neil Taylor, she was happy to pay it.

Which is why, for the last week, Delilah had been working a lot from home. She told herself that it was easier, given the weather and her need to keep her current project a secret. That her period of self-enforced purdah was largely the result of her argument with Samson, she didn't allow herself to think about. Basing herself at the small table in her kitchen, she'd thrown herself into redesigning Taylor's website, only venturing down to the office building twice.

Both times Samson had been there. Both times Tolpuddle had been reluctant to leave once her work was done, mournful eyes reproaching her as they left Samson in his office, bent over his laptop.

She'd been determined not to weaken. Not to get pulled back into the easy relationship that had developed between them and blinded her to the fact that he couldn't be trusted. Whatever anger she'd felt the day of the shooting had been replaced with wariness. A sense of self-preservation which made her keep her distance. She'd exchanged pleasantries with him, but when he'd dangled the Thornton case in front of her, she'd made her excuses and left. Only to have to return some minutes later to coerce Tolpuddle after her.

Although, by the look of frustration on Samson's face as he tapped away at his computer, she sensed nothing much had been happening in the quest for Livvy's death certificate. Or in the search for the mystery sharpshooter. And she knew for a fact that Samson had yet to inform the police about the incident up at Rainsrigg because if he had, it would have been all over town by now.

Telling herself that none of it was her concern and she was better off out of it, Delilah had done her best to block the Thornton case, and Samson O'Brien, from her mind.

She'd seen more of his father in the last week than she had of him, having called in on Joseph every other day since he'd admitted he was struggling to control his addiction. The older O'Brien was still refusing to tell his son about his predicament or accept professional support, so Delilah could do little more than sit and chat to him, but it seemed to be helping. She found herself looking forward to her visits to Fellside Court and Joseph's stories about Samson's youth, the joyous years before cancer tore their family apart and alcohol filled the void. The fact that she was vicariously spending time with the very person she was supposed to be avoiding, Delilah chose not to dwell on.

A whimper from the back seat made her glance in the rear-view mirror. Tolpuddle had his head on his paws, looking dejected. While Delilah might be able to feign in-difference to the absence of a certain person in their lives, Tolpuddle wore his heart on his sleeve. The hound was missing Samson.

And now she was dragging the poor dog out into the cold on a fool's errand.

Hands tense on the steering wheel, she eased the car along the narrow, wall-lined road that snaked across the lower slopes of Pen-y-ghent, windscreen wipers slapping, the skies dark above. Just gone midday and it was more like midnight. Thankful that someone had cleared the worst of the snow to the sides, Delilah was equally glad that her little car had come equipped with winter tyres, and it wasn't long before the ramshackle collection of buildings that was Mire End Farm came into view. Deciding against risking the rough farmhouse track, a cover of thick snow lying across it, she pulled into a partially cleared area by a gate. Better to park here and be able to get out, even if it meant a bit of a trek.

'Ready for cold paws, Tolpuddle?'

The dog lifted an ear. Not a huge sign of enthusiasm. About as much as she had herself, the excitement she'd felt earlier in the day having waned – a result of the tricky drive, combined with a growing acceptance of the impossibility of the task she'd set herself. There was only so much a dating profile – no matter how brilliant – could achieve.

It had all come together the day before when Clive Knowles had called her, irate that she hadn't been in touch since his visit to the office a fortnight ago. But in the excitement of the Livvy Thornton case, Delilah had neglected her own business and had nothing to show her client after two weeks' work. Understandably annoyed, Mr Knowles had given her twenty-four hours to produce a dating profile, further insisting that she deliver it in person to his farm. Otherwise he would take his business elsewhere.

That threat had been enough to make Delilah focus. Faced with his ultimatum, she'd spent the rest of the day trying to compile a description of him that didn't deceive, but didn't tell the blunt truth either. The idea she'd finally settled on was unusual, to say the least. She hoped he'd like it.

Most of all, she hoped it would work, bringing the farmer a wife, and her business a much-needed injection of cash. But looking out across the snow-covered fields to the dilapidated barns that guarded the farmhouse from view, Delilah felt that hope might be short-lived.

With a resigned sigh, she opened the car door and stepped out into the snow, her boots ankle-deep. Tolpuddle followed and the pair of them began walking into a bitter wind towards the property, where the welcome sign of smoke was spiralling out of a chimney. At least they'd get warm. And at least she was out of the house.

Mundane!

Samson slammed back his chair and stood up, restless at being confined behind a desk for so long. A week on from the incident-packed day that had culminated in the second anonymous letter, the Livvy Thornton case had hit a lull. A quick conversation with PC Danny Bradley had established that Oscar Hardacre was a member of the Bruncliffe gun club, confirming what the cluster of androgynous figurines holding guns on the sideboard in the Hardacre kitchen had made Samson suspect. That Jimmy Thornton, while not a club member, was also a frequent participant on the local range and a decent shot according to the young policeman, made things interesting. But other than that, Samson had unearthed nothing new to help identify the mystery shooter.

Which was frustrating as he was convinced now, more than ever, that exposing the person trying to obstruct the investigation would be pivotal to breaking the case.

Given the lack of progress, Samson had even debated taking Delilah's advice and going to the police, in an attempt to shake things up. But with ever-decreasing resources, the local force wouldn't act on mere speculation. Which was all he had.

The suspicion that Carl Thornton had killed his daughter. It wasn't enough to go on. Even the threats that had been intended to stop the investigation were of no substance. Some haphazard letters cut from a magazine and a shattered car window. Hardly sufficient to get forensics involved. And what motive did he have for whoever was behind the threats? A vague sense that Jimmy wasn't telling everything he knew, and a hunch that Oscar still nursed a grudge against a dead girl.

With everything at a standstill, Samson had been reduced to going back over the file and making sure he chased every lead, knowing that was how most investigations got solved. As for the threatening letters, there had been no more. Probably because, to all intents and purposes, the Livvy Thornton case had ground to a halt.

So in the quiet of the office building, Samson had filled the days with a couple of background checks he'd been asked to run for a small business in the town. One was on a new employee. The other on an au pair being employed by the owner.

Not exactly high-octane stuff.

He missed his old life at times like this. That tingle of anticipation when an investigation came together; the moment of complete calm before a raid. It was easy to forget the hours spent in cramped conditions staking out potential targets, or the days spent trawling bars trying to get information. Bars that were peopled with unsavoury types. And all while trying to maintain his cover – whatever it was in that particular case.

Did he really miss it? Or was it more that he missed his old life here, in Bruncliffe? The life he'd had for the last four months, but which had suddenly changed. The office no longer populated by an anxious Weimaraner. Or an insane Metcalfe.

Date with Mystery

It was so quiet. Even Ida Capstick seemed to be spending less time here of a morning. Her cousin was in the process of moving over from Bridlington and somehow this meant Ida didn't have time to linger so long over tea and biscuits. Samson didn't understand why, but he did know that some days his chat with the cleaner was the only meaningful conversation he had.

What he'd give to have Delilah here storming around. Making her undrinkable cups of tea and offering her opinion on everything, as was the Metcalfe way.

Instead she was staying away, claiming to be working from home because of the weather. He glanced out of the window at the snow that had started again, spattering against the glass and smearing the gold letters that arched across the glazing. Some excuse when she lived up the hill, within easy walking distance.

There was no denying it. Delilah was avoiding his company – as frosty as the weather outside in the couple of dealings he'd had with her over the last week.

It had started the day of the shooting up at Rainsrigg Quarry. She'd arrived back from her mystery assignation in time to see DC Green leaving the office. And then she'd found the second menacing letter and had lost her temper with him. Somewhere within those events was the cause of her withdrawal. And while being shot at would normally be grounds for someone to take offence, knowing Delilah Metcalfe, Samson couldn't believe that was the reason for her sudden detachment. She was much more likely to tackle something like that head-on. So what was it?

With a week of nothing much else to occupy him, he had allowed paranoia to flourish.

Did Delilah know about his suspension? Had Rick somehow found out what Samson had fled from? The property developer had been threatening to discover the reason for his return to Bruncliffe since October. Maybe he had finally succeeded. And knowing the man, the first person he would tell was Delilah Metcalfe. With that knowledge fresh in her mind, she'd overheard Samson talking to DC Green. How much had she heard? Enough to validate whatever Rick had told her?

Samson paced the lino from window to wall, impatient at the lack of activity in the Thornton case and anxious about his past, which seemed to be getting closer. Passing the desk, he picked up his mobile. He'd call her. See if he could tell anything from her tone. Then he tossed the phone back down.

Work. It was what paid the bills. He resumed his seat, staring at the laptop, Facebook open on the screen. He'd had the idea of tracing some of Livvy's friends from when she was at school – friends who'd moved away and married, changing their names in the process. But social media wasn't his thing. Being instantly contactable wasn't exactly something an undercover officer aspired to. So he'd hesitated, unwilling to create the necessary profile to get started.

Delilah could help him with this. A legitimate reason to contact her. He reached for his mobile again and heard the back door open.

'Delilah?' he was up and in the hallway in one swift movement. But instead of seeing his landlady, he was faced with Matty Thistlethwaite, eyebrows prominent above a scarf wrapped around the lower half of his face, his shoulders dusted with snow.

'Cold out!' the solicitor exclaimed, stomping his feet as he unwound his scarf. 'Any chance of a brew?'

Delilah was on the edge of her seat. Literally. When she'd laid her hand on the back of the chair, preparing to pull it out and sit down, her fingers had encountered a greasy residue and she'd had to discreetly flick some food off the seat before she took her place across the table from her client.

She'd been met at the door of Mire End Farm by Clive Knowles, who'd grunted and turned back into the gloom of the hallway, the tiles muddy, dirty boots cluttering the floor. Above them a coatrack hung drunkenly on the wall, tipping under the weight of a motley collection of wax jackets and waterproofs, torn and stained from years of service. Against the opposite wall was a sideboard riddled with woodworm and with one door missing. Drawers gaped open, too full to close, a spool of twine spilling out of the top one and trailing to the ground, and a mound of paperwork littered the flat surface – along with a broken ram harness, a set of foot-rot shears, a couple of clipper blades, various jars of ointment, several coils of rope and three traps for rats, judging by the size of them. The farm office.

Delilah had followed the farmer into the kitchen, a bare, low-watt bulb doing little to dispel the shadows in the room. But at least there was a fire burning in an open grate, an aged sheepdog lying before it. Too old to object, the dog had merely opened an eye as Tolpuddle crossed to the hearth and settled down next to it, less fussy than Delilah about the conditions he found himself in.

As though trying to prove his marital potential, Clive Knowles had insisted on making tea. So now Delilah was perched on the rim of a chair, a chipped mug that she could have aged from the rings of old coffee on the inside placed in front of her, and surrounded by a kitchen that probably hadn't been cleaned since the current owner's mother passed away more than three decades before. To say it lacked a woman's touch was an understatement.

Mire End Farm was making her think more than ever that finding its owner a wife was beyond the realms of her abilities.

'So, you've found me someone?' the farmer asked, pulling a couple of biscuits out of a tin and offering one to Delilah with grime-covered fingers.

'I'm fine, thanks,' she politely declined.

'Watching your weight?' he grinned, a blast of bad breath accompanying his words. He dunked the biscuit, half of it falling into the cup and sploshing tea over the table. He wiped his sleeve across the liquid, smearing it across an even larger surface. 'Happen I should think about dieting, too,' he said, patting the paunch underneath his jumper. 'Wouldn't hurt my chances.'

Delilah could think of a lot more pragmatic steps he could take to enhance his chances. A good bath, to start with.

'I've devised a new profile for you,' she said, pulling her Surface Pro out of her rucksack and placing it on her legs. There was no way she was putting it down on the table. With a couple of swipes she opened his file. 'See what you think.' She tried not to flinch as she passed the computer into his grubby grasp.

He read her description of him slowly, lips moving silently, a broad finger tracking the words. It had taken all of her skill to write it. After many false starts, it had been a throwaway comment from Samson when they'd been on the train to Leeds that had given her an idea. Ralph, Clive Knowles' prize-winning Swaledale tup – Samson had jokingly suggested that Delilah would have more success if she used a photo of the ram as the farmer's profile picture. Sitting in her kitchen, struggling to complete an honest portrayal of her client, those words had suddenly seemed inspired.

She'd compiled the dating profile in terms anyone in farming would understand.

BREED CHARACTERISTICS
Body: Medium length; shoulders broad; back strong.
　　Good firm loins.
Head: Long-faced, dark-complexioned. Eyes bright.
　　Firm jaw. Some grey.
Legs: Well-set legs of medium length. Walks well.
Fleece: Thinning with age.
General: A bold and hardy specimen, well suited
　　to harsh environments. Robust. A good thriver.
　　Of strong constitution.

Biting her lip, she watched Clive Knowles finish reading. Then he scratched his head and stared at her, eyes wide. 'You've made me sound like a tup at market!' he exclaimed.

'That,' said Delilah, 'is exactly what you are. It's my job to make you sellable.'

'Sellable?' he grunted.

She nodded, sensing she was losing him. Losing the

payment that would come with the completion of the job, too. 'By putting this on the Dales Dating Agency website, you are effectively offering yourself up to the highest bidder. I thought that if we approached it from the angle of a livestock sale, we might have more success . . .'

A light came on in the farmer's eyes. 'Aye,' he muttered. 'It might work.'

'But,' continued Delilah, deciding it was time to bite the bullet, 'a sales pitch isn't enough on its own. I'm sure you know what it's like when you turn up at the mart and the catalogue spec doesn't match the beast in the pen?'

Clive Knowles squinted at her, then glanced down at himself. At his hole-ridden sweater, his dirt-rimmed finger-nails. He ran a hand over his chin, stubble scratching his hand.

He nodded, the penny finally dropping. 'You mean I'm to preen myself up if I want the chance of fetching a good price?'

Delilah laughed. 'Exactly. Although I won't ask you to go as far as trimming your gigots or colouring your fleece.'

He grinned. 'Right,' he said, passing her back her computer before brushing the biscuit crumbs off his chest and sitting upright, something akin to hope on his features. 'What else do we need to do to get this on the internet?'

'A photo is essential. Perhaps one with you and Ralph?'

The farmer stood and crossed to the sideboard in the hallway. Amidst the chaos he somehow found what he was looking for and returned with a framed photograph, which he passed to Delilah.

'Malham Show,' he said with pride, finger tapping the glass beneath which he was captured posing with his prize-winning tup, a rosette adorning the broad back of the sheep.

It was perfect. More of Ralph than of the farmer, which was no bad thing. Delilah checked the back of the frame and saw the sticker for a photographer she knew from the shows. She'd contact him for a digital copy. One without thumbprints on it.

'Anything else?' Clive Knowles asked.

'This should do the trick.' Delilah got to her feet, aware of her boots sticking to the floor.

'Good, good,' he muttered. He held out a hand, shaking hers furiously. 'Thanks, lass,' he said. 'I reckon this might work.'

Finding the farmer's sudden optimism heartbreaking, Delilah busied herself with slipping her Surface Pro back into her bag and waking up a reluctant Tolpuddle. For the reality was, no matter how clever her profile and no matter how her client tried to spruce himself up, there was no way any woman would be willing – or stupid enough – to marry Clive Knowles. Not when the hovel that was Mire End Farm was part of the package.

The car started first time. Shivering with the cold, Delilah cranked the heating up high, apologising to Tolpuddle on the back seat who was regarding her dolefully, no doubt wondering why he'd had to be ripped away from a blazing fire. She wasn't sure herself. The snow was falling hard now, the tracks from her arrival already covered on the lane, drifts reaching almost to the top of the stone walls that edged the road.

It would be a trickier drive home.

Taking her time, Delilah eased the car back onto the track and turned it round, careful not to edge too far into the deeper banks of snow that lined the roadside.

'Home soon,' she promised the dog as she put the Micra into second gear and pulled away from Mire End Farm.

Soon wouldn't be soon enough. The weather didn't look good, black clouds overhead, the flanks of Pen-y-ghent obscured by the flakes falling thick and fast. The windscreen wipers were having trouble keeping up. And the narrow lane was getting even narrower.

Stupid! She was stupid for having come out in this. It was the kind of thing newcomers did, not realising the risks. It would have been far wiser to have told Clive Knowles she couldn't make it, despite his threats, and then she wouldn't be trying to drive through a blizzard in a vehicle not entirely suited to the conditions.

'Home soon,' she muttered again. Reassuring herself as much as the dog.

But when a rabbit ran out across the road ahead of her, a brown smudge of fur against an expanse of white, she knew it would be a while before she'd be going anywhere.

It was instinctive. Slamming on the brakes. In slow motion the car began to slew across the track, tyres struggling and slipping on the icy surface. It pirouetted full circle while skidding sideways towards a deep bank of snow. There was a muffled yelp from the back seat, a curse from the front, and a crumpling sound as the bonnet buried itself in the snowdrift.

'You okay?' Delilah was already checking the dog, who was adding indignant to his repertoire of expressions. She patted him, just to make sure, and he rewarded her with a lick on the hand.

He was fine. As was the miscreant who had caused the crash, the small rabbit skittering along the road in the distance.

More in hope than expectation, Delilah restarted the car and put it in reverse. The whine of a wheel spinning uselessly was her reward.

Unclipping her seat belt, she got out to survey the damage.

'Damn!' She thumped the roof of the car in exasperation. The Micra was stuck nose-first into a wall of white in the middle of nowhere. Surrounded by the bleached landscape, the silence wrapping itself around her, Delilah remembered the sharp crack of the air rifle the week before. She felt her skin prickling in concern.

20

'How frustrating.' Matty Thistlethwaite finished his coffee and placed the mug on Samson's desk. 'And there was I thinking this would be straightforward.'

Samson shrugged. 'Sorry, but there's not much more we can do. I'm going to set up a Facebook group to see if we can get in touch with friends of Livvy who have moved away. Perhaps that will yield something. But other than that, we really don't have anything to go on.'

'So Livvy Thornton has effectively become a missing person,' Matty mused. 'A missing person we suspect may have met a dreadful end. In which case, we need to think about formally notifying the police.'

'You sound like Delilah,' said Samson dryly. 'She's been pestering me to get the police involved. Personally, I don't think they'll have any more success than we have.'

'You're probably right. But we have an obligation to tell them if we suspect a crime may have been committed. And that's what you're suggesting, isn't it?'

'From the little we've uncovered, it does seem likely that Carl Thornton had something to do with Livvy's death. But there's no proof.'

'And what about the letter warning you off? Any developments there?' asked Matty.

'Nothing new,' said Samson, lying with practised ease,

aware that the risk-averse solicitor would have him and Delilah off the case if he knew someone had taken shots at them. 'Probably someone messing around. I'm not exactly Bruncliffe's most popular person.'

Matty leaned back in his chair, fingers steepled under his chin in his characteristic manner as he thought about the unexpected mess that the Thornton case had become. 'How curious. No death certificate. No record of burial or cremation. No newspaper reports,' he murmured. 'It makes you wonder . . .'

'Why Mrs Thornton left Livvy in the will in the first place?' Samson was nodding. 'I've been thinking that. Did she do it deliberately, knowing we would uncover this mess?'

'You mean that's what she wanted?'

'Why not? What other explanation is there for a mother bequeathing half her estate to her dead daughter.'

'Half her estate and a shoebox,' stated Matty.

'What?'

'Along with fifty per cent of her mother's assets, Livvy inherits a shoebox and its contents.'

Samson stared at the solicitor. 'Any particular shoebox?'

'It's explicitly stated in the will. One from Beryl's Shoes in Skipton.'

'Do you know what's in it?'

'According to Jimmy, some letters from Livvy, baby memorabilia, postcards from a penfriend . . . that kind of thing.'

'You haven't seen it yourself?'

Matty shook his head. 'I mentioned it to Jimmy and he's put it to one side. You think it might be important?'

'Put it this way,' said Samson, 'Mrs Thornton had her own reasons for including Livvy in the settlement. So anything she stipulated in that document might be worth a look.'

'You could be right,' agreed Matty. 'Give Jimmy a call and tell him I've authorised you to collect the box.'

'Will do. And I'll take Delilah with me,' Samson added, thinking about the state they'd left the farmer in and that he might be more receptive if Delilah was there.

'Good idea. In the meantime, I'll have a word with Sergeant Clayton later this week. Tell him what we suspect and let him take it from there.' Matty rose from his seat and pulled his coat on, looking out onto Back Street with a grimace. 'It's getting worse,' he said, taking in the thick flakes of snow falling outside. 'I'd leave it a day or two. No point going out in this if you don't need to.'

'Don't worry,' laughed Samson. 'I've no desire to test my winter driving skills. Especially not on a Royal Enfield.'

Matty wound his scarf around his face, looking every bit like the infamous Turpin, as opposed to the staid solicitor of the same name whose business he'd taken over. 'Let me know how you get on,' he said as he headed for the door.

Samson stood on the doorstep watching the solicitor disappear into the awful weather. 'Only idiots would go out in this,' he muttered, shivering as he closed the door and hurried back into his office.

She was an idiot.

After fifteen minutes' hard work trying to shovel out the front wheels of the car with no success, Delilah was hot, bothered and more than cross with herself. It wasn't simply that she'd ventured out into bad weather in a small car. It was more the jittering nerves that had overwhelmed her in the short time she'd been stranded.

This was her countryside. The place she felt at home in. Safe in. Yet here she was casting apprehensive glances at the fellside above, scouring the landscape for the sign of a marksman, her stomach in knots.

It was daft, she admonished herself. Apart from the fact that no one other than Clive Knowles had known her itinerary for the day, who in their right mind would venture out in this weather on the off-chance of stumbling across her? Besides, Samson was right. He'd been the focus of the mystery letter writer's wrath. She had nothing to worry about.

'Bloody hell,' she cursed, aiming a kick at one of the tyres that wouldn't do anything more than spin and slip, digging the car even further into the snowdrift. Accepting defeat, she threw the shovel back in the boot and pulled her coat back on, trying not to think about the great target it made, a red flare of colour in the surrounding snow.

She was going to have to ask for help. And in doing so, she would have to admit to others just what an idiot she was. Reluctantly, she considered her options.

Not Will. Definitely not Will. He'd never let her out of his sight again if he knew. No point calling Ash, either, as the youngest of the Metcalfe lads was working over in Skipton, fitting kitchens for Procter Properties.

Her father? She looked at the thick snow falling around her. Did she really want to drag him out in this? Besides, calling her father would mean Will finding out for sure, as her father would need to use the Land Rover to pull her out.

And as for Samson? A week ago he'd have been top of her list. But now . . .

So who then? Clive Knowles? She shuddered. It was the only alternative. Better that than standing around out here twitching at shadows. She sighed, reaching into her coat pocket for her mobile. It started ringing before she even laid a finger on it, the sudden trilling in the eerie silence sending her heart scampering.

'Samson?' she said, answering the call with a burst of relief, a slight tremble in her voice.

'Dee . . . is everything okay?'

She heard the old nickname, his instant concern, and she felt a rush of affection for this man who infuriated her.

'Fine,' she muttered, not willing to admit how vulnerable she was feeling.

There was a pause at the other end of the line and Delilah had to fight the urge to tell him. To blurt out how much she wanted him to come and fetch her.

'I was calling to ask if you could come down to the office,' he continued. 'I need your help with something.'

She looked at Tolpuddle sitting in the car and then up to the heavens, wondering which deity was taunting her. 'Sure,' she said, finally grasping the lifebelt she'd been thrown. 'But I could do with a bit of help myself first . . .'

Jimmy Thornton didn't allow something like the weather to stop him. He was used to working in inclement conditions and had the vehicles to cope with it. So when he decided he'd had enough of the whole fiasco surrounding his mother's will, he didn't think twice. He got in the Land Rover and drove over to Rainsrigg, passing not a car on his journey.

Bruncliffe had gone into hibernation. Over a bit of snow. It was ridiculous.

At Quarry House, he cleared the path to the back door and then lit the range in the kitchen, trying to get a bit of warmth into the property as he set about completing the task he'd abandoned the week before. Dishes, glasses, tins of food and jars of home-made jam. He boxed the lot, leaving the cupboards bare. When he was finished he moved upstairs, bagging and boxing what was left in the bedrooms after his initial attempt to clear them a full two weeks ago.

A fortnight. How had it taken that long? And still the issue of the will wasn't resolved. Burning with resentment at the insinuations Samson O'Brien had made about his father and frustrated at his mother for leaving such a mess behind, he worked like fury. Before long, the hallway was lined with stacks of boxes and Jimmy Thornton felt he was finally getting somewhere.

He'd take it to Age Concern tomorrow – Matty Thistlethwaite be damned! It was time to move on.

Heading back into the kitchen, he noticed the falling snow, the heaviness of it. That's when his eyes fell on the spade, outlined in white. He'd left it there when he'd gone to dig up the rhubarb the week before.

Berating himself for treating the tool so neglectfully, he pulled on his boots and coat and slipped out into the quiet of the garden. It was beautiful. The rock face that normally scowled down on the house had been transformed into a soft backdrop filled with ripples and patterns where the wind had blown the snow. Beneath it, the bare earth of the vegetable patch had been merged with the path and the old barn had lost some of its menace, the scene more like the innocent interior of a snow globe than a place filled with sorrow. And death.

Perhaps even worse, if Samson's beliefs were to be trusted.

Was there any credence in them? Jimmy had been tormenting himself with that question all week, ever since Samson and Delilah had called in and dropped their bombshell.

None of it made sense. Not just the lack of documentation for Livvy's death, but also what had happened at the time of her accident. He'd never thought about it until now, when, confronted by the brutal facts, he'd had no option but to reassess his childhood; to view his parents in a different light.

The funeral. Why hadn't he been allowed to go? And why would his mother have claimed Livvy was cremated in Leeds if that hadn't been the case? Where had she been cremated? He remembered the ashes, brought home in an urn by his mother, who had scattered them in Hawber Woods amongst the wildflowers Livvy and Red had loved walking through. Mother had taken Jimmy with her, his hand clasped in hers, the urn held tight against her chest as they walked up the hill into the trees. They'd stood on a carpet of fading bluebells, the smell of wild garlic scenting the air, and Mother had solemnly opened the urn and let the ashes be taken by the wind. Father had been at work.

But now Samson was telling him that Mother had lied.

Date with Mystery

About the cremation. Had she lied about the accident, too? Was the truth behind Livvy's death a lot more sinister?

A burn of anger and frustration caught at Jimmy's chest. Bloody family. So dysfunctional. He strode across to the upright spade and pulled it from the ground, the shock of dark soil on its blade a contrast to the snow. He thrust it back into the earth, feeling a release in the physical effort. Damn his parents! And damn Mother's precious rhubarb.

Another shove. Another levering of soil. The earth beginning to yield, the snow falling from the dying plant, the crown exposed.

Damn all of them. Samson. Matty. Every bloody last one of them!

Another plunge of the spade. More soil lifted up, his anger fuelling each furious strike. No thought of the rhubarb now, the plant tipped to one side by the frenzied digging. Jimmy Thornton was only aware he was crying when he felt the tears on his cheeks. And when he had to blink to focus on the hole he'd created.

What was that? Something in the soil.

He crouched down for a better look, hand still on the spade, and saw a black bin bag. Ripped open by the sharp edge of the shovel. A piece of fabric was sticking out of the jagged edges. Fabric he recognised. And protruding from it was what looked like . . .

Horror propelled him back onto the path, scrabbling crablike away, the spade falling over into the snow.

While Delilah was sitting in the car, engine running and heater on, anxiously awaiting rescue, Samson had been on the phone arranging suitable transport. As time ticked by and Delilah got out of the car, stomping up and down in the snow to keep the blood flowing to her feet and her nerves at bay, Samson was being driven out of town towards Horton. Fifteen minutes later, her annoyance at feeling so helpless having brewed into a temper, Delilah heard the sound of an engine coming along the lane.

Visibility was poor so it was a while before she could make it out. A grey tractor. Small. No cab.

A Ferguson TE20, affectionately known as a Little Grey Fergie, owned and lovingly restored by George Capstick, who was steering the vehicle through the snow with a broad grin on his face. Standing behind him was Samson O'Brien.

'Hello!' Samson called out, waving at her as if she wouldn't see them. As if arriving on a bloody vintage tractor made them invisible. 'Are you the damsel in distress?' he enquired with a laugh as the tractor pulled up and he jumped down into the snow. He had the sense to stand well back as he asked it.

'Not exactly subtle,' she muttered, glaring at the vehicle and knowing that the entire town would now be aware of the rescue mission, the arrival of the Ferguson in Bruncliffe to collect Samson not being something people would miss. Whatever the conditions. Consequently it wouldn't be long before everyone knew about her stupidity, too.

'It's not the weather for subtle,' Samson replied, as George started attaching the tow rope to the Micra and Tolpuddle deigned to emerge from the car, greeting their rescuers with far more cheer than Delilah had. 'It was either this or ask Will.'

Delilah folded her arms, conscious that she was being

churlish but smarting at having had to ask for help. Smarting at having everyone know she'd ventured out ill-equipped. And awkward at facing Samson properly for the first time since their argument.

'Besides,' added Samson with a lopsided grin, showing no signs of being ill at ease in her company, 'I had George pick me up at Hardacre's farm. Is that discreet enough?'

Hardacre's farm. On the Horton Road. Samson had walked across town to ensure that George Capstick hadn't needed to drive through the marketplace and attract attention.

'Thanks,' muttered Delilah.

'You're welcome,' said Samson. 'Are we ready, George?'

'Twenty-horsepower Standard wet liner in-line four-engine more than ready,' George replied, hands on his hips and beaming with pride.

It didn't take long for the Little Grey to extract the Micra from the snow, with George steering the tractor, Delilah behind the wheel of the car and Samson standing well back, a hand on Tolpuddle's collar.

'Now aren't you glad we came with this?' asked Samson, patting the grey bonnet of the Ferguson as George unhooked the tow rope.

'Thank you,' said Delilah with far more grace than earlier.

'But how on earth did you end up buried in there in the first place?' Samson had crossed the lane to inspect the mound of snow that now featured a Micra-shaped hole.

'A rabbit,' muttered Delilah under her breath, her cheeks going red.

'A rabbit?' Samson started laughing, George Capstick

casting her a shy grin. 'You were forced into a snowdrift by a rabbit?'

'It was a small one. Too cute to run over.'

Samson shook his head, laughing even harder. 'You're as soft as Tolpuddle,' he said.

She glowered at him, pointing at the platform that George Capstick had added to the Little Grey to accommodate passengers. 'If you want a cold ride back on a tractor, keep laughing.'

He grinned, undaunted by the threat. 'Might be safer than putting my life in the hands of someone capable of getting stuck in a couple of inches of snow. What do you think, George?'

Samson made the fatal mistake of turning his back on her. In one fluid movement, Delilah bent down, scooped a fistful of snow and had it compacted and flying through the air just as he started laughing.

It caught him on the side of his head, showering icy particles all over his face.

'What—? You bugger!' He was quick to retaliate, hurling a snowball back at her, but even as it left his fingers, a second shot caught him on the chest.

She was good. What could you expect with having five brothers? Already she was behind the Micra, gathering and throwing in smooth movements, hitting her target – him – with a high percentage.

'Surrender,' she called out with a laugh, Tolpuddle darting between the two of them, leaping up at the snowballs flying over him.

'Never,' Samson shouted, taking another hit to the body, his black parka now smeared with white. He ducked behind the tractor, seeking shelter, and turned to George Capstick, who was standing by the bonnet, watching the fight with an amused expression. 'Help me,' he whispered to his old neighbour, before firing another couple of snowballs in Delilah's direction and getting the satisfaction of a yelp from the vicinity of the Micra.

George gazed at him blankly and Samson thought it was a lost cause. But then one of Delilah's efforts landed on the Little Grey, whumping onto the bodywork. George Capstick's eyebrows shot up, his lips compressed, and he glared across no-man's-land at the transgressor.

Whump. Another missile, hitting the grey paintwork.

'You're losing,' laughed Delilah, stretching above the car to fire again. She was mid-shot when it hit her. A huge snowball, catching her full on the chest.

She let out a small squeal as she fell back into the snow, arms splayed out like a scarlet angel. 'I surrender,' she yelled, still prone, Tolpuddle rushing over to lick her face.

Samson cast a look at George Capstick, calmly wiping snow from his hands. 'Good shot, George,' he murmured, before hurrying over to help a laughing Delilah to her feet. He was brushing the worst of the snow off her back, thinking about the perils of getting between a man and his tractor and how good it was to hear the sound of Delilah's laughter again, when his mobile went.

'Hello,' he said as he turned, cupping the phone to his ear.

'Come quickly!' Jimmy Thornton, shouting, his voice quavering. 'I've found her . . . Livvy . . . she's here.'

21

They found Jimmy Thornton standing at the kitchen window up at Rainsrigg, staring out into the garden with a look of horror.

'I was splitting the rhubarb,' he muttered, gaze fixed on the dark gash in the snow he'd created. 'Just digging. And I found—' He gulped, throat working. 'It's Livvy, I'm sure of it. You were right.'

Delilah moved over to his side. 'Come on,' she said, leading him to the table. 'Sit down. We'll take over from here.'

Jimmy sat, back to the window and its macabre view, while Delilah put the kettle on.

'Have you called the police?' asked Samson.

'No. Just you.'

'Do you mind if I go and have a look?'

Jimmy shuddered. 'As long as I can stay here.'

'You can look after Tolpuddle for me,' said Delilah.

As if sensing he was needed, the dog came and sat by the table, leaning into the farmer's legs until Jimmy lowered a hand onto the grey head, leaving Delilah to follow Samson back out into the cold and the falling flakes.

'Are you sure you want to see this?' Samson murmured, closing the back door behind them.

They'd ridden up to the quarry on the back of the

Date with Mystery

Little Grey, the two of them huddled with Tolpuddle on the makeshift platform, knowing the road over Gunnerstang Brow would be too challenging for the Micra in the wintry conditions. Having seen how shaken Jimmy Thornton was, Samson was glad Delilah had insisted on accompanying him, her interpersonal skills far surpassing his. He was also glad he'd told George Capstick to head home after dropping them off, the man not being equipped to deal with drama. Or death. Seeing the upturned earth in the Thorntons' vegetable patch, Samson was expecting both.

'We're on this case together, remember,' Delilah said, reinstating herself into the investigation with more bravado than she felt, aware of the vast space around them; the trees and the rocks providing cover for anyone wishing them harm. The place felt menacing, despite the purity of its winter coating.

In tense silence they walked in Jimmy's footprints up the snow-covered path to where a spade lay abandoned on the ground, not far from a brown smudge in the surrounding white. Samson squatted down beside the hole and brushed off the thin layer of snow that had settled in it, the tattered edges of black plastic buried within it discernible. Jutting out of the rent in the plastic was a piece of fabric, colour faded, some kind of pattern on it, like the petal of a flower, a rusty stain across the white leaf. But it was what that fabric contained that made Samson straighten up, blood draining from his face.

'Are they . . . bones?' gasped Delilah, a hand over her mouth.

'Afraid so.' Samson was already retracing his steps, heading for the house to use the phone.

Sergeant Clayton, a policeman who had grown into his role over the years – literally, in some ways – was accustomed to a certain type of crime. Quad-bike theft. Sheep rustling. The odd fracas outside the Fleece on a Saturday night – never inside it, as Troy Murgatroyd was more than capable of turfing out troublemakers before they caused any damage to his pub. Nothing to spark any major concern. Nothing that would elevate the heartrate.

Since the return of Bruncliffe's black sheep back in October, all that had changed. They'd had a spate of murders that had culminated in complete mayhem up on the fells. A series of malicious attacks on the elderly residents of Fellside Court. And now this.

The possible remains of a young woman, uncovered at Rainsrigg Quarry. A woman who was supposed to have died twenty-odd years ago in Leeds.

He pushed back his helmet, scratched his head and glared at Samson O'Brien, the man who seemed to be the catalyst for the recent outburst of exotic crimes in this part of the Dales. Not that there was anything exotic about this. Standing out in the bitter cold getting covered in snow and staring down into a hole that contained bones, young Constable Bradley next to him, looking like he was going to faint at the sight.

When the call had come through to the station, Gavin Clayton had been sceptical. Not least because he didn't fancy the drive up Gunnerstang Brow in the current conditions. But mostly because he remembered Livvy Thornton.

'Delilah?' Samson was frowning.

'Hi,' she said, trying to control the heat that was coursing up her face. 'I was about to ask if you wanted a coffee. I didn't realise you had visitors.'

'No, no need for coffee.' He turned to the woman, ushering her out of the office and towards the back door.

No introductions. The woman giving the smallest of smiles as she walked past.

Delilah kept an eye on them as they walked into the yard, Samson saying something, the woman nodding. Then he was opening the gate and she was gone.

Who was that woman? And the bit Delilah had overheard – Samson declaring he didn't need babysitting – what the hell was that all about? And what was it that Samson didn't want the people of Bruncliffe to know?

The back door slammed and Samson was coming towards her, a smile on his face.

'Didn't take you for someone to listen at doors, Delilah.'

She blushed. 'And I didn't take you for someone so secretive.'

'Can't a man even have a private life around here?' he asked, grinning. 'Or do I have to go to York to get away from prying eyes?'

It threw her. The mention of York. Was that the woman he'd spent Valentine's Day with? The one with the sultry voice? She'd been expecting someone more . . . sophisticated. Not a child with ink smeared on her lips and her hair all over the place.

Thoughts churning, she turned towards the stairs, only for Samson to call after her.

too. So why would he go
rd on a wild goose chase,
long way from here?
ad insisted they respond,
n't waste their time. So
was bound to mean a
anging about in freezing
solation was seeing the
down his breakfast.
r, seeing as she died an
sergeant grunted.
'Let's go inside in the

turning away from the
wards the back door of
ion of a decent brew or
ne, it wasn't clear. They
boots on the mat and
slabs cold on the feet.
yton said to the farmer
xt to him at the table.

up in reply, merely
Delilah Metcalfe had
sn't it?' he muttered.
the sergeant. 'We'll
e I go and do that, I
. Like why you think

mmy shot a sideways

glance at Samson. 'Tell him. You figured it out, so you tell him.'

It took a while. To detail the will, the missing death certificate, the lack of evidence in the newspapers. The growing suspicion, fuelled by Tom Hardacre's story about the shotgun and his belief that Livvy came home before she died. When he broached the topic of Carl Thornton, Samson tried to make it more palatable for the sake of the son sitting there listening. But there was no avoiding the brutal truth of what he was suggesting.

'So let me get this straight,' said the sergeant when Samson had finished. 'You think Carl Thornton killed his own daughter when she was home on a secret visit. And that the whole story about Livvy being killed in a hit-and-run accident was fabricated to cover that up?'

'I'm saying it's possible,' Samson countered. 'But like I said, apart from a lack of paperwork to support the idea of Livvy having died in Leeds, there's no evidence for any of this.' His gaze fell on the patch of earth beyond the window, already merging back into the white landscape. 'Not yet.'

Sergeant Clayton shook his head in dismay. 'What a mess.'

Jimmy snorted. 'That about sums up my family,' he said. 'A bloody mess.'

Delilah reached across the table and took his hand. 'Don't, Jimmy. This might turn out to be something and nothing.'

'Delilah's right,' said Sergeant Clayton. 'Until we get the experts in, there's not much point in making assumptions.'

'And when will that be?' asked Samson.

The policeman glanced at his watch and then cast an eye towards the weather outside, snow still falling fast. 'Not today, that's for sure. They come over from Harrogate nowadays. It's already late and there are roads closed all over the place, so tomorrow morning at the earliest, I'd say.'

'So what do we do with . . . that . . . in the meantime?' Jimmy pointed towards the garden.

'Cover it over and protect it from the elements for now. And wait for the cavalry.'

'More bloody waiting,' muttered the farmer. 'But I can tell you now, that's Livvy.'

Sergeant Clayton leaned across the table. 'What makes you so sure, lad?'

Jimmy raised his head, face twisted in grief. 'James – the band. Livvy was mad about them.'

The policeman looked puzzled, but Samson was already making the connection. The fabric in the hole outside. The pattern. The big petal. It was part of the daisy motif favoured by the Manchester band in the nineties.

'That's Livvy's T-shirt out there for sure,' continued Jimmy. 'So unless you can come up with some other explanation for how my sister's bloodstained clothing is buried in our garden along with a load of bones, I'm thinking that the blood and bones are probably hers, too.'

Accepting that there would be no further progress on the case that day, the two policemen and Samson covered the gruesome discovery with an old tarpaulin from the barn – a temporary measure until a police tent could be brought up from Bruncliffe. Jimmy Thornton had been persuaded to return home, having left a set of keys to the property with Sergeant Clayton. And Constable Bradley had come to terms with the fact that he'd drawn the short straw and would be on duty at the quarry overnight, standing guard over the find. Promising to return to the empty house with provisions to keep the young constable going, Sergeant Clayton had led Samson, Delilah and Tolpuddle out to his car, leaving poor Danny Bradley to his unenviable task.

The drive back into town was slow and sombre, the sergeant negotiating the slippery slope of Gunnerstang Brow with care, no one inclined to talk. On being dropped off at the office, neither Samson nor Delilah was in the mood for company in the form of the clientele at the Fleece, but both of them were starving, breakfast a distant memory and the dusk already turning to dark. So when Samson offered to pop to the Spar and get supplies, Delilah acquiesced. Even though she wasn't supposed to be spending time with him.

An hour later, with Tolpuddle sound asleep in his bed across the hallway, she was sitting at the office kitchen table with Samson, pushing away an empty plate, the omelette and chips Samson had rustled up having been exactly what she needed.

'I guess that rules Jimmy Thornton out as our mystery letter writer,' Samson said, broaching the topic of the distressing afternoon up at the quarry for the first time since they'd got back to town. 'It's highly unlikely he'd try to stop us investigating and then unearth what could be his sister's grave up there.'

Delilah stared at him, eyebrows raised. 'Seriously? You thought Jimmy was the person shooting at us last week?'

'It crossed my mind. He hasn't exactly been forthcoming from the start, and I hear he's good with a rifle.'

'I told you before, he was as forthcoming as anyone around here would be when it comes to revealing skeletons in their closet.' She gave a dismissive shake of her head. 'I'd point the finger at a lot of others before I'd lay the blame on Jimmy.'

'Like who?' asked Samson, a glint of challenge in his eyes.

It was bait. Delilah knew it. Samson O'Brien was luring her back in, piquing her curiosity and getting her engrossed in the case again. She felt her will to resist crumble.

'Oscar Hardacre,' she said, beginning to tick off a list on her fingers. 'He has a history with Livvy that doesn't sound healthy; he's still bitter about the way she left; he knows that path between the two properties like the back of his hand. And he's inherited the Hardacre talent with a rifle.'

'Those trophies at the farm aren't just his?' asked Samson.

'No. Shooting runs right through the family – his grandparents were national champions. But Oscar's no slouch on the range. Pretty nifty with clays, too. My money would be on him. Not that I've given it much thought,' she added with a mischievous grin.

Samson laughed. 'Clearly not.'

'You've not tried speaking to him again then?' Delilah asked, tone light as she skirted the subject of the last week and her self-imposed exile from the office.

'I called him a couple of times, but he hung up on me.'

'I could—'

'No!' Samson cut her off before the offer could be made. 'Whatever Jimmy's uncovered at Rainsrigg is going to make our mystery letter writer desperate. And desperate means dangerous. I've got away twice with placing you in harm's way. I'm not willing to chance my luck – and your brother's wrath – a third time. Leave Oscar Hardacre to me.'

Instead of her habitual defiance, Samson saw consternation in Delilah's expression. 'So you think this might bring the shooter out of the woodwork? They might strike again?'

Samson nodded. 'Which means I'll be keeping an eye on Oscar.'

'And watching your back,' said Delilah.

'That too.'

She fell silent, eyes on her empty plate. When she spoke again her words were laced with sorrow. 'Do you really think it could be Livvy that Jimmy's found?'

'There's every chance of it. We both know this case has been spiralling closer and closer to home. And with the history of Carl's violence . . .'

'Not just Carl. I keep wondering if Oscar might have had something to do with it.' Delilah shuddered. 'Unrequited love can lead to drastic actions.'

'It's crossed my mind, too. When Tom came home that day knowing Livvy had sneaked back to Rainsrigg, perhaps he told more than just his wife?'

'And Oscar decided to act on it. Watching the Thornton house with his binoculars and waiting for a chance . . .'

'Only flaw is,' said Samson, 'why would Carl and

Marian Thornton lie for all those years about how Livvy died, if Oscar was the cause of her dying?'

'And conversely, why would Oscar Hardacre be trying to stop our investigation if Carl Thornton killed her? The whole thing is a mystery,' Delilah muttered, dropping her head into her hands with fatigue. 'What a day!'

It was shock. The hassle of getting stuck in the snow, followed by the sight of those bones . . . So upsetting, the oddly familiar shapes nestled in the fabric. She knew she would be dreaming about them that night.

Not that she was the only one stunned by what they'd discovered at Rainsrigg. She'd been in the kitchen with Jimmy when Sergeant Clayton and Constable Danny Bradley arrived and she'd watched them follow Samson up the garden. Seen young Danny wheeling away as he registered what was down there.

'You okay?' Samson was regarding her with concern.

She nodded. 'Just not used to seeing things like that. Being involved in things like this. I don't know how you do it for a living.'

He gave a half-smile. 'Like I said before, it's easier when you don't know the people involved. Putting Jimmy Thornton through all that today was hell.'

'Did you become inured to it? The violence? The death?'

She watched him consider the question, placing his cutlery on his plate and leaning back in his chair before replying. 'I'm not sure "inured" is the right word. The way I dealt with it was to put it in a black box and never lift the lid.'

'How very Bruncliffe,' she said with a light laugh.

He grinned at her. 'Yeah, it's not exactly what the police shrink would advocate.' The smile fell from his face. 'Seriously, if you need to talk . . .'

'Thanks. But I think I just need something to take my mind off it all. And it's not exactly good running weather out there.'

'In that case, I may have just the thing.' Samson got to his feet, cleared the plates into the sink, put the kettle on and disappeared downstairs. He was soon jogging back up to the kitchen, laptop in hand. 'I need a Facebook profile,' he said, placing the computer on the table and giving her a smile.

'You're going on Facebook?' She couldn't help the laugh that escaped her.

His smile morphed into a wounded look. 'What's so funny?'

'Nothing – just I didn't think . . .' she started stuttering, then saw the twinkle in his eyes.

'You're right,' he said, grinning again. 'Not my thing at all. But this is for work.'

'The Livvy Thornton case?'

He nodded. 'I had the bright idea of setting up a group for her old friends, maybe seeing if any of those who've moved away can shed light on what happened in the days leading up to her death. If Livvy came home in secret—'

'She might have met up with one of them!' Delilah was already pulling the laptop towards her. 'What a brilliant idea.'

'Thanks. But when it came to setting up an account, I was terrified of getting something wrong.'

'And ending up telling all of Bruncliffe what you were having for tea?' she teased.

'Or worse! Seeing as there's an expert on the team, however . . .'

'Sweet talk doesn't work on me,' she said, concentrating on the screen, her fingers flying over the keys. 'Luckily for you, coffee does. And chocolate.'

Samson took the hint. Delilah didn't even hear the front door close as he made his second trip to the Spar. Nor did she pay him any heed when he returned with a bag full of chocolate. And she devoured the Cadbury's Dairy Milk he placed in front of her without even glancing up from the computer.

'Done!' she exclaimed not long after, her smug smile offset by an endearing smear of chocolate on her cheek. 'That's your profile set up. I've made sure it's as invisible as you can be on Facebook, but there's still a risk of being found by some old school friend you'd rather not hear from. Or an old flame.' She grinned. 'So before I press the button and go live, are you sure you want to do this?'

'How big a risk?' he asked, thinking that school friends and former girlfriends were the least of his worries when it came to being tracked down.

She shrugged. 'Bigger than if you left Facebook alone.'

He thought about the trouble in London. Could doing this put his head too far above the parapet? Make him an easy target?

Then he thought of Livvy Thornton and poor Jimmy, his life being turned upside down by the past. This might help solve the mystery that was causing such upheaval.

'Of course,' continued Delilah with a glint in her eye, 'if

you've got something to hide, we could always set up the group for Livvy's friends using my profile.'

Samson sensed the reservation beneath the quip. She didn't trust him. Not fully. It made him reckless.

'Do it,' he said. 'Press the button.'

Delilah clicked on the screen and Samson found himself hoping he wouldn't regret the decision to step out from the shadows he normally dwelled amongst.

Shadows. Turning to dark. At Rainsrigg Quarry, PC Danny Bradley was standing outside the evidence tent Sergeant Clayton had sent up, trying not to get spooked as the night staked its claim.

At least the snow had stopped. It was scant consolation for the constable, stamping his feet to ward off the cold and wishing he was in the warmth of the Fleece, enjoying a game of darts with his mates. Anything rather than keeping watch over a grave of bones in the middle of nowhere.

The edges of the tent flapped sharply behind him, making him start.

'Just the bloody wind,' he muttered to himself, heart rattling against his ribs, eyes peering into the surrounding blackness, unable to rid himself of the feeling that he was being watched.

Danny Bradley was already counting the hours until he was relieved of duty.

Facebook made no sense to Samson O'Brien. Likes. Friend requests. Privacy settings. Status. Check-ins. After half an hour sitting next to Delilah as she walked him through the basics, his head was reeling.

'People actually enjoy all this?' he asked, face twisted in pain.

Delilah laughed. 'You'll get the hang of it. In the meantime, I'll monitor it for you. So don't go doing anything private on here for now, as I'll be able to see everything you do.'

Samson shuddered. 'I won't be doing anything apart from watching the group.'

Entitled *Friends of Livvy Thornton*, Delilah had kept it simple. What she'd called a 'pinned post' was at the top of the page, explaining the reasoning for the group and making it clear that the Dales Detective Agency was behind it. It included a brief explanation about the search for a death certificate and encouraged people to discuss their memories of Livvy, especially the last couple of weeks of her life.

'That ought to get people interested,' she said. 'I've kept it closed, too, which should prevent unwanted visitors.'

'So how do we get Livvy's friends to join?' Samson asked.

Delilah pointed at the list of members on the sidebar, several names showing there despite the group having been live for such a short time. 'Word gets around,' she said. 'Plus I've invited a few key people, like Jo from next door.' She gestured towards the salon. 'She'll spread the news. I reckon by bedtime tonight you'll have a lot of discussion going on here.'

As she spoke, a red circle appeared at the top of the screen.

'More requests to join,' she said.

Samson watched on, impressed by the speed with which she navigated what to him was an incomprehensible world, as she clicked on the mouse and brought up the names of three women.

'Oh, Lisa Baldwin,' she exclaimed, leaning in closer to the screen. 'She used to have a massive crush on Will. What's she up to now?'

Delilah clicked on the name – one Samson barely recalled from school – and the image changed, the entire screen now devoted to one particular woman.

'It's Lisa's personal profile,' explained Delilah with a grin. 'And I'm being nosy.' She scrolled down: holiday photos, pictures of kids, the odd joke all rolling past. 'Tut-tut,' scolded Delilah. 'She's not got her privacy settings very secure. I can see everything. Let's see who she's friends with.' Another click and they were looking at rows of mug shots.

Samson was mesmerised by the sheer number of people claiming to be Lisa Baldwin's friend. And the places they came from. Bruncliffe, obviously. But also London, Manchester, Leeds, quite a few in France, several in Spain, quite a few in the US and a couple in Australia. 'How does she keep in touch with them all?' he asked.

Delilah laughed. 'It's Facebook. It's not about keeping in touch. It's about showing off! That's why most profile photos are shots of people on holiday.'

He turned to look at her. 'Have you uploaded a photo for my profile?'

She grinned. Clicked the mouse a couple of times. And there it was. Samson O'Brien's profile.

'Like I said, it's all locked down, with minimal personal info. No marital status or anything.' She grinned again.

But he was staring at the screen. At a photo of him and

Date with Mystery

Ryan Metcalfe when they were in their teens, Samson astride a quad bike, Ryan leaning against a barn to one side. Both of them were wearing T-shirts and jeans and squinting into the camera, the sun full on their faces, giving them something of a cowboy air – James Dean, Dales-style.

'Where did you get that?' he asked, overcome with memories.

'It was on my phone. The original photo was pinned to Ryan's bedroom wall when he left to join the army. After he died, I took it. Made a digital copy. Sorry,' she said, sensing his emotion. 'Do you want me to change it?'

He shook his head, forcing a smile. 'No. It's lovely. Just a shock.'

A shock because he remembered the day vividly. Ryan had come over to help get the hay in. It had been a sublime summer's day, the two of them working hard alongside George Capstick under a hot sun, sweat running down their backs. They'd broken off at midday, returning to the house for something to eat. And his father had met them at the door. Camera in hand.

It had been a rare moment of sobriety for Joseph O'Brien. He'd insisted on taking photos, capturing the event for posterity, as he kept saying. All the while Samson was watching him for the first sign of trouble, the squinted glance in the image not merely because of the sunshine in his eyes.

But Joseph had turned all expectations on their head. He'd ushered them into the cool of the kitchen where he'd laid the table, the provisions Samson had bought in preparation already made into sandwiches, tea brewing in the pot. Not a drop of alcohol in sight.

And now . . . ? Samson suppressed the memory of his father at Fellside Court and the niggle of concern that accompanied it. The old man was fine. There was nothing to worry about.

'Thanks,' he said, glancing at Delilah. 'It's a lovely photo.'

She grinned in relief. 'I'll say. I reckon you two teenage gods will encourage a few women to get in touch. Now, in terms of privacy settings—'

Samson interrupted her with a raised hand. 'Enough,' he pleaded. 'No more Facebook. Not tonight. How about we head across the road for a quiet drink instead?'

She opened her mouth, as though she were about to say yes. Then she glanced at the kitchen clock. 'Damn! Sorry. I lost track of the time. I've got to go.'

And like a modern-age Cinderella, she jumped up from the table and ran down the stairs. He heard the front door slam and crossed to the window to see her still struggling into her coat as she began hurrying away, the street lights reflecting back up from the snow-covered pavements.

Seconds later a Range Rover pulled up alongside her, the blond head of Rick Procter visible as the window wound down. He said something. Delilah laughed. And got in.

Under Samson's sullen gaze, the Range Rover drove off towards the marketplace. A pumpkin coach being driven by a rat. When he turned from the window, Samson half-expected to see a silver shoe lying in the doorway.

Instead he saw the mournful features of a dog. Tolpuddle. Delilah had run off and forgotten him.

'Come on, boy,' Samson said. 'Let's go to the pub.'

*

'Just drop me there.' Delilah pointed at the bright facade of the Happy House Chinese takeaway on the junction of Church Street and Fell Lane.

'Are you sure? I don't mind waiting and giving you a lift back,' said Rick as he pulled the Range Rover into the kerb. 'How long can it take to choose a few books, anyway?'

He turned to look at her with a warm smile, his blond hair glinting in the light streaming from the takeaway. And Delilah thought she must be mad.

Rick Procter, good-looking to an insane degree. Incredibly successful self-made businessman. Well known for his charitable donations to local causes. And, more importantly, held in high esteem by the Metcalfe clan, even Will having nothing but good things to say about the man.

So why, when it was clear that he was interested, was Delilah not encouraging his advances? She'd even thought twice about getting in the car with him when he'd offered her a lift, but decided it would seem churlish not to.

She was definitely mad. Preferring instead a reprobate with a chequered past and a dangerous profession.

'Thanks,' she said, 'but the walk home will do me good.'

'We still haven't had that drink you promised me before Christmas,' Rick reminded her as she reached for the door handle. 'How about tonight? After you've been to the library.'

'Not tonight. Sorry. It's been a long day. But soon, I promise.'

Rick smiled and leaned over to kiss her cheek, but Delilah was already out of the car.

'Thanks again,' she said, waving as the door closed.

She waited until the Range Rover was out of sight before walking up Fell Lane towards her supposed destination. She'd had to think fast when Rick had asked where she was going; the library was the first place she'd thought of. Glancing over her shoulder to make sure no one was watching, she continued past the building with its shelves of books inside the windows, lights bright against the dark of the night, and on to Fellside Court.

No one needed to know about her visits here. Because no one needed to know about Joseph O'Brien's struggle. If word got out, all of Bruncliffe would hear and the man would be condemned in an instant.

She looked at her watch. She was late. Joseph had invited her round for tea and she'd completely forgotten. Still, she had plenty to tell him. Just wait until he heard that Samson was on Facebook. She was smiling with anticipation when Joseph O'Brien opened the door to her.

Delilah didn't notice the car parked in the shadows of an alleyway, lights off, the driver watching her walk straight past the library. And on to Fellside Court.

From the dark interior of the Range Rover, Rick Procter kept his eyes on her all the way up Fell Lane.

She'd not been telling the truth. He'd known it straight away. Delilah Metcalfe had to be one of the worst liars he'd ever met, those big eyes revealing her every emotion.

It had been pure chance that had placed him on Back Street as she left her office building, the slippery conditions underfoot providing him with the perfect excuse to pull over and offer her a lift. To try and persuade her to come for a drink.

Piqued by her refusal and her uncharacteristic deception, after dropping her off he'd turned left into the small lane just past the chippy and doubled back to where the alley met Church Street, providing him with the perfect vantage point for satisfying his curiosity.

Why would she lie about going to Fellside Court? Why the secrecy? She'd walked up the hill like she had something to hide, checking over her shoulder all the time.

He pulled out onto Church Street, heading back towards the marketplace, thinking hard.

Somehow it had to be linked to bloody O'Brien. The returned detective had been haunting his thoughts since that call from Leeds. What had he been doing at the house on North Park Avenue, trespassing where he had no right to be?

The man was a curse. A constant malign presence, sticking his nose where it shouldn't be. He'd been poking around Fellside Court before Christmas, a situation that had troubled Rick. But with reports from Leeds saying the second intruder had been a woman, it looked like Delilah could be involved as well. For Delilah's sake, he hoped that wasn't the case. He liked her. Really liked her. And he'd rather not have to deal with her in the way it was looking like he'd have to deal with O'Brien.

If it came to it, however . . .

Fingers tapping the steering wheel, the property developer drove slowly across the quiet marketplace, the snow and the cold keeping people at home on a dark evening. He turned the Range Rover into Back Street and saw two familiar figures crossing the road. O'Brien with that stupid hound of Delilah's. They headed into the Fleece, unaware of his scrutiny.

It was only as he was passing the burnt-out ruins of the rugby club on the edge of town that Rick Procter wondered about what he'd seen. O'Brien was in the pub with Delilah's dog. Yet Delilah had been heading into Fellside Court. Something she hadn't wanted anyone to know about.

Were they in cahoots? Was she helping him investigate another of Procter Properties' holdings?

Pulling into the kerb, Rick reached for the mobile in his jacket, ignoring the latest-spec iPhone stowed between the seats. It was time to do something about the returned detective. No more waiting for official channels to take him down. The man was too dangerous. And given his tenacity, Samson O'Brien wouldn't stop until he'd uncovered the truth behind the successful business that Rick had spent so long building up.

There were too many people involved to let that happen. Too many dangerous people.

On the prepaid mobile he entered the number he knew by heart.

'Boss?' A deep voice. No names. An added precaution.

'That problem we talked about,' said Rick. 'I've thought of a solution. Two birds with one stone.'

'I'm listening.'

Less than a minute was all it took. Rick Procter ended the call and slipped the phone back in his pocket, smiling at the neatness of it all. The sheer bloody brilliance of it.

The scourge that was Samson O'Brien would soon be taken care of. Permanently.

*

Many hours later, at a time when most of Bruncliffe's lights had been extinguished and the majority of its residents were tucked up in bed, a yellow glow still spilled from the window of the Dales Detective Agency.

Samson O'Brien was staring at his laptop, a cold cup of coffee and a half-eaten sandwich to one side, the dog bed in the corner empty. There was something about the Livvy Thornton case that he was overlooking. Like he wasn't seeing it right. A blind spot obscuring his view.

He sighed. He was getting nowhere. He logged off the computer, switched off the light and headed up to the second floor and the room he'd appropriated as a bedroom, aware of the silence in the building. It wasn't something that normally bothered him. But after a day with Delilah and then a couple of hours in the pub with Tolpuddle, Samson was missing the company.

Likewise, in the small cottage on Crag Lane, Delilah Metcalfe had yet to join her fellow townsfolk in slumber. She was sitting on the couch nursing a hot chocolate, Tolpuddle in his bed by the wood-burner. Luckily the hound was the forgiving type and had given her a warm welcome when she called in at the Fleece to collect him on her way home, having unwittingly abandoned him with Samson.

Now the dog was sleeping like an angel and Delilah was wide awake, tormented by the idea that poor Livvy Thornton had met such an awful fate.

Those bones. Every time she closed her eyes Delilah saw them, swaddled in fabric and soil.

Not wanting to be alone, she lay down on the sofa,

covered herself with a throw and listened to the soft snoring of the sleeping Weimaraner.

Up above the town, in the shadow of Rainsrigg Quarry, Constable Danny Bradley was wishing he was in bed. Instead he was sitting at the kitchen table of the Thornton house, the range ticking away quietly behind him. A quick cup of coffee and a chance to get warm. No one would blame him for abandoning his post, not when he could see the silhouette of the police tent through the window, its ghostly outline marking the evidence he'd been tasked with guarding.

Five minutes and he'd head back out.

He settled back in the chair, his eyes gritty and tired. He closed them. Felt the heavy blanket of sleep enfold him. Then he jerked awake. Senses alert.

A light. Muffled but visible by the side of the tent.

Someone was out there.

Jumping up from the table, the young policeman went scrambling for the door, throwing it open and running out into the night.

'Hey!' he shouted. But the light had already started moving away, flitting into the distance like a will-o'-the-wisp.

Danny scrambled for his mobile, fumbled it out of his pocket and turned on the torch, a thin beam of illumination picking out a path as he ran, feet slithering and slipping on the snow. Already the tent had been left behind, the trespasser heading towards the quarry, its inky nothingness looming ahead.

'Come back,' Danny shouted, his years of fell running

giving him the advantage as he began to gain ground. 'Stop!'

Still the dancing light moved away, deeper into the dark and the dangers of the quarry. Given better light and better luck, Danny would have caught it. And the person carrying it. But luck wasn't with him.

As he ran headlong into the hollowed-out arena that was littered with debris from its working past, his left foot snagged on something solid, tripping him, sending him flying. He sprawled across the rocky ground, felt his cheek smack against the cold earth and heard his mobile smash. Danny Bradley was plunged into darkness.

22

Early the following morning, the isolated solitude of Quarry House was broken.

With the snow having stopped and the snow ploughs finally getting the roads clear, under a cloudless sky streaked with the first fingers of light the forensics team and a couple of detectives had arrived. Now several police cars, radios crackling, were parked outside the cottage along with an unmarked vehicle, and around the back people were working in the garden, their white suits merging into the landscape.

What had been the Thornton family home had become a potential crime scene.

'Bloody kids!' Sergeant Clayton was muttering as Constable Bradley finished telling Samson O'Brien about his nocturnal adventures. 'Mucking about like that. Someone could have been seriously injured.'

'You didn't see who it was?' Samson asked Danny, the young policeman showing the strains of his long stint on watch, black smudges beneath his eyes, his jawline unshaven. And an angry red welt along his left cheekbone.

'Not a chance. It was pitch-black. All I saw was the light bobbing into the distance. And then I fell.' The constable shrugged, bony shoulders sharp beneath his uniform. 'I reckon Sarge is right. It was kids larking around.'

'But you didn't hear them?'

'No. Not a peep. Which is odd. But why would anyone else have been up here?'

'It was kids,' the sergeant reiterated. 'Trying to get gory photos to put up on Facebook or the like. Makes you wonder what the world's coming to.'

Samson didn't offer any rebuttal. Neither did he concur. For he had his own theories about who may have been trying to see inside the evidence tent, which was now busy with activity, and he wasn't keen to share them.

'Do they know if it's Livvy yet?' he asked.

Bruncliffe's sergeant rubbed a hand over his face as though he too hadn't slept well. 'Too early to say. We'll have to wait for the boffins to do their job. But I'm hoping it's not. Livvy Thornton was a lovely lass.'

'Did you know her well?' asked Constable Bradley.

'Not that well,' admitted the sergeant. 'She was a couple of years above me at school. Like everyone else, I was shocked when I heard she'd been killed. But I didn't for a moment doubt the version of events the Thorntons gave.'

Constable Bradley was frowning.

'Penny for them, Danny,' said Samson, knowing from past experience that the young man was astute when it came to crime, despite his lack of years on the force.

'I was thinking overnight . . . I mean, how could it be possible? To deceive people for that long in a community this tight-knit?'

'The Thorntons weren't from here,' said Sergeant Clayton. 'That would make it easier. No family to contradict their stories. And once Carl Thornton died, there was only Marian left who would have known the truth.' He shook his head in dismay. 'I just can't believe it. That Marian Thornton could be capable of such a cover-up. She was such a good woman. A regular churchgoer.'

Samson stayed quiet, thinking of all the people he'd come across who had masqueraded as decent folk while hiding heinous crimes. Going to church was no indication of innocence.

'But it doesn't make sense,' continued Danny, brow still furrowed. 'I mean, if Mr Thornton killed his daughter like we're presuming, then Mrs Thornton must have known about it.'

'You'd think so,' agreed the sergeant.

Danny shrugged. 'So why put Livvy in her will?'

'What's your point?' asked Sergeant Clayton, not as sharp as his protégé.

'My point is that if Mrs Thornton hadn't named her daughter as an heir, we'd be none the wiser about any of this.' He waved a hand towards the white tent billowing in the breeze, police tape fluttering around it. 'We'd have carried on believing Livvy died in Leeds. So why do something that would expose everything after years of covering it up?'

Sergeant Clayton gave Danny a world-weary look. 'Guilt,' he said simply. 'Mrs Thornton couldn't bear to go to her maker without unburdening herself. When you've been in this job as long as I have, son, you'll realise how powerful remorse can be. In fact,' he continued, turning to Samson, 'I wouldn't be surprised if that's what was behind Carl Thornton's death, too. Couldn't live with himself after what he'd done, so he took his own life. Aye,' he said, concentrating on the white-suited figures moving around the garden. 'That'll be it all right.'

Satisfied that he'd solved the mystery, the sergeant turned towards the house. 'Wonder how that tea's coming on,' he said, heading for the back door. 'Come on, Danny. Get yourself a brew and then we'll get you home.'

The young constable followed his boss into the farm-house, leaving Samson with his thoughts. And his foul mood.

He'd barely got settled in the Fleece last night when he'd got a text from Delilah, apologising for leaving Tolpuddle with him. He'd offered to drop the hound home, but she'd insisted on coming to the pub to collect him when she was done. Whatever it was she'd been doing. No doubt eating out with Rick in Procter-Properties-owned Low Mill, the converted mill at the edge of town that now housed trendy apartments and some upmarket boutiques. Plus a brasserie. A place Samson couldn't afford a coffee in, let alone a meal.

An hour and a half after her initial text – during which time Samson had been cajoled into playing darts with some of the regulars – Delilah had swept into the Fleece, all flustered, cheeks flushed, thanked him for looking after Tolpuddle and then, dog in tow, promptly left. With the darts game over, Samson had wandered back to the office feeling morose.

It was a feeling that had evolved into irascibility thanks to a fitful night's sleep, his dreams haunted by Rick Procter. Consequently, at this early hour thinking wasn't something Samson felt equipped to do, his mind sludge-like, synapses firing as poorly as his Royal Enfield engine on a cold morning. But Danny Bradley had triggered something.

Samson stood there in the shadow of the quarry, feeling the wind picking up, its sharp bite bringing the temperature down despite the emerging sunshine. He stared at the garden. And the old barn, the scene of Carl Thornton's suicide.

Then he gave up trying to force his brain into action and turned back towards the house. He'd had enough of the cold for one morning. And he'd had enough of watching what could be Livvy Thornton's grave being dug up by strangers.

In the kitchen of Quarry House, Delilah was making tea. Vats of it.

After a night sleeping on the sofa, she'd been woken by Tolpuddle leaping on top of her with his characteristic enthusiasm for the day ahead. Unfortunately, she hadn't shared his joy. A foul mood had descended on her overnight, leaving her tetchy and irritable, her eyes gritty from her restless sleep and her body stiff and sore from the cramped conditions of the couch. The prospect of a day sorting out her taxes hadn't brightened her temper. So when Samson had phoned to offer her a lift to pick up her car from Horton, she'd jumped at the chance to get out of the house and away from the tedium of her accounts. Luckily she had a dog-sitter already sorted, Joseph O'Brien having suggested the evening before that walking Tolpuddle occasionally might be good therapy. Given her Weimaraner's anxiety issues, Delilah thought the therapy might work two ways. Over the last week Tolpuddle had seen a lot of Joseph and was completely at ease in his company. It would be a good test to see if that affability remained once she was out of sight.

Fifteen minutes later Delilah had been handing over Tolpuddle's lead to Joseph in the marketplace, along with a packet of Dog-gestives to be used as bribes.

'Thanks, Joseph,' she said, leaning in to kiss his cheek. 'Call me if there's any problem.'

'No need to thank me. And don't worry,' Joseph said, registering the uncertainty on her face. 'We'll be fine. Won't we, boy?'

Tolpuddle looked up, ears cocked, and then nudged Joseph's pocket. The very same pocket containing the dog biscuits.

Joseph laughed. 'He's a fast learner.'

Man and dog had walked away without a backward glance, leaving Delilah to meet Samson at the office.

If Delilah's mood could best be described as waspish, Samson was like a bear with a sore head. On meeting her in the back yard, his greeting had taken the form of an acerbic comment about the missing Tolpuddle, asking Delilah where she'd abandoned him this time.

She hadn't graced him with an answer, her fuse way too short to risk replying and her conscience still smarting over her canine neglect. Instead she'd climbed onto the back of the Royal Enfield in silence. But while she may have been holding her tongue, she spent the entire ride out to Horton aiming silent curses at the broad back in front of her. When the bike pulled up alongside her Micra, Samson waited for her to get off before flicking up his visor and brusquely informing her that he was heading up to Quarry House, but there was no need for her to bother joining him.

'I'm sure you have better things for doing,' he'd muttered.

She'd thanked him for the lift, cleared the remnants of snow off the Micra's windscreen and promptly followed him. All the way up Gunnerstang Brow to Rainsrigg.

It was petty. She knew it. Watching him riding ahead of her, checking his mirrors to see the Micra still behind him. Knowing she was irritating him. But the pleasure she got from needling him quickly turned to guilt when they arrived at the Thornton house in tandem and the sombre context of their visit was emphasised by the collection of official cars. She'd quickly made herself busy.

Tea. Sergeant Clayton had brought supplies for the troops up with him but had done nothing more than dump them all on the kitchen table, possibly hoping that the tea-fairy would arrive and take care of it all. Or a woman, judging by his comment when Delilah appeared.

'Get a brew on, there's a good lass,' he'd suggested. 'We're all parched.'

Delilah had time to note Samson's look of surprise as she calmly turned and entered the house without the merest rebuke for the sergeant. Knowing there was nothing she could do to help the experts carrying out their work in the garden, she figured she might as well do something useful. If that meant conforming to Sergeant Clayton's stereotyping for once, so be it.

Raiding the boxes in the hallway for mugs, plates and utensils, she'd soon had tea brewing, bacon sizzling in a pan and a plate of doughnuts on the table. And now she had several hungry people hovering around the kitchen, all talking about the grisly discovery in the garden and the incident in the night.

Apparently Danny Bradley had disturbed someone at the evidence tent. He'd given chase, but the intruder had run off into the darkness of the quarry.

Delilah kept her suspicions to herself as she listened to the detective sergeant who'd come with the forensics team dismissing the episode as a prank. He broke off as the door opened and Sergeant Clayton walked in with a bruised Danny Bradley.

''Ey up, it's Forrest Gump,' said the detective sergeant to much laughter, Danny blushing scarlet at the attention. 'Shame it wasn't a sheep, eh, lad. You've probably had more experience running after them.' A lewd wink accompanied the comment, causing more amusement.

But Sergeant Clayton wasn't laughing. He was glowering ominously at his counterpart. Sensing the tension, Delilah stepped between the two sergeants, the first batch of bacon butties held out before her.

'Help yourself,' she said, placing the plate next to the doughnuts, bringing conversation, and potential acrimony, to a halt. She was refilling the frying pan with rashers when the back door opened again and Samson entered, face solemn. She caught his eye but he shook his head before making himself a cup of coffee and taking a seat next to Danny Bradley.

No news.

Delilah concentrated on the bacon curling in the pan, not wanting to think about the work being carried out beyond the window.

*

In the cosy kitchen of Quarry House, with the range kicking out heat and the smell of bacon frying, it was easy to forget what was happening outside. Samson sipped his coffee, surprised to find he had a raging appetite.

'There you go.' Delilah placed another plate of bacon sandwiches on the table, pushing it in his direction.

He took one and bit into it, feeling his mood lift slightly.

'What a mess,' Sergeant Clayton was saying between bites of doughnut, addressing his observations to the detective sergeant, the more senior of the two plainclothes policemen who had come with the forensics team. 'I never thought I'd see the like of this on my patch.'

'How long will it take?' Danny Bradley asked, glancing in the direction of the garden.

'Depends what they find,' said the detective. 'If it's random bones, it could take a while to determine their origin. Either way, we're treating the whole place as a crime scene for now. Which means nothing can be removed from the garden. Or this house.' His voice held more than a hint of warning and his gaze fixed on the two local policemen and Samson.

Sergeant Clayton bristled at the unnecessary explanation. 'I think we know how to treat a crime scene,' he muttered, finishing his doughnut and reaching for a second. 'Don't we, Constable Bradley?'

Noticing Danny's unease at being thrown into the tense atmosphere that was developing between the two sergeants, Samson changed the topic.

'How are you getting home?' he asked.

'I'll get a lift with someone,' said Danny.

'I can take you.' Delilah had turned from the stove. 'I won't be long here.'

The young man's face lit up, his tiredness pushed to one side, and Samson had to hide a smile.

'Or,' Delilah continued with a grin, 'you can persuade Samson to give you a ride back.'

Danny's gaze swivelled to Samson. 'Did you come up on the Royal Enfield?'

Samson nodded, still eating his bacon butty.

'Oh.' The poor lad. The dilemma was so clear. Have a lift down with the legendary Delilah Metcalfe, former Queen of the Fells. Or ride on the back of a vintage motorcycle.

Amused, Samson watched on as the constable tried to decide, not sure which option he would have plumped for at the same age. Now, it was a no-brainer. He'd combine the two and have Delilah up behind him on the motorbike.

'I think,' the lad said hesitantly, afraid of causing offence, 'I'll go with Samson. If that's okay.'

Chasing his sandwich down with a doughnut, Samson merely nodded again. But he caught Delilah's amused look before she turned back to the stove.

'Any more mugs?' The younger of the two detectives had entered the kitchen and was looking at the teapot with longing, slapping his cold hands together.

'In a box by the front door,' said Delilah, busy adding more bacon to the pan.

'I'll get them,' said Samson. He gestured for the detective to take his seat and headed into the hall.

Away from the warmth of the range, the hallway was chilly, a slight smell of damp coming from the cold slate floor. Lined along the walls were boxes and bin bags, evidence of Jimmy's hard work clearing the house, and halfway down the row was an open box full of crockery. On a pile of boxes next to it was a beige shoebox.

Beryl's Shoes.

It had completely slipped Samson's mind, the conversation with Matty Thistlethwaite seeming so long ago – Marian Thornton's bizarre bequest to her dead daughter.

'You taking young Danny home, then?'

The voice behind him made Samson start. Sergeant Clayton had followed him out from the kitchen and was now squeezing past him, heading for the stairs and, no doubt, the bathroom.

Samson nodded, heartrate picking up. He reached into the open box, making a show of pulling out a couple of mugs.

'Good, good,' said the sergeant, already partway up the stairs.

Samson waited until he heard the click of the bathroom door – the loud humming issuing from behind it telling him more about Sergeant Clayton's bathroom routine than he had a desire to know – then he grabbed the shoebox and moved to the front door.

Locked. No key in sight.

He was going to have to take it out through a kitchen full of policemen. Smuggle potential evidence away from what was now a crime scene, despite having been warned. Because even though he knew he would have Jimmy Thornton's permission to take the box, the minute the detectives or Sergeant Clayton sensed that what he held in his hands could possibly be linked to whatever lay in the garden, they would commandeer it before he'd had a chance to look at what was inside.

Samson was determined to prevent that happening. For unlike Sergeant Clayton, he had a gut feeling that the mystery of Livvy Thornton's death was a long way off being solved. In fact, he was hoping the contents of the shoebox would lead him closer to the answer. If only he could get it out of the house undetected.

The flush of the toilet told him he was running out of time. Box under his arm, he looked frantically around the hallway, hearing the click of a door upstairs, the humming getting louder, steps already on the landing.

Panic made Samson desperate. He grabbed the only option available to him and prayed he wouldn't get caught.

23

Afterwards Delilah would remember how focused Samson seemed when he came in from the hall up at Quarry House. But at the time, with her back to the room as she wiped down the worktop, she merely heard the clink of crockery as Samson set the mugs he'd gone to fetch on the table.

'Thanks,' she said over her shoulder.

Samson nodded, leaning back on the dresser, gaze fixed on the assembled policemen who seemed in no hurry to get back out into the cold. The red bundle on the dresser behind him didn't catch Delilah's eye.

'You off then, Danny?' Sergeant Clayton was coming through the hallway door.

'If that's all right, Sarge.'

'Aye, lad. You've done your shift. May as well take them back to the station on your way.' The sergeant pointed at the remaining doughnuts. 'Give them to the lads and lasses down there.' He turned to the detective sergeant with a sarcastic smile. 'Unless they're considered part of the crime scene?'

The detective scowled at him.

'Good.' Sergeant Clayton was rubbing his hands together, eyes still focused on the doughnuts, and Delilah was just forming the suspicion that his magnanimity might have sprung from more selfish motives when Samson spoke up.

'Best if Delilah takes them,' he said. 'Danny's with me on the bike. That okay with you, Delilah?' He was already reaching for the shopping bag Sergeant Clayton had brought everything up in.

'Fine,' she said, busy stacking the dishwasher.

She heard the rustle of the bag and then the scrape of chairs on slate as everyone got ready to go back to work.

'We'll let you know when we hear anything, O'Brien,' Sergeant Clayton said as he pulled his boots back on.

'O'Brien?' The detective sergeant was staring at Samson. 'Samson O'Brien?'

'The same,' said Sergeant Clayton before Samson could respond. 'Bruncliffe's finest. No doubt you've heard of him? He's been down in London working with the Met.'

'Oh, I've heard of him.' The detective's eyes narrowed, a knowing smile forming on his lips as he turned to Samson. 'I hear you've got a busy couple of months ahead.'

Samson didn't respond. He simply picked up the shopping bag and crossed to Delilah. 'There you go. I put your coat in there too, so you don't forget it.'

'Thanks,' she said, focused on him rather than the bag he was putting on the floor, trying to work out what had caused the tension in the room. She squeezed his arm. And he winked at her.

Hiding a grin, she turned back to the dishwasher. Unaware that she was about to become a criminal.

Samson followed Sergeant Clayton and Danny Bradley out of the door, glad to be away from the detective's scrutiny. And wondering if he'd done the right thing. Would Delilah get caught? She was so useless at lying, he hadn't felt able to tell her the truth. Better if she was unaware of the crime she was committing.

'Obnoxious bugger,' muttered Sergeant Clayton as they turned the corner of the house, heading for the Royal Enfield parked out front. 'Treating us like country bumpkins.' Then a grin split his face. 'He'd heard of you though, O'Brien. You're putting Bruncliffe on the policing map.' He slapped Samson on the back.

'I wouldn't go that far . . .' Samson said weakly, passing a helmet to Danny and getting the keys for the bike out of his pocket.

'Nonsense. You've achieved more than that runt ever will. I have to admit,' continued the sergeant while Samson started the bike, the throb of the engine echoing in the quarry, 'I wasn't happy when I heard you were back. Now I'm only hoping you'll stay.' He shook Samson's hand, gave him another slap on the back and then turned to Danny Bradley.

'You've got a perfect role model here, lad. Watch and learn.' With a nod of his head, he walked back towards the crime scene, leaving the young constable with a massive smile on his face and Samson with a sour taste in his mouth.

Gavin Clayton wasn't the sharpest of coppers. And he certainly wasn't one of the fittest. But he was honest. Having a man like that eulogising him was more than Samson could bear. As was Danny Bradley's look of admiration.

Slapping his helmet on, he pre-empted any further false praise and tried not to think of all the people he'd be letting down when his suspension – and the causes of it – became public knowledge.

*

Dishwasher on. Stove wiped down. Table cleared. It was only then that Delilah picked up the shopping bag, ready to go home.

The weight of it surprised her, first of all. Heavier than a few doughnuts and a bundled-up coat. But it was when she went to pull the coat out and put it on that she realised. Something was hidden inside it.

Keeping her back to the detective sergeant, who was still standing by the table talking quietly to his colleague, she peeled the red fabric away to see what it was concealing.

A shoebox. The Beryl's shoebox that had been out in the hallway.

She hastily covered it back up, heart thumping.

It hadn't got there by accident. Just jumped inside the bag of its own accord, wrapping itself in her coat for good measure.

Samson. The bugger! He'd been out in the hallway getting mugs. He'd taken the box and used her coat, hanging on a hook out there, to hide it. And now he was using her. Getting her to smuggle potential evidence away from a crime scene. Like she was his own personal mule!

She glanced at the two detectives. She could tell them. Or she could simply go back out into the hall and leave the box where Samson had found it. No one would know.

The young detective sniggered and then she heard Samson's name, rising from the hushed conversation. They were talking about him. It wasn't complimentary either, judging by the sly nature of their exchange.

Delilah's stubborn loyalty kicked in. She picked up the bag, said a cheery goodbye and walked out, neither of the detectives questioning why she was heading into the cold without a coat on.

To be fair, with the fear of getting caught and her anger at having been used burning inside her, Delilah didn't feel the cold at all.

She was going to be furious. And while Samson knew there would be no avoiding it, perhaps there was something he could do to dampen the blaze of her ire.

'Two Americanos, please, Lucy. And a couple of your lemon-and-ginger scones.'

Lucy Metcalfe smiled at him from the other side of the Peaks Patisserie counter, a smear of flour on her face. 'They're Delilah's favourites.'

'I'm banking on that,' he said, grinning.

Lucy raised an eyebrow, still smiling. 'In trouble with my sister-in-law, are you?'

'This is Delilah we're talking about,' he said. 'Of course I'm in trouble.'

'Well, if the scones don't work on her,' came a voice from behind him, 'pop next door with them. They'd buy my forgiveness any day.' Jo Whitfield from Shear Good Looks had joined the queue and was giving Samson a saucy look.

'I'll bear that in mind,' he said, laughing.

'How's your case going, anyway?' she asked, turning serious as Lucy put his order together. 'Any closer to finding Livvy's death certificate?'

'No definite leads as yet. I'm hoping the Facebook page might trigger something. Thanks for spreading the word, by the way.'

'Least I could do. It's a great idea.' Jo grinned. 'Good to see you've joined the modern age at last and signed up too.'

'Facebook?' Lucy was placing the coffee and scones in a paper bag. 'You've joined Facebook, Samson?'

He grimaced. 'Of sorts. I'm in a bit of a rut with the Livvy Thornton case and thought it might help. I don't feel very qualified to use it yet, though.'

Lucy laughed. 'I don't think any of us do – apart from our teenage kids. Any specific problems?'

'Nothing major. Just a general sense of inadequacy and a fear of doing something wrong. Although I wouldn't mind knowing what to do with friend requests from people I don't even know.'

'I'm the last person to offer advice on that,' said Jo, grinning. 'I ended up befriending a couple of people I've never met, thanks to a few glasses of wine on a Friday night. Now I'm too worried about causing offence to un-friend them, even though one of them is on the other side of the world!'

Lucy was laughing as she took Samson's payment and passed him the coffee and scones. 'The perils of social media,' she said. 'Almost as tricky to negotiate as a Metcalfe in a bad mood.'

'Here's hoping this does the trick,' said Samson as he took the bag and headed for the door.

Outside the air still held a bitter chill, the wind blowing from the east and refusing to be warmed by the bright sun above. He rode across the marketplace, spotting the Micra outside the front of the office as he cut along the top of Back Street.

Delilah had beaten him back from Rainsrigg.

343

He wasn't surprised. He hadn't exactly hurried on the journey into town. He'd waited outside the police station while Danny logged off his shift and had then taken the lad home, to one of the Victorian terraced houses on High Street where he lived with his parents. They'd stood for a while, talking about motorbikes, and then Danny's mother had appeared and started fussing over her son's bruises. She'd tried to persuade Samson in for a cuppa but he'd politely declined, making his way back to the marketplace and Peaks Patisserie to buy the sweetener for Delilah.

He knew he'd been stalling, delaying his inevitable return. She was going to be fuming. But at least she was home. Whether she'd managed to smuggle the box out, too . . . ?

Parking the Royal Enfield in the yard, he crossed to the back door. He'd barely got a foot inside the porch when he was met by a blur of grey. Tolpuddle, jumping up, happy to see him.

'How's her mood, boy?' he whispered, fondling the dog's ears and hoping his presence was a good sign. At least Delilah hadn't been so enraged she'd forgotten to collect him from wherever he'd spent the morning.

Tolpuddle just barked. And then sniffed hopefully in the direction of the scones.

'Not for you, I'm afraid.' Samson lifted the bag out of dog-range and passed through the ground-floor kitchen, which came with his tenancy but which he never used, and into the hall.

Would she be upstairs? He edged forward towards his office, the door open as always, and peered around the doorjamb.

She didn't even look up, chin resting on a hand, dark hair falling across her face as she stared at the contents of the shoebox splayed across his desk.

'I've brought treats,' he said with a cheeky grin, holding up the Peaks Patisserie bag.

Finally she lifted her head and stared at him, eyes steely, a scowl darkening her features. 'After the stunt you pulled this morning, there had better be more than just coffee in there.'

'What if I'd been caught?'

'But you weren't.'

'But what if I had been?'

The coffee and scones had dampened Delilah's rage, as he'd hoped. They hadn't extinguished it completely. Still sitting behind Samson's desk, the contents of the shoebox all packed away, she was leaning forward, hands flat on the surface as she glared across at him.

'You left me there surrounded by police officers and carrying stolen property.'

'Trust me, Delilah, if I'd told you what I was up to, it would have been worse. You're a hopeless liar.'

'How about just not including me in your hare-brained scheme in the first place?' she hissed.

He grinned at her. 'Are you sure that's what you want? To miss out on the thrill of being part of the Dales Detective Agency?'

Her lips snapped together and she frowned. And he knew he had her. She gathered up the plates and moved the empty coffee cups to one side and then pulled the shoebox towards her.

'It wasn't worth the risk anyway,' she muttered, lifting the lid and laying the objects back out on the desk.

Some photos of Livvy. A baby's shoe. A swimming certificate. An old rag doll and a home-made Mother's Day card. Some postcards from Australia. A tea caddy filled with Livvy's letters from Leeds. And a jeweller's box.

'It's just junk,' said Delilah, not hiding her disappointment.

Samson picked up the rag doll. Checked inside the pockets of its calico dress. Felt the soft limbs. Nothing hidden there. He did the same with the tiny baby's shoe, running his fingers around the edges, looking for something that would indicate it had been tampered with.

Another blank.

'Told you,' said Delilah with resignation. She opened the jeweller's box, the interior empty, its size suggesting it had once held a ring. 'I mean, why would you hold on to this?'

Samson took it from her, giving it the same scrutiny he'd applied to the doll and the shoe. But its velvet lining yielded nothing.

She was right. None of it was of any value, beyond sentimental. None of it threw any light on the case.

'I don't get it, either,' he muttered. 'I wasn't expecting this.'

'You didn't know what was in the shoebox when you decided to steal it?' she asked, incredulous.

'Not a clue. But seeing as it's mentioned specifically in Mrs Thornton's will, I thought it was worth a look.'

'*This* is in the will?' Delilah stared at the shoebox and back up at Samson. 'In what respect.'

'As part of Livvy's inheritance. Matty said she was left half of the estate and everything here.' He waved a hand over the objects cluttering the desk.

Delilah shook her head. 'Why would a mother go to the effort of listing all this in a will for a daughter who's already dead? It doesn't make sense.'

'Danny Bradley said exactly the same thing this morning. And he's right.' Samson flipped the jeweller's box closed and placed it back with the other items. 'Nothing about this case makes sense. But I was hoping this lot might have revealed a bit more about Mrs Thornton's motives.'

'You make it sound like all of this was deliberate. Part of a plan of some sort.' Delilah looked sceptical.

'Perhaps it was. However Livvy met her fate, Mrs Thornton knew she was dead. Yet she included her in the will. That's what I keep coming back to. Why would a mother do that?'

'So you think Mrs Thornton knew exactly what she was doing? That it wasn't all an indication of the early onset of dotage? Or merely a last wish to acknowledge her daughter in some way?'

Samson studied the objects before him for a moment and then looked at Delilah. 'I think Mrs Thornton has been leaving us clues.'

'Clues?' Delilah gave a wry laugh. 'Really? Like what?'

'First of all, including Livvy in the will. Mrs Thornton knew we wouldn't find a death certificate. Because there isn't one. She knew we would be forced to investigate. And in doing so, there was a high probability of us digging up the past—'

'And finding out about Carl Thornton's abuse of his family. You really think she wanted us to know that?'

'I'm beginning to suspect she wanted us to know everything . . .' Samson paused, remembering the first day they'd met Jimmy up at Quarry House. 'Rhubarb!' he said.

Delilah was looking at him warily. 'What about it?'

'Jimmy mentioned it, the very first time we went up there. He said his mother loved her vegetable garden. That one of the last things she'd said to him before she died—'

'Was to look after her rhubarb.' Delilah shrugged. 'And?'

'I thought you were a country girl,' said Samson with a grin. 'How do you look after rhubarb?'

'Trim it back in winter. Split the crowns—' Delilah's hand went to her mouth. 'Split the crowns! You have to dig it up to do that.'

'And when Jimmy did as his mother asked and dug up the rhubarb . . .'

'He found Livvy!' exclaimed Delilah. 'Good grief. Do you really think Mrs Thornton was that calculating?'

'I'm starting to think so.'

'But she must have known what would be uncovered. Not just Livvy, but the whole past . . .'

'And why would she do that, when she'd spent more than twenty years covering it up? Danny asked the same question up at Rainsrigg.'

'So? What's the answer?'

Samson stared at the baby shoe, the rag doll, the tin of letters. Then he looked up at Delilah.

'Revenge.'

Delilah flinched. Glanced down at the objects and back

at Samson, eyes wide. 'Really? You think that's what's behind all this? Marian Thornton is getting even with her husband from beyond the grave?'

'It's one way of looking at it. Let's face it, without her bizarre bequest, we wouldn't know any of this. Carl Thornton's abusive past would still be a secret and the lies about Livvy's death would still be believed.'

'But this is so . . .'

'Extreme. I agree. But at the moment there's no other explanation for any of it.'

'And the intruders Danny intercepted last night? Do you believe Sergeant Clayton's theory that they were just kids mucking around?'

'If they were, they were the quietest kids ever. Danny said he didn't hear a thing. No laughter. No carrying on.' Samson shook his head. 'I think it was more likely—'

'Our anonymous letter writer,' said Delilah, nodding. 'I agree. And given the conditions, Oscar Hardacre is looking like the most suitable candidate. Getting up to Rainsrigg in that weather would have proved difficult for most folk. Oscar only had to walk up the track from the farm. But what was he after?'

'Tampering with the evidence?' suggested Samson.

'Which would mean he knows what's buried up there,' Delilah replied, looking appalled at the implication. She reached out a finger to stroke the calico dress of the rag doll lying on the desk. 'Poor Livvy. She didn't deserve—'

A crash of a door slamming open came from the back porch, interrupting her. Samson shot to his feet, crossing the floor in silent strides and pulling Delilah behind him as he stepped towards the doorway into the hall. Body tense, fists clenched, a roused Tolpuddle by his side growling softly, he inched along the wall. The clatter of footsteps running towards them and then Samson was moving forward, hands raised, grabbing hold of the figure that appeared around the doorjamb and, in one swift movement, flinging him against the wall, hand against his throat.

'It's me!' squeaked Danny Bradley, his lanky frame held up by Samson's grasp, the welt on his face lurid against his reddening cheeks.

'Jesus, Danny!' Samson released his hold, the policeman slumping back on the wall, an affectionate Tolpuddle nudging against him. 'Knock next time.'

Danny rubbed his throat, eyes full of admiration. 'Wow! You have to show me how to do that.'

Delilah meanwhile was watching on in shock. Those reactions. It wasn't the first time she'd seen Samson go into Ninja mode. The man was expecting trouble. Serious trouble. More than was justified by a handful of threatening letters or even a potshot with an air rifle.

Frank Thistlethwaite's warning echoed in her head.

'So what did you want that was worth risking getting flattened?' asked Samson with an apologetic grin.

'The bones,' said Danny, remembering why he was there. 'They've unearthed all the bones.'

'And?' whispered Delilah.

Danny was already shaking his head. 'It's not Livvy.'

24

'Sarge called me,' Danny continued. 'He said there's no doubt about it. That's not Livvy buried up at Rainsrigg.'

Delilah was staring at the young policeman, unsure how to react. Relief that Livvy hadn't met such an awful fate, or confusion that the mystery surrounding her death still remained unsolved.

'How can they be so sure so soon?' Samson asked.

'Because the bones belong to a dog.'

Delilah gasped, hand flying to her mouth as she collapsed onto a chair. 'Red!'

'What?' Danny looked puzzled.

'Livvy Thornton's dog,' said Samson. 'She had a collie called Red. He went missing at the time of her death.'

'Mrs Thornton told everyone he ran after the car involved in Livvy's accident . . .' Delilah paused, taking in the significance of this new information. 'It was all blatant lies. All the time Red was buried in the family garden.'

'The important question is why would Mrs Thornton lie about that?' mused Samson.

'Maybe because the dog was shot.' Danny's comment triggered another gasp from Delilah and a frown from Samson.

'You're certain of that?' he asked.

'Pretty much. Preliminary findings at the site are point-ing that way, but it'll be a while before we get official confirmation.'

'And what about the T-shirt. The bloodstains. Are they going to investigate those, too?'

'Thanks to Sergeant Clayton, yes, they are. The detec-tives didn't want to pursue it any further but Sarge insisted that, with the lack of a death certificate for Livvy Thornton and the allegations that her father threatened to kill her, we're looking at what is technically a missing-person case now. So the bloodstained clothing is going to the lab. Sarge has also suggested that the rest of the property be searched, but that'll need authorisation from higher up.'

Samson nodded, satisfied that Sergeant Clayton was tak-ing the case seriously. Then he noticed Danny Bradley's gaze.

'Is that . . . ?' The policeman was pointing at the shoe-box, its contents strewn across the desk, the photos of Livvy giving the game away. 'Did you take that from . . . ?' He looked at Samson, who grinned.

'From the crime scene? Yes, I did. But don't worry, I won't tell anyone you saw it.'

Danny was already picking up the items one by one, feeling them the same way Samson had. Searching for clues.

'It's just junk,' muttered Delilah, still thinking about poor Red, her chin on her hand, Tolpuddle's head on her lap.

'One man's junk . . .' murmured Danny. He flipped open the jeweller's box and stared at the empty interior, before turning to Samson. 'What is all this?'

'Mrs Thornton left it to Livvy. Along with half of the estate.'

'Samson's convinced she was actually leaving clues,' said Delilah. 'Although how an empty ring box can be an indicator of anything, I don't know.'

'Perhaps,' said Danny with a shrug, 'it's the fact it's empty that's significant.'

Delilah groaned and dropped her head into her hands. 'Honestly, this case. It's like a Chinese puzzle. I don't see how we'll ever solve it.'

Danny was already heading for the door. 'Much as I'd love to stay and help, I need some sleep. I'm dead on my feet.'

'You came over just to give us the news?' asked Samson, taking in the policeman's dishevelled state for the first time – a creased hoodie over a T-shirt and jeans, his hair standing on end as though he'd risen from his bed.

'I thought you'd want to know straight away,' said Danny, rubbing his throat with a grin. 'Next time, though, I might just call.'

'Much appreciated,' Samson said, shaking hands with the young man before he disappeared down the hallway the way he had come.

The back door slammed shut, leaving Delilah and Samson looking at each other.

'What now?' asked Delilah.

'Now,' said Samson, 'we have to start all over again. Because we still don't know where Livvy is.'

Delilah made tea while Samson got out his laptop. He was engrossed in his notes from the case when she returned to the office with two mugs.

'Are you getting anywhere?' she asked, placing the tea on the desk.

'God knows.' He sat back, running a hand through his hair in exasperation.

Delilah sat down opposite him, pen and paper in hand. 'Perhaps it might help if we try to fit what we've just discovered into the order of events.'

'A timeline, you mean?'

She nodded. 'Yes, but not for Livvy. For Red.'

Samson looked up from the computer screen. 'That's not a bad idea. Let's start with what we know.'

'Okay – so Red was in Bruncliffe up until Livvy left town.'

'How can you be so sure?'

'Because,' said Delilah, writing on her pad, 'according to you, neither Jo Whitfield nor Mrs Walker mentioned him being absent from the salon before Livvy moved to Leeds.'

'Good point.'

'So Red was here—'

'And alive,' Samson added.

Delilah bit her lip. 'And alive at that point.'

'After that . . . we were told he went to Leeds—'

'But he ends up shot and buried in the back garden of Quarry House.' Delilah shook her head. 'How is that possible? Do you think Livvy brought him back with her when she came home in secret?'

'Possibly – although we have no evidence of him ever being in Leeds. By contrast, we know he wasn't here during that time. Tom Hardacre was adamant that the postman would have been aware if Red was still around. And the same goes for Jimmy.'

A sigh of exasperation escaped Delilah's lips. 'We're going round in circles. Red is here right up until Livvy goes. Then he's missing while she's in Leeds. Yet the poor dog ends up buried beneath Mrs Thornton's rhubarb. It's not possible—'

'The shotgun.' Samson got to his feet and began pacing the floor. He stopped at the window and then turned to Delilah. 'Red was dead before Livvy left for Leeds.'

'How do you know that?'

'Tom Hardacre's testimony.'

Delilah cast her mind back to the farmhouse kitchen in the company of the Hardacres. 'Tom heard a shotgun fire when he was walking Jimmy back to Quarry House,' she whispered, piecing it together. 'Red . . .'

'Red was shot the night before Livvy left.'

'How awful.' Delilah cast a glance at the snoozing Weimaraner in the dog bed in the corner. 'Livvy must have been distraught.'

'Enough to make her leave home.'

'But who . . . why . . . ?'

'I suspect the who will turn out to be Carl Thornton. We know he had a quick temper. As to why he would kill a dog?' Samson leaned on the windowsill. 'I've a feeling that might be at the heart of this mystery.'

Tolpuddle stirred in his sleep, legs twitching as he chased something across his dreams. It was enough to trigger Samson's memories. Up at High Laithe, Lucy Metcalfe's place, in November. The time he'd been faced with certain death.

Tolpuddle had saved him. Leapt in front of a knife to save Samson, regardless of the danger.

'Red . . .' Samson muttered, toying with the idea. A small kitchen. A room filled with violence. One that had witnessed violence before. Add to that a shotgun and a loyal dog – the shotgun aimed at the one person that dog wouldn't allow any harm to come to.

'The shotgun wasn't meant for Red.'

Delilah stared at him. 'You mean Carl Thornton was going to kill his wife?'

'No. He was going to kill his daughter.'

Delilah was standing now, shock driving her to her feet. 'Livvy? She was the one he was aiming at? Why?'

'You heard what Jimmy said about trying to come between his father's rage and his mother. What if the same thing happened that evening? Carl flew into a temper, started beating his wife. Both Tom and Jimmy testified to Mrs Thornton having bruises, remember.'

'So you think Livvy tried to intervene, to stop her father?'

'That's exactly what Livvy was like. She would have tried to put a stop to it. But Carl got even angrier. Fetched the shotgun, intent on teaching his daughter a lesson . . .'

'And Red . . .'

Samson nodded. 'Red did what Tolpuddle would have done.'

Tears filled Delilah's eyes. 'He saved her. He saved Livvy's life.'

'He jumped up as Carl fired. Came between Livvy and the danger, like Tolpuddle did with me up at High Laithe.'

Delilah was nodding, tears on her cheeks. 'That's it.

That's why Red didn't go to Leeds with her. He was already dead. He sacrificed himself for Livvy.'

'Which means,' muttered Samson, 'he wasn't around when she came back to Rainsrigg.'

Delilah raised a hand to her mouth. 'Oh God.'

'If Carl Thornton was moved to raise a gun against his own daughter once,' continued Samson grimly, 'what would stop him a second time? What would stop him from killing Livvy when Red was no longer there to protect her?'

They were back at square one. The bones up at Quarry House didn't belong to Livvy Thornton and they were no closer to finding a death certificate for her than they had been when they started the search two and a half weeks ago. Apart from the fact that they now suspected she'd been killed at the hands of her father, rather than through the recklessness of an anonymous driver. And that Livvy had become a part of their lives.

For Samson, this case had become more than just a paperchase. It was personal. He was driven to discover what had happened to the vivacious young woman all of Bruncliffe remembered. They'd already let her down once, failing to intervene in the Thornton family with the simmering violence at its heart. He was determined the town wouldn't let her down in the matter of her death.

He would find her.

With the afternoon ticking by, Samson stood up from his desk, stretched his arms above his head and heard the click of tired bones. Too long sitting. He rolled his shoulders, loosening his neck muscles, and found himself cursing the weather. There was still a lot of snow on the ground, despite a day of sunshine. Too much for an out-of-condition runner like himself. He wouldn't risk going up on the fells today. Maybe tomorrow. When the hillside would be less treacherous.

He stretched once more and then stared at his desk. The contents of the Beryl's shoebox lay haphazardly across the surface.

He was still none the wiser as to their significance. If there was any. The way this case was going, it was more than possible that the objects in front of him were nothing more than they seemed – a random collection of memorabilia from a dead young woman's childhood.

Following Danny's revelations and their speculation about the fate of the beautiful Red, Samson and Delilah had spent an age looking at each of the items. Trying to pin some kind of relevance on them. But nothing had sprung to mind. They'd also talked over what remained an anomaly in the case – the anonymous letter writer. No matter how they looked at it, neither of them could find a way to fit Oscar Hardacre into the puzzling tangle of the investigation. If he was the mystery shooter, what was his motive for trying to protect the past? A question made even more perplexing if they were to believe that Carl Thornton probably had a role in Livvy's death.

Finally, after it was clear they were making no progress, Delilah had announced that she had to go, muttering something about a client in the mysterious manner she'd assumed of late. The lie was written all over her face.

Quelling the urge to ask her outright if this person who was taking up so much of her time was Rick Procter,

Samson had instead offered to look after Tolpuddle, earning himself a grateful look. In return, Delilah had agreed to accompany him on a security risk-assessment for Bruncliffe Social Club the following morning, Samson wanting the benefit of her technical knowhow when it came to the latest security gadgets.

Having fully intended to return to the Thornton case once Delilah was gone, when the back door closed and he was left in silence with the snoozing hound, Samson's concentration began to slip. Rather than carrying on trying to unpick the tangle of evidence, he found himself googling Procter Properties. Stalking Rick Procter across the internet.

Disgusted at his adolescent behaviour, he'd forced himself back to work. Half an hour later and he was ready for a break.

'Fancy a walk?' He directed his question at the dog, who was likewise stretching, paws extended over the edges of his bed.

They turned left out of the office along Back Street, past the salon next door and on past the antique shop, before crossing the road and cutting through a small lane which brought them onto High Street. Turning left again, they headed away from the town centre, shops and cafes giving way to residential properties and Bruncliffe's two schools. All the while, Samson's thoughts were on the case.

It seemed unsolvable. Yet the answers had to be there. They just weren't looking at it the right way.

As he walked beside the dog, wandering towards the outskirts of town, he forced himself to focus on what they knew, putting the events into chronological order.

Livvy Thornton had left home because of her father's violence and his threats to kill her. The night before she left, her dog had most likely been shot and killed, probably by her father. She'd moved to Leeds, where she lived and worked for several months, writing to her mother via Ida Capstick. When her father put an end to that communication with more threats, she had visited her mother in secret, a visit noticed by Tom Hardacre. A week later her family announced she was dead, killed in a hit-and-run in Leeds. There was no record of the accident. And no death certificate had been found as yet. Less than a month after that, Carl Thornton took his own life. Finally, more than two decades later, Marian Thornton died, leaving half her estate to Livvy in her will, including a shoebox full of mementoes.

With the facts laid out so clinically, it was easy to see how Carl Thornton had become their prime suspect. His history of domestic abuse, not least his promise to kill his own daughter if she came home, only damned him further.

But . . . the mystery letter writer. That was what was colouring the case. Twisting everything, so that what should be straightforward became complex.

Whoever the person was, why were they going to such lengths to protect the secret of Livvy Thornton's death? If, as Samson suspected, Carl Thornton had killed her, who would be trying to cover that up now that he and his wife were both dead? Not Jimmy Thornton, that was for sure. Whatever reservations Samson had harboured about the man, there was nothing staged in the agony the farmer was going through, as his childhood home became a crime scene and his childhood memories became nightmares.

Who then? And why?

What was he missing?

He stopped. A flash of comprehension like quicksilver across his mind. There, then gone. A fleeting idea that probably would have had a better chance of forming if Samson O'Brien hadn't suddenly become aware of his surroundings.

He was standing in front of Low Mill, deep in the heart of enemy country.

Samson stared at the old mill that had been converted into exclusive commercial premises and upmarket apartments, and the development that spread out from it: a collection of executive homes and town houses, all sold or under offer, according to the placard at the entrance to the complex.

Yet another successful Procter Properties project. The man had the Midas touch. And Delilah was in his thrall. She was probably in there right now, being wooed in the plush surroundings of the restaurant.

'What are we going to do about that, eh, Tolpuddle?' Samson looked down at the dog, who barked in the vague direction of the mill before turning away, tugging at the lead, far more interested in the nearby river.

All thoughts of the Thornton case chased from his mind, a dejected Samson turned his back on the symbol of Rick Procter's prosperity and walked down to the tumbling waters of the Ribble.

One day, he vowed to himself as he watched Tolpuddle run up to a group of ducks and scatter them into a squawking flapping of feathers, he would bring it all down. The entire kingdom of Procter Properties. He would expose its rotten core and bring it toppling to the ground.

'He's a good lad, no matter what Bruncliffe thinks.'

Sitting on the sofa in Joseph O'Brien's lounge, Delilah looked up from the photograph album laid across her lap, pictures of a young Samson arrayed on the page. Idyllic photos taken on Twistleton Farm. Samson in his pram, all chubby legs and cheeky smile. Samson on his first bike, gap-toothed and brave. Samson with his mother, a prize-winning tup between them, both of them laughing.

The images ended dramatically, the last few pages of the album blank. The record of his life had stopped when Samson was eight. When his mother died.

What would those missing photos show? The descent of his father into despair. The drinking. The hard work keeping the farm going.

But also the delinquency. The fights. The growing notoriety. The whispered scandals that delighted the likes of Mrs Pettiford. Then Nathan's christening, when this cherub of a child in the photo before her had turned on his own father and attacked him in public, before leaving town for good. On his father's Royal Enfield.

'You still think that, after everything he did?' Delilah asked gently. 'Despite what happened before he left?'

Joseph shrugged, a gesture reminiscent of his son, as though the weight of opinion from the town counted for nothing with him. 'There's a lot folk don't know about my boy.'

If the shrug had reminded her of Samson, so did the determined set to Joseph's face. There was no point in asking him to explain. To give the other side of the story. The O'Briens were past masters at playing their cards close to their chests.

'I'll have to take your word for it,' she said with a light laugh.

Joseph smiled. 'No need for that, Delilah. You're working with him every day. You'll know better than any what kind of man he is. I just wish the rest of the town would give him a second chance like you have.' He reached across from the armchair and patted her hand. 'You're a good friend. He's lucky to have you.'

She felt instantly guilty. And ashamed at how quickly she'd allowed rumour to sway her. A whispered warning from a man she'd only just met and she'd taken it as gospel. Ignored the evidence of the last few months working alongside Samson in favour of Frank Thistlethwaite's take on him. Which was based on what exactly? They hadn't even served in the police together.

Yes, Samson O'Brien had secrets. But so did plenty of folk in Bruncliffe. It didn't make him a bad person.

She closed the album and laid it back on the coffee table before reaching into her coat pocket and pulling out an envelope.

'Here,' she said. 'I came across this the other day. Thought you might want a copy.'

Joseph took the envelope and pulled out a photo. He stared at it and then looked up at Delilah, tears in his eyes. 'I remember that day.' He gave a choked laugh. 'Out of all of the fog of those years, all the memories lost in a bottle, this day I remember.'

He stood, crossed the room and placed the photo of a

teenage Samson and Ryan – the same one Delilah had used for Samson's Facebook profile – on the bookshelf, next to the silver-framed image of Samson and his mother.

'Thanks,' Joseph murmured, coming back to Delilah and putting his arms around her in a warm embrace. 'Thanks for everything.'

Delilah wasn't sure how to tell him that it was she who was grateful. Grateful that someone had made her see how bigoted she had been in danger of becoming.

She walked back to the office a while later with a lighter step than she'd had in a while. Samson O'Brien was a good man. Her instincts told her so. No matter what Bruncliffe and the likes of her brother thought. Besides, she was a fine one to be judgemental about his secretive nature when she was keeping him in the dark about his father's struggle to stay sober. Filled with a sense of shame, she entered the empty building and saw the shoebox still sitting on Samson's desk. She realised there was a way to make amends for her unjustified mistrust.

He'd be furious with her if he knew. But he wouldn't need to know until it was all over.

A couple of phone calls and it was arranged, an appointment that might just crack the Thornton case.

That it might also place her in danger, Delilah didn't allow herself to dwell on.

It wasn't until much later, as night crept in over the Dales, that the isolated solitude of Quarry House was re-established. The evidence tent had been dismantled, the forensics team had gone home, and with the bones exhumed from the shallow grave and the bloodstained clothing having been sent to the lab for testing, the two detectives had seen little cause to spend their department's sparse resources on establishing a guard at the house. What was there to protect?

Consequently there was no one present to witness the dark shape moving up the path, treading in the well-established footprints that patterned the snow. Likewise, the muffled crunch of glass attracted no attention. As for the torchlight that began moving through the empty house, it was so faint that, even if there had been someone around, it's doubtful they would have noticed.

Fifteen minutes later the figure re-emerged, hurrying across the exposed land in front of the quarry to disappear into the trees.

25

'There's been a break-in at Quarry House.'

Nine o'clock the next morning, with the sun out in a blue sky and the snow finally beginning to melt, Samson was exiting the lane that ran between Back Street and High Street, his mobile pressed to his ear. He ducked into the doorway of the bakery, trying to shield himself from the hustle and bustle of Bruncliffe on market day so he could better hear Danny Bradley. 'When?' he asked.

'Last night. Plainclothes lot didn't see any point in leaving a guard up there. Whoever it was had the place to themselves.'

'And no chance of being disturbed. Was anything taken?'

'Not that we can tell. Jimmy's going up there later this morning to check.' A slight shuffling noise came over the phone and when he next spoke, Danny's voice was significantly quieter. 'It might be worth giving Jimmy a call and telling him you've got that shoebox full of stuff, if you haven't already. You know, save any awkward explanations in front of those detectives who already think we're hicks.'

Samson smiled, grateful for Danny's shrewdness. 'I'll get straight onto it,' he said. 'Thanks. Any idea as to who it was?'

'Sarge reckons the same kids that were up there two nights ago.'

'What do you reckon?' Samson set far greater store by the constable's intuition than by that of his boss.

There was a pause, Danny considering his answer. 'Seems odd,' he admitted. 'Kids don't normally go to the bother of breaking in and then taking nothing. There was no graffiti left behind, either. But for a broken pane of glass, you wouldn't know there'd been anyone in there.' Muffled shouting came through the mobile. 'Sorry, got to go,' said Danny, 'Sarge is calling me. I'll let you know if we hear anything back from the lab about Livvy Thornton's T-shirt.'

'Thanks. I owe you.' Samson ended the call and sent Jimmy a quick text to tell him that the Beryl's shoebox was at the office. Before he'd put his phone away it beeped with Jimmy's reply, the farmer relieved to know that at least his mother's odd bequest hadn't been stolen.

Would it have been? Samson wondered. If it had been left at Quarry House, would the box of mementoes have been taken?

The person who'd interrupted Danny Bradley's vigil and run off into the quarry was most likely the same person who'd made the most of the empty house last night. And probably the culprit behind the two letters and the air-rifle incident.

Oscar Hardacre? Was it him? And if so, what had he been looking for? Could it have been the shoebox, the only thing Marian Thornton had specifically left to Livvy? Whoever it was, they were getting desperate. Cornered by their inability to keep the past a secret, they were becoming more reckless; more ruthless. A lethal combination.

Head spinning with the impossible case and yet another night of restless sleep, Samson stared at the bakery window, trays of sausage rolls and savoury pastries displayed inside it, the smell of fresh baking tormenting his senses. He tore himself away from temptation, promising himself a treat when the morning's meeting was done, and crossed the road to the Georgian property that housed Bruncliffe Social Club to wait for Delilah.

Security appraisals. They were a long way from the excitement of undercover work. But they brought in much-needed money and were a heck of a lot easier than locating Livvy's death certificate had turned out to be. It would make a nice change, Samson decided as he stood outside the front door of the social club. It was a place he hadn't frequented in years. Not since he'd dragged his father away from the bar that final time, a couple of weeks before leaving Bruncliffe for good. So he was glad Delilah had agreed to accompany him, not just for the moral support, but also because her expertise when it came to modern gadgetry was something Samson thought would add to the business.

He was looking forward to spending the morning with her.

If she ever turned up.

He scanned the street, expecting to see her hurrying towards him along the slush-covered pavement. Instead he saw his father in the distance, walking towards the marketplace. Assailed by guilt, Samson shrank back into the doorway of the social club.

Date with Mystery

Damn! It was already two weeks since that visit to Fell-side Court when his father's shaking hands and averted gaze had been enough to cause him worry. Two weeks in which he'd done nothing about it. He'd pushed it to the back of his mind and allowed the Thornton case to occupy his time, persuading himself that he was too busy to get involved.

In the cold light of a March morning, as he spied on his parent in the centre of town, Samson had to accept the truth behind his lack of filial responsibility. He hadn't done anything because he didn't want to admit his father might be drinking again. Anything but that.

From the cover of the building, he watched the familiar figure walk past Peaks Patisserie with a steady gait, a smile on his face. Reassuring himself that there was no need for concern, Samson was about to pull back out of sight when a shift in shape caught his attention. He squinted into the distance, hand shielding his eyes against the bright light as Joseph O'Brien stepped off the pavement, preparing to cross the road. There. That grey shadow beside his father. Was that—?

A deep bark echoed down the street.

Tolpuddle. His father was walking Delilah's dog.

Samson was puzzling over the presence of the hound when his mobile beeped again. Another text. He read it, stared back up the road at the distant figures of his father and Tolpuddle, and frowned.

Delilah Metcalfe was the world's worst liar.

He turned and entered the building alone, wondering where she really was. Because according to the text she'd

369

just sent, she'd cancelled their appointment in order to take Tolpuddle to the vet.

Trying to persuade herself that this wasn't a stupid idea, Delilah parked the Micra and took a moment to calm her growing nerves.

It was broad daylight. What could possibly go wrong?

She looked at the pristine glass in the passenger window, the echo of the shot loud in her memory. Perhaps she should send Samson another text, with the truth this time.

She picked up her mobile, but instead switched it to silent and slipped it back in her pocket. He wouldn't approve of her plan. He might even turn up and she would lose the chance to have a snoop around. And they would lose the chance to solve the Thornton case.

This was up to her. She was the only one who could do it.

Getting a grip on her shaking hands, she got out of the car, the sound of the closing door reverberating between the buildings to signal her arrival. In the doorway of the barn, overalls making his bulk look even bigger, he appeared.

Oscar Hardacre. A scowl on his face, thick arms folded across his massive chest, he didn't look overjoyed to see her. Neither did he look like a man interested in love.

Taking a deep breath, she crossed the yard towards him. Delilah Metcalfe was going undercover.

'Did Mother put you up to this?' The growl came from inside a pen of lambs, Oscar Hardacre feeding two with bottles while four more butted against his legs.

He'd led the way into the barn which was set up as a lambing shed, the large space marked out in smaller enclosures mostly containing ewes waiting to give birth, a few holding mothers and their newborns, and two set aside for lambs that needed hand-rearing. A warm smell of wool and straw draped over it all, punctuated by the tremulous bleats of the new arrivals. It was a scene familiar to Delilah, but even so she felt a tug of nostalgia and the awe and excitement which accompanied every lambing season.

All combined with the fear of knowing she was in the company of someone who might be dangerous.

'Cos I'm warning you,' the farmer continued, 'I don't have much patience for such talk this morning. Been up all night with a yow even Herriot couldn't save.'

'Guilty as charged,' said Delilah, forcing a grin. 'It wouldn't hurt to try. You might get lucky.'

'I've no interest in dating.' Oscar scowled. 'Women are more bother than they're worth.' He turned his attention to the lambs he was feeding, his solid back towards her.

As investigations went, it was not going well. Under the pretext of calling in to invite Oscar Hardacre to the next Dales Dating Agency speed-dating event, Delilah was supposed to be sounding him out about the past while pretending to sort out his love life. But she wasn't exactly getting the man to open up. And time was ticking. While Annie Hardacre had happily agreed to drag her husband to Bruncliffe market for the morning and leave the coast clear for Delilah to try and enrol Oscar in the dating agency, Delilah knew it wouldn't be long before Tom Hardacre was itching to get back to the lambing shed.

She was going to have to take a more direct approach. So she said the first thing that popped into her head.

'Was Livvy that mean to you? Did she put you off women for life?'

He jerked upright, triggering a furious bleating from the lambs whose milk had been abruptly taken away. Then he turned, face thunderous.

'Don't talk about her,' he snapped.

Delilah knew she should heed his warning. But there was something incongruous about the man standing there filled with rage while a small flock of tiny lambs stumbled around his legs.

'What did she do to you?' she asked, curiosity overcoming her caution. 'Everyone else in town is happy to talk about her. But you . . . I thought you loved her?'

He stared at her, stunned by her directness.

'I didn't know her,' she continued, 'but from what people say, she was wonderful. So I don't understand why you—'

Oscar stepped out of the pen, bottles still in hand, and advanced on Delilah. She took a step back, felt a metal barrier against her legs, trapping her, setting her pulse racing. He was inches away from her, leaning in, face up close and solid jaw set in anger.

'I'll not talk about her,' he snarled. 'And neither will you.' He raised his huge fists towards her. She flinched. Then she felt the milk bottles being thrust into her hands. 'Now make thyself useful and finish the feed. There's a yow needs seeing to.'

He stomped across the barn to a pen where one of the pregnant ewes was bleating loudly, leaving Delilah to enter the lamb enclosure. Trying to hold the bottles steady in her shaking hands as the lambs eagerly resumed feeding, she assessed her progress so far.

Information uncovered – zero.

Ability to annoy target – full marks.

But then she'd always had that talent. Growing up with five older – and much bigger – brothers, she'd been like a mosquito around a herd of elephants. Only able to get noticed by making a nuisance of herself. Oscar Hardacre, with his trigger temper, was a lot easier to provoke. Which might not be a good thing. It certainly didn't seem to be getting her anywhere.

She needed to have a look around. See if there was anything that might identify Oscar as the anonymous letter writer. Looking down at the now-empty bottles, Delilah realised she had the perfect excuse.

'These two are done,' she said, holding up the bottles. 'Want me to make another couple up?'

Oscar glanced across from the back of the barn where he was checking over the upset ewe. 'Aye,' he said distractedly, a concerned look on his face. 'Everything's set up in the outhouse. You know what you're doing?'

Delilah nodded.

'Thanks,' he muttered, his attention back on the sheep.

Doing her best to act naturally, Delilah crossed the yard and entered the lean-to attached to the rear of the farmhouse. Inside, a metal counter ran along one wall, a couple of tubs of milk-replacement powder stacked upon it, along with a kettle, a large plastic bowl and a container of clean bottles and teats. Adjacent to it was a sink, a plastic bucket on the drainer filled with more bottles in sterilising fluid.

As a veteran of the lambing season, Delilah was impressed. It was like a hospital. Clean. Organised. Even Will Metcalfe, the most conscientious farmer she knew, would have approved; Oscar Hardacre knew how to look after his sheep. He even had bags of Maltesers and liquorice allsorts on a shelf for those shifts in the wee hours when instant sugar was needed.

But she didn't linger to admire the farmer's set-up. Instead, leaving the dirty bottles by the sink, she moved across the room to the door at the back and turned the handle.

It was unlocked. The door swung open and, out of sight of the barn, Delilah entered the farmhouse.

By nine-thirty Samson was walking back down High Street. The meeting had gone well, despite Delilah leaving him in the lurch, and he'd drawn up a detailed security plan which the social club had accepted, asking him to oversee the installation of the system the following month. The Dales Detective Agency had a new client.

That the investigation into his alleged gross misconduct might well be under way by then and his position in Bruncliffe tenuous, to say the least, Samson hadn't made public to the club's management. He was living each day as it came, on a constant knife-edge of expectation that the lid was about to be blown off his past.

Delilah's erratic behaviour of late wasn't helping. If Rick Procter was privy to Samson's looming trouble, he hadn't told her. Not judging by her demeanour over the last couple of days. Since the snowball fight at Horton, she'd been her old self. Less distant. Apart from her odd disappearances. Like now.

He took out his mobile. Should he call her? He had every right to, given that she'd cancelled their appointment and he knew she was lying about the reason. But what if she was with Rick?

He ducked into the doorway of the bakery once again, phone in hand.

A few minutes of frantic searching in the Hardacres' kitchen, which had felt more like a year with her heart galloping and her palms sweating, and Delilah had found nothing. She'd opened cupboards, peeked into drawers and even rifled through a wallet lying on the table by a vase of daffodils. Not that she knew what to look for. A pair of scissors and a pot of glue next to some writing paper perhaps? Or a picture of Samson with a target drawn on his chest?

It had been a stupid idea. And she'd been gone long enough for Oscar to be wondering where she was. Plus she didn't think her nerves could take any more. It was time to make up the milk bottles and return to the barn.

She turned towards the door that led to the lean-to and in her haste, kicked a plastic container on the floor by the bin, sending it flying.

'Damn!' she muttered, scrabbling to pick up the papers and magazines that had come tumbling out. She was stuffing them back in the recycling bin when her hand froze.

On the slate tiles in front of her was January's edition of the *Dalesman*, a snowscape of white stone walls and rolling fields on the cover. Stretched over the top was the magazine's masthead, in vibrant yellow.

She stared at it, thinking of the jagged characters that had formed the second threat. Fingers trembling, she took out her mobile, flicking through her photos to find one of the anonymous letter. There.

Next Time I won't Miss.
Leave the Past alone.

She zoomed in and held it against the magazine. The 'a' of 'Dalesman'. It was identical to the 'a' of 'alone'. And the yellow 's' matched the final two letters of 'miss'.

The letter writer had used the *Dalesman* to help form the threats. And Oscar Hardacre, chief suspect, had access to a ready supply of the magazine.

A quick glance out of the window showed an empty yard. No sign of Tom and Annie coming back from the market. No sign of their son.

Delilah rifled back through the papers and magazines she had just replaced, pulling out copies of the *Craven Herald* and several editions of *Yorkshire Life*, until she came to the compact form of another *Dalesman*.

December. Masthead in bright red, with snow decorating the tops of the letters. None missing.

She carried on, aware of the clock on the wall ticking in the silence. Aware that the sands of her luck were slipping out, grain by grain. It had to be here . . .

There. Caught up inside a *Farmers Weekly*. February's edition of the *Dalesman*. Yellow masthead.

It was minus a letter.

A very neat hand had cut out the letter 'a'.

Heart truly thumping now, she flicked through the magazine. It was intact. Apart from that gap on the front. She looked at the masthead again. It was definitely the same. Was it proof? Enough to pin the blame—?

A door banging. In the lean-to.

Panicked, Delilah thrust the magazines in the bin, shoved it back into place and was heading for the kitchen door when she heard footsteps in the hallway beyond. It was too late. She was trapped.

She spun round, reached for the kettle and, when the door slammed open, forced herself to breathe calmly.

'What the hell are you up to in here?' growled Oscar Hardacre, blocking the doorway, face dark with suspicion.

'Cup of tea?' asked Delilah, turning towards him as she filled the kettle, sweet smile in place.

It took all of her effort to maintain it. Oscar Hardacre was holding an air rifle.

Voicemail. She must have her mobile turned off.

Samson shoved his phone back in his pocket. Where was she? First thing on a Thursday morning wasn't exactly a time for romance. Especially as Rick Procter was a busy man. Surely she couldn't be with him.

Forgetting his promise to treat himself, Samson turned from the bakery window to walk up the lane to Back Street. Perhaps he'd been too cavalier with those threatening letters? Dismissed them too easily? If whoever was behind them was desperate enough to break into Quarry House, then maybe they'd resort to other means to prevent the past from being uncovered.

Which would mean anyone investigating the Thornton case could still be in danger. Delilah included.

Where the heck was she?

With a growing sense of unease, Samson emerged onto Back Street, the office building opposite. When he saw PC Danny Bradley standing on the doorstep looking grave, he started to run.

'I don't have time for tea,' muttered Oscar, laying the gun on the table. Delilah tore her eyes away from it, her smile rigid.

'No,' she said. 'I suppose not.' She made a show of checking her smartwatch for the time, felt her throat constrict to see a missed call from Samson. She could do with him here. Now. 'Goodness,' she said breezily. 'I really had better get on.'

She moved towards the doorway, Oscar still between her and the only exit.

'I've changed my mind,' he growled, stepping in front of her. A large hand grabbing her upper arm, fingers digging in through her coat.

She froze. Thought of all the things she could have been doing this morning instead of putting herself in danger. Then Oscar was reaching towards the table. Towards the gun.

Fear soured her throat. She glanced out of the window, hoping to see a car turning in. Nothing.

'Here,' he said roughly, shaking her arm. 'Take it.'

She turned back to see he'd grabbed the wallet lying next to the weapon and was holding out a twenty-pound note.

'Put me down for that bloody date night.'

'Will do,' said Delilah weakly.

She took the money with trembling fingers and left, her feet moving quickly across the snow-streaked yard. Collapsing into the driver's seat of the Micra, she turned on the engine, shoved the car into gear, and pulled away. It was only when she was some distance from the Hardacre farm that she reached up under her coat and pulled out a copy of the *Dalesman* – the February edition with its yellow masthead.

Her foolish gamble had been worth it after all.

'It's human blood,' Danny Bradley announced, sitting at Samson's desk.

'They're sure of that?' asked Samson. He'd ushered the constable into the office, half-expecting to hear some dreadful news about Delilah. So Danny's revelation about the stained T-shirt they'd found with Red's bones was met with some relief.

Danny nodded. 'Definite. It'll take a while longer to know if it's Livvy's or not. But it's looking likely, given that it was found on her clothing.'

'So what now?'

'Sarge has been pushing for a more detailed search of the grounds up at Rainsrigg, on the basis that Livvy Thornton is effectively a missing person. Now we know it was blood on the T-shirt, there's more chance of that happening.'

'Poor Jimmy,' Samson murmured. 'What a thing to have to go through.'

'At least he'll get closure this way,' said Danny. 'He'll find out one way or the other what happened to his sister.'

One way or the other . . . This case which had started out as a search for a piece of paper had taken a macabre twist. One Samson wasn't enjoying.

'So given these developments,' continued Danny with an apologetic look and a gesture towards the desk where the shoebox with its puzzling contents was on display, 'perhaps that ought to find its way back to Quarry House.'

'Consider it done. I'll drop it up today,' promised Samson.

'How will you sneak it back in?'

Samson laughed. 'I'll think of something.'

'Did you get anywhere with any of it?' Danny had picked up the Mother's Day card and was reading the inside.

'Nowhere,' muttered Samson. 'If Mrs Thornton was leaving us clues, they're beyond my grasp. I've been looking at this lot for hours and still haven't found anything to link it all together.'

'Maybe it's not all meant to be linked.'

'How do you mean?'

Danny shrugged. 'I don't know. Perhaps some of this is just . . . camouflage.' He put the handmade card back in the shoebox and then looked at Samson. 'I mean, Mrs Thornton kept this whole mess a secret for more than twenty years. She was hardly likely to gather together a bunch of objects which would make that deception obvious straight away.'

'So you think she put some red herrings in here,' mused Samson. 'You could be right. Trouble is, how do we know which is a clue and which is merely a smokescreen?'

Danny scratched his head under his helmet, gave a

bemused laugh and got to his feet. 'Think I'll stick to formal police work,' he said with a grin. 'I'll keep you posted if there are any updates.'

Samson walked him out and was just closing the front door when the back door slammed and Delilah came rushing round the corner from the downstairs kitchen, face flushed, eyes wide.

'Samson! I think we've got him!' she exclaimed. In her hand she was brandishing a copy of the *Dalesman*, a glaring void in the masthead across the top.

Delilah Metcalfe definitely hadn't been to the vet's.

26

'You could have been killed!'

'You sound just like my brothers. And that's not a compliment.' Delilah glared at Samson across his desk, hands on her hips in defiance. 'You could at least acknowledge I did well.'

Samson sighed, collapsed onto his chair and stared at the magazine on the table. There was no arguing with her. And he had to admit, she had done well. Getting inside the Hardacre household without arousing suspicion. Having the presence of mind to stick the magazine up her jumper when Oscar caught her in the kitchen. And the calmness not to give the game away when he arrived with the gun.

Even so, the thought of what could have happened chilled Samson to the bone.

'Good work,' he said grudgingly.

She grinned at him, her anger dissolving in the face of his reluctant praise. 'And you haven't heard the best bit,' she said, brandishing a crisp twenty-pound note as she sat down opposite. 'I even got him to sign up for the next Speedy Date night.'

Samson burst out laughing despite himself. 'That really is good work. And you're saying Oscar had no idea why you were really there?'

'Not a clue.'

'Did you get any sense of a motive when you were talking to him?'

She shook her head. 'He wouldn't talk about Livvy. Closed the conversation down straight away when I broached it, and I didn't dare ask again. Especially not once he introduced a gun into the equation.'

'So we still don't know why he's doing this. *If* it's him.'

'It's got to be him!' Delilah leaned over the desk and tapped the copy of the *Dalesman* she'd brought back. 'How else do you explain this? Oscar Hardacre is our mystery person.'

'One magazine,' said Samson. 'You only found one with missing letters.'

'Only because I didn't have time to search the rest properly.'

Samson stared at the gap-toothed title. She was right. The font from the magazine was an exact match for some of the characters in the threatening letters. But something was still niggling at him.

Why? The same old question. What reason did Oscar Hardacre have for keeping Livvy's death a secret?

'You don't believe it, do you?' Delilah was staring at him in disbelief.

'Alibi,' he muttered. 'Let's establish whether Oscar was with anyone two nights ago when Danny disturbed the intruder. Or even last night.'

'Last night? What happened last night?'

'Quarry House was broken into.'

'You're joking! Was anything taken?'

Samson shook his head. 'No on both counts.'

Already Delilah was looking at the shoebox on his desk,

quick on the uptake. 'Do you think that's what they were after?'

'It makes sense. As much of any of this does. Could it have been Oscar?'

She shrugged. 'It's lambing time. Oscar's doing most of the work, which means long stretches out in the barn overnight. He could easily have nipped up to Rainsrigg and back without being seen.'

Oscar Hardacre. He had the history – obsessed with Livvy. He had the gun and the skill to use it. And now they knew he had access to the materials used in the anonymous letters. Samson was willing to bet that if they could pressure him into talking by threatening to go to the police, his motive would soon become clear. And the Thornton case might be solved at last.

'Although, hang on a minute . . .' Delilah was leaning forward in her chair, frowning. 'Oscar mentioned something about having trouble with a ewe . . .' She stared at the lino, trying to remember what she'd heard the farmer say through the fog of her fear. Then she groaned. 'Bugger!'

'What?'

'Herriot was with him last night,' she said, referring to James Ellison, the town's vet – otherwise known as Herriot, for obvious reasons.

'What time?'

'Oscar didn't say. He just muttered something about being up all night with a yow even Herriot couldn't save.'

Samson already had his mobile in his hand, calling the vet. He heard it ring several times and then the automated tones of voicemail. He left a brief message asking Herriot to call either himself or Delilah, and hung up.

'He'll be busy,' said Delilah with frustration. 'It's that time of year.'

'We'll just have to wait,' said Samson, standing up and putting his jacket on. 'We can't go accusing someone if there's a chance they're innocent. In the meantime, call in on Danny at the station and see if they have a rough idea what time the break-in happened. It could help establish one way or the other whether Oscar is indeed our man.'

'Yes, sir,' she quipped, pulling a mock salute. 'Anything else?'

'Tolpuddle. I reckon he's probably had enough of Dad's company by now.' Samson was pleased to see the surprise on her face.

'How did you—?'

'Delilah, this is Bruncliffe! Of course I know.'

She laughed. 'And you? Where are you off to?'

Samson was reaching for the shoebox. 'I've got to sneak this back into Quarry House without being noticed.' He grinned at her. 'Are you volunteering to help?'

Her look of response was pure Metcalfe.

It was a sudden decision. The type that often turned a case on its head.

Preoccupied with the prospect of Oscar Hardacre being behind the attempts to stop the investigation, Samson had set off for Rainsrigg on the Royal Enfield. The thought of confronting the farmer didn't worry him. What did concern him was Delilah Metcalfe and her attempts to go undercover. Until they could establish the veracity of Oscar's alibi, Samson wasn't willing to underestimate the man. Or the possibility that Delilah hadn't been as covert as she thought. Given how poorly she told lies, Samson was afraid that Oscar could have seen through her ruse. In which case, she'd placed herself in danger.

He should have told her, warned her to stay safe. But Samson knew that if he said anything she would dig her heels in and refuse to hide away. So instead he'd tried to steer her into company. Danny's. His father's. And he'd tried to make sure that faithful Tolpuddle was back by her side.

It was all he could do until they knew one way or the other.

With concern gnawing at him, when he reached the turn-off for Rainsrigg he made the snap decision to ride straight on.

Over Gunnerstang Brow and down the other side, he turned right at the main road, following the curve of tarmac around fields before taking a left, back on narrow lanes. Past farms and stone walls and sheep. Always sheep. Finally, at a remote crossroads, he turned towards the dark mass of Bowland Knotts.

The land soon changed as he climbed higher up the moor, the patches visible where the snow had melted no longer the softer green of the lower pastures but harsher, browner. It was a lonely place in human terms, isolated houses hidden from the road, the occasional track signifying their presence. Compared to the quarry, however, it was paradise.

Spotting a rough track up ahead, Samson swung the bike off the road and was soon dropping down to a farmhouse nestled in the hillside.

*

The bones were from a dog. The blood was human, possibly Livvy's.

In a farmhouse high up on the Keasden Road, the narrow lane which wound up over Bowland Knotts, Jimmy Thornton had been trying to make sense of it. Gemma was at work, a part-time teaching assistant in Bruncliffe Primary, and so the farmer was all alone with his thoughts. It wasn't a situation he liked finding himself in of late.

Over the last couple of weeks he'd had to re-evaluate his entire life and the role his family had played in it. Livvy, the older sister he'd adored, hadn't been killed in Leeds as he'd been told. Instead it looked likely she'd met a terrible end at Quarry House. And his mother, whom he'd had on a pedestal all his life, had turned out to be a liar. A teller of untruths who, in dying, had finally told a truth of sorts, leaving behind a document that would reveal the mess she'd kept so well concealed. As for his father . . .

For years Jimmy had blamed himself for his father's suicide. That argument he'd tried to prevent. His mother's harsh words. It had culminated in his father coming home from the pub and shooting himself in the old barn. Impossible, then, for a young lad of eight not to feel guilty – to believe that his actions had triggered the events which took his father's life.

Looking back with the benefit of recently acquired hindsight, things took on a hideously different complexion.

His father had been the one feeling guilty. His mother was the one who had fuelled that guilt. Co-conspirators in the mystery of Livvy's death – one carrying it out, the other concealing it – in the court of Jimmy's mind, they were both convicted.

He didn't think he could ever forgive either of them.

The purr of an engine outside disturbed his thoughts and with relief, he got up to see who was calling on him. He recognised the scarlet-and-chrome motorbike straight away.

'Are you sure I'm not disturbing you?' Shoebox under his arm, Samson took a seat at the wooden table in the heart of the kitchen, a wood burner blazing behind him.

'You've no idea how glad I am to be disturbed,' muttered the farmer.

'You've heard the news then?'

'About the bloodstain?' Jimmy nodded. 'Don't like to think what it might mean.' He sighed. 'Is that why you're here? Have you come up with something?'

'Not as such.' Samson placed the shoebox on the table. 'I was returning this to Quarry House and thought I'd get you to tell me what you make of it.'

The farmer approached the table, taking a seat opposite Samson and pulling the box towards him. 'Mother's legacy to Livvy.' He gave a wry laugh.

'Have you got any idea why your mother would have gone to the effort of listing this separately in her will?'

Jimmy was sorting through the contents, frowning. 'Not a bloody clue. Same as with this whole business. It's like I missed something growing up. Something the rest of my family were in on but neglected to tell me about.' He pushed the box away and rubbed his face in frustration.

'Do you think you could have another look? See if anything in particular stands out?'

'Stands out?' The farmer's laugh was devoid of humour.

'What, apart from my father possibly having killed my sister, and my mother having covered it all up? For twenty-four years?'

'Sorry. If you'd rather not . . .'

A large hand waved away Samson's apology and Jimmy reached into the shoebox and began placing all of the objects on the table.

They were so familiar to Samson now. The well-loved rag doll. The home-made card. The postcards, the photos and the tea caddy filled with letters. The swimming certificate. The tiny shoes. And the jeweller's box.

'Stands out . . .' muttered the farmer, frowning. He picked up the ring box and flipped it open. 'This.'

'Why?'

He gave a shrug. 'It shouldn't be empty. Mother used to keep her engagement ring in here.'

'She didn't wear it all the time?'

'No.' Jimmy grimaced. 'I always thought it was because it was too precious. That she was afraid of losing it. Now I wonder if it was because of how Father was. The way he treated her. And us.'

'Do you remember when you last saw the ring in there?'

'No.' A memory came to the farmer unbidden. A hand reaching out to touch his bruised face, the sparkle of diamond catching his frightened gaze. 'But I know when I last saw Mother wearing it. It was the night Father killed himself.'

'You haven't seen it since?'

'I don't think so. But I couldn't swear to it.' He gave another dark laugh. 'I'm not much help. It's probably with all the other important stuff, like birth certificates and so on.'

'You didn't come across it while you were clearing out?'

'Not yet, but then I haven't finished going through the dresser. What with everything that happened . . . I haven't felt much like going up to Quarry House lately.'

Samson totally understood. Especially now that the grounds were about to be dug up as part of the investigation into Livvy's death. 'Don't worry about it,' he said. He picked up the postcards, fanning them out, images of kangaroos and koalas and Sydney Harbour Bridge amongst them. 'And these?'

'Livvy's penfriend. She lives in Melbourne. They'd been penfriends for years. And then after Livvy died, she kept on writing to Mother. A couple of postcards a year. A Christmas card. That kind of thing.' The farmer shrugged. 'Right nice of her, really. To keep writing after everything . . .'

Surprised, Samson turned the cards over, the terse greetings on the back printed in a neat hand. He hadn't noticed the postmarks. Partly because they were smudged and almost illegible. Now that he looked closely, he could see the dates. All after Livvy's death, as Jimmy had said.

He slipped them back in the box.

'Is there anything missing that you would have expected to be in here?' he asked.

'Apart from Mother's engagement ring, you mean?' asked Jimmy with a wry smile. He scratched his head. 'I can't think of anything. To be honest, I'm surprised at this lot. Mother wasn't the sentimental type. She didn't make much fuss about Livvy's anniversary. She set more store on her birthday, marking it with flowers on the windowsill each year.' He shrugged. 'I guess we each have our own ways of acknowledging death.'

'One last question' said Samson, getting to his feet and picking up the shoebox. 'Did you tell anyone else that your mother had left this to Livvy?'

'Just Tom Hardacre,' said Jimmy. 'I tell him pretty much everything. He's like a father to me.'

Samson nodded. 'Thanks for your time. I'd best get this back to the house. And if you don't mind, not a word to Sergeant Clayton or the other detectives about me having taken it off the premises.'

Jimmy gave a sad smile. 'My lips are sealed.'

They walked out to the waiting motorbike, pillows of white clouds blowing across a backdrop of blue, the fields below the farm beginning to green up where the snow had melted.

'I'm sorry you're having to go through all this,' said Samson as he got on the Enfield.

The farmer gave a tired shrug. 'I'm trying not to be bitter about it,' he admitted. 'But it's difficult. Especially when it comes to Mother . . .' He shook his head. 'How could she have covered for him? Concealed the murder of her own child?'

'We don't know for sure—'

'Oh, come on!' said Jimmy, cutting off Samson's attempt to mitigate the involvement of Livvy's parents in her death. He cast a dark look at the fells, beyond which lay Rainsrigg Quarry. 'I think we all know what's going to be unearthed over there. I just have to find a way to come to terms with it.'

Samson didn't attempt to dissuade him a second time. He left the farmer standing in front of the farmhouse, a large man confused by the sudden turns his life had taken.

The news from Danny didn't clarify anything. Quarry House had been broken into between ten at night and eight o'clock in the morning.

A large stretch of time to play with.

Promising the constable that she'd go for a run with him sometime, Delilah left the police station and walked up to Fellside Court to collect Tolpuddle. She stayed for a short while, chatting to Joseph and his friends, and then headed back to the office. She was only just in the back door when her mobile rang.

Herriot. With the sound of bleating in the background, he answered her questions briskly, keen to get back to work.

She thanked him, hung up, and then thought about her morning.

She'd been an idiot. Putting herself in harm's way like that. Because it turned out that Oscar Hardacre's definition of all night was a lot shorter than Herriot's. The vet had testified that he'd left the Hardacre farm at one o'clock.

Oscar had had seven hours in which to visit Rainsrigg and break into Quarry House.

Feeling a sudden need to be cautious, Delilah broke with Bruncliffe tradition by returning to the porch and locking the back door.

Jimmy Thornton wasn't the only one confused. On the ride back into town, Samson didn't notice the scenery. His head was filled with missing engagement rings and flowers on windowsills. And something Ida Capstick had said.

Marian Thornton would have died for her daughter.

Ida was a sound judge of character, someone Samson would trust as a witness in any court. But her portrayal of Mrs Thornton didn't fit with a woman who'd covered for her murdering husband. The same woman who now seemed intent on the world knowing the extent of her sins.

Which was the real Mrs Thornton? And why did he have the feeling that he was missing something?

He let his thoughts roam over the facts of the case once more, sensing the answers were tantalisingly close now. And as he hit the outskirts of Bruncliffe, it came to him.

The missing piece of the puzzle.

Could it be . . . ?

By the time he reached the office, Samson could feel the quiver of anticipation that heralded the cracking of a case.

Delilah spent the rest of the morning trying to concentrate on the next Dales Dating Agency speed-dating night. Choosing to sit at Samson's desk with Tolpuddle by her side – thinking that at least from there she could escape out of the window if Oscar Hardacre came calling – she'd worked through the guest list, jumping like a nervous cat every time there was the slightest sound.

If this was what going undercover did for you, she wasn't sure she was cut out for it.

When she finally heard the solid thump of someone walking into the back door, followed by muttered cursing at it being locked, she felt relieved.

Samson was home.

Home. What was she thinking of?

Flustered, she got up and followed Tolpuddle into the hallway.

'The back door was locked!' Samson said in surprise as he entered, rubbing his forehead.

'I took the precaution of locking it,' she said. 'Oscar Hardacre doesn't have an alibi.'

He nodded, walked past her into his office, sat at his desk and opened up his laptop.

'Did you hear me?' she repeated, feeling slightly miffed that her news had been met with such composure. 'It's looking like Oscar is our man.'

'Yes.' He glanced over. Smiled. And turned back to the computer.

Intrigued by what was holding him so transfixed, Delilah leaned over his shoulder to look at the screen. 'Facebook? You're just in the door and you're already on there? You're getting as nosy as Mrs Pettiford.'

'What?' He glanced up again.

'I said you're becoming nosy. That's what Facebook is for. Keeping tabs on people.'

He stared at her, before looking back at the website, the Livvy Thornton page displayed before him. He clicked on the followers, opening up Jo Whitfield's profile. 'Keeping tabs,' he muttered.

'So when are we going to confront Oscar?' she asked.

He grunted, his focus on the screen. She heard the repeated click of the mouse.

'Should we go this afternoon? Strike while the iron's hot?'

'No need,' he said, without looking up. 'It doesn't matter now.'

She was about to argue when he froze like a pointer on the scent. He glanced quickly at the photos on his mobile, Delilah recognising some of the items from the shoebox. Then he shot to his feet and took her startled face in his hands.

'You,' he declared, kissing her on the forehead, 'are a genius.' He turned from the computer, grabbed his mobile and his jacket and headed into the hallway.

'What's going on?' she called after him.

The closing of the back door was his only response.

'What the—?' Delilah looked at Jo Whitfield's Facebook profile on the laptop, the hairdresser smiling out at her, and then down at Tolpuddle.

The hound simply raised an ear and tipped his head to one side. He had no idea what was going on, either.

He needed time to think. Away from the laptop and his office. Time to make those final connections, to see whether his growing suspicion had any foundations before he took action.

Because action would need to be taken.

With his parka zipped up against the sharp air blowing from the east, Samson turned onto the narrow path that bordered the tumbling waters of the river. Walking north, towards the distant white-capped fells and away from the town, he let his mind wander.

It was so obvious. Now that he was thinking straight. He was kicking himself for not seeing it before. He'd been intent on looking for what was there instead of looking for what was missing, even when Delilah had been so close to the answer. But how to go about sorting it?

He walked on, unaware that the sky was beginning to darken as afternoon yielded to evening. It was only as he arrived at the scattering of houses that heralded the boundary of Horton that he took any notice of where he was. And how far he'd come.

Feeling suddenly weary – and hungry – he turned back towards Bruncliffe. By the time he reached the marketplace he was footsore and starving. Picking up a takeaway from the Happy House, he got back to a darkened office building. No Delilah. No Tolpuddle.

Instead there was a scrawled note on his desk.

> *Have you cracked it? Call me if so. D x*
> *PS. Do I need to lock my doors?!*

He smiled. Sent her a brief text in reply. Then sat down to eat his meal alone.

He wouldn't be calling Delilah. Even though he was pretty sure he knew what had happened to Livvy Thornton. For if he was right, this was going to turn the town on its head all over again. And if he was wrong . . .

'She must be here somewhere.' Sergeant Gavin Clayton surveyed the garden of Quarry House and the small hole under the rhubarb that had sparked the police excavation. 'We'll find her. We'll solve this mystery and get the lass a decent burial.'

Danny Bradley was standing next to him, the cold wind filtering through his uniform, making his bones ache. He watched the forensics team wind up their search for the evening after a day digging into the soil under the menacing quarry face. And he felt a pang of sadness for the young woman he'd never known who'd met her fate in such a lonely place.

27

'You won't tell me?' Delilah was standing at the top of Pen-y-ghent, hands on hips, glaring at him as he struggled to catch his breath.

'Nope.'

'I thought we were partners?'

'I still can't tell you,' he gasped.

A jut of her chin and that glare he knew so well greeted his words.

'You're being ridiculous,' she spat. 'Come on, Tolpuddle.'

In a flash of trainers and grey legs, Delilah and her dog started back down the fellside, leaving Samson still recovering from the climb.

She was impossible.

Less than twenty-four hours on from what he'd been sure was a breakthrough in the Livvy Thornton case, Samson knew he had a long wait ahead of him, killing time until the news arrived that would tell him what he needed to know. Aware that the news might never come.

It was bad enough that he had to endure the agony of an investigation in limbo, without Delilah being in on it, too. Plus there was every possibility that he was wrong . . . So he'd decided to keep her in the dark, ignoring the texts begging for an explanation that she'd sent him the evening before.

But Delilah Metcalfe was no fool. As Samson had slipped out of the back door at seven that morning, intending to spend the day out of reach, she'd been coming up the path, a determined look on her face.

'You're here early!' she'd announced, taking in the motorbike parked in the yard with a frown of surprise.

'Actually, I was just leaving,' he muttered, thrown by her unexpected presence. Any earlier and she'd have walked in while he was in the shower, uncovering more than just his illicit use of her premises.

'Where are you going?' she demanded.

His normally quick wits deserted him, his heart still pounding at the close shave. 'Nowhere special.'

She'd grinned. 'Good. You can accompany me on a run then. It'd be a shame to waste such a lovely day.'

He could have said no. Just walked past her and ridden off, finding somewhere to while away the hours out of range of her burning desire to know what he'd unearthed in the Thornton case. But the devil in him had accepted her offer. Perhaps it was the definite hint of spring in the air. Or maybe he'd had enough of being on his own. Which was ridiculous – an undercover specialist no longer comfortable being alone. Either way, he'd said yes, telling himself that there wouldn't be much talking on a run up the fells . . .

He hadn't banked on a run up Pen-y-ghent.

She'd nearly killed him.

When the questions she'd fired at him on the drive over to Horton elicited nothing to satisfy her curiosity about the investigation, she'd set a gruelling pace on the first section of the climb, Tolpuddle loping along easily beside her. Samson had done his best to keep up, but before long he was struggling. Finally she'd waited for him, a glint in her eye.

'So,' she'd said as he staggered up to her. 'Feeling any more talkative?'

He'd managed to shake his head.

'Oh, come on,' she'd demanded. 'Tell me what you've uncovered.'

Another shake of his head.

'Why not?' she asked.

'I'm not sure I'm right,' he said between gasps.

'When will you know?'

He'd shrugged, gestures using up less of the precious oxygen he was sucking into his lungs.

She'd made a noise akin to a growl and ran off, Tolpuddle following her, up and up, towards the top of the fell.

She hadn't waited for him again. Not until she reached the peak. And now she was haring down the steep slopes back towards the car park. In the mood she was in, Samson didn't expect the Nissan Micra to still be there when he made his own way down.

With a sigh of resignation, he began running after her.

She was impossible. But she made life a lot more interesting.

The man was impossible.

Delilah felt her sour mood thumping into the ground with every footfall as she hurtled down the fellside. Why was he being so secretive?

Since he'd leapt up from his laptop and disappeared the day before, she'd heard nothing from him. Apart from a terse text saying 'Don't worry', in response to the note she'd left him. He was keeping her in suspense about the Thornton case and whatever it was he'd hit upon.

If he'd hit upon anything, of course. Perhaps it was all a show of pretence? Maybe he was no closer to solving the mystery than any of them. No closer than her. Or the poor sods turning over the soil up at Rainsrigg.

They'd be into another day of the search up there, which, from what Danny had told her yesterday, wasn't getting anywhere. According to the constable, they only had twenty-four more hours and then the manpower would be taken away. Budgets, he'd said with disdain, when she'd asked how that could possibly be enough time to conduct a comprehensive search. For while the garden of Quarry House was limited, the surrounding quarry stretched out into the distance, bordered by trees and woodland.

Livvy Thornton could be buried anywhere out there.

The situation filled Delilah with frustration. And now Samson had discovered something and was refusing to share it with her. Not even the morning run, which she'd orchestrated hoping to prise the truth from him, had made him relent.

Samson wasn't going to tell her anything about the Thornton case.

'Let's leave him to walk home,' she muttered to the dog as they ran the last stretch of track back to the car. 'See if that loosens up his tongue.'

But when Samson staggered up to the Micra ten minutes later, Delilah Metcalfe found she wasn't sadistic enough to make him suffer any more. Taking pity on the man, she held the door open and watched him collapse on the passenger seat, Tolpuddle leaning over from the rear to lick his ear.

'Thanks,' panted Samson. 'Does this mean I'm forgiven?'

She slammed the door shut and got in the driver's side. She might not be cruel enough to kick a man when he was down. But when Samson doubled over in cramp halfway home, she didn't hold back in showing her delight, her laughter finally breaking the heavy silence.

Ida Capstick was running late.

She'd arrived at the Dales Dating Agency – the official name in Ida's view, as that agency had pre-dated the subsequent one that now had its initials decorating the glass out front – a bit later than normal. And had been surprised to find the scarlet-and-chrome contraption that so fascinated her brother out in the yard, but no Samson inside.

Calling his name loudly, she'd made her way up to the top floor and knocked firmly on the bedroom door, hoping to prevent an incident like the one back in November. An incident that had left the image of a naked godlike figure lunging at her out of the dark seared on her consciousness. With that in mind, she knocked even louder. Then she turned the handle to release the latch, stood to one side and kicked the door open, keeping her eyes firmly fixed on the bathroom the entire time.

'Is tha in there?' she'd called out, gaze still averted.

There'd been no response. And when she finally plucked up the courage to look, she'd seen an empty bed. No sign of his sleeping bag which she knew would be stowed away, no evidence of his occupation of the room ever being left out on view.

Deprived of a chance to chat – this morning, of all mornings, when she had so much to say, with her cousin driving her demented – she'd made her way down to the first-floor kitchen. A cup of tea on her own, then.

She'd sat at the table, a couple of biscuits on a plate, mug in hand, and grumbled away to herself about her impossible relative, who had arrived the weekend before and was already proving unbearable.

'*Not clean*,' she'd muttered. 'Who does she think she is, saying my range isn't clean?'

Caught up in the turmoil of her domestic problems, Ida had sat longer than she intended. Consequently she'd been still up on the first floor when she heard the knocking.

Chuntering about folk calling round at ridiculous hours, she made her way down to the hall and was approaching the front door when she heard the knocking again.

It was coming from the back. Someone was at the porch.

Ida frowned. What kind of person knocked at a back door and then waited? Folk from Bruncliffe, where back doors were nearly always unlocked, knew better than that. Knock and enter, that was the custom when calling round the back.

Grumbling about modern habits, Ida made her way along the hall, through the rear kitchen and into the porch.

'What's tha wanting that can't wait for a decent hour?' she demanded as she flung open the door. Then she blinked at the figure standing there. 'Tha'd best come on in.'

*

'I can't believe you laughed at me. What kind of fiend laughs at someone when they have cramp?'

Delilah grinned at Samson as he limped up the back path, his right calf still giving him pain. 'Serves you right for keeping me in suspense. Or haven't you heard of karma?'

'Voodoo more like,' muttered Samson, stooping to pat Tolpuddle while Delilah fished her key out of her pocket. 'I can just see you sticking pins in a doll.'

She laughed, turning towards him as she opened the door. When she turned back she was face-to-face with the stern features of Ida Capstick, arms folded and standing sentry in the porch.

'Ida!' Delilah stepped back in surprise. 'What are you doing still here?'

'Most folk stay in when they know visitors are coming,' the cleaner said enigmatically, staring at Samson in disapproval. 'Tha's got some explaining to do, young man.'

Samson frowned and then his eyes widened. 'Already? I wasn't expecting . . . so soon . . .'

Delilah looked from the cleaner to her tenant and then back again. 'Perhaps,' she said, 'one of you would like to explain what's going on.'

Ida led them through the porch and the rear kitchen and past her cleaning bucket in the hall, before stopping outside the closed door of Samson's office. She put a hand on his arm.

'I hope tha knows what tha's doing,' she said.

Samson nodded. 'I think so.'

'Think? Tha needs to be more certain than that. There's a lot at stake here.'

Delilah watched him, his face pale, the glow of the exercise having faded in the shock of whatever Ida knew. Whatever lay behind the door.

'I'm certain,' he said. He looked at Delilah.

'Do you want me to wait out here?' she asked, sensing the delicacy of this situation that she didn't understand.

He shook his head, reaching out a hand to squeeze hers. 'No,' he murmured. 'I need you with me.'

And like a ringmaster at the circus, Ida opened the door and ushered them into the office.

'You came.' Samson was walking across to the figure standing by the window, back to the room, a hood pulled up. It wasn't someone Delilah recognised.

'Yes.' A woman's voice from behind the hood. Soft. Sensuous. 'I wasn't sure. But your message . . .'

'You didn't reply. I wasn't sure you'd come . . .' Nerves. Delilah could hear it in his voice. Samson was nervous about whatever this woman represented.

'I had to.' The figure at the window turned. Auburn hair tumbling out of the hood. Tears on the face – a beautiful face Delilah thought she should know, but couldn't place. 'He's all I have left.'

'I'm sorry—' Delilah began.

Samson turned at her words. 'Delilah Metcalfe,' he said, 'meet Livvy Thornton.'

28

'I think I need to sit down,' said Delilah, gaping at the woman standing the other side of Samson's desk.

'Tea,' said Ida from the doorway. 'Good and strong.' She turned, her heavy footsteps on the stairs breaking the ice.

'Strong tea,' laughed Livvy. 'I've missed that.'

'Here, let me take your coat.' Samson was holding out his hand, showing Livvy to a chair, the woman's beauty made even more vivid by the shabby surroundings of the office.

'Hello, darling,' she was saying, a hand on Tolpuddle's head, the Weimaraner clearly smitten. 'What a gorgeous dog. Is he yours?'

'Yes. But . . . how come . . . ? I thought—' Delilah didn't know where to start. She looked over at Samson, who was staring at Livvy, a huge smile on his face. 'You knew? This was your secret?'

'I thought I knew. But I wasn't sure.' He shrugged. 'Perhaps now you understand why I couldn't say anything.'

Delilah looked back at Livvy. 'Jimmy . . .' she said.

Livvy bit her lip. 'I'll go and see him. Put it right.'

'But I don't understand,' said Delilah, turning to Samson

again. 'How on earth did you find her? She's supposed to be dead.'

'About that . . .' Livvy looked up from petting Tolpuddle. 'It's probably best if I start at the beginning.'

Ida Capstick didn't think she'd ever heard the like in her life. A young woman returning from the grave after twenty-four years. It wasn't the sort of thing that happened in Bruncliffe.

As a consequence, she made the tea extra strong. Good for shock. Plus that lass looked like she needed fortifying – all those years away from home, amongst strangers.

Armed with tea that could fell an ox and a plate piled high with biscuits, she returned to the office. Livvy and Delilah were sitting next to each other at the desk and Samson was leaning on the windowsill. Ida took the remaining chair. There was no way she was going to miss out on what would be the story of the century for the town.

'It got unbearable,' Livvy was saying. 'He'd drink and come home violent. Then it got to the point where he didn't even need the drink as an excuse to hit her.'

'Was it always aimed at your mother?' asked Samson.

Livvy nodded. 'Always. He only turned on me when I tried to stand up for her.'

'So is that what happened? The night you left?'

'Yes. Jimmy was down at Hardacre's lending a hand with lambing and I was helping Mother get the tea ready, when Father came home drunk. He started shouting straight away. His meal was cold. The house was dirty. The dog was annoying him.' She shook her head. 'It didn't take much to set him off. Mother tried to placate him but it only made him worse, and then he hit her.' She reached in her pocket for a tissue, twisting it between her fingers. 'It was the last straw for me. I was seventeen. Old enough to leave home and start a new life. But I couldn't. Not while he was there. Not while he was treating Mother that way. I remember hearing the crack of his hand on her cheek and I snapped. I went for the shotgun.'

Livvy paused, the silence filled with the clank of the radiator and the soft sighs of a dozing Tolpuddle, the unremarkable contrasting sharply with the extraordinary tale unfolding.

'Were you intending to kill him?' asked Samson.

'I don't know.' Livvy frowned. 'I've asked myself the same question so many times . . . I think I probably meant to frighten him. But things got out of hand—' Her voice broke, the tissue in her hands twisted to tearing point.

'He took the gun off you?' Delilah asked gently.

'Yes. He turned and saw me in the doorway and he started laughing – like a demon – saying that if you picked up a gun, you had to use it . . . that he'd teach me a lesson—' She gulped, her voice dropping to a whisper. 'He wrestled it out of my grasp and knocked me to the floor. Then he pointed it at me. And then Red . . . beautiful Red . . .' A tear slipped down her cheek.

'He saved your life.'

Livvy nodded. 'Red jumped up, putting himself between me and the gun . . . There was this loud noise and it took me a moment to realise . . . Then I saw Red. And the blood.' She wiped the back of her hand across her face. 'Father had shot him.'

'Were you injured, too?' asked Samson.

'Yes. A couple of the pellets caught my shoulder. But I didn't realise it at the time. I was too focused on Red, crawling across the floor to him. He was dying . . .'

'And your father, what did he do?'

Livvy grimaced. 'He pointed the gun at me again. Shouting that it was all my fault. That I was to blame . . . I thought I was going to die. But then he just threw the shot-gun on the table, told me that if I was still there when he came back he would kill me, and walked out.' She reached for her mug with a trembling hand and took a drink of tea.

'How long was this before Ted Hardacre brought Jimmy home?'

'Not long at all. I was still cradling Red on the kitchen floor when they knocked at the door. Mother grabbed a hand-towel from by the sink and I gathered Red up in it and carried him into the pantry. I don't know how she covered up the blood. But somehow she managed to get Jimmy in and up to bed without him seeing anything. By the time she came back down, Red was dead.' Livvy lowered her head, her bottom lip trapped between her teeth. 'We buried him in the garden. I wrapped him in the T-shirt I'd been wearing – I wanted him to have something of mine with him . . . And when we got back in the house, Mother said I needed to leave.'

'It was your mother's idea? To go to Leeds?' asked Delilah.

'Yes. She was afraid. Afraid that Father would make good on his threat.'

'So she sent you to Mrs Larcombe.'

A smile flitted across Livvy's face. 'She was lovely, Mrs

Larcombe. A real lady. She helped me find a job. Let me come and go as I pleased. It was a totally different life. I was singing and getting paid for it and had almost completed my training at the salon . . .'

'And all the while you were writing to your mother in secret.'

'Thanks to Ida.' Livvy smiled at the cleaner, who waved away her gratitude.

'How did you father find out about the letters?' asked Samson.

Livvy shook her head. 'I don't know. Mother thought he must have seen one in her handbag or something. Either way, he told her to stop writing to me.'

'Humph. It was a bit stronger than that,' muttered Ida. 'He told tha mother he'd find thee and kill thee if she wrote again.'

'I know. She told me. Begged me not to contact her any more.'

'But you couldn't do it. You came home in secret to see her,' said Samson.

'How do you know about that?' asked Livvy, surprised.

'Tom Hardacre. He called up at the house about some chickens and heard you singing.'

Livvy laughed softly. 'Good old Bruncliffe. I've missed it so much.'

'So was that when you decided to die?' asked Delilah. 'When you came home that time?'

'Kind of. Mother wanted me to go away. Far away. And never see her or Jimmy again. But I couldn't do that. I couldn't leave them to his mercy. So I suggested that we fake my death . . .'

'It was your idea?'

Livvy nodded. 'Mother wasn't keen at first. So I said it was either that or go to the police. To try and get Father locked up. But Mother didn't want the trauma of testifying, of airing all the Thornton dirty laundry in public with a court case. So I convinced her that this way we could still meet up and he would never know. And when Jimmy was older, we could tell him I was alive . . .'

'Did your mother ever consider leaving? Taking Jimmy with her?' asked Samson.

A harsh laugh greeted his question. 'You didn't know my father. He'd have tracked her down. There was no way out for her. Or at least she couldn't see one. We were desperate . . .'

'And you were only seventeen,' said Delilah. 'Such a load to bear.'

Livvy nodded. 'I look back and I think of all the ways we could have done it differently. But at the time, there seemed to be nowhere to turn.'

'So where did you go after you . . . died?' asked Samson.

'To Southampton. The plan was to get a job on a cruise ship as a cabaret singer. I'd be gone for a couple of months at a time, but I'd be able to meet up with Mother in between. And there was little chance of bumping into anyone from Bruncliffe at sea.'

'But something went wrong . . .'

'Everything went wrong,' said Livvy bitterly. 'It was all my fault. I'd had an offer from an agent for one of the major cruise companies, who'd heard me singing in the Fforde Grene in Leeds. He knew I was underage, but he didn't seem worried about it. So I was all set to go abroad and disappear for a while. But I wanted Mother to know. So I sneaked home.'

'A second time?' asked Delilah, surprised. 'When was this?'

'In the June after . . . after I'd supposedly been killed in the accident. No one knew. Not even Tom Hardacre,' said Livvy with a dry laugh. 'I caught the train to Horton and then walked back across the fells and up through the trees to Rainsrigg. It was night-time. Dark. Only the owls out in the woods.' She stopped. Took a drink and then placed the mug back on the desk, her hands shaking. 'I was coming out of the trees when I heard the shotgun. I started running, thinking that this time he'd done it. He'd killed her. I ran so fast, across the quarry, and then as I reached the edge of the garden, I saw the light. In the old barn. I ran towards it—'

Delilah's hand crept to her mouth. 'Oh no.'

Livvy nodded. 'Father – he was there . . . the shotgun . . . It was awful.'

'You came home the night your father killed himself?'

'Yes. Talk about bad timing.' Livvy rubbed a hand over her face, as though erasing the memories. 'I was standing there, not knowing whether to be relieved or sad, and then Mother appeared. She took charge. Ushered me away. Told me no one could know I'd been here. That they'd think I'd done it. That my fake death would look suspicious now . . . I could be tried for murder.' She gave a weary sigh. 'I left on the cruise ship two days later. When it arrived at its destination, I got off. And I never came back.'

'Even though your father was dead?' Delilah asked quietly.

Livvy's smile was twisted. 'Yes. Such an irony. We were finally freed from his tyranny and yet, thanks to our attempts to escape it, I was no longer able to come home.'

'You weren't prepared to take your chances with the police? To explain what had happened?'

'I was. Mother wasn't. She said she couldn't bear for my life to be ruined any more than it had been already.'

'Where did you go?'

'Australia.'

Delilah looked over at Samson. 'The postcards.'

He nodded. 'They weren't from Livvy's penfriend as Jimmy thought.' He turned to Livvy. 'That was how you kept in touch with your mother, wasn't it? Postcards and the odd Christmas card, supposedly from your old pen-friend.'

Livvy nodded. 'Mother didn't even want that. She was so afraid someone would stumble on our secret and start making accusations. But I couldn't leave her not knowing I was okay.'

'Which is why you followed people on Facebook. To keep tags on what was happening at home.'

'On Facebook?' Delilah looked puzzled.

'It was Jo Whitfield who mentioned it first,' Samson explained. 'She said something about a friend request from someone on the other side of the world she'd never heard of. When you accused me of being nosy the other day, I was already toying with the idea that Livvy was still alive, and it seemed so obvious – if you want to stay in touch these days, you use Facebook.'

'So you found my fake profile,' said Livvy, impressed.

'Once I knew what to look for, it wasn't hard. I started

looking at the profiles of the women you were at school with. I searched their lists of friends, trying to find a common denominator. And there it was, a profile for a Vivian Walker. In Australia. I took a chance and sent her a message. And here you are. Although I have to admit, I thought it would take you a lot longer to get here.'

'I was already in London. I knew Mother had died . . . there was a notice on the *Craven Herald* website—' Livvy's voice trembled and she took a deep breath before continuing. 'I found out too late to make the funeral but something drove me to come home anyway, so I flew back a week ago. But I couldn't find the courage to take the next step. And then I got your message.'

It had taken Samson an age to compose the brief lines, trying to think of the right words that would tempt Livvy out of hiding. Sending it to an unknown person through the medium of Facebook and hoping to God that his hunch was right.

'"Come home. Jimmy needs you,"' murmured Livvy. 'You couldn't have chosen anything more likely to get me back here.'

'But how did you know Livvy was still alive?' Delilah asked Samson.

'Danny. He said we should be focusing on what was missing from the shoebox.'

'What shoebox?' asked Livvy.

'Your mother left you a shoebox in her will. That's what triggered all of this.'

Livvy's hand flew to her mouth. 'She put me in her will?'

Samson nodded. 'She wanted us to find you.'

'I thought you'd just found me by accident. I didn't realise . . .'

'I'm sorry,' said Samson as tears sprang to Livvy's eyes. 'I didn't explain when I contacted you. I thought it might frighten you off.'

'So you don't know what's been happening, then? About the missing death certificate and our search for evidence that you were dead?' asked Delilah.

Livvy shook her head. 'I just thought you'd got in touch because Mother had died. I had no idea what she'd done.' She wiped her damp cheeks with the shredded tissue in her hand. 'Poor Mother. Carrying that secret to her death . . .'

'It was her way of protecting you,' said Delilah. 'She wouldn't want you to distress yourself over it.'

'Aye,' said Ida Capstick, patting Livvy's hand with firm strokes. 'The lass is right. Just be thankful Marian left thee in her will. Tha's been given a way out of all of this.'

'Thanks to a shoebox,' said Livvy with a hiccup of a laugh at the absurdity of it all.

'A shoebox full of clues,' said Samson.

'So explain how you knew Livvy was alive thanks to some postcards, a rag doll, a pair of shoes and a jewellery box?' Delilah smiled at him, trying to lighten the atmosphere.

'Like I said. Danny Bradley pointed out that not everything in the box might be relevant. And that what was missing might also be important.'

'The engagement ring.'

Samson nodded. 'Mrs Thornton gave it to Livvy the night she left town for good. Am I right?'

'Yes.' Livvy looked surprised. 'Mother didn't have any money at the house. So she told me to sell it. To help finance my new life.' She stared at Samson. 'That was it? You worked out I wasn't dead because of an empty ring box?'

'Not quite. There was also the matter of Mrs Larcombe at the house on North Park Avenue. She denied any knowledge of you when Mrs Atkins at the salon enquired where you were after you failed to show for work. If you had really been dead, why would Mrs Larcombe tell people she'd never heard of you? It made me think she was hiding something.'

'She was hiding me,' murmured Livvy. 'We thought we could get away with telling people here that I'd died in Leeds. But for those living over there – it would have been too easy for them to uncover the truth. So as far as they were concerned, I just moved on.' She shook her head. 'So many lies. Over so many years. And yet you unearthed the truth so easily.'

'I wouldn't say it was easy,' said Samson with a wry smile. 'Your mother didn't exactly leave an obvious trail. In fact, if it hadn't been for Ida, I might never have spotted the clues.'

'Me?' Ida sat up in her chair, chin sticking out. 'There's nowt I've said that caused any of this. I'm not one for gossip.'

'It wasn't gossip, Ida,' Samson said, hands out to calm the indignant cleaner. 'It was something you said about Livvy's mother. When you told me why she'd stopped writing to Livvy, you said that Mrs Thornton would die for her daughter. But she wouldn't allow her daughter to die for her.'

'Aye. And what of it? That woman had a heart of gold. Just a pity she married such a wastrel.'

'It made me think,' continued Samson, turning to Livvy. 'About all the ways you can die for someone. Like giving them up, so that they can have a life free from an abusive father. I'm sure being separated from you was torture for your mother, a small death every day. But she did it so you could be free. And then continued doing it because she feared the consequences if the truth came out.'

Livvy broke down into fresh tears, Ida putting her arm around her and stroking her back.

'Enough,' said Delilah softly, taking pity on the sobbing woman. 'I think we've talked enough about the past for now. It's time Jimmy was reunited with his big sister and put out of his agony. And it's time,' she said looking at Samson, 'that Sergeant Clayton was told to stop the search.'

Samson organised a taxi to take Livvy up to the farm on Bowland Knotts, while Delilah showed her to the bathroom so she could wash the worst of her grief off her face. Then they gathered at the back door to see her off.

'It's good to have thee home, lass,' muttered Ida, embracing Livvy once more. 'Bruncliffe's in need of folk like thee.'

'Thanks,' said Livvy, kissing the older woman on the cheek. Then she held out her hand to Samson. 'And thank you. Both of you,' she said, turning to Delilah. 'If it hadn't been for your tenacity . . .'

Delilah put her arms around her, hugging her tightly. 'You were worth the effort,' she said, making Livvy laugh.

'I'll walk you to the taxi,' said Samson as Livvy pulled up her hood, tucking her distinctive hair under its cover.

With Ida and Delilah waving them off, they turned right out of the gate, Samson having asked the driver to wait on a side street out of sight of prying eyes, knowing the speed with which news of strangers travelled around Bruncliffe.

'Thanks,' Livvy said again as they walked down the ginnel. 'It feels so much better getting everything out in the open.'

Samson paused, Livvy stopping alongside him. 'Everything?' he said.

Her gaze dropped to the floor, then her chin lifted and she stared at him. 'You guessed?'

He shrugged. 'Not straight away.'

'Do you think anyone else will?' she asked, bottom lip trembling.

'Probably not. They'll be so caught up in having you back.'

'It was an accident . . .' she whispered. 'It all happened so fast. He was there. Cleaning the gun.'

'And he saw you?'

She nodded. 'He went into a rage. Knowing we'd deceived him. He started loading the gun . . . All I could think of was what he'd said to me the night Red died and I knew he was going to kill me. So I threw myself at him. Trying to get the gun off him.' Her voice dropped even lower. 'It was an accident,' she repeated, 'a horrible accident . . .'

'And your mother?'

'She was in the house. She came running when she heard the shot—' Livvy broke off and Samson took her hand in his.

'She knew straight away, didn't she? That you couldn't come back. That with you dead, she could pass off your father's death as a suicide caused by grief. But with you alive, there would be reason to suspect murder.'

Livvy nodded, too upset to speak.

'So she let you stay dead in order to let you have a life. And even in death, she left things so that if there was any blame, it would fall on her.'

'I don't know if I can live with that . . .' whispered Livvy. 'Letting her take the blame, if it ever comes out.'

'You have to,' Samson said. 'You owe her that.'

She nodded, glanced down at her hands and then back up at him. 'Will you tell anyone?'

Samson laughed softly. 'Not me. I'm the world's best secret-keeper.'

Relief washed over Livvy's face. 'Thank you. For everything.' She stretched up on tiptoe and kissed his cheek. Then she turned and walked towards the waiting taxi.

His last image of her was of that auburn hair, spilling out from underneath her hood as she twisted on the back seat of the taxi to wave goodbye.

When he got back to the office, Ida could be heard up on the top floor, finishing off the cleaning; Delilah was sitting at his desk, staring at the anonymous letters.

'It's all so obvious now,' she said, looking up as he entered. 'These were never meant to conceal Livvy's death.

They were written to protect her secret. The fact that she's alive.'

Samson nodded. Waited for her to make the connections he had made, once he realised that the missing piece of the puzzle was the most obvious one – the lack of a dead body.

'She was seen,' Delilah continued. 'Home when she shouldn't be. When she was supposed to be dead.'

He nodded again. He knew she was working through it all. The gun. The carefully crafted letters. The intruder at Quarry House, driven by the shock of hearing Livvy's body had been found when they knew it wasn't possible. The attempt to remove the shoebox in case it gave the game away.

He saw her hand move to her mouth. A gasp of realisation.

'Oh my God! What are you going to do?' she asked.

'First I'm going to shower and change into something more suitable,' he said, gesturing at his running kit. 'Then I'm going up there. And before you ask, you're not coming. This one I need to do alone.'

For once, Delilah Metcalfe didn't argue.

The farmyard was quiet. He parked the motorbike and walked across the yard. From within the barn he could hear the faint sound of a radio over the bleating of lambs, the silhouette of Oscar Hardacre visible stooping over a sheep pen.

Samson veered away towards the farmhouse, opened the back door, shouted a greeting and went in. Through the porch and across the hallway until he reached the kitchen door. Turning the handle, he entered the welcoming room, with its cluttered sideboard and the smell of baking.

'Oscar's in the barn.' A lone figure, standing by the sink. 'He says he's willing to talk.'

Samson shook his head, reaching into his pocket. 'It's not Oscar I've come to see. I wanted to talk about these.'

He placed the letters on the table, the mishmash of coloured letters garish against the wood.

A glance at the letters. A worried frown. Hands working nervously.

'I've worked it out,' Samson said gently. 'It took me a while. The rifle, you see. I didn't think—'

'That a woman could fire a gun?' said Annie Hardacre with a small smile.

Samson smiled back. 'Not quite. But I must admit, when Delilah said shooting ran in the family, I didn't think of you.' He glanced towards the trophies on the sideboard. 'How many of those are yours?'

'Most of them. I keep my hand in.'

'I'm grateful,' said Samson wryly.

She looked contrite. 'I was going to hit the bodywork, but you ducked down, offering me a better target with the window. It meant less damage to Delilah's car.'

Samson was struck by the consideration for Delilah, even as the act was intended to threaten.

'She nearly drove him mad,' Annie was saying, looking out of the window towards the barn where her son was working. 'Livvy Thornton. She was all Oscar talked about. All he thought about. And then she just upped and left . . .' She turned back to Samson. 'He was distraught. Obsessed. It wasn't healthy.'

'And when Livvy died?' Samson asked. 'Things got better?'

Annie nodded, fingers twisting in the folds of her apron. 'Yes.'

'Which is why you wanted her to stay dead.'

A sharp gasp gave her away, even if he hadn't already guessed the truth. 'You know? How—?'

'I found her. In Australia.'

'How is she? Is she well?' The concern was genuine.

'She's fine.' He wondered how much more to press. Whether it was better to leave the rest undisturbed. Another secret for Bruncliffe to harbour. But Annie Hardacre, after twenty-four years, had the look of a woman who wanted to share the burden. 'You saw it all,' he said.

A slight nod. As if words didn't come easily after all this time guarding them.

'You went up the path to the house for some reason and saw Livvy, alive when she was supposed to be dead. And her father . . .'

'He was shouting at her. Goading her. Then he started loading the gun—' She wiped a hand across her eyes, tears on her cheeks. 'I've never regretted not telling. He deserved it.'

'You helped her escape. Possibly even helped Marian stage the suicide.'

She nodded, more forcibly this time, as though un-ashamed of her actions. 'Marian was a wreck. We got Livvy out of the way and then . . . sorted things. No one ever guessed.'

'So when you heard we were investigating the lack of a

death certificate for Livvy, you panicked. Worried that someone would uncover the truth.'

'Yes.' There was a flicker of guilt in Annie's face for the first time.

'Worried, too, that Livvy would come back?' asked Samson gently. 'And ruin Oscar's life all over again.'

A hand went to her mouth, stifling a quiet sob. 'I didn't know what to do. I just wanted to stop you. I would never have hurt you.'

Samson crossed the kitchen and put his arm around the woman. 'It's okay,' he said, 'it's okay.'

Oscar Hardacre didn't notice the motorbike for some time. A couple of ewes lambing and feeding time for the orphan lambs – it was enough work for two, with his father off up the fells rounding up more sheep. Deciding to ask his mother for help, he emerged from the barn and in the bright sunshine saw the gleaming chrome and scarlet paint-work of the Royal Enfield. The back door opened and his mother appeared with O'Brien.

They exchanged a few low words, then the detective threw up a hand in greeting as he crossed to his bike. Oscar nodded in reply, aware that his mother was coming towards him.

'What did he want?' he asked brusquely, watching the departing motorbike.

His mother looked at him, a look of concern. And love. He shifted uneasily.

'Well?' he asked.

'Livvy Thornton,' his mother said, words so quiet he

had to strain to hear them. 'She's alive, son. And back in Bruncliffe.'

Oscar stared at the ground. The solid concrete of the farmyard. The familiar sound of the sheep behind him. The sun warm on him. He felt it all shift slightly. Then resettle.

'Right,' he said. 'Good. Best get on and get these lambs sorted.' He walked off, feeling the weight of her worry on his back. Then he stopped, turned, went back to her.

'I signed up for that bloody speed-dating session,' he muttered.

He knew she was smiling as he returned to work.

Jimmy Thornton was just in from feeding the yows. He'd taken off his boots and overalls and was drying his hands at the sink in the utility, savouring the smells of baking coming from the kitchen.

'Swear I heard a curlew on the moor,' he shouted through to Gemma, who was pulling a cake from the oven.

'Like heck,' she retorted with a smile. 'You're hearing things. They're a good couple of weeks off yet.'

'I know what I heard,' he said with a laugh. Then he spotted the taxi pulling up outside. ''Ey up,' he muttered, peering through the window. 'Who's this?'

It took a moment for him to realise. The implications of a taxi up here. It had to be bad news. They'd found something up at Rainsrigg.

He stepped out into the yard. Heart thumping. He saw the rear door open, a woman get out, hood up. She paid the driver and turned towards him, the car pulling away. Then she spoke.

'Hi, Jiminy Cricket.'

He thought he'd misheard. The nickname. The one only she used.

The woman put down her hood and he saw the hair. The face.

'Livvy . . . ?'

She was nodding, coming towards him, her arms open. He felt the tears on his face, heard Gemma calling from the house. And then she was hugging him. His sister. His very own Livvy. Back from the dead.

29

'What a rum do!' muttered Sergeant Clayton, pushing back his helmet and staring at the desolate landscape. 'She was alive all this time.'

'The *Craven Herald* will have a field day with this,' said Danny Bradley, eyes wide with amazement.

'As will Mrs Pettiford,' muttered Delilah, provoking a laugh from Samson standing next to her.

On Samson's return from Hardacre's farm, the two of them had ridden up to Rainsrigg on the Royal Enfield to break the news about Livvy's return. In the grounds of Quarry House, the forensics team were already packing away their equipment under the wall of rock that reared above them.

'We'll need a statement, most likely,' said Sergeant Clayton.

'I'm sure Livvy will be happy to produce one,' said Samson.

The sergeant scratched his head, pulled his helmet back into place and hitched his trousers up over his generous waist. 'Well, well, well,' he murmured. 'I don't think we've ever had the like around these parts before.'

'Will there be an investigation?' asked Danny.

'Into what?'

The young constable shrugged. 'I don't know. The lies. The reasons behind them.'

'Seems fairly cut-and-dried to me,' said the sergeant. 'A man beating his wife and daughter. Threatening to kill them. I'd lie, if it meant I could get away from that.'

'And they haven't broken any laws, have they?' asked Delilah.

'None as I can think of.'

'I still think it warrants more scrutiny,' insisted Danny.

'Aye, well, when you reach my age and you've got a bit more experience under your belt – and I'm not talking just doughnuts – then you'll see it differently. The lass is home. That's a better result than we were expecting to find up here. As for what happened back then, it's like Livvy told Samson. Domestic abuse. It were a mercy Carl Thornton took the way out he did. Even if it was over misplaced remorse. So enough about investigations and the like, young Danny. How's about you get over there and help them lads pack up instead?'

The constable cast a glance at Samson, shrugged and then wandered over to help in the dismantling of the tent that covered Red's resting place.

'He's sharp, that one,' said Sergeant Clayton watching Danny walk away. 'Reminds me of you.' Then he turned to Samson and, from the look in his eye, Samson knew that Bruncliffe's sergeant wasn't fooled by the suicide of Carl Thornton. The man was a lot more astute than Samson gave him credit for. It was something worth bearing in mind over the coming weeks.

'Right, we'd best go rescue Tolpuddle,' said Samson, turning towards the bike.

Delilah laughed. 'Yes, Ida's probably polished his paws and dusted his ears by now.'

'Thanks, O'Brien.' Sergeant Clayton shook Samson's hand with a firm grasp. 'I've said it before, but I'll say it again. It's good to have you back. And as for you, lass,' he turned to Delilah, taking a step back, a twinkle in his eye. 'You know how to make a proper brew.'

She grinned. 'I'll take that as a compliment.'

Shouting a last goodbye to Danny, Samson and Delilah walked away from the garden of Quarry House to the motorbike out front. The snow had melted, leaving the green of the lawn vibrant and sprinkled with the drooping heads of snowdrops. In the borders, a few early daffodils were opening in bursts of yellow, new life coming with the spring.

'We make a good team,' said Delilah.

Samson grinned. 'Of sorts.'

'I mean it,' she continued. 'Not just this case, but the others too. And the work for the social club.'

'What work for the social club? You didn't even turn up for the meeting!'

'I was busy,' she protested. 'But it's not too late to add my expertise. We should go into business. Properly.'

'Let me think about it,' said Samson.

Delilah pouted. 'Don't spend too long thinking. I might withdraw the offer.'

They reached the motorbike and Samson paused, turning back to her. 'You haven't asked,' he said. 'How I got on with the mystery letter writer.'

She smiled. 'Some things are better off not talked about,' she said. 'No harm done in the end.'

He stared at her, sensing a wisdom that sprang from a life lived amongst people – people she really cared about. Another one he'd have to be wary of in the coming weeks.

Then she took a deep breath of the fresh air that had a hint of warmth to it. 'So, back to the office? Amazingly, Clive Knowles has had a couple of enquires on his dating profile, which I need to field.'

Sensing she was as reluctant as he was to go back to work on such a lovely day, Samson shrugged. 'If you want. Although I thought I'd go and see my dad.'

'That's a great idea.'

He checked to see if she was being sarcastic, but she wasn't, her face flushed, slightly averted from him.

'Seriously, Samson,' she said, turning back to him with a smile as bright as the morning, 'that's a really great idea.'

Her smile and the sunshine made him reckless. 'Do you want to come, too? With Tolpuddle? We could go for a walk or something . . . ?' He grinned. 'Maybe even have a picnic down by the river. As long as we bring our coats.'

Delilah laughed. 'That would be lovely.'

Samson nodded, and was about to put his helmet on when he paused, head cocked towards the fells. 'Did you hear that?'

'What?'

'A curlew.'

Delilah listened, straining to hear the mournful cry of the bird that heralded spring in the Dales. She heard nothing but the caw of a distant crow and the whistle of the wind coming down through the quarry.

'You've been away too long,' she said, slapping her

helmet on. 'You've forgotten what a curlew sounds like. And besides, it's way too early.'

He laughed, got on the bike and started the engine, Delilah climbing up behind him. Thinking about families and secrets, and the burdens children were often made to carry, he rode down towards Bruncliffe. Spring was coming. On a day like today, it was possible to feel all would be right with the world.

Epilogue

'How long's he been in there?'

'Too early to say, guv.'

DCI Frank Thistlethwaite stood up, the smell of the canal mixing with the stench of the body lying on the towpath. It wasn't the best way to start such a lovely morning.

'Murder?'

'I reckon, guv. That jacket didn't get tightened round his throat of its own accord.'

Frank glanced at the tattered black fabric that was wrapped around the dead man like a garrotte. Whatever had occurred before the killing, the jacket had been torn to shreds in the savagery of it. 'Anything else of note?'

The sergeant held out a plastic bag. 'We found this in one of his pockets. Might be something. Might be nothing.'

It was a business card, a small laminate wallet protecting it from the watery grave that had held the man's body. Frank turned it over, taking in the name on the front. And he knew it was something. Something big indeed.

'Samson O'Brien,' he muttered.

'A private detective, by all accounts,' said the sergeant, gesturing at the card in Frank's hands. 'Reckon we might need to talk to him about this.'

Frank handed back the bag. 'Keep me posted on this one.'

He walked away deep in thought. Thinking about Samson O'Brien. The man was trouble. And it looked like trouble was about to catch up with him. In more ways than one.

Acknowledgements

As the third instalment of the Dales Detective comes to a close, it merely remains for me to express my gratitude to a brilliant bunch of people who have helped shape this novel. All of them have offered up their expertise willingly – what I have chosen to do with their advice in no way reflects on them. I owe each and every one a couple of Mrs Hargreaves' steak-and-ale pies!

First up, a massive thanks to forensic scientist Kevin Jack, whose patience with my rookie questions is unfailing and whose enthusiasm for his subject is contagious. Another man who shows no disdain for my amateur approach to his profession is Harry Carpenter – thanks for keeping the police bits as real as they can be in a work of fiction, Harry (and for providing great shelter on a bike!).

Someone else who keeps me company on a bike while sharing her knowledge freely is Catherine Speakman of North West Equine Vets. Being blindsided with random questions about Weimaraners and alcohol doesn't seem to faze her. I'll have to try harder. Equally, thanks to my two cousins (two of many), Josephine and Laura Taylor, who didn't blink when I bombarded them with queries about the note-taking habits of the younger generation.

A special mention in this book must go to the wonderful ladies that make up Austwick WI. Not only did they invite me to speak at one of their sessions but together they helped me name Tom Hardacre who walks across these pages – I only hope he doesn't disappoint you, ladies! And as always, I have to acknowledge the amazing support of my family – in a busy year, particular thanks to Claire for finding the time to read the first draft of *Date with Mystery*. Cheers, ears!

Three books in now and the team at Pan Macmillan are still excelling. A big thanks to my editor, Vicki, for putting me through my paces and encouraging me to produce my best, and to her fabulous assistant, Matt. I'm also indebted to the editing crew of Natalie, Mandy and Fraser, whom I continue to learn from and love working with. On the PR side of things, Alice remains the best publicist I've ever had the pleasure to work alongside – arigatō, Alice – and the sterling efforts of Andy have ensured that every bookshop in the north of England knows about the Dales Detective series. Last but not least, thanks to my agent, Oli – a great champion of my writing and a lovely man to have a pint with.

Finally, my eternal thanks go to the gods that sent me Mark – you're an absolute rock and after a manic twelve months, I reckon it must be my turn to cook by now. Luckily I know where I can get some cracking steak-and-ale pies . . .

The Dales Detective series continues in

DATE WITH POISON

Spring is in the air in the Yorkshire Dales, but not everyone is filled with the joys of the season.

Samson O'Brien of the Dales Detective Agency is being questioned by police about a murder, with the truth about his policing past about to be brutally exposed.

Delilah Metcalfe is busy defending Samson to everyone in Bruncliffe, when her nephew runs away from home and a frantic search begins. And with attention elsewhere, only a local vet is paying attention to a worrying spate of canine poisonings happening throughout the village.

Bruncliffe is turning toxic and with suspicion raining down on him, Samson knows he has to ask Delilah for help. Can she forgive his transgressions and help him so that they can find the missing boy and the poisoner, or has the poison already spread too far?

Read on for an extract . . .

Prologue

Half a kilo of minced pork. Half a tablespoon of salt. A light sprinkling of nutmeg and sage – not enough to overpower. Then a careful measurement of the secret ingredient, mixed in with a wooden spoon.

Outside, beyond the grime-covered window high above the worktop, darkness held the dale in its grip. But here, in the makeshift kitchen, the contents of the mixing bowl glistened beneath a stark bulb, a grey skein of empty casings spooled beside it.

Skins.

Fingers working them now, pulling them into place over the funnel, a routine so familiar. Slowly, to avoid any splits, the mixture was oozed into place.

A twist. A cut. Repeated.

Before the first light of dawn could penetrate the room, six sausages lay fat and tempting on a metal tray. Tempting. But toxic.

1

On an early spring morning, with a pale sun casting more light than warmth upon the town nestled amongst the fells, Bruncliffe's private detective was feeling none of the joys commonly associated with the season. In fact, he was feeling besieged.

Sitting in the office he'd occupied for the last four and a half months, Samson O'Brien was wishing he was as far away as possible. Up on the hills running. Down in London working undercover like he'd done in the life that now seemed a century ago. Anywhere but here in the room with the metal desk and rickety chairs, lino curling up at the edges of the floor and garish red-flocked wallpaper decorating the walls. With Ida Capstick sitting opposite him, her head thrust forward and a grim expression on a face that hardly ever relaxed into mirth.

'Tha has to help me,' she stated.

'What can *I* do?' Samson asked. 'This is a family matter. You'll just have to sit her down and tell her how you feel.'

Ida snorted, her head snapping away from him in disgruntlement. 'I've tried that. And I'm done trying. This needs sorting.' She turned the full glare of her gaze back onto him. 'Permanently.'

Silence fell on the room, broken only by the clank of the radiator as it struggled to combat the cold of the March morning which had blurred the glass of the window with condensation.

'I'm not sure I know what you mean,' said Samson, still captured by Ida's powerful stare.

Ida shrugged. Glanced towards the closed door and pursed her lips. 'She's got to go. By whatever means necessary.' The determined nod of her head underlined her resolve.

Samson gave a startled laugh, quickly choked back as that formidable gaze refocused on him. 'You're not serious?'

'I most certainly am. Tha must know someone? Someone from down in London? I'm willing to pay.'

And with that, Ida Capstick, Samson's former neighbour and current cleaner of the Dales Detective Agency, reached into her pocket and pulled out a roll of banknotes held tightly with an elastic band. She threw it onto the desk, where it rolled to a halt in front of him.

'I want thee to hire someone to persuade my cousin to leave. Before I kill her.'

Samson stared at the money and then up at the granite features he knew so well. 'I think,' he said, rising from his chair, 'we could both do with a cup of tea.'

In the office one floor above, Bruncliffe's purveyor of love, Delilah Metcalfe, was struggling to placate a customer of her own.

'He's an animal!' exclaimed the stylish lady sitting on the other side of the desk from the youngest of the Metcalfe clan. 'He smells like a farmyard, he could do with a good wash and as for his house . . .' A shudder rippled across the woman's shoulders as her face pulled into an expression of disgust. 'And if that wasn't bad enough, he knows nothing about romance. His idea of a first date was to take to me to the auction mart in Hawes!'

Delilah felt a bubble of laughter escape her, which she smothered into a hiccup. 'I'm sorry—'

'*Sorry?* I should think so. A day spent inspecting sheep is hardly an ideal backdrop for courtship. I half expected him to demand to see my teeth so he could assess my viability.' The woman drew herself upright in indignation. 'Anyway, I called in to say that if this is the calibre of clients on the Dales Dating Agency's books, I will be cancelling my membership immediately.'

The words were enough to quell any levity on Delilah's part as, with loans weighing down both her dating agency and her web-design business, the bank manager was shadowing her door. She could ill afford to lose a customer.

'I'm sure we can find someone more suitable for you,' she swiftly countered, turning to her computer and pulling up the disgruntled woman's file. 'In fact, how about taking part in a speed-dating evening? They're a great way to meet people in a relaxed environment and the next one just happens to be a week on Friday. I'm happy to waive the normal fee on this occasion . . .'

The woman's tense grip on her handbag eased somewhat and a small smile graced her lips. 'Thank you. I'd like that.'

Delilah nodded, adding the woman's name to the list of clients who had signed up for the event. An event that was technically already fully booked and now boasted a lopsided list of names. She was going to have to find another man to take part. And quickly.

'You're welcome,' she said, allowing none of her frustration to show. 'And again, please accept my apologies for your unfortunate experience.'

Unfortunate experience. It was a phrase that summed up Clive Knowles in a nutshell. A farmer from out beyond Horton to the north of town, with his low standards of hygiene and stubborn personality he was proving a hard man to find a bride for. The hovel that was Mire End farmhouse didn't help. But the man was desperate to get married – desperate enough to have offered Delilah a healthy fee if she managed to find him a wife in two months. Of which only just over a month remained. The prospect of that much-needed payment slipping through her grasp was a very real one because, as Delilah had suspected when she'd agreed to take him on, Clive Knowles was turning out to be a lost cause.

'For what it's worth,' said the woman, rising to her feet, her tone sympathetic now, 'I think you're wasting your time. Mr Knowles doesn't need a wife. What he needs is a cleaner!'

Delilah waited for the woman to descend the stairs and the front door to close in the hallway below before she allowed her head to hit her desk.

Across the other side of town, in a farmhouse just off the road that leads out past the dairy towards Bruncliffe Old Station, Liam Jackson was stepping out of the back door.

'You coming, old fella?' He glanced behind him at the border collie shuffling across the kitchen floor. 'Get a load of that fresh air. Spring's here!'

Alf, former English National Sheepdog Trials Champion

but now well past his prime, stepped stiffly over the threshold and out into the yard. He lifted his head and sniffed: daffodils from the verge that lined the road, and sheep from the lambing sheds down the track. Spring had indeed arrived.

In a routine established over the last two years since his working days had ended and he was granted the privilege of sleeping by the Aga, Alf hobbled forward, nose working overtime to compensate for his failing sight and muffled hearing. Making his way slowly around the perimeter of the large yard, he took in the scents that marked his world. The farm cats; oil seeped from the quad bike; sheep – always sheep; and . . . what was that? He lifted his head and sniffed again.

'I'll leave you to it, lad,' said Liam as Alf paused, head raised, nose twitching. Pained by the changes age had wrought in his former champion, Liam turned away, heading for the kennels where the younger dogs were waiting in eager anticipation of a training session.

Alf didn't hear him go. He was concentrating too hard on that unfamiliar yet tantalising aroma. Nose fixing on a direction, he shuffled towards the stone wall nearest the lane that ran between the farm and the back of the dairy. It was stronger there. A meaty smell. Tasty.

He almost walked past it, his eyesight so weak.

A treat. Tucked in by the wall.

Instinct made him glance back to where Liam had been standing, expecting to be told off. Warned away from an unauthorised snack.

But the yard was empty.

Alf lowered his head and bit into the unexpected delicacy. Two bites. Three and it was gone.

Warmed by the sunshine and the promise of life the season brought, he crossed to the house and settled down by the back door with a contented sigh. Head on paws, he was soon asleep.

2

'Tha'll sort it?'

'I'll do what I can,' said Samson as he escorted Ida Capstick down the hallway and through the ground-floor kitchen to the back porch. He had no idea how he was going to make good on that promise.

'Oh, and here,' said Ida, turning at the door and pulling a letter out of her pocket. 'It's a bit late getting to thee as George has been busy fixing a tractor. But then if tha will insist on living a life of deception, tha can't complain.'

Samson took the envelope she was holding out towards him, the line of disapproval that was her mouth letting him know, not for the first time, that she didn't approve of the lies he told on a daily basis. Lies about where he lived, concealing the fact from Bruncliffe – and his landlady, Delilah – that, thanks to a cashflow problem, he was temporarily camping out on the top floor of the office building amongst Delilah's old furniture.

'Thanks.' He glanced at the postmark. London. Five days ago. An official letter. It could only be one thing.

'Like I said, George didn't pick it up until yesterday. But then he won't have to fetch tha mail for much longer, will he?' Ida glared at him. 'Not now tha's been paid for the Thornton case.'

It was an arrangement Ida had never been happy about:

Samson living illicitly above his office while having his mail sent to his old address in the remote Thorpdale; an address where George Capstick, brother of Ida, was caretaker, looking after the farmhouse that had once been the O'Brien home but now lay empty, awaiting whatever plans the new owner had for it.

It was an arrangement Samson had felt was necessary for his safety – as well as his bank balance – protecting him from the dark past of his London life. But it was getting too difficult to sustain. And now that he had cash in his pocket following his last case, he was indeed taking steps to change it.

'I'm seeing a flat tonight,' he said.

Ida nodded, as much approval as she was going to show. 'Where?'

'Out by the Crown.' It was the best he could afford. A cramped one-bedroomed apartment in a converted Victorian house next to a pub on the outskirts of town. But at least the views would be good, out across the fells. And he'd be able to walk to work.

Ida's eyes narrowed. 'The Etherington place?' She didn't wait for his corroboration. Not that he could have provided it; after fourteen years in exile he'd lost track of the intricate network of connections that formed the social web of Bruncliffe. 'She's Mrs Pettiford's cousin. Shares the family trait for gossip, too. So tha'll have to watch thyself. Not one for cleaning, either. I'll call in when tha's settled and get it sorted.'

Samson smiled. Ida, doing her best to help. Like she'd always done, back when the O'Briens were the Capsticks' nearest neighbours. Back when Samson's world had started to fall apart.

'And if tha needs a reference,' Ida continued, stepping out of the door and into the fresh morning, 'I'd be happy to provide one.'

'Thanks, Ida,' said Samson, genuinely moved. Although he wasn't entirely sure that a reference in the cleaner's trademark brusque tone would be the glowing testimonial he'd need to overcome the prejudice he regularly encountered as the black sheep of Bruncliffe.

He watched her walk down the path, past his Royal Enfield motorbike gleaming in the sunshine, and out through the gate into the narrow ginnel that ran behind the row of terraced houses. The gate slammed firmly behind her and Samson was left looking up at the dark shape of the Crag, the massive limestone outcrop that loomed over the town, still cast in shadow.

Wishing he could run up onto the fells above it and never come back, he reluctantly opened the letter in his hand.

'Damn!' He thrust it back in the envelope. His day had just got worse.

'"Be discreet!"' A disdainful laugh followed the pronouncement. 'What kind of bloody order is that? Like he's some kind of royalty or something.'

Detective Sergeant Steve Cooper allowed his annoyance to infect his driving, sweeping the car too fast around a sharp bend, the stone wall on the left coming a bit too close for the comfort of his colleague in the passenger seat.

'Steady on, Sarge,' muttered the younger man. 'He's not worth dying over.'

'Not worthy of being on the force either,' retorted DS

Cooper as he accelerated along a rare stretch of straight on the sinuous A65. Either side of the road, fields rolled up the fells, walled in by grey lines of stone and populated with sheep. The bucolic setting only served to rile the policeman further. 'Sending us out into the back end of nowhere all because of him. I hope they throw the bloody book at the reprobate,' he growled.

DC Benson stayed quiet. He'd discovered that when it came to the topic of Samson O'Brien, it was best to let his boss rant, any interjections merely adding fuel to the fire. Not to say that he didn't understand the root cause of the animosity. Having secured a position on the force only after years of trying, Josh Benson couldn't fathom why anyone would be willing to throw away all that meant. Least of all someone who had attained near-mythical status within the ranks of Yorkshire's police. Even though he'd trained in North Yorkshire, Benson had heard about O'Brien's achievements – a star trainee in the West Yorkshire ranks, headhunted by the Met and then seconded onto the Serious Organised Crime Agency. When the organisation morphed into the National Crime Agency, O'Brien had stayed on, working undercover in the criminal fraternity of London. Until now.

Now he was living back in Bruncliffe and rumoured to be suspended, pending investigation, on allegations of corruption. And about to face—

'Bloody idiot!' A screech of brakes accompanied the exclamation as they came around a blind bend too fast and up behind a tractor, the two detectives thrown against their seatbelts.

From his position high up in the cab, the farmer glanced

over his shoulder and lifted a lazy finger of acknowledgement. But he didn't pull over. And as the road twisted and turned ever further into the Dales and closer to Bruncliffe, the car could do nothing but trundle along, the detective sergeant's temper building through every tortuous mile.

DC Benson was beginning to think their assignment would be anything but discreet.

The complete
Dales Detective series

'A classic whodunit set in the spectacular
landscape of the Yorkshire Dales, written with
affection for the area and its people'

Cath Staincliffe